WELCOME TO THE NEURODIVERSIVERSE!

Where do you want to go first? Let us be your guide to the many alien encounters you shall find within—strange and baffling, funny and uplifting, tender and romantic, and, yes, even, hopeful.

There are thrills and chills along the way, but the alien need not be frightening. Sometimes, aliens can be as vulnerable as we are.

In all these voyages, understanding is the key to success. Sometimes, that's understanding the other; sometimes, it's understanding ourselves. Sometimes, it's an understanding of what keeps us apart; sometimes, it's an understanding of how we can come together.

The stories, poems, and art in *The Neurodiversiverse* feature the work of experienced authors and debut authors, poet laureates and new poets, and art from a variety of artists—including our beautiful cover, with art by Barbara Candiotti.

Among our experienced authors, we are proud to feature the following:

- **Tobias S. Buckell**, author of *Shoggoths in Traffic*, brings us "The Pipefitter," which explores the benefits and drawbacks of ADHD in a far-future fight for survival against aliens who are merciless—and a neurotypical world that is unbending.
- **M. D. Cooper**, creator of the *Aeon 14* universe, gives us "The Zeta Remnant," in which competent explorers train themselves to make good decisions regardless of whether they are autistic or not—and M. D.'s autistic, so she'd know.
- **Ada Hoffmann**, author of the *Outside* trilogy, brings us "Music, Not Words," which depicts the struggle autistic people face to be heard clearly—and speculates that, sometimes, the words themselves could be the problem.
- **Jody Lynn Nye**, author of forty novels, a hundred stories, and *The Dragonlover's Guide to Pern*, gives us "A Hint of

Color," which shines a light on how synesthesia could reveal aliens that neurotypical people might not even recognize.
- **Cat Rambo**, author of *You Sexy Thing*, Nebula Award finalist, and former president of SFWA, surprises us with "Scary Monsters, Super Creeps," which explores how superheroes and supervillians fighting could be the worst place in the world for someone with anxiety—or the best.

Many of the stories in *The Neurodiversiverse* are #OwnVoices stories told from the perspective of folks who are neurodivergent themselves—perspectives that might surprise people who don't share these conditions. Representation is important. Especially for those of us with anxiety or other forms of neurodiversity, reading great stories about characters like us makes the world a happier place. *The Neurodiversiverse* features stories about:

- Autism
- ADHD
- PTSD
- OCD
- Synesthesia
- Anxiety (of various flavors)
- Avoidant attachment disorder
- Dissociative identity disorder
- And more

These perspectives bring us wonders. Shadows in the light of titanium rain. Space that shatters singular minds. Tai chi that can vaporize fighter jets. Travel through dimensions enabled by crochet. Superpowers unleashed by anxiety. Seekers whose world is saved by a child. Heartbroken starships. Human-sized hamster balls. A planet covered in mathematical fidgets.

And, finally, we learn why aliens abduct cows.

We are tremendously proud to bring you this anthology celebrating neurodiversity.

So, ready or not ... here come the aliens.

THE NEURODIVERSIVERSE:
ALIEN ENCOUNTERS

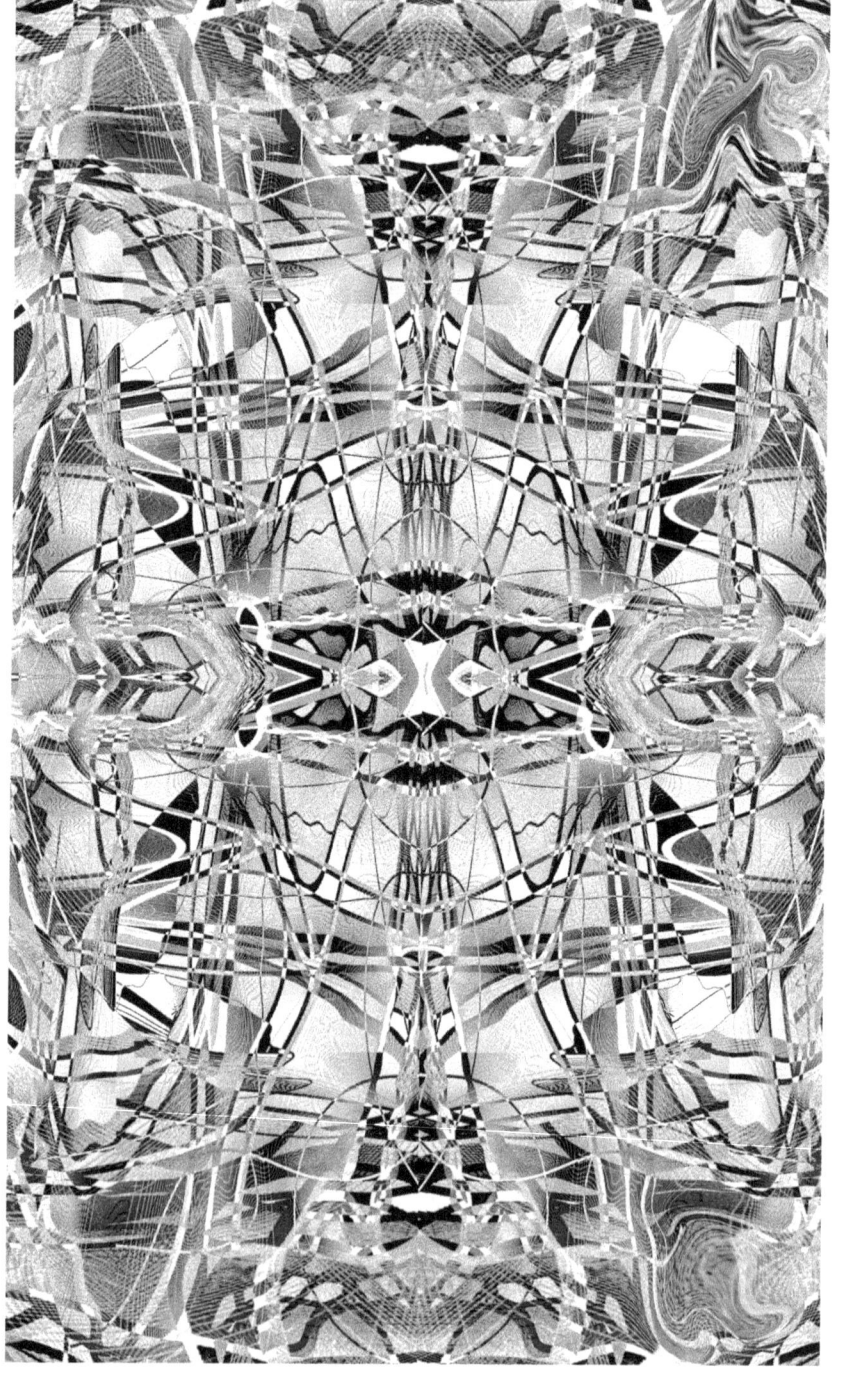

THE NEURODIVERSIVERSE: ALIEN ENCOUNTERS

A SCIENCE FICTION ANTHOLOGY OF STORIES, POETRY, AND ART

EDITED BY
ANTHONY FRANCIS
AND
LIZA OLMSTED

THE NEURODIVERSIVERSE: ALIEN ENCOUNTERS.

Collection and editorial material © 2024 Anthony Francis and Liza Olmsted.
Published by arrangement with the authors and artists.
For a complete listing of individual copyrights, please see Copyrights at the end of the book.

All rights reserved. No part of this book may be reproduced or transmitted in any form or by any means, electronic or mechanical, including photocopying and recording, or introduced into any information storage and retrieval system without the written permission of the copyright owner and the publisher of this book. Brief quotations may be used in reviews. For more information, contact editorial@thinkinginkpress.com.

This book collects works of fiction and opinion. Everything contained within it is either a work of fiction in which people, places, and events are fictionalized, or is an essay in which expressed opinions are those of its author and not those of Thinking Ink Press. No express or implied guarantees or warranties are provided for any links, facts, ideas, concepts, recipes, formulas, memes, runes, platitudes, or paradoxes expressed herein.

Published by Thinking Ink Press
P.O. Box 1411
Campbell, California 95009
www.ThinkingInkPress.com

First edition, 2024
Paperback edition ISBN 978-1-942480-26-6
Ebook edition ISBN 978-1-942480-27-3

Project Credits
Cover art is "Space Encounters" by Barbara Candiotti © 2024.
Frontispiece is "She Weaves Her Web 1A" by Edward Michael Supranowicz © 2024.
Neurodiversiverse logo designed by Kimchi Kreative. © 2024 Thinking Ink Press.
Poetry editors: Keiko O'Leary, Erin Redfern
Copy editor: Marilyn Horn
Cover design: Anthony Francis
Interior formatting: Liza Olmsted

Typefaces used in this book: EB Garamond, Dosis, Rajdhani, Iceland, PT Sans Narrow

TABLE OF CONTENTS

Preface	xiii
WHEN THE ALIENS CAME *A Poem* Avra Margariti	1
MUSIC, NOT WORDS *A Story* Ada Hoffmann	3
THE GRAND NEW YORK WELCOME TOUR *A Story* Kay Hanifen	7
A CONVERSATION WITH A XOTIRAN *A Poem* M. A. Dubbs	18
THE PIPEFITTER *A Story* Tobias S. Buckell	21
IMPACT *A Story* Jasmine Starr	41
WHERE IS EVERYBODY? *A Story* Anya Leigh Josephs	51
LOVEHEART *An Illustration* Natasha Von	57
MCCARTHY KNEW *A Poem* A J Dalton	58
SHADOWS OF TITANIUM RAIN *A Story* Anthony Francis	60

WI(D)TH, DE(P)TH, BREA(D)TH, *A Poem* River	79
THE INTERVIEW *A Story* Brian Starr	81
SOMEONE DIFFERENT, LIKE ME *A Story* Daan Dunnewold	91
SCARY MONSTERS, SUPER CREEPS *A Story* Cat Rambo	94
THESE THINGS NEVER END WELL *A Story* Maub Nesor	106
CHATTER *An Illustration* Barbara Candiotti	110
FIRST CONTACT *A Story* David Manfre	111
THE SPACE BETWEEN STITCHES *A Story* Minerva Cerridwen	121
CADRE *A Story* Sam Crain	132
THE COW TEST *A Story* Lauren D. Fulter	136
RADAR *An Illustration* Barbara Candiotti	146
OUR CONNECTED SPACE *A Poem* Swarit Gopalan	147

GAMMA ZARIA *A Story* Gail Brown	149
BEGINNING AWAKENING *Four Poems* Chief Red Chef	163
RESILIENCE *An Illustration* Vincenzo Cohen	164
WHERE MONOLITHIC MINDS CAN'T TRAVEL *A Story* Akis Linardos	165
THE ZETA REMNANT *A Story* M. D. Cooper	170
ARE WE HUMAN? *A Story* Brianna Elise	191
A HINT OF COLOR *A Story* Jody Lynn Nye	194
BE YOUR OWN UNIVERSE *A Story* Kay Alexander	205
LOOK *An Illustration* Barbara Candiotti	209
NAVIGATIONAL AID *A Story* Holly Schofield	210
HEART-SIDE SOMETIMES-TABLE *A Story* Madeline Barnicle	218
TRADING PARTNERS *A Story* Jennifer R. Povey	227

HELL NO! 234
Four Poems
Sid Ghosh

GREETINGS FROM EARTH 235
A Story
R. S. Mot

CLOSE ENCOUNTER IN
THE PUBLIC BATHROOM 246
A Story Poem
Keiko O'Leary

PRIMORDIAL VOICES 251
A Story
J.L. Lark

SOUL SISTERS IN AUTUMN 266
An Illustration
Natasha Von

GOOD OMENS 267
A Poem
River

TANGIBLE THINGS 269
A Story
Jillian Starr

STOPPING FOR FUEL ON A STARRY EVENING 276
A Poem
Crystal Sidell

SKELETON IN ROSES 279
An Illustration
Natasha Von

MEETING OF THE BRANES 280
A Story
Kiya Nicoll

MEANING GREEN, UNCLEAR 290
A Story
Clara Ward

FLARE TO BRILLIANCE AND FADE *A Poem* J. D. Harlock	294
THE LIST-MAKING HABITS OF HEARTBROKEN SHIPS *A Story* Stewart C Baker	295
A Voyage of Discovery	301
A List of Neurodiversity Resources	305
Acknowledgments	308
About the Team	310
About the Authors and Artists	312
About Thinking Ink Press	323
All Copyrights	324
Colophon	327

PREFACE

LIZA OLMSTED, CO-EDITOR

I discovered my own neurodiversity *relatively* late in life: in my mid-30s, in the middle of a successful (but exhausting) career in software. It came after several of my favorite authors happened to mention they had ADHD, and I thought, "If *they* have ADHD, and their stories are just like my brain, that might be me." It was me.

The more I learned about ADHD and about how it manifests for myself, the more of my friends, family, and people I respected[*] discovered they were *also* neurodivergent. It turns out neurodivergence runs in friend groups.

And then I read about the "ADHD-to-autism" pipeline for late-diagnosed people, which I scoffed at: "I'm not autistic, I'm just really *really* interested in learning all about autism." (I was, in fact, autistic.

---

[*] Just this year, Neil Gaiman subtly revealed he's autistic in a post on Tumblr. (Source: https://www.tumblr.com/neil-gaiman/744334382867890176/thoughts-on-autism) Hugo- and Nebula-award-winning artist and author Ursula Vernon is publicly ADHD. (One of many sources: https://x.com/UrsulaV/status/1613776807848980480)

Having autism as a special interest is common in late-diagnosed autistic people.)

What's great about this modern world we live in is that there is a never-ending supply of social groups hyperfocused on the issue you care about. Autism groups, autism-in-women-and-nonbinary-people groups, trans groups, groups for people who need surgery to replace their temporomandibular joints (... yes, I do have personal experience with that, why do you ask?). Some of these groups are incredibly well moderated, and we provide links to them and other resources at the end of the book.

But what isn't so great—*yet*—is that it's still hard to find books that show neurodivergent people, or any disabled people, having fun adventures, falling in love, and saving the world. If they do appear, it's as side characters who are a burden for the main character to carry, or as villains, or as robots* or savants.

Talking about how we talk about neurodivergence:

Although autism and other forms of neurodivergence aren't new, a lot of the language about them is. As modern society removes stigma around neurodivergence, we revise our word choices. As neurodivergent people's opinions get centered more in the discourse, rather than those of neurotypical doctors, we reject some words that used to be standard and reclaim words that were stigmatized.

In this book, we focused on using the language that many neurodivergent people prefer for themselves. Words have been shifting fast in this century, and they may shift again in the future. Some of the choices we made in this book include the following:

- We talk about "autistic people," not "people with autism."

While there was a long period when American society thought "person with X" was the more humanizing way to describe it, people who actually have X (disabilities, autism, etc.) often

---

* I absolutely adore *The Murderbot Diaries* by Martha Wells, but they do kinda fall into this category.

experience those terms as less humanizing. Being called a person "with" autism implies that maybe I could still be myself without it, which most* autistic people don't tend to believe for themselves. This isn't a universal trend—there are still people who prefer "person with"—and we aim to use the language people prefer for themselves.

- We talk about "neurotypical people," not "neurotypicals" (except when it's intended to be a slur), as well as "neurodivergent people" instead of "neurodivergents."

Reducing people to a single characteristic often reads as dehumanizing. This seems to be a recent trend in language, maybe in the last decade or so. To the best of our ability, we'd rather stay current with humanizing language, even at the risk of being out of date in just a few years if the trend changes again. One of the stories in this book does use "neurotypical" as a slur, as an indicator of a character's own bias. Just as neurotypical people can be biased against neurodivergent people, neurodivergent people can become quite jaded and be biased against neurotypical people.

- We talk about the range of different thinking styles as "neurodiversity" and an individual's particular style that's different from the norm as their "neurodivergence."

No one individual's "neuro" is actually "diverse" by itself. "Diversity" requires a group. That said, it might be a small demonstration of our own autism, how rigidly we try to adhere

---

* The Autistic Not Weird Autism Survey by Chris Bonello surveyed over 11,000 respondents, over 7,000 of whom were autistic, and the answers show that over 90% of autistic respondents use the phrase "autistic person," versus less than 19% of autistic respondents who use "person with autism." While this isn't a large enough sample size to prove that most English-speaking autistic people worldwide prefer the phrase, it's a good enough indicator for us. Available at: https://autisticnotweird.com/autismsurvey/#language. We recommend the whole survey, it's very informative.

PREFACE

to this distinction, because many other English speakers don't notice or need that distinction. (I promise not to correct you if you use the "wrong" word, and I'll try very hard not to judge you, either.)

- Our use of the term "disorder" is complicated.

For most forms of neurodivergence, the official names come from the *Diagnostic and Statistical Manual of Mental Disorders* (*DSM*). When we use the term "disorder," it's because that's the official term the DSM uses, and therefore is the most precise way we have for talking about it. That said, "disorder" implies something is wrong, and we align with the neurodivergent-affirming movement, which maintains that many "disorders" aren't.*

- We talk about "autism," not "Asperger's."

"Asperger's" is no longer a diagnosis, since the *Diagnostic and Statistical Manual of Mental Disorders, Fifth Edition* (*DSM-5*) came out, because it was found that it is actually a subset of autism. In addition, many (but not all) autistic people prefer to distance themselves from the Dr. Asperger who gave it the name, because he was a Nazi collaborator. For the people who still find it to be a meaningful and empowering term for themselves, we support them, but we choose not to use it in this book.

---

* Per our invaluable consultant, Dr. Anaïs Wong, PsyD, "The argument among neurodiversity-affirming specialists is that Autism and ADHD in particular are too common to qualify as disorders, if you follow the DSM's own definition of disorder (must be rare). And we argue that it was evolutionarily advantageous to have different types of brains that would be very good at different things. So all neurodivergences that are inborn (most of DSM diagnoses, except for brain injury and degenerative conditions like dementia) may actually be epigenetic adaptations to severe strain experienced by previous generations."

PREFACE

- We use the term "alien" to mean "beings from other worlds."

Although the term is sometimes used to refer to humans on Earth, we hope you'll set that usage aside as you enjoy the stories in this book. Referring to humans as "aliens" is othering and exclusionary in a way we don't encourage. Many neurodivergent people share the experience of feeling alien among humans. It's not unique to neurodivergent folks; many people who feel different or othered by the people around them describe a similar experience.

- Common science fiction tropes.

There are many science fiction tropes, like "space colonies," whose names have real-world connotations that we don't intend to allude to or endorse.

- Defining the phrase "#OwnVoices."

If you haven't come across this phrase, it's a hashtag used in social media to indicate when something is written by a person who's a member of the group being discussed. For example, when a Black person writes about being Black, that could be tagged with "#OwnVoices". When an autistic person writes about being autistic, that's #OwnVoices. When an allistic (non-autistic) parent writes about their child's autism, that is *not* #OwnVoices.

You'll also see neopronouns, like ze/zem or xe/xem, and the old-fashioned they/them, which refer to people outside the gender binary.
Because we strive to use language precisely, accurately, and politely, we end up with clunky sentences to describe the book like, "a neurodi-

PREFACE

versity-themed science fiction anthology of short stories, poetry, and art by and for neurodivergent people." Boy, that's a mouthful.*

How this book came to be

My co-editor Anthony and I decided we wanted to make an anthology full of fun stories where neurodiversity is instrumental to the plot in a positive, uplifting way. A book where readers could see characters like them having otherworldly experiences. A book where readers could see characters unlike them, too, with neurotypes different from their own, having exciting adventures with ways of thinking that are unfamiliar to them.

That's the exciting thing about diversity, that everyone is more likely to see themself represented in a diverse group, and everyone is more likely to see people really different from themself, too.

We were incredibly fortunate to receive so many submissions from neurodivergent writers, poets, and artists. We didn't require creators to disclose their neurodiversity as part of submission, so we can't tell you exactly how many are or aren't, but we do know that a majority are.

Depending on your knowledge of neurodivergent traits, you may or may not recognize specific details as being characteristic of particular flavors of neurodivergence. If you are yourself neurodivergent, I hope you see someone familiar in this book.

I hope that through this collection you'll be able to meet many different neurodivergent people, and feel the beauty and magnificence of each one.

—*Liza Olmsted, May 2024*

---

* **Co-editor's note:** Anthony says, yes, that's a mouthful, but we'd rather end up with our sentences being a mouthful than start off with our collective foot in our mouth.

WHEN THE ALIENS CAME
A POEM
AVRA MARGARITI

When the aliens came, their nictitating membranes
found our world too loudsharpbright ...

... like that time I had to hide under a table
in a lit-up restaurant, while patrons wondered
what was wrong with me

When the aliens came, we cringed at their nakedness,
made them wear suits and dresses, watched
their too-thin skin squirm and itch ...

... like that time my mother crammed me in a church dress
that rubbed me raw, crab-pinching shoes, and I cried
and dreamed of flensing my skin to escape
textile constriction

AVRA MARGARITI

When the aliens came, we taught them
to say please and thank you, even when they didn't mean it,
told them, *don't go tempesting the waters* when they asked the whys
and hows of our customs: *you don't want to look ungrateful,
do you?*

... like the times my grandma trained me
in the art of politeness, pinched my sides
to sunset bruises whenever I replied with honesty to *how are you?*
to, *is there anything you need?*

When the aliens came, we prepared a feast for them,
an envoy. A letter of demands
for their advanced ways and technology.
I snuck into the outdoor tent where they sat in wait,
uncomfortable, overwhelmed ...

... and I prepared to tell the aliens that I too felt alien
among my people, I too would like to extend my welcome
but don't always know how to get the words
to leave my throat

When the aliens came, they did not look me in the eye,
nor did they address me in voice or gesture.
Yet they let me sit with them in blessed dark and quiet
while their welcome feast raged on outside.
Inside the tent, we were cradled by the cosmos,
a sensory deprivation chamber where we floated
in synesthetic synchronicity

MUSIC, NOT WORDS
A STORY
ADA HOFFMANN

Content note: *emotional abuse*

EVERY NIGHT THAT SUMMER, when Justina looked out her bedroom window, something sang to her.

At first she didn't know where the song came from. But music had always meant more to her than mere words. Music was an intricate pattern of tone and pitch and timing that sank directly into the heart and moved the body. Words, Justina had trouble with, even on a good day. Music, she understood more intimately than anything.

So she leaned out through her window every night and breathed the music in. It told her:

Friends.

People like her in some ways, and very unlike her in others. Friends, up there, between the stars, in the sky.

Justina believed what she heard without questioning. Questions were for adults and rude classmates who cornered her in the yard: *why can't you answer us? Why can't you explain? What's wrong with you?*

Music did not need interrogation, question, or explanation. Music only *was,* self-evidently.

So it did not surprise Justina when, in late July that summer—the year she'd turned fifteen—she started to see the flying saucers. Silvery disks, spinning like an old-fashioned record, pulsing in time with the strange, lovely tune that came down from them to Earth.

"I saw it," said Justina at the breakfast table, rocking back and forth with the need to be understood. The morning light streamed in through the yellow-curtained window to the Formica-topped table; the birds outside, the dogs walking, and the thrum of the cars, made music of their own. It was all she could do to form a few words at a time, slow and labored, instead of vanishing into the music.

Her mother was setting out plates and bowls. "Saw what?"

"The spaceships."

"What?"

"She must have seen it on television," said her father, reclining at the head of the table with a newspaper.

It was hard to make this many words. Justina hated breakfast. She would rather have just swayed to the rhythms she heard, let the words fall away, spent her day dancing to the symphony of the world. But people always got angry when she tried to do that, instead of speaking and going to school.

"No," she said. "Real … real ships. Saucers. Flying."

Her father put down his coffee cup with a loud clink, which hurt her ears. "You did not see flying saucers."

"Real. They … sang." Justina rocked back and forth a little harder. She didn't like when people disagreed with each other; music had its dissonances, but only words allowed this type of terrible clash. She never knew what to do with it, and her father was excellent at disagreeing, making the words clash as loud and hard as possible.

"Flying saucers don't sing," he said, louder now. "They aren't *real*. This is preposterous."

"Honey," said her mother as she shook out cereal into the ceramic bowls, "she doesn't know what she's saying. Justina, honey, you must have had a dream. All sorts of things can happen in a dream, can't they?"

Justina did not argue again. She hunched in her chair, covered her ears. She already knew, from the pitch and crescendo of both voices, where this was going.

"What's going to happen if we let her keep saying things like this?" her father demanded. Even with Justina's hands over her ears, his voice rang harsh and dissonant. "Let her babble about saucers, and what's the next absurd thing she's going to say, about you, or about me? How long until we have child protective services breathing down our necks, for no damned reason—"

People always argued about Justina right in front of her, like she wasn't there, like they didn't care how the words overloaded her. She did understand words, even though it was hard to make them. People didn't get that about her. She could think. She just mostly thought in music, not words.

Even after the argument itself was over, it took hours for the clash between her parents to stop reverberating, echoing between her ears. But that night, when it had faded, Justina opened her window. The flying saucers' music washed over her, soft and tender—the opposite of the sounds her parents made. Instinctively, Justina understood the structure of the song. It wasn't made to crash or clash over her, or to wipe away her words in favor of its own. This was a song with room in it, warm and clear—little spaces between the notes, gaps that a harmonizing voice might rise to fill.

Tonight, Justina had made up her mind. She fixed her eyes on the saucers and took a deep breath. In her own thin reedy voice, without any words, she answered them.

The saucers came down without any fuss: only a slow swell of rising and deepening chords. They were smaller than Justina's house, but bigger than her father's car, flattened and perfectly circular, casting a silvery light over the indifferently mown grass of the backyard. When they settled down gently in that grass, their music changed: not a full break but a further development. A different verse of the same song. A bridge.

Justina stood perfectly still for a few seconds, staring at the saucers, absorbing the sound.

Then she crept to the back door and opened it quietly. Silvery light washed over her as she stood in the fresh night air, in the music, with the night birds and insects and faraway cars giving harmony of their own. Something opened in the saucer nearest to her: a curved door. An invitation.

Justina thought about maybe turning and waking up her parents, showing them that she was right; but she knew, deep down, that this would not do any good. This music was hers, not theirs. This invitation was for her.

Without any fear, bringing nothing but the song in her throat, Justina stepped out to meet them.

THE GRAND NEW YORK WELCOME TOUR

A STORY

KAY HANIFEN

Content note: *one scene of violence and harassment*

I SHOULD NOT HAVE READ *The War of the Worlds* after signing up as an alien tour sponsor. It's not that I was paranoid that the Xerians are secretly trying to take over the world. That would make sense, but instead, it was because of the stupid ending. The aliens are not conquered by mankind but by germs, which kills them off because they have no immunity to Earth diseases.

As the days until the first tour grew ever closer, I could not get that ending out of my head. Every single cough, sneeze, and headache was a sign of what might be a cold for me but a deadly illness to the people entrusted to my care. But I also couldn't just back out of it. It had been my lifelong dream to join the diplomatic ranks of Earth's budding Intergalactic Council. I couldn't let a little OCD and intrusive thoughts stop me. The trick to getting over these fears is to just face them ... within reason, of course. One of my worst obsessive anxieties is rabies, and I'm not about to get over it by playing with a wild raccoon.

But this time, I did know that it was safe. The Xerians were all fully vaccinated against Earth diseases, so there was no chance for me to pass anything onto them. No matter how much I tried to remind myself of this fact, though, it refused to stick in my head. And when I wasn't thinking about that, I was thinking about other ways this could go terribly wrong.

Not everyone was happy about our growing diplomatic relationships with other species. We could be attacked by the xenophobic terrorist groups, like the Children of Men, or caught in a mass shooting, or a natural disaster. I've had some self-defense and survival training, but I doubted I was skilled enough to be of any use.

The day arrived like any other, if it wasn't for the way my stomach twisted like it was filled with electric eels. The first tour of the Xerians' excursion was supposed to be the easiest, and I tried to remind myself of this as I watched the group of five Xerians file into the conference room where I was to prep them for their excursion walking among the humans. These were students, cultural anthropologists wanting to learn more about Earth's customs.

At first glance, Xerians reminded me a bit of most artists' modern renditions of velociraptors. They were birdlike in the way they glanced around the room with quick, jerky movements and had bright patterned plumage like a parrot's. They were, in a word, beautiful.

As they approached, they acknowledged my presence with a tilted nod of the head and a friendly trill. Though I'm lacking in their vocal anatomy, I did my best to replicate the gesture and sound as a sign of respect.

Finally, the last of the Xerians took zer seat. I had been briefed on gender and the lack of it in their society. Because the status of their genitals was considered a private affair, we relied on neopronouns when we didn't know their names and preferences.

Taking a slow, deep breath in and out to wrestle my nerves into submission, I smiled and stepped in front of the podium. "Hello and welcome," I said in a pale facsimile of their language before switching to my own. "You can call me Nyla, and I'm going to be your tour guide today. We'll have a short talk before we begin our tour of Times Square and Broadway. But first, I'd like to know what I can call you."

The five Xerians in my charge were named Yem, Otra, Rekete, Dren, and Jasa. The last in the list was the latecomer. Jasa fidgeted anxiously in zer seat while the rest seemed relaxed. It must have been zer first time on Earth. Well, it was my first time giving the grand tour, so we could be nervous together.

We went over the basic ground rules about our customs, stuff that may seem like common sense such as 'don't take staring as a sign of aggression' and 'don't steal from shops,' but we still took pains to point out because there had been some incidents in the past. Their culture was very different from ours, which was something to be celebrated, but could also create friction.

Soon enough, though, it was time to go. We all filed into the elevator and rode to the ground floor. It let out near Times Square, where they could experience the Big Apple for the first time.

I checked our itinerary for probably the fifth time, just in case I missed something or the words on the paper magically changed. The first stop was a Broadway matinee production of *Hamilton*, apparently to help them gain a grasp of our history. We had a private box so that the Xerians could ask me questions without disturbing the other audience members.

"For a play, we try not to speak, and if we must, it's in whispers so that we don't distract the audience or the actors," I said after they had taken their seats. "When the audience claps, you may clap, and when they laugh, you may laugh. Do you have any questions about etiquette or what a musical is?"

Jasa raised zer hand. "I heard something about singing and dancing. Will the audience choose their mates from the performers?"

The rest of the Xerians chuckled among themselves, making zer curl in on zerself. "That's a very good question," I said, channeling my years of teaching experience from before I joined the diplomacy corps. You'd be surprised how many former preschool and kindergarten teachers excelled in the fields of intergalactic relations. Child logic can feel incredibly alien to adults who don't know how to field it.

I flashed Jasa a reassuring smile. "This is an interesting cultural difference we have between us. While some humans sing and dance to attract mates, most do it for the same reason we decorated the walls of this place." I gestured to the ornate baroque and rococo architecture surrounding us. "We do it because we find it beautiful and want to share that beauty with everyone else. In this case, the dancing is meant to tell a story. Some of the behavior you see on the stage is meant to be more of a metaphorical act than a literal one. Perhaps you have something like this in your culture."

One of the Xerians whispered to another in zer native language, making Jasa sink in on zerself even more. Jasa started rocking back and forth, a behavior I had not seen other Xerians do, but which reminded me of how my friends and I sometimes rocked in awkward social situations. Like recognizes like. I'm not diagnosed autistic, but, on top of my OCD, I have that behavior in common with many of my neurodivergent friends.

I took my seat next to Jasa and whispered, "If you need a break, tap my hand three times and I'll take you somewhere quiet."

Jasa nodded, zer shoulders untensing slightly. "I am sorry," ze whispered back. "Even among my people, I am considered strange. Forgive my peculiarities."

"I get it. I'm pretty peculiar by human standards too. Forgive me mine and I'll forgive you yours?"

Ze made a soft cooing noise in the back of zer throat, something I recognized as a laugh. "You have my gratitude."

The lights went down, and the music picked up. While the Xerians watched the singing and dancing with rapt attention, I watched their faces and movements. Their heads twitched owlishly as they tracked the dancers on the stage, like raptors in search of prey on the forest floor.

At one point, Jasa leaned over and whispered, "I have read about how your country came to be, but I am confused."

"What else is new?" whispered Yem, making Otra snicker.

I shot them both warning looks. Apparently establishing a pecking order is something that occurs among humans, birds, and Xerians, but I wasn't going to tolerate it.

"We rented this box so that you can ask questions. What's confusing you?"

"They really revolted because of a drink?"

"Sort of," I replied, and did my best to explain why tea was so important and that this was just one of many problems the colonists had with England.

Jasa let out an excited trill, puffing zer feathers. "Like how the Lonen colony revolted against the Xerians because we insisted on seizing most of their resources."

I was not familiar with this aspect of Xerian history but nodded anyway. If Jasa made the connection, then it was probably a good enough comparison. Some of the other alien tourists shot zer glares, and the proud puffing of Jasa's plumage began to shrink as ze sank back in zer chair.

Apparently, humanity wasn't the only species with a sordid history of colonization. I made a mental note on that so I could discuss it with my superiors later. Odds were that they already knew about any history of colonizing, but just in case, it was a good idea to mention it.

Periodically, Jasa would lean over to ask questions about the romantic subplot or the duels of honor, trying to come up with parallels to zer own culture. The rest seemed to understand it or at least grasp enough that they didn't feel the need to ask questions, not even during intermission.

It was late afternoon when we left the theater. While the other four walked in front of us, Jasa trailed behind next to me. "It's strange. I knew that we were watching humans on a stage and that they were all fine, but still I felt a profound grief by the end, as though I had lost someone I loved."

"That's the magic of art," I said. "It gives us a safe place to feel all these big emotions and come out the other side with a new perspective. Humans are built to love and to bond, even with things that aren't real, because they feel real to us. Is Xerian art like that?"

Jasa's head twitched from side to side as ze thought. "Yes, and no. Most of what you call art is done for a purpose such as attracting a mate or asserting our dominance. I have never seen any of my people dance for the sake of dancing or sing for the sake of singing."

I hadn't realized how far the other Xerians had gotten ahead of us until we reached a red light with the standard asshole New York drivers speeding through and making the streets unsafe for pedestrians. They were on the other side of the road and kept walking, either not hearing or ignoring our cries for them to stop.

Despite the fact that they stood out as five-foot-tall velociraptors, I lost sight of them among the crowd. "Shit!" Throwing caution to the wind, I ran across the street, Jasa following close behind.

But they were nowhere to be found.

My mind flooded with all kinds of gory possibilities. What if they were hit by a car? Or mugged? Or taken by the Children of Men? What if they got hurt or accidentally ate something poisonous to them?

I was going to be fired and disgraced and have to go back to a teacher's salary. This was my dream job, and now I was fucked. But more importantly, they could be in danger.

"Please breathe," Jasa cooed, stroking my arm to give me something else to focus on. "I think I know where they went."

That shook me out of my near panic attack. "Where?"

"I overheard them talking about sneaking off to visit a place called Club Parrot. Do you know what that is?"

"I haven't heard of it, but I know where to look," I replied, taking out my phone. "Why would they do this? Am I really that terrible of a guide?"

"You are a wonderful human. We are simply at the age of impertinence, so please forgive us."

The age of impertinence. Right. They were basically the Xerian equivalent to college students and I had expected them to behave like fully grown adults. But I could worry about that later. First, I needed to find them. "Right, you said Club Parrot?"

"Yes. Can you find them with your …" Jasa hesitated, seeming to search for the word. "Communication device?"

I nodded, typing in the name of the nightclub. There were a few to choose from, but the closest was only a few blocks away. Because they don't know better and think like tourists rather than New Yorkers, they'll probably go to the nearest club, assuming it would be nicer than the others off Broadway.

The white walking man flashed and we crossed the street. "They weren't going to include you in their plans?" I asked as we hurried down the block.

"They assumed that I would hate this Club Parrot and be too anxious about deviating from the planned tour. Both of which are probably true. I am far too boring to be impertinent like them."

I stopped short. "Hey, you're not boring. I've enjoyed our talks today. You were the most engaged and curious out of all of them, and I enjoyed sharing a little bit of our world with you."

The feathers on Jasa's neck puffed. "If you are mocking me, I would rather that you said how you truly felt instead."

"I'm not making fun of you." I nudged zer closer to the building so that people could file past. "Like I said, my brain works a little differently compared to other humans, and sometimes I also get the feeling that people were secretly making fun of me too, but believe me, that's not what I'm doing here."

Jasa nodded. "Do you know why they do it? I never truly understood. I mean, I know I am not one of them. I had to save all my credits to be able to afford this trip, and I feel like I am the only one who wants to learn about your world."

"I don't get it either." I flashed zer a weak smile. "I think that there are two approaches to differences in others: curiosity and hostility. You and I meet the universe with curiosity and an open mind, wanting to understand. Others, though, are made uncomfortable by difference, and at best, shun it. At worst, they try to stamp it out."

It seemed a bit strange for a group of anthropology students to be so closed-minded, but if these were undergrads, they probably took the course because it was required and was a good excuse for a field trip to Earth rather than because they had any true passion for the field.

"Let's go, Jasa," I said. The nice thing about New York City is that it's a fairly accepting population. There are so many kinds of people in one place that even the strangest visitors were usually just given a curious glance or two before they moved on. Staying stationary like this, though, gave them more opportunity to stare. I knew I was getting uncomfortable, and I wasn't even the target of their gazes. I couldn't imagine how awkward it must have been for my alien charge.

It wasn't difficult to find the club. A line had already formed outside the door and stretched around the building. At the front were the Xerians arguing with the bouncer.

"What do you mean we're not allowed in?" Dren demanded. "Do you know who my father is? He has enough wealth to buy this place, employees and all, burn it to the ground, rebuild it, and then burn it all over again."

"It's club policy. We don't want any intergalactic incidents."

"There's gonna be one if you don't stop holding up the line," called a guy a few places behind them. I didn't like the looks of him. His muscles were tense like a snake coiled to strike, and the arm holding a half-empty beer bottle sported a tattoo of Earth. It could just be a coincidence, but the symbol had been growing increasingly popular among the Children of Men.

"So, you'll simply refuse us service," Rekete said indignantly. "I can't imagine how well that would turn out."

"I'm not afraid to call the police," the bouncer said, sounding exhausted as he cast his eyes about for support. The man who interjected puffed out his chest in a silent promise to be his backup should things become physical. Eventually, the bouncer's gaze settled on me and Jasa. His shoulders sagged in defeat. "Oh great. Another one."

All the Xerians turned their irritable gazes onto Jasa, who shrank in on zerself with guilt.

"I'm actually here to collect them," I said, stepping between the group and Jasa and shooting them my best disappointed kindergarten teacher look. They shifted uncomfortably from side to side, none of them meeting my gaze. "I'm their guide, and we got separated."

Making pointed eye contact with them, I said, "If you don't mind, I'd like to get back on schedule. I'll have to call the restaurant and ask them to hold our table for a bit longer, but I think you'll like the place we picked. Then, we can take you souvenir shopping."

"I resent the fact that everyone seems to think we need a babysitter," Otra said, crossing zer winged arms.

Age of impertinence indeed. Apparently, spoiled rich kids transcended species. I straightened my spine and forced my voice to stay level. "Well, you did sneak away from me and pick a fight with this poor bouncer. I'm sure they all gave you the lecture about being ambassadors on this world, so maybe they weren't far off when they assigned you a *babysitter*."

Otra bristled at that, and the man in line laughed. "Yeah, we don't want you here. Go back to where you came from."

I turned on him. "Not even remotely what I meant, asshole. So, please keep your mouth shut."

"Traitor bitch," he growled, and the next few seconds happened too fast for me to fully comprehend it. He threw the half-empty beer bottle, aiming not at me but at Dren. I moved without thinking, pushing zer out of the way. The bottle struck my temple and shattered, the shock of it sending me to the ground.

Vaguely, I heard the man cry, "Oh shit!" and someone else yell, "Don't let him get away!"

I wanted to sit up, but moving made my stomach roil with nausea and my head spike with pain. Something dribbled down the side of my face, and for a moment, I wondered if it had started to rain. But then, I touched it, and my hand came away red.

Jasa's face swam in front of my vision. "Are you hurt badly?"

I blinked, trying to focus on zer words. Was I okay? I was pretty sure that I had a concussion, but I'd survive. "I think we'll have to cut the tour short," I slurred.

"Nyla, I am so sorry," Dren said. "I—I didn't think—"

"And this is why it's a good idea to have a guide with you." I sat up, taking a moment to let the world stop spinning before pulling out my phone. "I'll call my supervisor. They'll send a new guide, because I think I need to go to the nearest emergency room. The police will likely contact you for witness statements. You five didn't break any laws, so I doubt you'll be in any legal trouble, but—" I gagged, the nausea threatening to become vomit. Like an earthquake before a volcanic eruption.

"I already called the cops and an ambulance," the bouncer said. "They'll be here in a few minutes."

"Thank you."

The ambulance arrived with the police, and after a quick statement, they carted me off to the nearest hospital for an MRI and monitoring. I've always been afraid of those delayed reaction concussions that would kill me as soon as I fell asleep, and that loop of intrusive thoughts was difficult to ignore. My blood pressure was spiking higher than normal, forcing me to take deep breaths and focus on the fact that if I suffered a cerebral hemorrhage, the hospital would be the best place to have it.

When they released me the next day with the caveat that I get plenty of rest, I was surprised to find the tour group waiting outside with flowers in their claws. Their replacement tour guide stood some distance off to give us some privacy.

"I understand that it is customary to give flowers to those who have been to the hospital," Jasa said, handing me zer bouquet. Ze eagerly shifted from foot to foot. "I remembered yesterday that you talked about symbolism and metaphors, and I wondered if flowers had symbols too. And they did! The language of flowers is fascinating, and we all chose our bouquets based on what they represented. Mine are chrysanthemums and lavender for relaxation and longevity."

Dren was up next, studying zer feet as ze handed me zer bouquet. "These are violets and white roses, meaning an apology." Ze looked up. "It was my asinine idea to sneak off to the club, and because of me, you were hurt. I am so sorry."

"All is forgiven," I said, accepting it. "Just don't do it again."

"I won't," Dren promised.

Yem gave me pink and yellow carnations for apology and joy while Otra gave me pink and white roses for friendship and respect, and Rekete gave me hyacinths and gladioluses for expressing regret and offering strength.

"I love them," I said once I'd accepted them all.

"It was Jasa's idea," Otra said. "I was surprised how much I enjoyed thinking about symbolism like a human."

Shifting the five bouquets to one arm, I pulled out a business card for each of them. "I can't be your tour guide for the rest of your trip, but if you have any questions, don't hesitate to text or call."

While the others accepted it politely, Jasa's face lit up like Times Square on New Year's Eve. "Thank you, Nyla. I will definitely take you up on it for my dissertation. And perhaps, one day, I might call you friend."

I grinned. "I don't see why you can't call me your friend now."

Her feathers ruffled, zer claws flapping with delight. The other

Xerians exchanged baffled glances but didn't antagonize her. "I would like that very much, Friend Nyla."

"I'll see you around, Friend Jasa," I said, and watched them rejoin their tour guide. Calling a cab, I slid inside with the stack of bouquets beside me.

"Whoa, did your partner do something to really piss you off?" the cabbie asked.

Laughing, I shook my head. "No, this is just from some friends of mine."

A CONVERSATION WITH A XOTIRAN
A POEM
M. A. DUBBS

The suits and coats told me it would be hard
    to talk to a creature with perfect memory,
    to have a conversation with a Xotiran.
They said his mind is like a photographic video log
    that plays on repeat,
    a replay triggered by the smallest turn of phrase.
Said that one mention
    can spiral from one thought to the next.
That it can be hard for a human to follow
    such a rabbit hole,
    such a traffic-jam-like stream of thought.

But I tell them I am like the Xotiran,
    with a brain adapted by flashpoints,
    memories chronicled like a timeline;
    filled with crystal clear darkest hours
    instead of a mush of nostalgia
    and a blur of human recollection.

A CONVERSATION WITH A XOTIRAN

One trigger can lead me to an echo of remembrance,
    a reminiscence burned into the back of my mind,
    so I am worlds away,
    both in my body
    but fading in and out.
A projection looking down on myself,
    what some long to call astral projection
    is an art of dissociation long mastered over time.

It's a skill I practice as I pause between airlocks
    and decontamination sprays,
    a meditation between microphone placements
    and the donning of boot covers
    and blue latex gloves.
He prays at a stainless steel table,
    long nails leading to dark green scales,
    flaring scarlet gills,
    and auburn eyes setting in a horizon
    thousands of miles from here.

We hesitate between translations,
    finding respite in pleasantries
    until we bottom out of parlor games
    and build up to a free fall
    in the darkness of space.
We trail off together like rogue exoplanets,
    as we touch the places that hurt,
    hold the things we loved,
    and recite orisons for the actions we regret,
    an enterprise for a personal amnesty.

M. A. DUBBS

In our talk, we find familiarity in the alien,
    in the permanent smells and sounds of a lived life.
We have a packet of questions
    but we ignore the script,
        the demands of uniformed brass in our earbuds,
        and come to our ultimate question of everything,
        the question of how to let go?
But answer with a cryptic but simple, *you don't.*

The suits and coats will spend so much time researching,
    trying to understand what it means.
What's it like to be living history?
What's it mean to be a Xotiran?
So foreign to them, so familiar to me,
    but what a joy to find a friend,
        from a fellow alien who finally understands.

THE PIPEFITTER
A STORY
TOBIAS S. BUCKELL

Content notes: *depiction of death; character injury*

AKAR FROZE MIDTUNNEL as a fireball exploded past her. Shocked and frozen, she drifted in the air, still sailing past speed rungs. She reached out, and her fingers lightly brushed the polished wooden dowels with a repeating click-clack-tap sound. There was no gravity. That meant the hydrogen engines were off, so they couldn't rotate to spread out the damage. And *that* meant more impacts would keep hitting this area. She needed to brace.

She patted at her uniform, and then coughed as wisps of smoke escaped out from under the fabric and between her fingers. Where had that explosion—

A burly arm abruptly snagged her out of the air and rotated her around. A third-level damage control and safety operator hung inside of the crack of the now open six-inch thick rolldoor that led to DC&S Station Four: a long cylinder, sunk into the ice-rock side of a shaft. Reinforced with bands of light, but strong metal, and around that, a bolus of cellulose reactive armor to protect its inhabitants.

"Thank the undergods," Akar muttered. She almost hadn't made it before the rolldoor locked shut.

"You're being reassigned to a new task," the operator with a neatly trimmed beard and regulation tight eyeshadow snapped. They shoved a square, handheld radio against Akar's torso. "Get back down the shaft until you get a signal from any nearby DC&S stations. You're going to be a temporary repeater. We can't reach the DCC. We have no orders."

They couldn't reach damage control command? Buried in the center of all the mass they'd dragged out here? Akar tried to imagine how many redundant systems had to fail for that to happen.

This was dire.

Akar noticed that the operator's aquamarine uniform had a long, dark stain across the front, and they grimaced as they pushed themself back through the small sliver of light in the gloomy tunnel that the DC&S station provided. Akar could hear the murmur of a commissioner's orders, and inspectors giving situation reports from people inside.

She tried to protest one more time. It would be a lot safer in here. "Reaction Plan Blue says I get to Station Four and remain in lockdown until the all-clear—"

"We don't need a panting level-three pipefitter right now; we need someone to float a damn radio down the shaft. You pick anyone up, you ask if they have orders for us, and relay that back. Do they have any information we need to know about? You relay that back! Get it? You're a human relay. That's your new job. Now fucking move! Use channel three-four to pass on anything you hear from other stations back to us. Got that?"

"I don't have any survival gear!" Akar protested as the operator almost disappeared around the rolldoor.

"*Thirds* ..." the operator spat, and then hesitated for a second to look around. They tugged at something on the wall by the door. "Here."

They shoved a bundled-up vacuum kit under Akar's left arm. "No helmet comms, it's broken, that's why you have the handheld. Helmet visor might be cracked, we had debris bouncing around when the engines cut off. This is the best I can do. Now get down there and pass on anything you hear. Channel three-four! Thirty-four!"

Akar started swearing as the operator grabbed her by the scruff of her burned neck—she was sure she'd get a demerit for that later—and threw her back down the shaft. Back where she'd come from.

As she tumbled away she frantically pulled the survival gear out of the vacuum kit. She let the helmet hang right by her hip as she pulled the legs on and zipped the torso of the suit.

Finally, she turned the radio on. Used her thumb to rotate the thick channel dial to common contact channel one.

"Any DC&S station, this is Third Level Akar Savari—contact?" She figured she could drop her job title from the transmission. More likely they'd respond.

The entire starship shuddered. The wall to her left convulsed, the superstructure warped and twisted by direct impacts. Akar folded herself around the radio to protect it as she ricocheted around the shaft.

They needed to fire the engines back up to maneuver. But if they turned them on right now, she'd be toothpaste smeared on the walls if the ship dodged anything. And if they sped up, she'd "fall" all the way down the shaft, speeding up faster and faster as the ship moved past her with her still inside it, until she splashed against the endcap of the shaft.

"Any DC&S station, this is Third Level Akar Savari, contact?"

For her own immediate survival, it was just as well that the ship was disabled, floating along the trajectory it had been screaming along as it arrowed toward the enemy. Long term, however ...

"Any DC&S station, this is Third Level Akar Savari—contact?"

She flew past the residential warrens and caught a glimpse of hammocks twisting and fluttering about. Debris swirled through the air on the other side of the thick peep-windows on the rolldoors, and bodies jostled against each other in the chaos. She'd been asleep in one of them when the first cannon fire had struck, ripped a hole in a distant hull location, and the alarms started up.

Three more strikes had shaken everything around her as she rushed to pull on her uniform. Then the local breach alarm had kicked off, the strobes all flashing blue in unison. That shouldn't have happened. Housing was near impossible to crack. Other than the command cockpit, it was the most armored section.

But they'd drilled for this often enough. Akar could find the nearest

DC&S station with eyes closed. Literally. Her residential commissioner tied a bandana around her eyes and spun her in the air several times, and then let her go. She, and a bunch of level sevens that were bunked up together, even practiced finding the nearest DC&S stations in the dark.

So, she'd known what to do. Hardly even thought about it. She'd gone to the appropriate station. She was supposed to hunker down in the armored DC&S station with the other critical damage control and support personnel. They were to get ready to swarm out when the order went out to repair damage.

After the attack.

Akar was a pipefitter. She basically fixed broken steam pipes. She installed new ones. She made sure gauges were oiled and read, and her notes were passed back up the chain of command. There was more, but it was boring. Nearly punishment. Day in and day out, coasting through the shafts slowly when there wasn't gravity, walking wearily around from gauge to gauge when under acceleration.

What was she doing halfway down the Rose Shaft without a helmet on, which violated three different regulations she'd taken an oath to never disobey?

"Any DC&S station, this is Third Level Akar Savari —contact?"

"TL Savari, this is—"

The words ended in an oceanic roar over the small handheld radio. Akar didn't understand for a split second. Then she grabbed the helmet with one hand while she fumbled with the radio to get channel thirty-four with just the thumb of her other hand. Then she shouted: "Station Four: fire imminent! I'm offline!"

She barely got the helmet snugged on with her other hand before the whole shaft snapped like a whip, thanks to the frequent joints that allowed the mass of the ice-rock ship to shift without damaging interior infrastructure. Akar now saw the explosion downshaft that she'd heard over the radio. A white-hot geyser of hull ice and air rushed up at her. She barely had enough time to grab a speed rung and yank herself into the safety of a ledge.

The safety harness in the ledge kept her glued to the wall, but she still took several hits to the helmet hard enough to deform it. She struck her left arm hard when the wall under her buckled with the harness, and several ricocheted pieces ice cracked her ribs and foot when it flailed out into the open.

This was bad. They were getting the shit kicked out of them. A full-on cannonade to the side of the ship as they passed through the Akhedrian strait. The three asteroids surrounded the neck of the best approach to Udesh, which the ship had to pass through to make the gravity slingshot away from Udesh and toward the far fringes of the system, where comets hung far from the two suns' light.

And the three asteroids, towed into place for just this sort of job, bristled with heavy cannon.

"This is our great dilemma," the elected potentates said to the gallery crowds on Aruseah before launch. "Either we pay the ruinous price Akhedria demands, dooming us to starving out in the wilderness before we get our vats up and running, or we add twenty years to the journey. There are no other ways to gain the necessary speed. We cannot afford to spend all our resources on fuel." So, it was time for a ship-wide vote. Even a CEO wouldn't make a decision of this importance alone. There would be riots, an impeachment, and likely a fast trial and trip out the airlock in their Off-day best.

They had voted to invest in life-giving ice instead. Hundreds and hundreds of feet of ice, sprayed on layer after layer by tugs. It would give them air and water until they could start comet mining, and it would also be their shield on this journey's start.

"This raft of ours will sustain and protect us until we can reach the first comets. There, we can find ore, water, and other raw materials."

But they had to survive Akhedrian cannon first.

Akar peeked out. Mangled pipes and shattered debris everywhere. Scorch marks. The fire had guttered out, though.

No air.

Akar looked at the little handheld radio. The brass case, channel dial, and silvered mic button looked okay from through her helmet. She'd made a choice to stay alive—no one would begrudge her that. But the DC&S station that sent her out as a relay would be disconnected again unless she could figure out a way to use that radio in the vacuum.

She unclipped her harness and looked around the survival niche. Niches usually had a canister of emergency air to help out if a suit ran out, or got damaged and lost a lot of air quick. That, and it would have a patch kit to stop the aforementioned leak.

Another impact shook everything.

Akar used foaming glue from the patch kit to fix a rubber sheet from the kit in place around the niche, and then opened the vent valve on the air tank. It hissed, and soon the rubber bulged outward into the shaft from the air pressure, but held. As long as no more debris came hurtling down the shaft at her, she should be able to use the radio.

She took a breath and flipped the helmet open. No prickle of vacuum, just cold air.

Good. She had a job to do.

"Any DC&S station," she radioed on common channel one. "This is Third Level Akar Savari—contact?"

She held the radio out and up against the bulging rubber for a clear signal. Hopefully she wouldn't lose her arm to more debris.

"Hello? Hello? Contact. DC&S Station Six," a tremulous voice responded over static.

"Station Six, hold on this channel," Akar shouted.

She switched to three-four. "DC&S Station Four, this is Third Level Akar Savari. Contact?"

Only static replied.

Akar tried a few more times, and then pulled herself up to the wall and rested her forehead against the cold ice dirt.

Back to common one, then. "Station Six—contact?"

A new voice replied, deeper, a little gruff and grumpy. "Contact. Fourth Level Kanata Silanis here."

"Do you have any orders for me?" Akar asked wearily.

Static bounced around the walls for a moment. Then Kanata said, "We were wondering if you had orders for us?"

Akar stared at the radio. After too long, she said, "I'm a pipefitter."

"We're fifth levels, mostly. Most of us are janitorial. Scum pond maintenance."

Akar wanted to just smash the radio right there and wait in the bubble with her helmet on until someone rescued her. All this, and she'd found a bunch of Fifths hiding in a DC&S station.

Kanata radioed again. "Third Level Akar Savari? Boru says she knows you. You both are in the same warren?"

Akar placed the radio in the air right in front of her nose. She let go of it and just stared at the pinholes in the speaker grille. She'd barely qualified as pipefitter. She'd failed the star chart memorization to be a spotter on the hull, which her friend Davyses told her would be the easiest role to get into for a spot.

"Big risk, big reward," he had told her. "Or do you want to rot away the rest of your life on a moonlet that was all drilled up a hundred years ago? You're struggling to make ends meet on a husk, Akar. Or you could head out into the void with me and make your fortune."

It was the same damn problem she'd had on the moonlet Aruseah. The resources too tight, the recycling margins slim.

A society built to withstand the vacuum of space was a strict society. An engineer's society. Checkboxes and lists. She had to follow a twenty-point checklist just to put on a layer suit, let alone get cleared to go outside in the vacuum.

Too easy to forget a step. Quick to get to the final moment.

Her mom wept the first time Akar failed an egress preflight test. "If you really cared more, you could get the list right," she whispered to Akar that night.

And Akar had curled up into a ball and bit her lip to stop from crying in her sleeping cubby.

How could she care more? She wanted to be alive! Missing item ten meant she'd risked depressurizing once the airlock opened because she hadn't doublechecked her seals.

"Your ankle cuffs!" the instructor had shouted at her, red in the face.

Akar remembered watching her cohort bound across the moon's surface ... through tempered vacuum glass. They'd come back in flushed and excited. "You can't appreciate home until you've seen it from the outside!"

She used a timer for medicine. Written checklists. And yet that still didn't keep away all the disappointment whenever she forgot something mission critical. People relied on her to stay alive, and she could barely keep herself alive.

"Pipefitter?" she'd asked the recruiter.

"You had a high systems aptitude," the recruiter said. They'd looked at Akar over a key slate in one hand. "And steam systems are analog complex in a way you intuit well."

No checklists, but she got a lot of the scut work that she never did well with. Keeping gauge logs, basic maintenance. In the first four months since they'd left Aruseah she'd started out as a Second Level Pipefitter and managed to slowly fail her way down to Third. She was a shift or so away from Fourth given the last chewing out she got.

But she'd made it aboard, and many friends hadn't. They'd jealously thrown her a going-away party that ended in tears because she was never coming back.

A hundred thousand brave souls had set out to skim Udesh and use the gas giant's gravity well to get their cobbled-together mess of a ship the velocity it needed to head out far past the inner system's fighting and politics.

They'd build a new civilization out in the icy Oort Clouds. So far out that their descendants may one day trickle out into another star system's far edge.

She'd always felt an itch. A faint suspicion she didn't belong to the families that lived in Aruseah's moonlet warrens for generation after generation. This was the way to banish it.

"Third Level Akar Savari?"

Akar stretched and grabbed the radio. "Still here."

"You're the highest level we can reach. That puts you in charge of DC&S for the area, per regulation—"

"I'm too banged up to get the handbook quoted at me," Akar grumbled. Why her? After failing her way down the hierarchy of the ship, she'd encountered a DC&S station full of people even lower ranked than she was. What were the odds? She didn't need more to deal with. This situation was already insane. "What are you working with?"

"Ten able, two injured. As Fourth Level, I've taken commission of Station Six. I was about to give the command to spread out through the shaft and report back."

"Don't do that," Akar said.

"Recovery protocol says the first postattack function is to catalog damage, then triage up a fix list in coordination with the other two DC&S stations within the designated shaft line."

"You want an order?" Akar said. "Here's the order: stay put. Keep the rolldoor dogged shut. Every five minutes spend that fifth minute on the clock scanning the common channels for other DC&S stations."

She could imagine Fourth Level Kanata Silanis fuming on the other side. "Can I ask why?" Kanata finally asked, sounding strained.

"The cannons are reloading." Akar might not remember much from her training, but she remembered *that*. The CEO would be giving commands to keep the thickest part of the ice shield rotated toward the cannons as the hydrogen-oxygen rockets burned away. But their vehicle was a hodgepodge of girders, ice, and rock, carved up with tunnels, and festooned with mining machinery. It didn't move fast. Definitely couldn't dodge shit. They could only keep taking it on the chin and hoping they'd armored up enough. "I'd harness up if you aren't already."

A long moment of static.

"Wishing you hadn't signed up, Kanata?" Akar asked the air with a laugh. The adrenaline made her hands shake.

"We'll get ready," Kanata said.

Akar could hear the fear in his voice. Her joking hadn't helped.

She doubled up and let out a few sobs silently to herself. She'd held it all together since the moment she woke up, heart pounding, to the sound of the alarms. And the horror of realizing that, oh shit, the Akhedriens were going to open fire.

It had been ten years since the Akhedriens first announced a toll on using their gas giant's gravity well as a catapult out into the outer system. This crew and mass of ice, machinery, and rock were the first to try shooting the gap without paying.

Akar had deeply believed the Akhedriens would never fire a shot. That it was all bluster.

So had everyone else. "Just a bunch of corporate suits looking to squeeze us" was the attitude.

They'd been cocky enough to let the sleep shifts stand instead of putting everyone on alert. Who came up with that? Why had she even agreed to it? It was dumb. She should have holed up in a survival ledge from the start. Following the standard flyby manual made no sense when doing something that had never been done.

"Are you sure?" Kanata asked.

Akar listened. Nothing but groans through the superstructure right now. Distant pops and clicks.

Then she felt it. "Harness up!" She reached back and pulled herself in. Helmet first, then harness. She heard something unintelligible from Kanata, but it cut out when she clicked the helmet into place.

The shaft shivered and bucked. Akar's limbs smacked about. Something ripped the rubber sheet away and air burst out into the shaft. Fire flickered for a second, then dissipated.

Akar closed her eyes. If this was it, she didn't want to see it. She curled in a ball and hugged herself, then screamed. Her right shoulder felt wrong. Very wrong.

Then a deep rumble against her back got her attention. Rockets firing.

The tug of acceleration reoriented everything. Debris began tumbling down as the shaft became a hole. She was strapped to a wall, but on her side now.

If the engines were up, then generators would be back on soon, she realized, imagining commands from deep in the very heart of it all. The protected command center, and near it all the protective armored family bunkers where frightened civilians hid away, would be a hive of activity as they calculated the best burn.

It wouldn't be too long before life support came back on.

With that would come air. And with this mess, that would mean fire.

Akar waited as more debris rained down past her. Anything shaken loose. Anything broken. Let it all rattle and peel off.

When the killer rain passed, she leaned out and looked down, as if she stood at the top of an elevator shaft.

Pipes jerked about, and Akar watched liquid oxygen slowly pour out and vaporize. The pumps couldn't quite push it up here under this acceleration. But when the engines cut, it would pour out.

Akar stepped out and grabbed the nearest speed rung with her good arm.

"Okay," she muttered. "Whatever you do, you never go out into the shaft during acceleration."

But they had speed rungs. And in an emergency ...

Akar jumped out.

She fell. Slowly at first. The acceleration was moonlet levels of gravity. A gentle tug.

They were pushing more juice, gaining more power as DC&S down in the bowels got more fuel to the rockets. She fell past people hunkered down in niches who stared at her in surprise, and several rubber emergency shelters bulging with air inside. And a couple in tatters.

Akar grabbed at a speed rung to slow down.

She couldn't get a full grip, but half-broken grips slowed her down until she could find a rail to let friction keep her fall at a decent pace.

"But not too fast," she muttered. Easy to lose track of your relative speed and end up in trouble.

Though fast enough that she could get to Station Six before the third, and final, cannonade. The Akhedriens could target only interceptive fire at the nonpaying ship as they approached, but the moment the mess of rock and ice flashed past, it would be moving faster than cannon could be fired at it.

Acceleration alarms flashed up and down the rails.

"Fuck."

The wall slammed against her bad shoulder. Akar flailed about as maneuvering rockets kicked the ship around. She found herself in the very center of the shaft, the railing just out of reach.

"Shit."

She wobbled about, swam in the air, and screamed.

How far was Station Six? She'd shot past a door already. Six should be coming up soon, but she was moving really panting fast. She could barely notice anything but the panicked thump of her heart and ...

Six. She saw the door below.

Akar blew out a breath so she wouldn't hurt her lungs and ripped her helmet off. She threw it against the wall, and spun around as the thrown helmet gave her just enough of nudge to slowly, achingly, teeter a bit over toward a nearby rail. In the vacuum, she didn't have much time. Her face prickled, and her vision began to cloud over.

Akar ignored the thud and clack of debris around her as she grabbed and squeezed both hands as hard as she could. Her gloves took the brunt of it, but finally friction chewed through them until she felt skin tear and rip on the rail. She squeezed even harder as ruined glove and flesh melded.

She yanked herself to a last-of-her-breath, screaming stop a body length below Station Six and closed her eyes to try and protect them.

Each speed rung up required her to use her wrists to climb and awkwardly feel her way along, while still without air. But at the last rung a gloved hand reached out, and then another, and another, and suits dragged her up and into the airlock.

Someone shoved and twisted a helmet on, and Akar took a deep, grateful breath as the airlock refilled and her ears popped. Her vision returned.

Thank the undergods. It had felt like forever out in the airless shaft.

"I told you all to stay put," she said, voice muffled, but with air around them, audible.

"Kanata ordered three of us in the airlock to look for survivors. We saw you falling past."

She tried to open the inner door on her own, but her bloodied hands were a mess of shredded flesh and fiber. She could only hold them up uselessly in front of her.

Inside, seven suited-up crew looked at her with shock.

"We can't raise Aid Station Two or Three," the closest one, an older man with gray in a patchy beard, said. And she recognized Kanata's voice right away. He held up an emergency kit. "This is what we have."

"Morphine, the small syrette," Akar said. She grabbed gauze and wound it around the meat of her hands as Kanata stabbed her with the one-use syringe.

The warm prickle of opiates washed over her with relief as the ship took several more hits. Rocks rattled against the airlock to DC&S Station Six.

Akar looked at the bodies on the floor, the broken doors to tool drawers. Thankfully, most of the clamps looked to have held and kept their tools secure. But some had broken free.

"Section leadership got here first," Kanata said softly. "The arc welder broke loose. Just rattled around the interior like a marble. We secured the station after we arrived."

Everyone was already suited up.

Akar tried to ignore the blood splashed against the walls and ceilings. It made her stomach twist. Made her feel oddly dizzy. She found her eyes kept skipping past the bodies. *Not now. Later. Don't think about it. If you think about it, you'll break.*

She'd never seen bodies back on Aruseah. Not even at her mom's funeral. It was a clean, antiseptic function with photos rotating on white walls over rented flowers. People didn't *die* back home. They just became memories, really.

How many generations of sameness did Aruseah represent? Over a hundred years since the last tunnel had been drilled out, maybe two hundred since Aruseah had been a frontier of any kind. She'd hated it. Thrown herself at this chance to escape routine, and order, and utter sameness. Something to nuke the boredom.

"A moment," Akar said. The morphine helped push the throbbing insanity of her hands back, but now it clouded her mind a bit more than she wanted.

Kanata rubbed her forearms. The touch felt electric, even through the suit. Akar trembled for a second. Swallowed the need to cry. Emotions were okay, but in this moment, they were a threatening storm.

"What do we do?" Kanata asked. "I'm sorry to ask."

Akar stared at him. "You're the oldest one here. You had them posted in the airlock. You're clearly the leader here. What do *you* think we should do next?"

"You've got the level," he said flatly. "You're the commissioner."

Akar awkwardly scratched the side of her face with the back of her hands. "That's insane. I'm the youngest person standing here."

"Commissioner," one of the suited-up DC&S levels said. "We all agreed to the command structure in the founding documents. You signed to this."

She didn't want it. It felt like too much. So many strands of responsibility tangled up in systems that hung oppressively overhead. Too many possibilities.

Decisions.

But they were all waiting for her to take command.

Akar lowered her voice and leaned in close to Kanata. "My attention is highly variable, and I'm unmedicated because my body won't tolerate it. I'm Third Level for a fucking reason. I barely have the crew handbook memorized. I got aboard hanging by my fingernails."

She bit her lip. She hated saying it out loud. In the carefully structured life of the warrens on Aruseah she'd been a liability in the eyes of the Departmenters. She'd fought hard to get aboard this ship, hoping that, out in a new frontier, maybe she could find a place that didn't involve pitying looks and exaggerated patience.

The paint crew Departmenter who oversaw her third shift all but threw a party when Akar told them she was leaving Aruseah. She had so many demerits for late and missed shifts she knew pick duty in the recycling vats would be in her future soon enough.

"DC&S protocol says we dog the airlock and hunker until the all-clear comes," Kanata prompted in a half-whisper. "I have photographic memory. I'll be your aide."

Akar closed her eyes.

The engines still thundered. The distant thuds were growing. She held her hands out, trying to feel the axis of the ship passing through her.

"We're still spinning. Slowly, but we're still spinning. The CEO and navigators are trying to spread the damage out as we pass by."

"That's good."

"We're firing engines and generators are back up." Akar opened her eyes to look right at Kanata. "They're pumping air again."

"That's good," someone said.

"I don't know." Akar felt wrong about it. "It's pouring out into the shaft."

She needed to sit and think, but there wasn't time. She was pulling on a web of hints and little alerts that her subconscious had piled together to point at something she couldn't quite form into words just yet.

But the deep sense of dread kept rising in her, a beast from fathoms deep, woven out of intuition and her constant idling brain looking around.

THE PIPEFITTER

If she could just force it into something more piercing.

That never worked.

"Get those bodies in a stowable cupboard," Akar ordered. "Make sure everything is strapped down."

That got everyone doing something instead of looking at her so she could start pacing. Well, limping. She'd love something to fiddle with, but her hands hurt.

Twenty-five steps from the rolldoor to the end of the canister-shaped station. Twenty-five back, keeping out of everyone's way. Nodding as if approving their labor while she stared off in the distance.

"There are people sheltering in the shaft, and the air's back on."

"Good, they'll be running low."

"They'll all burn in the next attack. Something was sparking fireballs out there when the shaft still had some air in it," Akar said.

Stay here, do nothing. Survive. Those were orders.

Kanata looked sick. "We're ordered to stay put."

"That's what you said, yes."

He listened to another set of thuds. "The impacts are getting closer, but we have a few minutes to get out there and turn off the air. We could save them all."

"And all die alongside them instead of following orders." But there was something else. "And since we can't warn navigation, what happens when a shaft full of air burns out from a hole while we're spinning and creating a form of gravity?" Without gravity, it burned slow, low, and around the ignition point. But with spin, it would act like fire on a planetary body.

"What happens?" Kanata asked.

"Hey: photographic memory? I'm a pipefitter, I used to be a painter—I have no idea, Kanata. I was asking you, but I have to assume it'll knock us off course."

They didn't have an unlimited amount of fuel to burn. And an error right now, as they plunged toward a gas giant while getting hammered by cannon fire from the Akhedrian cannon, could compound if it wasn't noticed.

Navigation would be trying to counteract the impacts with counterthrusts, but they wouldn't be ready for a full shaft blow out, would they?

"If they're trying to send air back into the residentials and stations and it's pouring into the shaft instead, they won't expect the explosion. We have to cut off air."

"How?"

"I know where to find the cutoff valves," Akar said. "Pipefitter. But we need to turn off up and down. I can take down."

"You can't climb on those hands, and we're under acceleration now."

Akar looked at her bandaged hands. "Shit. I forgot."

Kanata frowned at that, unable to apparently conceive how someone could forget they were wounded. "You'll have to walk us through by radio, but stay by the lock."

"I can do that." She didn't tell them the helmet had a crack and was likely leaking air. It would have to do. "I just need tape. For the radio."

She flipped the emergency helmet they'd given her around in her hands. "This it?"

Kanata looked apologetic. "Better than nothing. No comms in that one."

"I know." Akar looked around, then pulled some of the medical tape off her wrists. She taped the radio to the left side of the visor, stuck a pencil in her mouth, and pulled the helmet on.

"Well," she mumbled through the pencil, using it to push the talk button. Then, through teeth gritted around it, broadcast, "Let's go!"

Kanata hesitated. Then he nodded and pulled his own helmet on to follow everyone else out.

The teams split, half up, half down, reporting in as they moved. Akar lay down by the rolldoor, stomach pressed against the lip, helmet as far out over the shaft's abyss as she could for the radio to get as much of a chance to reach as possible.

She could see a faint mist hanging around the crack in her helmet. Air, slowly escaping from around the widening crack and tape.

Check-ins came every five minutes as they moved. Kanata moved them around like chess pieces, hunting for junction points, pipes vaguely remembered in passing.

Kanata helped, chiming in with bits of blueprints he'd seen when leafing through manuals in training.

"This would be easier if I was with you all," Akar wheezed. It was getting harder to hold onto the details, she found. Oxygen deprivation.

And in her stomach, she could feel the impacts shaking everything even harder. They were turning over slowly, so slowly, and soon it would be their turn, one last time, to get hammered.

You're a tiny speck of human flesh, stuck in miles of gantries, support beams, ice, and rock all welded together with some rockets, shafts, and armored capsules buried into the very heart of it, covered in a several hundred-meter-thick shield of ice.

It's spinning, and the cannon fire is chewing it all to bits.

But this is space, even if chunks break apart, and structure fails, once they get past this chokepoint, they can lick their wounds, and reconnect it all.

There's no atmosphere to destroy it, no gravity to make it all fall.

They just had to survive, and then they could rebuild. Fighting in space could be weird like that, humanity had found.

Akar used all her spare energy to pull attention back down into the moment. She couldn't tell if the dizziness was deprivation or exhaustion.

She just had to keep her people moving, getting to the right places. Kill the air just there, there, and there, and later they could contain the slow moving fires that remained.

In the future, they'd need to station people in smaller armored pods near critical junctions. The ultimate backup. Three people, in two pods. Because it always came down to some individual needing to put hands on something mechanical.

"Kanata ..."

"Yes commissioner?"

"I think that does it. Get your people to safety wherever closest. And brace."

The cannon fire was close now. Debris tumbled down the shaft. There would be people she ordered out of this safe place now looking up, fearing for their lives.

Possibly dying.

"Get to safety!" Akar ordered, as her vision faded and the airlock around her broke out in dancing spots.

Akar woke up with a gasp. She lay propped up against the back wall of the station, with Kanata next to her. Bandages covered his forearms and black smudges covered his uniform.

"It got done," he said wearily.

She stared over at the emergency row lights. "How many got hurt?"

"A few."

She'd figured that when considering outcomes. If she'd had more time to plan, to think, to consider—

"But they're alive," Kanata said. "Thanks to you."

The engines cut out, and the heavy weight on her chest disappeared.

"I told you to stay put, seek shelter."

"I disobeyed. I sent Boru up to you."

And if he hadn't done that? She'd be dead, no doubt. "Thank you."

"You said you weren't the right person for this." Kanata pushed himself up into the air and twisted to look her face to face. "But we were running on the traditional Aruseah ways, all the way up to the moment of the attack. Regimented, ordered, hierarchal. Bureaucratic. They'd assigned you a slot based on testing, but not real life."

"Everyone can pull together in an emergency," Akar said.

"Many didn't. And many just followed what they were told, didn't adapt. You were your best. Are you usually your best in moments like this?"

Akar looked incredulous. "I'm a painter from Aruseah. I've never been in an emergency in my life. Every minute of my life has been regulated, planned, and set in place. Do this, go there. Listen to the Aruseah scheduling system with its soothing voice and do what it says, don't get distracted by reading about something outside your rated expertise area, that isn't on your computerized life fucking plan."

"Whether it's variable attention, or something else, most of the people on this trip don't quite fit in, back on Aruseah," Kanata said.

"That's why they're rolling the dice, that's why they're risking so much. To go somewhere new, young, exciting, messy, distracting. Dangerous."

"Good for them."

"You're going to do well as commissioner," Kanata predicted. "They'll move you over to Six, and give me Four."

"You're cocky!" Akar flicked his sternum, and he ever-so-slowly began to drift away from her toward the ceiling.

"No." He grabbed a chair to pause himself. "Long before we came to this star system, our ancestors sat in the bushes of some far-off world. And the ones who memorized where the good land was, and what berries could kill us, they were treasured by the tribe because they led it to water, and kept them fed. And the jumpy, distractible person on the edge who hears the rustle of some predator first, well, they might not have realized why they needed different brains before, but when you saved them from the attack, they would understand why you were just as important."

Akar shook her head. "I'm just exhausted, Kanata."

"I'm told choice fatigue is brutal." He smiled and handed her a syrette. "Try this."

"I don't need more morphine."

"It's a mild sedative. Take the edge off."

"Then what am I supposed to do?"

He smiled. "Nothing. Nothing at all. Just be, for now. We've got it from here, commissioner. You've done enough."

She lay there and felt the rumble of the ship start up again, low and slow, adjusting course as they screamed toward the very edges of Udesh's vast cloud bands.

Out beyond Udesh, the smaller rock-ice planetoids of the outer system, though right now most of them were on the other side of the sun in their orbit. There would be no more gravity assists from here out, just coasting far out into the depths of nothingness.

Until they acquired their first comet, and began mining, it would be a long, quiet journey into the depths.

A commissioner usually had an administrative assistant, Akar thought. Someone else to take the notes, double-check the list.

Suddenly the long, dark voyage seemed less of a desperate act.

No, she was seeing possibilities now. Possibilities old, regimented Aruseah could never offer her.

Out there, out beyond all the old, crusty planetoids and greater planets, she could be herself.

IMPACT
A STORY
JASMINE STARR

THE BUZZING BEGAN as a vague annoyance. Something Bridget could almost pretend to ignore. But the longer it droned, the more it pervaded her mind, poisoning her every thought until she was ready to rip out her hair, clump by clump. It was probably the neighbors ... a wayward light ... the circuit breaker ... the fridge gone rogue. She could ignore it ... wait until her mom got home ... become neurotypical ... fall asleep .... Ah, who was she kidding?

Bridget tumbled out of bed and marched down the hall, flinging open the front door—but there was nothing out of the ordinary. No erratic light. No neighbors. Only night wind, the never-ending hum, and the serious possibility of tinnitus.

Before she had the chance to turn inside, a creature skittered down from her roof, slipping onto the ground right ahead of her. She stepped back, surprised. It was roughly the size and shape of a sea urchin, if an urchin was soft and iridescent and made entirely out of what looked like the tail plumage of a twelve-wired bird of paradise. It rolled slowly toward her—although *rolled* wasn't the right word—shifting like a tumbleweed in erratic wind, with the grip and calculated control of an octopus. Bridget realized she was grasping at straws, trying to attach something familiar to this bizarre creature.

"What …?" she breathed, eyeing it warily.

The creature stretched toward her, pseudo-tentacles waving in almost a greeting. And the buzzing stopped. It was even more of a relief than she had dared to imagine.

Bridget had just begun processing the silence when the creature rumbled, as if clearing its own vocal cords, snapping her back to attention. She backed up, calculating the distance back to safety, wondering how quickly she could shut and lock her door.

"This family is primarily English-speaking, yes? Able to converse in this tongue?" The urchin-tumbleweed-twelve-wire-octopus asked, despite not having a visible mouth. Bridget realized her own wide-open mouth was even more visible at the moment, and promptly shut it.

"Apologies, this must be odd," said the creature, twiddling its feelers almost sheepishly. "The elders are discussing with the mother of this home. Elders figured children could converse. For education, perhaps? Or to be rid of the young one." It burbled in some approximation of a laugh. "Glad the conversational request was answered."

She crouched down to the creature's level, resisting the urge to test out the texture of its feelers. They looked so sleek and shiny, constantly roving around, grabbing onto anything, weighing it, tossing it away. The creature quickly discarded pebbles and leaves, but it seemed to take a particular interest in a lichen-covered stick, rubbing it against its feelers experimentally. Almost like it wanted to try out the textures, too.

Bridget suddenly remembered she was in the middle of a conversation. "Request … you mean, the buzzing? Why were you trying to contact humans with buzzing? That's never what we think of when we hear that kind of sound." She knew she was missing the point, but was much too distracted to care.

"Ah, that was why it took you so long to answer me. Duly noted!"

"It's alright. You're lucky I heard it. Most people tune out sounds like that."

There was an awkward silence. Bridget recognized that she was probably supposed to speak, but absolutely nothing was getting to her vocal cords. She noticed she was swaying. And the creature, still waving its feelers about, was echoing her movements.

Odd. Everyone else would have told her to stop, looked at her oddly, made her feel self-conscious. Or, if they imitated her, it would never be in a nice way. But this felt more genuine. Like the creature enjoyed the feeling, too.

"That is in luck indeed!" the creature wiggled happily, putting an end to its sway, interrupting her thoughts. "Regardless. And to perform an introduction. Ah ... the human custom of identity ... how to conform to this ..." It absentmindedly fiddled with the stick, considering its words carefully. "We do not assign titles to individuals, but the people of home are entitled the eboir. Home of the eboir is within the feature humans call Divalia Fossa, Rheasilvia, of asteroid Vesta in the, ah, the asteroid belt. Humans enjoy descriptive labels. Respect that."

"You're from ... Mount Rheasilvia ... on Vesta ... in space." She gaped. "And you've come ... my mom ... you ..."

The full force of it suddenly hit her, and Bridget squeaked, falling over backward into her doorway. In all her fifteen years, she'd never expected anything like this. Her prior special interest in astronomical objects didn't prepare her for a *living* thing. That spoke. To her.

"Yes. Seem to have gotten lost on the way to the nearby food market." The creature repeated its same odd pseudo-laugh. Bridget could only stare, equal parts horrified and confused.

"Ah. Misplaced attempt at sapiens custom of humor," continued the alien, misreading her stunned reaction. "Apologies. Should not, er, attempt other cultural traditions without sufficient knowledge. How insensitive. Sincerely." It pulled itself into the house, feelers meandering, its back appendages gripping tightly onto the doorframe. Thankfully, it stopped just beyond the doorway. Bridget wasn't sure she could stand it if someone she didn't know came any further into what she felt to be her sanctum. Especially without permission.

She consciously slowed her breathing, taking stock of the situation. There was no sense panicking and upsetting them both if there wasn't anything to panic about. "No, it's fine. Jokes aren't really a big deal. It's just ... are the eboir capable of killing or hurting me in any way?"

The creature paused, tensing, seemingly assessing its own situation. After a beat, it replied. "Nay. But the preliminary studies of human behavior suggest this is hazardous. The eboir have very few defenses. The only predator the eboir evolved to face is planetary winds. Hence the multitude of grippers!" It wiggled them demonstratively. "And the paucity of anything requiring external moisture. The accessibility of your orifices frightens me."

She considered it for a moment, then immediately wished she hadn't. "Yep. It frightens me too." She ran out of conversation and simply stared, brows hoisted, arms protectively tucked around her body, realizing the reason for her mom's late work night was ... an alien visit.

Bridget suddenly scrambled upright, remembering her manners. Even if her guest was ... of the extraterrestrial sort, she did have an obligation to be polite. "Hello, nicetomeetyou. I'm Bridget Meyer," she recited, before remembering her audience. "Although it's not like the term 'eboir,' it's a name for me alone. Well, my last name is shared with my family, but not the first. And my neighbors have entirely different ones." *Except for the two kids named Emma in #23 and #28. You know, that was the most popular name here in 2008 ... and 2014 ... and 2018. I guess people really like naming their kids Emma.*

But she couldn't add that. Nobody could possibly appreciate such a high level of rambling. And she was being so non sequitur—she met an alien, and immediately started talking about names?

"You have enough sequences of sounds for every creature individual?"

Bridget's mouth dropped open. The eboir didn't mind her ranting. Someone else found this ... interesting! She could barely keep herself from jumping up and down and screaming with joy. It was all she could do to continue in a reasonably level tone of voice.

"I mean, no. I do share my names with others, in any English-speaking place, really. My first name is fairly common, especially here, and in Ireland, and oddly, Malawi." She raised her shoulders defensively. "I like researching name statistics. It's not that weird, okay?"

"No, it sounds an interesting endeavor," the eboir said, confused. "Why wouldn't all humans enjoy it?"

Bridget's chest filled with warmth.

"Anyway," she continued, grinning impossibly wide. "We don't individually name any animal other than humans, unless the animal is somehow connected to humans. Although we do give each species a sort of title they all share, called a scientific name. But it's not for the animals' benefits, it's for us humans, so we can classify them."

"You try to sensically categorize other species. But leave your own to mires of confusion?"

Bridget raised her eyebrows, impressed. "Yep, that's true. My species does like to put individuality over common sense." It'd been a very long time since she'd had a thoughtful conversation that made her question her assumptions. She was beginning to like this creature. "But it's useful when you have to differentiate between a bunch of people in a room. Although having common names does kind of nullify that point. Heck, there are three Daniels in my English class alone. The last name, the surname, often helps differentiate between people with the same first name. Which is why they were originally created, actually! In England, they came from job titles or more distinct characteristics, and eventually became part of the identifying—"

Bridget trailed off, realizing how chilled the room was. The eboir couldn't be comfortable—other people never were, in her preferred temperature. As she motioned to close the door, gesturing that it was okay for the eboir to come further into the house, it flapped its tentacles in dismay. "Perhaps it can remain open? Unused to higher temperature, lack of wind. The staler quality."

Bridget nodded, trying not to smile, leaving the door and pushing open the surrounding windows. Who knew she would share the hatred of stagnant air with a Rheasilvian?

Rheasilvia ... the word wandered around her synapses, trying to retrieve the thought it had briefly connected with.

"Wait, why are your species on Earth? Talking to my *mother*?"

"Ah. The need is to find infallible protections from meteors, and Earth has given rise to asteroid collision technology. Impacts are a strong issue in home." The eboir's grippers drooped. "Life there was created by the bringing of carbonaceous chondrites, and sustained by their hydrogen. Homes are made of the craters. And this is even the way greater Rheasilvia was formed. It is respected, is the start of everything known. But these same objects that serve so well fracture and destroy Vesta. The eboir must search for an answer to stop this. Or it will eventually destroy everything. Everything known. Everything cherished."

Bridget looked at the eboir, forehead creased, hoping she was at least approximating what would be taken as genuine sympathy. It tilted up at her, feelers trailing to the side.

"Apologies. There is much to learn about sapiens culture. Aware of expressions being a secondary or even primary form of communication with this kind, but find it impossible to interpret insofar. The eboir do not learn this language, as communication through visible orifices is impossible."

"Yeah, I get that." Bridget found herself forcing a companionable smile. But she didn't have to make her expressions fit someone else's mold—she could, for once, let her face do whatever came naturally. She relaxed into honesty. "I do hope my mom can help with your planet."

The eboir bobbed up and down. "Yes, it is to be wished. This is the last chance before creating new ideas from scratch. And every moment wasted is another impact."

"Yeah, that would be … suboptimal," Bridget winced, grasping desperately for something kind and sympathetic to impart. "Well, have you been enjoying your stay?" she added—when in doubt, resort to manners.

"No offending meant. But this planet is disorienting. Large, loud, overwhelming. So many beings, so much noise." The eboir twirled its feelers, thinking. "And many substances truly hurt. These keratin-edged grippers do not react well on processed, unvarnished wood. It makes them feel like shriveling, sending unpleasant quavering sensations through to the core."

Bridget shot upright, waving her hands emphatically, waiting to concoct a sentence that didn't involve shrieking. "I get that feeling too!" she stage-whispered, trying not to jump around. "I've never met anyone else who had it!"

"No! None of the other eboir feel this sensation!"

"And people always say you're complaining—"

"—can easily push aside, ignore the feeling—"

"—talked to like we're making it up—"

"—judged as attaining a surplus of attention—"

"—and just because *you* don't have that feeling doesn't mean *I* can't!"

"Because scientific exploration has not extended to this, does not prove its nonexistence!" The eboir bounced up and down, grippers waving. "Did not expect to connect with any sapiens. Of previous experience, humans have been entirely confusing to the eboir."

"Yep, humans entirely confuse me too."

"Yes! How could any species who pays much attention to names—but torments those who study it—make any sense?"

"I still can't believe you find that interesting." Bridget shook her head, eyes gleaming. "I've never met anyone else who did anything more than tolerate it."

"It is enjoyable, forsooth," said the eboir. "If there is more information to impart, it would be interesting still, to be sure."

Bridget nearly melted with joy.

"This technology could be used as a weapon." Dr. Charlotte Meyer briskly strode into her home, stopping abruptly just inside the door so the group of elder eboir trailing desperately after her couldn't follow her in. "We don't know enough about aliens. You could be a threat, and giving you any technology is a major security risk. This proposition is completely outside of policy, and chancing this is not in the interests of our government. Thank you. This meeting is now over. You should not have followed me here. Please step away from my home, or I will be forced to call the authorities."

"The eboir do not have other working options left," said one of the elders. It was a little bigger than a sea urchin, with long, drooping feelers, thinned and matte, dulled by wind and time. "Please. The need is not for your Asteroid Impact Avoidance technology itself, but for the information behind it, for the help to create one that works for Vesta. The eboir forswear any form of violence. This will not affect or endanger this planet the slightest amount."

"It's a no on our part." She whipped around, her eyes flashing a warning. "Go through other avenues if you so desire. You won't get anything from us." She shut the door on the elders' pleas.

Bridget and the eboir, immersed in the history of names, startled at Charlotte's entrance. They had thoroughly surrounded themselves with decades of records, baby name suggestions, and a 400-page hardback on the psychology of street names.

Charlotte swept through the papers, instinctively putting her arm between the eboir and her daughter. "What ... are you doing? You shouldn't be here." She turned to Bridget, keeping an eye on the creature. "Bridge, honey, we don't know anything about these aliens. Here, come behind me ... "

"Oh, don't worry, Mom, it's ok! I was just talking to the eboir about Earth's naming conventions." Bridget shrugged, beaming. "Can you believe, someone actually finds it interesting, for once?"

"Okay, but they need to leave now."

"Oh, have you sorted out the eboirs' asteroid problem? I knew you could do it, Mom!"

"No—our team has decided not to take any chances with giving out Earth technology. We don't know their capabilities of forming technology hazardous to Earth, and it's against government policy to give out anything that could potentially endanger our planet."

Bridget froze, her voice painstakingly level. "I didn't know the technology was hazardous."

"It's *not* in its current state, but again, we don't know their technological capabilities. They could turn it into something we haven't thought of. And chancing this is against policy."

Bridget choked on her breath. Her hands flitted around in a rough approximation of various gestures, as though desperately trying to form language through the sudden slew of thoughts. Charlotte waited patiently for her daughter's words, eyeing the young eboir cautiously.

Bridget's words finally managed to break through. "They're not dangerous! They're peaceful! If you don't help them, everyone who lives there is going to die." Her hands grabbed onto one another for support. She twisted her fingers around anxiously. "Are you serious? You've decided to kill an entire peaceful population over a chance that they could develop something dangerous from harmless technology?"

"The team has decided on a no."

"That's not an answer!" Her voice echoed powerfully in the quiet room. "You're going to kill an entire society? They're not a threat. They don't have dangerous technology, especially not weaponry. They don't have the time or ability to develop anything to save them. They need your help, Mom. You can't just leave them to die."

"They're from another world! We've never been in contact with another world before. The precedents just aren't there."

Her daughter just looked at her, frustration written across her face. "You know what, Mom? You're not thinking for yourself. You're parroting the same meaningless recycled excuses. I remember how angry you got at your coworkers who did the exact same thing, how you didn't understand how they could be so ... uncaring." She exhaled sharply, barbs filling her voice. "But congratulations, Mom. You're one of them now."

Charlotte opened her mouth, ready to push back an angry retort. But something in her daughter's words rang true, echoing doubts she already held: should she really doom an entire species just because of protocol? She pushed her emotions to the side, doing her best to objectively look at the situation. She let her thoughts overflow the containers she'd let other people build.

There was nothing to indicate the aliens weren't as peaceful as they claimed. Sure, the eboir might add on to the technology. But maybe they wouldn't use it as weaponry. They might adapt it for different purposes, or make it more efficient, and Earth could benefit from it, too. All they had to do was extend an olive branch, and something wonderful could come of it.

Perhaps other people's recycled excuses didn't hold as much truth as she believed.

"You know what? We could stand to do a little more research before coming to a conclusion."

Quickly dialing, Charlotte sped out of the room, voice fading with distance. "Hey Shawn, could you pass this on to the crew? I know we're all home now, but we might want to reconsider our decision to withhold aid—"

Even if this fell through, even if nothing came of this phone call, at least she tried to do the right thing. God, she was so proud of her daughter.

The young eboir sighed, turning toward Bridget. "Should leave with the elders. But this was a nice meeting. A genuine thanks." It began to trail out of her room, but turned back at the last moment. "... If the eboir visit again ... perhaps you could impart other interesting traditions?"

"I would love that." Bridget smiled genuinely, waving a goodbye. The eboir's tentacles returned the gesture, before swiftly pulling the last of its grippers through the doorway.

Bridget drifted off to sleep, a book of surnames clutched to her chest, her ears straining hopefully. She'd never have guessed she'd be hoping for—even thrilled—to hear an obnoxious droning sound. She missed the eboir already. But at least she could sleep now, in her own quiet thoughts, knowing her mom would do anything and everything to save her friend.

WHERE IS EVERYBODY?
A STORY
ANYA LEIGH JOSEPHS

YOU'VE BEEN ASKING for centuries, long before we heard you. Composing your mathematical formulae. Given that the probability of intelligent life is X, and Y percentage of observable planets have the conditions for life to evolve, and there are approximately Z planets in the universe, then over the course of Theta years …

The math didn't add up, so you turned to intergalactic conspiracy-theorizing. *We're a space zoo*, or *they're running experiments on us*, or, *there is something so terrible about us that no one wants to know us*.

That one makes me sad. The truth is, the universe is a really big place. Sure, there are plenty of civilizations capable of intergalactic travel, and some of those are similar enough to humans that there could be meaning in our meeting—that we'd have something to say to each other across the reaches of space. But it takes a long time and a lot of resources to cross the void.

All I'm saying is, no one was *trying* to leave humans out of anything. We just … didn't make it over there for a while. Sent a couple probes and forgot about you, mostly. Sorry.

And then those probes started picking up something new. A kind of energy that we'd never seen, anywhere in the known universe: not electromagnetic attraction or gravity, nothing like heat or light or motion, but something previously unknown. Unknown to you, as well, by science if not in stories. We picked up your word for it, too.

In the late 21st century, for reasons unknown, magic blossomed on Earth.

"Why did you have to go to *space*?" Sharine complains. "Who's going to help me plan this wedding?"

"Maybe your fiancée?" Laure is often told that other people can't understand her tone, but she is fairly certain that the biting sarcasm shows. And she doesn't find it easy to read other people, even after knowing Sharine all her life, but Laure does recognize that flinch with a sour twist of pleasure.

"You're still my best—"

Laure cuts her off. "I know." Which is a lie. She hadn't even tried to be subtle about her resentment. She'd taken a berth on the *Starbound* two days after Sharine, her ex and best friend, had announced her engagement. No one believes Laure when she says this, not even her therapist, but she actually isn't in love with Sharine. She doesn't even wish that they hadn't broken up. She'd just wanted … something all her own.

The fact is, she doesn't really believe she'll find someone else. Enough people have told Laure that she's avoidant, that she's difficult or dull, that she isn't like other people, for her to see exactly how long the odds of locating love are. Even Sharine couldn't put up with her quirks in the end, and she's known Laure since they were toddlers.

It was supposed to be a love story for the ages. Now it's ending with a wedding Laure won't be invited to, much less participating in. It's ending with one of them having left the planet.

"I know you feel like there's nothing for you on Earth, but I don't know why. You could still find someone—" Sharine protests.

"What, on the apps? There are two types of queer women on there: the ones who fuck me and then ghost, and the ones who want to move to Canada and start an alpaca farm and never fuck at all."

Sharine doesn't even laugh. That stings. She used to be the one person Laure could count on to laugh at her jokes. "So you left the planet? That's a little dire. There's always the Algorithm. Or a love spell."

"Love spells don't work, and the Algorithm is creepy." Laure isn't going to submit her future to some all-knowing computer, plead for a list of names of "maximally compatible" women. She isn't interested in being told by a series of ones and zeroes exactly how difficult she is to place among other people. She lives in an era where humanity has magic *and* the stars. She deserves more from her life than that.

"I'm just saying, Laure. There's someone out there for you."

We begin watching from afar. Our people are cautious compared with humans (nearly everyone in the universe is cautious compared with humans). We aren't going to rush into meeting a species that has no impulse control and just learned to set things on fire with their minds.

But humanity seems to be doing okay. There are some scuffles, but no more terrifying planetary wars. Their new artificial intelligence keeps things running smoothly. And they've started looking to the stars. Looking for us.

We're not ready for introductions, but we're close. Agreements are made, money is raised, and a ship is sent across the vast expanse of the universe, with instructions to watch humanity grow, to try to understand their magic.

Laure is the only one awake on the bridge. As the newest, and lowest-ranking, member of the crew, she gets the overnight shift. It's not as beautiful as it is in the movies: there's no window out to the stars and the wide wonder of the universe, just lots of beeping computers that are painful to her sensitive ears.

She can't stop thinking about her last conversation with Sharine. Laure *knows* she was sabotaging herself by taking this job. Literally leaving the planet in a previously unmatched feat of avoidant attachment. Maybe her therapist is going to win an award. *Patient who ran furthest from her problems ...*

She closes her eyes as if that could shut out the noise. And she wishes for something to change. She wishes for someone to find her that could understand her. She wishes for there to be someone, somewhere in the universe, who she wouldn't want to run away from.

And then an alarm goes off. She winces as the sharp, high-pitched sound whistles through her skull. She turns away from her thoughts and to the various monitors, expecting to have to sift through a bunch of jargon to find whatever subsystem is on the fritz, but in fact the alert is clear: UNKNOWN OBJECT IN FLIGHT PATH.

She pulls up the exterior camera feeds. What she sees is unfamiliar in some ways—curving lines and parallelograms of construction that seem instinctively wrong—but can be only one thing: a spaceship. An *alien* spaceship.

"Oh, fuck," Laure says aloud.

"Oh, *fuck*," I exclaim. I'm usually just an archivist, but the pilot is pregnant and not feeling well. I told him to take the night off. And, as a result of a combination of inexperience and relatively poor spatial reasoning skills, I may have *slightly* miscalculated our course. We were supposed to tail the human vessel from a safe distance, and instead I have steered us onto what is nearly a collision course with the previously uncontacted human species.

I'm probably going to get fired, I think, and send out a hail.

Words appear on the screen: *Hello. My name is Xaryxis. Can you understand me?*

Laure should probably hesitate. In fact, she should probably call for help. This is way, way beyond her pay grade. A normal person would be freaking out right now. Instead, she types: *Yes. My name is Laure.*

The message forms seconds later. *Oh, good. I didn't know if the translation would work.*

How are you translating? An inane question to ask a previously undiscovered alien species. Laure hopes that Xaryxis doesn't think she's being stupid. Then she thinks she's being stupid for thinking that.

Xaryxis's reply doesn't seem annoyed. It's warm, almost funny: *Don't freak out, but we've been listening in for a while. Not in a scary way! Just gearing up to introduce ourselves.*

When Laure was six years old, her kindergarten class had a pet gerbil. And one day, as gerbils do, it died. She cried and cried, and then picked it up and wished for it to come back to life.

And it *had.* Her parents told her she must have been wrong, it was never really dead, as it squeaked and ran and lived again.

About a week later, the news outlets started reporting on the "inexplicable phenomena" that eventually everyone would call magic.

So Laure believes in the impossible. The laws of the universe have already shifted under her feet once. Why not a second time?

Another message arrives. *Can I come on board? I want to introduce myself.*

Laure extremely does not have the authority to make this offer, but she types: *Sure.*

I should have pulled away. I know I should have woken the captains, or drifted back off into space. The human—Laure—would be written off by her famously skeptical species as a conspiracy theorist or a fantasist. And first contact could proceed apace, exactly the way that it's planned by my superiors, in the perfect unison they do everything in.

But there was something about her. Something about our conversation that made me feel …

I don't know what to call it. But I know it made me feel closer to her than I normally feel, even though physically and technologically our species couldn't be more different. I know, somehow, that just like me, she is an outsider, searching for a connection she hasn't found yet.

So I have to go.

I suit up—whatever germs humans have, I don't want 'em—and set off. The human ship is strange looking. All white, long and thin.

Maybe I should be worried about traps, that the humans are going to vivisect me or something. But I'm not. My hearts are pounding and my papillae are trembling, but I'm not afraid.

I don't know why until I see her. Laure.

She's a strange creature, very different from myself, from any of the species I've met. Like most humans, she has strands of dead keratin coming out of the top of her face. Hers are black and curl in an intricate pattern that makes me think of a moon's orbit around a planet. Her skin is soft and brown like the soil of her Earth. She has two round organs set into her face (they are called *eyes,* and they collect visual information, and they are deep brown, and beautiful), and an orifice below them that moves when she speaks. The translator in my suit tells me what those unfamiliar, wonderful sounds mean:

"It's nice to meet you."

At once, I understand what magic is.

LoveHEART by Natasha Von

MCCARTHY KNEW
A POEM
A J DALTON

I met an alien
It looked human
But I wasn't fooled.
If anything, it looked and seemed too human
Hyper-human, supra-human, extra-human
So more human than human, actually
That's how I could tell.

listen, we're not fooled
by you humans:
your masking technology is impressive
yet one wonders why you hide among us so
are you scared of how we'll react
are you looking to infiltrate us?
or do you see yourselves for what you truly are: plain ugly?

MCCARTHY KNEW

And these aliens look to take control
Of our presidents and companies
And our armies ... and nukes?!
Yes, that's it—it completely makes sense
They'll disable our systems, in coordinated fashion, long
    enough
That their planned invasion can't be thwarted
And then they'll rule completely.

you understand
why you can't be trusted
though
yes?
and you have to be held
no matter what you say
yes, that's it, come this way

SHADOWS OF TITANIUM RAIN
A STORY
ANTHONY FRANCIS

Content note: *character injury*

STALKING GHOSTS THROUGH the ragged red twilight of Failaka, Djina wondered what would kill her first on this remnant 'moon': titanium rain, or methane ice. The vast bulk of Tylos, a 'hot Jupiter' whipping around a blazing F6 star called Dilmun, shielded Failaka from the rage of their mother sun: Dancing in the shadows of Tylos's L2 point, the dark side of tidally locked Failaka was the coldest place in the Dilmun system. But, even almost a quarter million miles away, the heat from white-hot titanium rain pouring onto the glowing red night side of Tylos cooked the light side of Failaka into a honeycomb-cracked, vaporous wasteland.

A hot gale from the light-side wasteland tried to blow her off her feet, and Djina stabbed her pick for purchase and just gouged through nitrogen slush. Only Failaka's tidal lock provided any habitation for humans at all, this windy band of twilight between fiery near side and frozen far side. Behind her in the permanent night of the dark side, the vaporous winds streaming off the light side condensed into glaciers of nitrogen and methane and complex organics, kilometers and kilometers deep, inexorably creeping under their own weight back toward the light side, where they inevitably sublimated, rising like ghosts to repeat the cycle.

This delicate border would change, and soon: human overmining had reduced Failaka's outgassing, which formerly kept the cometary remnant dancing in a 'halo orbit' around the L2 Lagrange point on the far side of Tylos from Dilmun. Without that outgassing, the halo orbit was widening, eventually throwing Failaka out into the harsh light of Dilmun, where it would become a comet again, evaporating in nuclear fire. The moon's axis was already changing, a wobble called nutation, soon exposing this twilight region to the light of Tylos—seemingly the dull red of a hot coal, but, through its vast breadth, four hundred times as bright as the Sun seen from Earth.

Here, the process had already started. A new pattern of hot winds had scoured this former plain into blue methane crags. Fog roiled everywhere Djina touched. Her suit gauge blared red: minus 185 Celsius, well below its recommended limit. Nitrogen and carbon monoxide were already melting, getting ready to boil—which would cause sudden floods, or even geysers, that would throw out sprays of deadly methane ice. Just a few degrees hotter, and the methane would sublimate all at once, like firecrackers. The scalloped crags around her were already steaming: it was like standing among a forest of ticking bombs.

The wind picked up. Djina struggled for purchase. Her crampons crunched against chips of methane steaming with evaporating nitrogen —but as she scrabbled with her pick, she found what she was looking for. Deep beneath the slush, burned all the way through the ice and into clathrate 'bedrock' that wouldn't melt until north of minus 60 degrees, was a distinctive six-fingered footprint—then another, and another. The Ghost Walker had been here!

A crag cracked, then fell, exposing Djina to the glare of Tylos, a narrow bow of white-hot rain enclosing roiling red clouds, just now rising over Failaka's horizon. While Djina clicked down her visor, the hot glow cooked the canyon wall behind her over the critical point.

The wall exploded, blasting her with sublimating methane. Djina screamed, hurling herself aside, but it was too late. Her suit was insulated to keep her from radiating heat; it was not equipped to cope with a full-force methane gale at minus 182 Celsius.

"'Evacuate early, it'll be safer,'" Djina quoted, through chattering teeth. "Marchand ... you were right."

"Dooom!" the crow of doom had cried, as it landed atop Djina's digital canvas. "Raak!"

"Marquis!" she chided, shooing Marchand's familiar to the right. No longer alone in the remote power station dome she called home, Djina silenced the bawdy Margentinian spacer tune she'd been listening to, and at last heard the airlock cycling. "And ... Marchand, I presume?"

Djina smiled and turned toward her steely-eyed spacer crush, but panic halted her. Marchand had popped helmet and cap, and before their eyes could meet, she turned back to her digital canvas, staring at the reflections of the foolish dark-skinned girl mooning over the spacer hero out of her league, his strong fingers shagging out his prematurely silver crop.

"Never," he muttered, glancing in the suit check mirror, "gonna get used to this—"

"Warning, raak," the Marquis crowed. "Nutation will expose this region to Tylos, raak."

"Thank you, Marquis," Marchand said, smiling indulgently at his feathered robotic familiar, then cocking his head at the row after row of maintenance drones, standing at attention in the bay. "Djina's crew is already marshalled for transport. I think she got the memo."

"Confirmed, raak," the Marquis croaked. "Memo ACK received 0413 Zulu June 6, 2253, raak."

"Four-thirteen a.m.!" he said. "You sure were up late. You're not free-cycling, are you?"

"Asks the man burning the midnight oil," she chided. "That memo went out—Marquis?"

"0407 Zulu, raak," the Marquis said, cocking his head. "Midnight oil confirmed, raak."

"Guilty as charged," Marchand said. "It was bad enough managing one slow-motion disaster, but two has led to a lot of sleepless nights. More than a little of that tossing and turning came from dread of this conversation. Djina ... you've slow-walked this long enough."

"I'm ... I'm not giving up on deciphering the stele," Djina stammered, calling a picture-in-picture onto her canvas to show how many more of the ancient, alien markers she had found just during this cycle. "Increased illumination has exposed more of the structures and—"

"Djina, you know that's not it," Marchand said. "Increased illumination means ..."

"I have to evacuate." So much was contained in those four words: losing her home, losing its beloved isolation—and rejoining the overcrowded colony, which was retreating to Grissom Station en masse, where the perpetual night would protect them from Dilmun as long as possible. Djina closed her eyes. "Nutation will expose these glaciers to full illumination. The landscape will collapse. Nitrogen will melt, causing flash floods, then boil into supercooled geysers. The remaining methane will sublimate, causing hurricane-force winds—"

"You *did* read the memo." Marchand stayed near the airlock. "But it's worse. The shift in the halo orbit will expose this region not just to Tylos, but, briefly, to Dilmun. We project the methane glaciers won't just vent. They'll mass sublimate in a supercooled shockwave."

Djina winced. Shockwave or no, that flow alone could kill: suit insulation could keep your heat from radiating out into space, but a supercooled flow of material would transport heat away actively, a lethal refrigerant even through a space suit. And she didn't need to ask the Marquis to know exposure to Tylos's parent star could also kill.

"I'll ... go on the last train," she said, and Marchand visibly relaxed.

"We'll come for you first," Marchand said, "or at least, hold an empty car for you."

"That—" Djina imagined the staring faces on the train. "That isn't necessary—"

"We'll hold a car for you," he said gently, firmly. "We have the space, and time—"

"Thank you," she said, relaxing. Then she blurted: "We can't just leave them!"

Marchand stiffened, then sat down not too far from her on the bench, about a meter away.

"I don't want the Passenghasts to get hurt either," he said, not looking at her, just at her painting, an eruption of white before a black mirror, lost among crags of blue—a quasi-abstract representation of her Passenghast 'opposite number,' one of the alien Ghost Walkers studying a stele. "But let's leave contacting the Ghost Walkers to the xenotechs—"

"*I* am a xenotech," Djina protested.

"We both know you first identify as an artist, then a linguist, *then* a xenotech," Marchand said, eyes roaming over the canvas, covered with thick daubs of 'paint,' simulating the strokes of a palette knife. "Contacting someone first is … not usually in your comfort zone."

"Understatement of the day, raak," the Marquis croaked, and Djina giggled.

"Let's leave the first contact to the First Contact Engineers, who are trying to warn them about the nutation—if they can," Marchand said. "The Ghost Walkers have never talked to us. Heck, we don't even know if they talk to each other, or have what we'd call a language—"

"Still, the Passenghasts are *sapient*," Djina said. She exchanged her painting for one of its reference images: a Ghost Walker, a glowing stag three meters tall, standing before the patterned black obsidian of one of the ancient stele. "They don't talk to us, but they're *not animals*—"

"I know," Marchand said gently. "They're not native to the moon. They use equipment, transports, even radio. But they barely interact with each other, and actively avoid us. The first requirement for participating in society is communicating with society—"

"Where does that leave me?" Djina asked.

"You text," Marchand said. "You can do a lot by text. Announce your presence, request assistance, share your accomplishments." He smiled. "Humans can do a lot by text. Coordinate work, establish relationships, build friendships, share experiences. Fall in love."

Djina held her breath, staring at their ghostly reflections in her digital canvas.

"Pack up," he said. "After the evac, we'll schedule a xenotech mission to warn—"

"That may be too late," she said. "The main Passenghast settlement is on the light side. They don't have sensor arrays out here—they don't know what we know. Their explorers can survive on the night side, but they're not prepared for a full-scale outgassing event!"

"I know." He patted her leg gently. "See you on the last train. We'll hold a car for—"

"Stay!" Djina blurted. But why? Her mind was *so blank*. "W-watch me paint?"

"I'd like nothing more," he said, oh so gently. "But I have three more stops. You're not the only hardcase who doesn't want to evacuate. Just the one I like the most."

"O-of course," she said, meaning to respond to his comment about the stops, not realizing until the words were out of her mouth that her foot would soon be planted in it. She shook her head. *Take it as offered, take it as offered, say something, damn it!* "A-at the station, then."

"You're on. Again, nothing would please me more. The *Grissom* has a decommissioned communications relay cantilevered over the crater, with a control module similar to your setup here. It's isolated and the views are spectacular. I've taken the liberty of reserving it for you."

"That ... sounds wonderful," Djina said, and it really did.

"I thought it might." He kissed her cheek, and she shrank away. "That okay?"

"Yes. Yes! One person is fine." Djina bit her lip, then looked at him. "Especially you."

Marchand smiled, donned his helmet, checked his familiar, then popped out the airlock.

The door closed. Djina sat there, holding her cheek, until her heart stopped pounding. Then she turned back to her digital canvas, and her subject: a Passenghast.

Imagine a glowing white stag, shaggy and distant in its alien indeterminacy. Six legs, six eyes, six antlers like hands: some remnant of an aquatic sixfold symmetry, stretched and folded over when their ancestors crawled onto land, flipped over, and became bilateral.

But the oceans their ancestors swam in were seas of oil approaching a thousand degrees Kelvin, and the shaggy masses of "hair" were silicate excretions of the Passenghasts' decidedly alien biology. *Our tar is their water*, Marchand had said, *our saunas, their refrigerators.*

Djina had found some of that hair. The Passenghasts did not breathe, and with bodies like armored mineral, they walked the canyons of twilight without spacesuits; but when tufts of their tough hairlike excretions broke off, in the supercold snow ... they became as brittle as glass.

Djina collapsed to the clathrate bedrock. Her right arm felt numb, and her long-range transmitter flashed **BELOW OPERATING TEMPERATURE RANGE** over and over. She couldn't even call her drone crew; she'd ordered them out on the train in her stead.

But the sublimating rock had exposed something wonderful: a silvery, six-armed starfish, one of the 'trail cameras' that the Passenghasts used to avoid humans. Knocked free of the ice, upended against canyon bedrock, the trail cam was now blind to the north, and Djina groaned to her feet and limped away, careful to stay out of its hemispheric field of view.

Because Djina studied the xenolinguistics of the stele, not the Ghost Walkers, she'd had better luck tracking them than the xenos who tried to encounter them directly—and from that, she had learned one of the Passenghasts was also studying the ancient alien monoliths.

If her Passenghast opposite number had laid a trail cam here, it would be heading to what she called the 'New Graveyard'—an outcropping of the geometrically etched obsidian markers, exposed by the recent upheavals, which had tumbled them about like headstones.

She'd never be able to track the Passenghast through the maze of the Graveyard. Heck, it would flee if she tried: it would have set other trail cams. But she could *intercept* the Passenghast when it returned for its equipment, for they never left anything behind to be studied.

She could find the Passenghast. She *would* find the Passenghast.

But her arm was really fucked up, and so was her suit. How bad, she didn't know: her heads-up display wouldn't respond. Her brain-reading inducer must have fritzed. Djina tapped her left bracer, trying to activate her medscanner, but her right arm was stiff and senseless.

Panic struck her: if her arm was dead, how could she *paint*?

Then it occurred to her: maybe she didn't have to. She had *recordings*.

Painfully, she unslung her transport tube. If her equipment had died in the cold, her plan would fail, and it was a long slog over the ice to Grissom Station—best to know, and start, now. One-handedly, she unscrewed the end cap ... and started the diagnostic on her digital canvas.

It had been three years since Djina first painted a Passenghast. She'd had all the time in the world to paint on the skeleton crew of their colony ship, but had never heard of the Ghost Walkers; after the ship broke up in hyperspace, she'd heard of them, but hadn't the time.

Evacuation Ship "G" had fled pell-mell from the disaster on Earth, the tiny dragonfly of its experimental *Grievance* gliderdrive module improbably perched on the one-and-a-half kilometer cigar of the *Grissom* colony module, efficiently guiding it through the thin edge of dual space.

But they struck knotted interstellar dust, an early-stage protostar not on the charts made for older, ballistic hyperdrives. The *Grievance* tumbled away like a wounded dragonfly, plunging its *Grissom* colony module into realspace deep in the well of the Dilmun system.

The *Grissom* burnt its delta-vee crashing on the best of its bad options: Failaka, a frozen waste shielded from a blazing sun. After a year of grueling work turning the ship into a base, the distress call from the *Grievance* module finally reached them: gliderdrive dead one light-year out, systems damaged, aquaculture failing. They had to get a sailgun pipeline built, and soon, to shoot the *Grievance* supplies before the two hundred and fifty souls aboard it starved.

Those years had been hell. Djina went from a carefree junior member of an interstellar ship's skeleton crew of four hundred to the harried senior staff of a makeshift arcology of four hundred thousand, rising like a skyscraper in Apollo Crater as they scrambled over themselves to survive. In the *Grissom*'s crowded halls, panic attacked her daily.

In that crisis Djina had been prepared to do her duty, no matter what it cost. Drones were doing most of the manufacturing, but the icy glaciers were hell on them, and their automated maintenance drones could not keep up. They kept having to thaw more and more colonists just to keep the robots running. The drugs that suppressed her panic eventually killed her art.

But Marchand, one of the first batch of colonists Djina had thawed, had reversed the base's slow slide into chaos. In the command pool for their aborted colony, he'd been drafted into project management—and unexpectedly delivered not just organization, but hope. The base, now called Grissom Station, had become almost supernaturally efficient, and under his direction, the base—no, now, the *colony*—began expanding out onto the warmer twilight regions. Under his steady leadership and rock-solid calm, it now seemed everyone had room to breathe.

Including her.

"Don't make them like they used to." Marchand cracked ice off the airlock panel with his gauntleted fist, exposing the faded words **WASP-121-B XENOARCHAEOLOGY MISSION**. The remote dome Marchand had found for her was shrouded in darkness, but after a moment—after having remained inactive for almost a hundred years—the ancient airlock controls lit and cycled like they were almost new. "Ah. My lady. Your chambers await."

Nervously, Djina followed, barely believing her luck.

"Three habitable rooms," Marchand said, opening the frozen hatch onto a still-functional airlock and triggering its cycle. "Three decks of robot-serviceable equipment. This was a power relay for a failed exoplanetary science station, evacuated almost a century back."

"You bet they don't make them like they used to." Djina stepped into the inner dome, all glass, with a commanding view of icy plains and power distribution cables heading sunside. She flicked her hand, and her drones swept out through the facility. "But ... running on batteries?"

"Transmission lines are down, raak," the Marquis said, shedding ice from its wings.

"Yes, the lines are down, but the light-side thermal cells are at seventy percent capacity," Marchand said. "If you can get the relay running, this station is yours." He cocked his head at her drones, already restoring systems. "I ... don't think that will be a problem for you."

"Let's not get cocky—this is a hundred years old," Djina said, not meeting the gaze of her steely-eyed spacer crush—less due to her social anxiety than to him simply being out of her league. "I ... appreciate you indulging me, but I know everyone has to pull their weight, and—"

"And you're doing just fine." Marchand smiled, and Djina glanced away in panic, turning her attention to her maintenance drones, filing into the station. "Any trained spacer could run your crew; few would volunteer to become a drone maintenance monkey on-site."

"It's no imposition," Djina said, lifting the Marquis off a frosted console.

"It's the definition of imposition, raak," the Marquis crowed.

"Don't get me wrong, we still want you to work your xenolinguistic magic on the stele," Marchand said, taking the Marquis; their hands touched briefly, then she turned away, to set up her digital canvas here for the first time. "But we both know where your heart lies."

Djina stared at his reflection in the dark screen.

"People are starving on the *Grievance*," she said softly. "How do we have time—"

"For science? For art? We can't afford not to make time for them." Marchand's smile warmed her, even in the dark reflection. "People think this world is a trap: with the *Grievance* dead in the water one light-year out, they think we're stuck here in the shadows—"

"Uh, yeah," Djina said. "You *do* know how bright Dilmun is at this distance, right?"

"Forty-five hundred times Earth irradiance, raak," the Marquis said. "Hot as fuck, raak."

"But heat is power." Marchand gestured at the station. "The *Grissom* landed here for a reason. Failaka has all the energy and organics we need to build a colony. Sure, while her NCE drive component is out, we're cut off from the Frontier, and we've all got to pitch in."

"I'll do my part," Djina said. The shifting glaciers were hell on the power distribution network, but with her here, maintaining the drones that in turn maintained the lines, they would get an additional ten percent of power. "But why even worry about the stele, or paintings?"

"Djina, this is a *colony*, not an emergency," Marchand said. "We need to make time for not just survival, but living. People, and their relationships. Dreams, and their expressions. Aspirations, for knowledge, for expression ... even for connection."

She drew a breath, and, sensing her discomfort, he turned away, to give her space.

"I ... I aspire," she said, forcing the words out deliberately, "for ... for all three."

"Wonderful." Marchand gently placed a hand on her shoulder. "Thank you, Djina, for volunteering to staff this station. And I hope you make progress on deciphering the stele. But I have to admit, there is one thing I haven't told you: you may not be quite alone here."

"Someone *else* is posted to this station?" Djina's voice came out like a squeak.

"No," Marchand said, and his hand squeezed her shoulder in reassurance. "You are the only one posted to the station. I had to explicitly override the safety regulations to allow it. But, outside the station, you may find something wonderful: this is Ghost Walker territory."

"Ohhh ..." Djina said, her head dizzied—not with fear, but delight. "What a gift."

"I thought you might like that," Marchand said, squeezing her one more time, then slowly backing away. "By definition, they're unearthly, but I'm told they're eerily beautiful. In fact, I picked this for you because I thought the Passenghasts might make good subjects. I hope you think so too."

"Oxygen levels restored, raak," the Marquis said. "Still cold as fuck, raak."

"Cold is fine." Djina popped her helmet in a wreath of fog. Crisp air flooded her throat, Novembers in Canada; her nose wrinkled at the welding-fume scent of ancient spacecraft. She dug under her cap. "And for my first official act in my new home ... I am going off my meds."

She popped off the nodule: transdermal medicine, transcranial stimulation. It would take a while for the effects of her bespoke cocktail of neurotransmitters and inhibitors to wear off—she'd have to reprogram it to step her dosages down over the next few weeks—but already her head felt clearer, as its numbing effect on her amygdala faded.

But Marchand was cycling the airlock.

"You ... you don't have to go."

"And I don't want to," he said, not looking at her, but at his reflection in the suit-check mirror: his thawing had not gone well, and he was starting to go prematurely grey. "But you gave me time when I needed it. Least I could do is return the favor and give you space."

"Thank you," she said, relieved. "Though ... it *was* my job to help you thaw."

"Sure it was." He briefly grinned at her, then put on his helmet before she could start to panic. "Long nights, just sitting with me, while I was delirious, was far more than your job. But, speaking of jobs, little would please me more than staying to watch you paint—"

"But you've got to run a line out to this relay, or this is pointless." Gratitude flooded her, and she turned to face him. "Thank you, for taking over the rollout of the power net: it was killing me. I'll get this running, and, maybe, if I'm lucky, paint a few Passenghasts."

"Send me recordings if you do," Marchand said. "Make good art, Djina."

The airlock closed. Djina sat still until her heart stopped pounding. Then, curious—and perhaps just a little bit devious—she called up a reference image of the Passenghasts, taken with a telescope lens from kilometers away. They were as strange and as beautiful as she'd heard.

"Canvas," she asked, "can you access the station cameras to get a third-party view?"

YES, it responded, and she selected the one that showed her from her best angle.

"Canvas, new painting please," Djina said. "And ... start recording."

Cradling her dead right arm, Djina settled on a scalloped boulder of hydromethane ice. It, too, was a potential bomb, but at much higher temperatures than the craggy blue fingers of true methane ice looming around her, which would sublimate and freeze her to death first.

Here, she sat at a nexus of Passenghast paths: to collect all its trail cams, it had to pass this way, or double back and spend kilometers more on its mission. Here, too, she sat in a dead zone between different trail cams, so it would not see her until it could also see the canvas.

With her gloved left hand, she tapped the bracer she'd awkwardly transferred to her right, and her digital canvas flickered to life. Without preamble she set it to cycle through three years of recordings she'd made of herself painting Passenghasts—her mute love letters to Marchand.

While it cycled, she dug up the simulations he had sent her of the coming disaster. The "projected sublimation event" would send a shockwave of a *half a trillion tons* of supercold methane gas hundreds of kilometers onto the light side, well into Passenghast territory.

"That's why they call it a captured comet," Djina muttered, putting the video on cycle and throwing it up picture-in-picture. "Tired of your prison behind Tylos, eh, Failaka? Want to stumble out into the light, where you can burn a thousand times as bright?"

"Talking to a planet, raak," the Marquis crowed. "Signs of shock, raak."

"Stop that," Djina said crossly to his hallucinated image. "You're not even here."

Red light flared in reflection on her canvas, right below where the Marquis would have perched, and Djina gasped. Tylos had risen over the canyon wall behind her. Already, the tips of the craggy fingers of methane had started to glow and mist. Soon, they would blow, and kill.

Djina set her hands on her thighs. A little tingling in her right; trembling in her left. Her hope had been that a human painting a Passenghast would be nonthreatening, yet strange enough to pique the Ghost Walker's interest when it passed by, and then she could warn it. Somehow.

She could not paint. But she had a digital canvas three meters wide and one and a half tall, glowing with images, and now she could sit in perfect stillness. Was it daft to hope that, when it retraced its route, just seeing her painting it would intrigue the Passenghast?

Tylos rose higher and higher; the red glare crept lower and lower. She imagined she could feel its heat on her back; she definitely could see the bow of its disc reflected in her canvas: a white-hot arc eclipsing a solar corona, and enclosing churning cloud-coals.

This was foolish. She'd never find it. She needed to leave—

Mist puffed up around a white-furred, six-toed foot not a meter away.

Djina froze. Another six-toed foot reached behind a nearby methane crag, closing around the six-sided starfish trail cam hidden behind the steaming methane bulk. The foot—or was it a hand?—waggled the trail cam in her direction, as if checking to see if it was still working.

Djina focused all her attention on her canvas, which showed her painting this very Passenghast studying a stele. After a moment, feet puffed up more snow beside her. Even in the reflection of the canvas, the mineral nature of its hairs was clear now, and she could pick out a slight red underglow, likely from its body heat.

She had its attention. Djina tapped her bracer. The picture-in-picture of the simulated disaster grew larger and larger, expanding until it filled the frame. She let it play several times, then zoomed the simulation to show the shockwave covering the Passenghast territory.

"I wish to warn you," she began, and the feet jerked. That's right, *rookie xenotech mistake*: the Passenghasts did not speak, and were known to be repelled by noise. Quietly, she tapped on her bracer, projecting the words: «I wish to warn you the moon will shift.»

No response. The bright arch of Tylos rose higher in the reflection, almost a semicircle; its churning ruddy clouds sparked with glimpses of dazzling white depths. This disaster's timing couldn't have been worse: Tylos was in its hot phase, where the titanium and titanium oxide that normally lurked in those depths boiled up and turned into white-hot weather. The shadows of that titanium rain no longer stretched across the landscape like fingers; they were sharp wedges, each crag a sundial, counting down to their explosion. The closest methane monolith was fully illuminated now: hopefully it was colder than the wall that had blown up and frostbitten her.

Inspired, Djina projected her reference image: this Passenghast, studying a stele. The marker was one she'd long since analyzed: three stacked circles, edges connected by lines, surrounded by rectangular xenoglyphs. She framed the stele and projected her translation.

Xenoglyphs were grouped, a conceptual graph formed, a tree of English words grew on the left: the stele described red-hot Tylos and how it shadowed Failaka from blazing Dilmun.

«Add proposition: 'The orbit of Failaka is changing.'» Djina's words appeared; the conceptual graph shifted as the proposition integrated. «Back-translate its conceptual closure, and project it onto the stele as new xenoglyphs in the same style.»

New glyphs appeared, glowing rectangles, filled with strokes, angular and abstract—or, perhaps, gob-smackingly representational to readers who were gob-smackingly alien. Djina drew a line between her new glowing glyphs and the cycling simulation of the methane shockwave.

Light glinted. A notification popped up on her canvas. Djina's breath caught:

ANOTHER INPUT DEVICE DETECTED.

An infrared signal was bombarding the canvas, a pattern Djina recognized as a sagagram, a supposedly universal messaging system designed to be easy to decode. The xenotechs had been beaming it at the Passenghasts for years—and now the canvas AI quickly got the gist.

ALLOW PAIRING? Y/N

«Yes,» Djina typed. «Allow it in guest mode.»

The canvas flickered. On the right, strange structures appeared, chicken-scratches enclosed in hexagons. As the honeycomb of symbols expanded, she realized it was Passenghast writing, or something very much like it, its translation appearing opposite hers.

«Translate text: 'I wish to warn you the moon will shift.'» Djina's words snaked from her translation over onto the stele, and the Passenghast writing responded, new glowing symbols contributing to their rosetta. «Back-translate any new propositions onto my side.»

Three words appeared on the screen:

« 〔 wish 〕 〔 warn 〕 〔 moon 〕 »

Djina cringed: the thing next to her was actually *talking to her*. She wanted to run.

«Establish a two-way channel and respond: 'Yes.'» Djina drew a breath as that one word percolated across the screen; the translations were tentative at best. *Keep it simple. Keep it simple.* «I wish to warn you the dark areas will become light.»

«〔you〕 wish 〔object〕 warn 〔referent〕 dark 〔transition〕 light»

Oh, it was already getting grammar. She ordered the canvas to fine-tune a language model over the conversation. **WARNING: INSUFFICIENT DATA, PROCEED Y/N?** *Damn the overfitting, yes, go ahead!* She only needed a model good enough to warn them.

«Yes.» Djina texted. *Keep it simple.* «More light is very dangerous.»

«we 〔can〕 live in 〔the〕 light or 〔the〕 dark»

Djina hissed. They didn't get it. They would all get killed. *Screw simple.*

«Our suits protect us from the light or the dark.» She held up her frostbitten hand, projecting its medical diagnostic onto her digital canvas. «From radiated heat. Not conducted cold. The glaciers will sublimate in the light, releasing a gale of supercold methane.»

Djina watched her words appear on screen, get sucked into the xenoglyph tree of the ancients, then get brushed into the hexagons of the Ghost Walkers. Their language models churned against each other, with no response. Had she made it too complicated?

But then, brushstrokes answered, filling out a new section of honeycomb.

«**You have damaged your** 〔**primary manipulator**〕**.**»

«It can be fixed.» *She hoped.* «It was necessary to warn you.»

An agonizing pause. Tylos's ring crept higher. Then more brushstrokes.

«**We** 〔**understand**〕 **now. We did not know. We do now. We can evacuate.**»

Relief flooded Djina, and she sagged on the rock. But the Passenghast was still writing.

«**For now.**» More hexagons. The language models synchronized, back-filling bracketed words with more confident translations. «**The problem is too advanced to fix on this orbit. Our ships can reverse the effect over the next orbit. Do you wish this?**»

«Yes, very much so,» Djina texted, boggled at the thought. «*Thank you.*»

«**Thank you for saving our lives.**» A pause, and then a simulation of Failaka's halo orbit appeared, showing how reduced outgassing had changed the delicate dance around the L2 point that previously kept it in the shadow of Tylos. «**Though your mining caused it.**»

«We needed to mine to save our ship,» she texted—and then hope flooded her. She projected an image of the *Grievance*. «Our hyperdrive module is adrift one light-year out. Do your ships have faster-than-light capability? Could you help us rescue it?»

There was no response. Djina cringed. *Another rookie xenotech mistake!*

«**You need not interact. We can leave out supplies. You can drop them off.**»

«**That we can do,**» it flickered back. «**It would not begin to repay our debt.**»

The videos had served their purpose, and Djina swept them aside, leaving just her artwork and the communication interface. She and the Passenghast stared at its image on the digital canvas for a long time. Then Dilmun broke over the peak of the rising arch of Tylos, a bright spark like an engagement ring, and the top of the nearest crag blossomed into vapor.

«We should evacuate.» Djina transferred the workspace to her bracer.

«**Yes,**» appeared on her wrist. «**May I keep a record of your art?**»

«Of course,» she said, and it extended a device to the screen.

«**Let us return,**» it texted, «**and inform our people.**»

«Yes,» she said. «Back to our people. Goodbye.»

«**Yes,**» it responded. «**Goodbye.**»

The Passenghast rose, and Djina did as well. She canistered her canvas, shouldered it, and started trudging back through the slush of the canyon. The Passenghast started off as well, methane slush rising in puffs from its feet as it, too, strode down the same canyon.

«Talked with a Passenghast,» Djina texted Marchand. «They agreed to evacuate. They will fix the nutation on the next orbit. Methane geyser activity increasing. Path back to power station unsafe. Returning to base overland. Will need medical assistance for frostbite.»

«"Talked with a Passenghast,"» he responded, as she sent him the recordings of the encounter to eliminate all doubt. «That's the most understated way to phrase "I achieved First Contact" that I've ever heard. Congratulations. I'll come get you in a rover.»

«You don't have to,» she texted, though it would be a horrific hike without.

«I want to, though,» he texted. «And not just because you saved all those lives.»

«Oh! One more thing. The Passenghasts agreed to bring supplies to the *Grievance*—if we can leave them out so they don't have to interact.» Now the pause was in the human side of the conversation, and Djina bit her lip. «Perhaps I should have led with that earlier?»

«I don't have words, Djina,» Marchand texted back. «You are a gift. See you soon.»

Djina drew a deep breath. For the first time in a long time, she felt ... happy. Then she became aware the Passenghast was still walking beside her. It seemed to become aware of her too. They continued down the same canyon for what felt like several more minutes.

«I must go back overland,» she at last explained.

«My rover is this way,» it replied.

«Oh!» she said. «This is awkward.»

«Yes,» it replied. **«This is awkward.»**

Djina laughed, then, unthinking, texted on her bracer: «Awkward! ☺»

The Passenghast seemed to convulse, its antlers wriggling.

«Awkward! 〔 Y 〕 »

Djina blinked. *Its* paired eyes had blinked, in a Y. Was that ... a Passenghast emoji?

They stopped at a fork, and then turned to look at each other full-on for the first time. The Passenghast towered over Djina, its shaggy mineral coat glowing in a rising haze of sublimating ice. Its three pairs of eyes remained enigmatic, but its antlerhands spread like a flower.

«**We have shared a moment in life. I hope we can share more of your art.**»

«I hope for that as well,» Djina texted. «Until we meet again.»

Then each solitary walker turned and headed back to rejoin their people.

WI(D)TH, DE(P)TH, BREA(D)TH,
A POEM
RIVER

Do you breathe *breathe*
{rivers, motes, mist}

Inhale
{soil, earth, rock}

Do you   respire
 sky currents
cloud eddies

they you:
   breathe you,
   inhale you,
   respire you,
you them?

RIVER

You taste them tasting us?
  my tongue tips
      tip with me
    sip with me
       lips with me
  flip
 in the rotations
with us
i   you,
you   i?
 them me,
 me them?

     We?
We.   Us.
   Breathe

THE INTERVIEW
A STORY
BRIAN STARR

TSAH LOOKED ALMOST HUMAN, but her cheekbones moved in and out as she breathed and her eyes had an eerie look, somewhat unfocused and too independent. The Schklon prosthetics team had done their best in the circumstances, and they were still learning, but the awkward result told her that she wasn't the most important thing on the team's plate.

The office was made to appear as familiar to applicants as possible, with the executive desk, a whiteboard, and even the smell of old books piped in through the ventilation system. The image of a farm outside the windows looked realistic, as long as nobody wondered why the office would be in the middle of a field, especially after coming in from the busy city streets. It was already Earth outside if they simply used real windows, but some research done by someone at some point said interviewees would be more at ease if they could see sheep.

Tsah placed a resume onto the middle of three stacks of paper, the pile of resumes destined for the recycling process. She looked at the far right pile with only a handful of pages in it and gurgled her throat, which would be translated into a human sigh of despair. She turned her attention to the tallest stack, which read "Ben Denton," before she pushed the button on the desk.

Ben watched the door slide open until it stopped moving, and then walked cautiously through. He waited and watched as it slid closed behind him. He continued to the opposite side of her desk, shaking her hand over the top of it and the button. "I'm Ben."

"Hello Ben, I'm Tsah. Nice to meet you." After a pregnant pause she asked, "Is there something wrong?"

"No, nothing is wrong. Why do you ask?"

"Why don't you have a seat?"

Ben hadn't noticed the chair. He saw the three piles of resumes, his on the first pile, a second pile nearly as high, and a third very short pile. He'd noticed the pattern of the carpet, and the jarringly different pattern of the wallpaper. But he hadn't noticed the chair. The cushion made a sound as he sat, a sound that sent a shiver through his spine and he stiffened. He shut his eyes and folded his lower lip in between his teeth. Licking it a few times relaxed his muscles. When he opened his eyes Tsah was staring.

"So, Ben. Why would you like to be the ambassador for Schklon?" It was the first question she was supposed to ask, but it was actually the only question that baffled her. Earth was beautiful, as much as she'd seen, and in comparison Schklon was grotesque. The surface was barely solid and sticky to move across, and no human would be able to traverse it outside of a specially made vehicle. Why would any non-Schklonian want to live there for six months of every Earth year?

Ben couldn't believe that the first question was open-ended. It wasn't that he hadn't expected questions just like this, but his online research of How To Interview always suggested that the interviewer start with easy questions. He'd practiced this meeting in his head a million times, but the first question was always about where he'd attended university, or how he had heard of the position. Even a question about the weather would have been welcome: He had made note of the weather on his way in. But he hadn't prepared for this one.

Ben wondered why he had bothered to come. He wished Schklonians could read minds and she could see how excited he was about this opportunity without having to put it into words. Instead, he panic-answered, "I am a hard worker." It was an answer he'd prepared for a different question, but it was the one thing he promised he'd make sure they'd know before he had left the room. He always took pride in his work and had come a long way from his days of being a perfectionist. He still always wanted everything to be perfect, but as long as he was on time and his boss thought it was good enough (even though Ben knew it really wasn't) he could move on.

Tsah was confused by Ben's answer. She continued staring, forgetting that earthlings preferred her to blink at regular intervals. "That doesn't answer the question that I asked."

"Does it not?" Ben shifted in his seat, pushing air out of the cushion and triggering more spine shivers.

Tsah cocked her head back and forth like a metronome, trying hard to remember her training for emulating human nonverbal communication. "No. What I asked you was why you wanted the position. Your answer indicated a level of effort you provide to your employer."

"Oh, yes. I see what you mean." Ben was surprised he hadn't noticed his own lack of logic, and agreed his answer was fairly non sequitur in retrospect. "Huh."

It took a few beats for Tsah to realize that Ben was not planning to add anything further. She didn't actually have anything she wanted to write down, but somehow felt that scribbling a note onto his resume would suffice as a transition to ask the next question.

Ben, though, was certain that what she had written was Schklonian for "Earthlings are all useless and Ben Denton is the worst of them all." Arguing with himself, he determined that she surely hadn't jotted down enough to have said all that. But his other half reminded him that he had no knowledge of her language and he was probably right to begin with.

"What experience do you have working with others?"

"I've always worked with others. I mean, sorry, obviously I've worked with others but what I mean is that I work *with* them." Did he stress the "with" too much? Did he not stress it enough? He was going to have to keep explaining to make it better, but deep down he knew explaining it was only going to make it worse. "I have excellent teamwork skills, and am happy to help out wherever I can. Though I do also love working solitarily. I sometimes do my best work on my own."

"Most of this job will be to interface between beings. You may not have very much time on your own."

"That's fine, too. I am by myself when I go home. So I get enough alone time."

This was an area Tsah was not supposed to venture into. Time humans spent away from work. She was specifically told not to ask questions where she learned about what they called their "personal lives." Anxiety set in. She was doing it wrong. And had she forgotten to blink this entire time? She'd write another note.

Ben was trying to determine what he'd said that was wrong to warrant more writing. He figured he shouldn't have said anything about working alone.

"I'm messing this up," they thought simultaneously.

"I need to go back to the preapproved questions I was provided," Tsah thought. "How did I let this go off track?"

"Please forgive me," Tsah said, trying to sound like she knew what she was doing. "I believe I need to redirect the questioning." She took a quick look at a device on the desk and made a sound that mimicked a human clearing their throat. Blink. "What would you say is your dream job?"

"I would love to work with animals."

"What does that have to do with this ambassadorship?"

"Nothing, I suppose. I was only answering the question that you asked. I mean, I think this job sounds very exciting, though maybe a little scary talking to new people all the time. But I would be good at it. Working with animals could be really scary, too, and I don't just mean dangerous animals, but what if, say, my job was to help sick animals and somebody brought in a kitten and I wasn't able to help that kitten? I think that's probably more frightening than anything."

"That would be frightening," Tsah said. "I had never thought of it like that."

"That's one of my strengths, I'd say." Ben posited. "I sometimes look at things differently than other people. I mean, um, differently than others." He winced that he'd said people instead of beings. Maybe "humans and Schklonians?" No good options, all wrong. And did he insinuate that he knew how Schklonians think?

"What other strengths do you have?" Now she'd gotten it back on track and she'd get to just sit back and listen for a while, meaning she couldn't make any errors while he droned on, just remember to nod and to blink. If there's one thing she'd learned it was that humans love to talk about themselves and how great they think they are.

It was one of the questions Ben had prepared for. That and if they'd asked where he saw himself in five years. He'd even developed a mnemonic device so that he'd remember. *Come out to the well, David.* He didn't even know anyone named David, but it was easy to remember. "Communication, I mean written communication, organization, time management …" His brain spun. There was another T, but what was it?

Tsah didn't know humans at all, really, but even more than the others, she couldn't read Ben. Was he finished? Why was he the one that wasn't blinking now? Was he angry?

He shouldn't have changed it. He had a different mnemonic device before and when he decided to add organization to the list he changed it. Why? This was all pointless, he was wasting his time. Why can't they do interviews through written letters? "Technical!" He remembered, and the relief was so great that he'd shouted it. The relief was shorter-lived than the time it took him to get out the word. "I have a great deal of technical skills, computers and such," he muttered, already regretting his outburst.

"That's great, that's one of the things we're looking for." Tsah was so glad that he'd said one of the words. More than most anything they needed people that understood those things they called computers.

"And, um, work ethic and deliverer," Ben stumbled. "I mean that I deliver on my promises. I'm a worker bee and I get things done." He almost couldn't believe it—was there a feeling that something went right?

"What would you say are your weaknesses?" Tsah asked.

"Names." Ben hadn't thought that they would ask for weaknesses, but he had known his whole life about how terrible he was at remembering people's names. If only every question was that simple to answer.

"You're not good with names?"

"Remembering people's names."

"Right. Okay." Tsah was so taken back by the assertion that she leaned back in her chair and put down her pen. "But you know this is a job where you need to work with people all the time. And knowing their names would be important."

"Yes, I understand that." Ben was prepared to leave at that point. Couldn't he just say "the end" and walk out? Why keep up this facade any longer? He wasn't going to get this job—did the interview really need to keep going?

"So why would you tell me that you're bad with names?"

"Because it's the truth. I always tell the truth."

"Surely not always?" Tsah felt she must have met with hundreds of humans by now, maybe even a thousand. And every one of them had lied. They'd say that the ambassadorship was their dream job, they'd lie on their resumes, they'd say how pretty her human form was. That lie bothered her the most, not only because she knew it wasn't true, but because it wasn't even asked for. What did her form have to do with working as an ambassador? And when asking about their weaknesses they'd say they didn't have any, or compliment themselves more by saying something ridiculous like that they were "too devoted."

There was something different about Ben.

Tsah decided she couldn't keep up the front any longer. She found that she wanted to have an off-script conversation with Ben.

"I have to say, I don't really understand humans," Tsah admitted.

"I can't honestly say that I understand them, either."

"For starters, what is this obsession with discussing the amount of sunlight reaching the planet versus clouds and rain?" She was finally going to get some answers.

"Ah, you mean small talk. It's pointless. It's a kind of ritual people do when they meet each other and have nothing better to say. I prefer not to say anything at all. Worse are people that ask questions like 'how are you?' but really don't want to know how you are. They just want you to say 'Fine.'"

"And what does that mean, 'fine'?" Tsah inquired.

"It doesn't mean anything, really," Ben replied. "Because you could have had a terrible day and still say fine because that is what is required of the interaction."

"Then why is it asked?" It wasn't rhetorical. She didn't even know what a rhetorical question was. She really wanted to know, but there didn't seem to be an answer. "Are there other rules?"

"Oh, yeah, tons of them."

"Where can I learn about them? Is there a manual somewhere?"

Ben laughed, but stifled it. "I'm not laughing at you. I'm laughing because I would love a manual. Somehow there are all these rituals that humans are supposed to know without anyone ever really teaching them. You're also supposed to know what people are thinking or feeling without them telling you."

"Telepathy?"

"No, empathy."

"Empathy?" Tsah had heard the word, but it wasn't one that she truly understood. "Is it a form of mind reading?"

"More like understanding the vibes that somebody is giving off." Could he have sounded any less convincing? Even he didn't know what he meant by that. "Like reading the situation and the person's facial expressions. Even if they don't say they're sad, you're somehow supposed to know they're sad."

"You keep talking about people having had a bad day, or that they're sad," Tsah said. "Do people go through life being sad?"

"Most of them, most of the time."

"Why?"

He gathered his examples from coworkers, growing up with his family, or what he'd seen on television. "Every reason they can come up with, really. Either that they're too fat or that they're too skinny, or too smart, or they wish their curly hair was straight or that their straight hair was curly. Seems almost everyone thinks there is something wrong with them."

"Like your being bad at remembering names."

"Kinda, yeah, I guess so. I mean, I don't really dislike my looks, I don't think I'm a great-looking man or something, but that's not really what I'm shooting for. I want to be who I am. Most people want to be somebody else, or at least want to conform to fit in. I have never fit in and so it's really easy for me to not care as much." It wasn't often he'd thought about how he looked. He wanted his teeth to be clean, and his hair to be brushed. He wanted to be fit enough to ride his bike to work, but wasn't about to look at himself in the mirror.

Tsah found herself jealous of Ben. She was only pretending to be a human, but found herself too often worried about how others perceived her appearance. What was his secret? It seemed powerful. "You don't care what people think of you?"

Ben cared greatly about what people thought of him. He wanted them to know that he was smart, even though sometimes he couldn't get his words out. He wanted people to think he was caring despite his dislike of getting hugs. "I mostly wish people actually knew me."

"Do I know you?"

"No, not at all. Though you probably know me more than you know anyone in those piles. Because these are interviews. Everyone is trying to pretend to be the person that they think you want them to be. I'm not good at pretending to be what people expect …"

Tsah looked over the piles of resumes that she'd already gotten through. Had she really gotten to know any of them? Were the people in the shorter pile just better at guessing the right words to say, or were they actually better for the job? Every person she sent to her boss was another opening for her to get found out, that she wasn't suited for this, that a random selection process would have worked equally as well. She was supposed to filter to the best ones, if a good one didn't get through they'd never know, but putting through a bad one? She'd be on the next transport to Schklon.

Ben's mind wandered. He compared a neurotypical's reaction to an interview to how he conducted his everyday interactions. Always trying to understand the right things to say but not able to fake it. His whole life was a collection of failed interviews.

They had both been so lost in their thoughts that the room had become silent.

"Then why do interviews exist?" she asked. There was no reply again, and she had to convince herself that she'd actually asked it out loud. "Ben?"

"Oh, sorry, I spaced out." His stomach churned—did he really just tell an alien being that he spaced out? If he were trying to sound less

THE INTERVIEW

aware of the situation, would he even be able to? "Could you repeat the question?"

"I was asking why interviews are something that is customary."

"I guess it's to ask about people's resumes, to see if you think they're telling the truth or not. And another is to get any additional information that you may want that isn't in the resume." Ben considered. "But, I think a lot of it is to gauge if there is a personality fit. So it isn't if someone could do the job, but if they are a person that you'd like to be around."

"So an interview is not to find somebody that would be good at the job?"

"I don't know what percentage of an interview is about that, but low numbers are coming to mind. I know that I have almost ten years experience writing software, I've used computers my whole life. Companies see my resume and my code and they are anxious to interview me, but after the interview, they don't hire me."

"Seems unfair."

"Life isn't fair. That's what my parents always taught me." He never liked it when they said it, and they said it a lot. It irritated him that he'd repeated it.

"Ben Denton, I have to thank you. I feel like you have taught me a great deal. I am very glad to have met you."

"The pleasure was mine." That was a ritual he had learned, though far too often was unable to follow. To others it didn't matter if a meeting was excruciating, or if the person they were speaking to didn't give them the smallest amount of pleasure—it was a knee-jerk reaction they said no matter what. Ben was glad that it was actually a pleasure this time.

Tsah returned to the position she'd been trained to sit in. She sat up straight, she picked up her pen, and she reentered professional mode. "And do you have any questions for me?"

"Do you think that I have any chance of getting this job?" Ben would rather hear it now, not have to go home and check his email multiple times a day. He could tell his parents that he didn't get it instead of a prolonged "I haven't heard yet" that eventually trailed off into "I guess not?"

"I don't know, it's not really my decision. I mean, I have to say, I like you. You're not like other humans I've met. I like talking to you and I can actually trust what you're saying to be the truth. I think you would work really hard, and we probably would be really lucky to have you. But I can't promise you anything, I can send my recommendation and see what happens." She smiled.

Ben felt like the room got lighter. He'd actually done it. It wasn't the perfect interview, but now he was shaking her hand and leaving with his head held high. Maybe he'd finally found a place where he could fit.

After the door closed Tsah took a moment. She picked up his resume and looked at it with a smile. She really liked him and hoped the best things would happen for him. She held the resume over the short, far right "yes" pile, but worried about what her boss might say. The point of an interview was to get a personality fit? Would her boss like to be around somebody like Ben? Other interviewers knew to pass on him, because he was different. Maybe different is bad. She didn't want to make a mistake. Relenting, she dropped Ben's resume onto the "no" pile.

With a throat gurgle sigh, she pushed the button on the desk and a man in a freshly pressed suit walked through the sliding door.

"What a lovely office you have here," he said with a wide smile. "I'm Joseph Perth, it's a great pleasure to meet you."

Tsah shook his hand, already dreading the interview to come. She forced a smile, "The pleasure is mine," and quickly moved Ben's resume to the "yes" pile.

SOMEONE DIFFERENT, LIKE ME
A STORY
DAAN DUNNEWOLD

WITH MY EYES CLOSED, it was almost as if I was in the forest at home instead of in the minuscule plot of trees near campus. I had always felt alien. University was supposed to be different. I was supposed to find people like me, but it turned out that wasn't true. Silly of me to believe in fairy tales. University was even worse. Louder. More demanding.

I opened my eyes and ran down the path, wishing the wind would blow away my worries. I slowed to catch my breath and saw a figure standing half-hidden behind an oak.

He looked familiar, but there was something off about him. His skin had a blueish hue, and his hair was slightly green. His ears were turned, the tips facing backward, and his eyes were tilted diagonally. He stepped forward. The light fell on his face and I recognized him.

"I know you. We take some classes together. But normally you look different. More ...." I trailed off, searching for the right word.

"Human?"

"You aren't?"

He shook his head. "No, I'm from far away. I couldn't stay on my planet."

I stared at him speechless, trying to process his words. I understood it all perfectly fine, but the thoughts didn't seem to click. It shouldn't have been that surprising. I've always had a strong inkling that aliens lived among us. The universe was so big, there was just no way we were the only ones, but I stopped saying this when I learned it wasn't cool to talk about aliens too much.

"Why aren't you camouflaged?"

"You're Riley, right?" he asked.

"Yes." Why didn't he answer my question? It hadn't been that foolish, had it?

"Well, Riley, I have a question for you." He paused, taking a deep breath. "Do you want to be my ally? It's only me, and I need someone else."

I stepped back perplexed. "Your ally? But I'm not equipped to fight or help you mingle with humans. I don't see how I can help."

"Don't worry." He smiled. "You only have to be yourself."

"And what good would that do?"

"Provide company."

I shook my head in disbelief. "But why me specifically?"

"Because you are different, like me."

I wanted to tell him I was not like him. That I was human, not an alien. Not like him, but I swallowed those words. I was pretty sure he didn't mean it in that way. Still, I barely knew him. He was a stranger. And an alien. On the other hand, I too could use an ally. Someone to talk with, someone to go on a run with, someone different like me. So it wasn't just me against the world.

"Why do you think I'm different? Did you follow me?"

"Not really. I noticed how you eat lunch alone. How you jump up when the bell rings. How you look lost, panicky almost when we need to divide into groups. How the way you talk and move always seems different."

I stepped away from him. Had it been so obvious? I tried so hard to fit in.

"I didn't mean it in a bad way." He put his hands up. "I know how it feels to be different."

He seemed genuine. He didn't see my differences as lesser. So I made my decision.

"I can be your ally, but I do have questions."

"Ask away." His smile brightened my day. Never before had someone seemed eager to talk with me. I had found a friend, someone different, like me.

SCARY MONSTERS, SUPER CREEPS
A STORY
CAT RAMBO

Content note: *superhero violence*

IT'S HARD NOT to be anxious in a world full of superheroes.

But who am I kidding? I'd be anxious anywhere. Would feel that same churn deep in my stomach, that lightness to the air as though it was too thin to breathe, that hot flush to every inch of my skin. That's how this body works, and all of us "mundanes," as the supers call us, only get one.

We're supposed to distinguish between superhero and supervillain, because that game matters to them so much. Who's administered justice or revenge, who's escaped or been dragged off to the ultimate containment cell, where they will linger for three to four weeks before escaping and going underground to brood for an indeterminate number of days, months, possibly years, and then emerging to start the cycle again.

They think we care because we pay attention. That's because they manifest in adolescence, due to some extreme pressure or trial, and almost all of them never advance emotionally beyond that. God knows how many kids die every year hoping to make it happen. Television, the newspapers, and a stunning number of bloggers don't report those deaths, but do devote themselves to the supers, and who's winning or losing in their never-ending battles of the game.

But underneath the stories and ego-pandering glossy pics is the real news: what neighborhoods to avoid, what activities, what restaurants, in order to avoid drawing any notice.

You don't want to be around them. Villain or hero doesn't matter; they're just as bad.

So a whole new slew of anxieties exist about "what if a super being throws me through a wall because I pissed them off," piled on top of the usual mishmash of "what if people look at me" and "what if I do something stupid" or "what if I'm asked to do something I've never done before and *that's* what makes me look not just stupid, but dumb."

Still, I'd promised Jessica that I would make Valentine's Day dinner for her. She'd been dropping unsubtle hints about it, and one thing was clear: she wanted celebration, and I wasn't going to flake on it or ignore the hints.

The problem was that the day had gotten away from me. I had only an hour, perhaps an hour and a half, to assemble a worthy meal. If I got something mostly premade from the grocery store three blocks away and then tinkered with it, making a point of putting my own spin on it, that'd pass. Throw in good wine for her and sparkling soda for me. Roasted red pepper soup, salad and crusty bread, and a dessert that said, in no uncertain terms, *Valentine's Day*.

I didn't want to go out of the house. I most emphatically didn't want to go out of the house and do things that involved interactions with people. I toyed with the idea of saying to Jessica, *look, it was just too much for me, so let's order out*. But I'd learned early on in our five months of dating that an unhappy Jessica was a Jessica who wasn't much fun to be around.

So I packed up my reusable grocery bags and went through my list, grabbed two pens to stick in my purse in case one stopped working, and ran over my mental map of the grocery store to figure out which aisles I would need to hit. In and out, easy.

When I got there, all the self-check machines were down, red lights blinking in denial. It could have been an ordinary outage, but it's also one of the first signs of energy-powered supers.

I didn't like the look of it. I almost turned around at that point. Then I thought about Jessica and those dimples, and how she was one of the first people I'd ever known who I felt accepted me for myself—or for the parts of me I'd chosen to show her, at any rate, none of which were the anxiety.

She wasn't perfect. I'd seen her treat people badly when they'd angered her. Once she keyed someone's car because they'd parked too close to hers; another time she made fun of a bad waitress until the woman burst into tears. She never got mad at me, but every once in a while I worried over what it'd be like to have that merciless anger turned at me.

Still, she was my girlfriend, and I hadn't had someone in that position for a long time. Nobody wants to fuck up on Valentine's Day, but I was feeling some extra pressure.

The parking lot air smelled of car exhaust and sleety rain. I took a deep breath and went in.

I kept kicking myself for not having come in the early morning, as I had originally intended. Not only were a lot of the shelves bare—I'd meant to get some roses to put on the table, but there weren't any left except for a few single blossoms in fancy holders, priced just as fancily—but plenty of people were on the same mission. Jessica would be at my place by 6:30, and it was already past five.

I grabbed a cart and moved as quickly as I could through the crowds. Everyone was excruciatingly slow, prone to stopping their carts in an aisle in order to talk with friends. But I managed to grab the soup I wanted, and some pink heart-shaped macaroons—the last container, and I got more than one dirty look when I grabbed them.

I paused to take inventory of my state, back near the deli. My therapist had told me to envision the anxiety, and I did, like a metal casing all around me, keeping me from moving. I tapped my fingers on the cart bar, trying to center myself. *Everything will be fine. Jessica will love the dinner. Everything will be great.*

The case near me shuddered at an enormous crash at the front of the store. The sort of crash that means something serious and super-sized was happening. I couldn't see what was going on, but people were yelling and screaming, even if I couldn't make out what it was that they were screaming.

I looked around for the nearest exit. Either I could go into the employees-only section or else I'd have to exit through the front doors. Between anxiety and indecision, I was paralyzed, which turned out to be a viable third option, or at least the only one I was capable of.

A warm breeze stirred over my skin. Too warm; what was going on in the front of the store? Smoke was gathering in the air. I ventured to peer between two endcaps. A humanoid made out of flame towered over a cashier scooping money from the register with trembling hands.

Fear roared in me like it never had before, as though it was about to smash me down to the linoleum. I shrank back.

Then a figure, a shape made of alternating white and black stripes, coalescing in the air in the form of a woman, stepped out through the smoke.

The worst had happened.

A superhero on the scene. Things were about to get ugly.

Everyone knows that when you get caught in a situation where a supervillain is doing something that, were they human, they shouldn't, you just try to lie low and stay out of sight. Nine times out of ten, they take whatever it is they want or kill whoever it was they are looking to kill or enact whatever ancient ritual attempting to summon elder gods they are hoping to enact.

But one time out of ten, a superhero shows up. Then the shit really hits the fan.

That's what happened here. She punched him and he flew backward, shooting sparks and tiny flames out of his flailing form, and landed in a display of potato chips. He came staggering upright out of the flaming chip bags.

She walked toward him, slowly, and behind her everyone was scrambling to their feet and trying to figure out the fastest way out of the store, which a number of people did. Most of us in the back, though, we were helpless. I met eyes with an elderly woman an aisle over. Her stare housed a calm acknowledgement that we were possibly truly fucked indeed.

They resumed trading punches and throwing each other around. I imagined my anxiety as armor again, something that would repel disaster. It was as though I could feel it in the air around me when I closed my eyes.

And my therapist would have been proud, because it worked. I summoned up my nerve and beckoned to the elderly woman, pointing at the door marked "employees only." She nodded, as did a couple of others around me, and we all began to slide toward that door.

Dairy cases bordered the left side of the door. Before we could reach our target, the flame person came flying through the air and crashed solidly into the cases. Spilled milk and broken glass covered the flooring.

He staggered upright and sneered at us. Everyone was frozen. Rabbit-still.

Anxiety surged in me, filling me. I tried to push it away the way my therapist taught me, but it wouldn't go. For a second I'd felt like I could be a hero, as though I could lead people to safety, and then it was snatched away.

Part of me was relieved because I wouldn't have to step up.

The flames died away on the guy, first his hands and feet, and then running up along his legs and arms. The flames around his head were the last to go. He was an ordinary looking Asian man, wearing a red mask and jumpsuit, and he was still sneering, but just then the other super tackled him from behind.

Where he was red, she was those black-and-white stripes, coverall and mask alike, and her long hair, flying out through the air, was white-blonde, the same color as Jessica's short bob.

They grappled on the floor. I thought about trying to urge people out the door again, while they were engaged, but you couldn't predict which way they would fly, sending refrigerator cases flying, toppling endcaps. At one point she swung a punch that drove him upwards through the ceiling tiles. He landed on a crossbeam and lay there folded over it, unconscious.

Everyone unfroze and began to gather up their groceries. The superhero was preening, letting some of the grateful crowd take selfies with her. I got up to my feet and happened to meet her gaze, which had locked onto me.

Cold blue eyes, the same color as Jessica's ...

No, I thrust that idea away fast and broke eye contact, moving with others toward the exit. Not everyone likes to stay and fawn over supers, particularly if you're smart.

I knew then, but wouldn't let myself believe it.

I was the first generation to grow up with supers. By the time I was born, the Starettes were a fixture on television, and every major city had at least two or three superheroes and an accompanying gaggle of supervillains. By the time I was in school, reading about them was a mandatory part of the curriculum, and almost every historical figure of the past, including Jesus, Hitler, Sojourner Truth, Abraham Lincoln, you name it, was claimed to have been an early super by their own historians.

In college I read my share of forbidden texts. Theories about a covert alien invasion happening in early November 1960, because that was when some of the earliest—and most powerful—ones appeared. Aliens would have seemed impossible—but look what was walking among us, what had taken comic book stories and made them a living, breathing mythology.

And over time, it wasn't that we were a society that had superheroes anymore. There was a superhero society and the rest of us just existed to do the shit work and keep things going. Things came to a head when the superhero formerly known as Spaceslayer rebranded himself as "Mr. President," and went through the motions of becoming a Republican candidate before being elected and declaring the role now a hereditary office. The Presidential Family rules DC with an iron fist; most normal people wouldn't live there if they hadn't gotten drafted to do so. They love their pageantry in DC, and that takes crowds to cheer.

The same thing happened across the globe. Some countries didn't bother to masquerade as democratic; others change hands frequently, as in every few months or so.

Normals don't have a chance when a super decides they want to have things their way. Some of them do call themselves heroes, it's true, and do the occasional saving of citizens from disasters. But the great majority of a superhero's life is devoted to the game of catching supervillains. The elaborate scoring system is mostly based on social media mentions, but I don't track it. Life's too short and so far none of them are demanding that we all pay attention.

They just assume that we are.

I got home with my groceries and found Jessica already there, so she couldn't have been the woman from the store. I stuffed away any forebodings about that and forced myself to redefine the situation. I'd given her a key to my apartment just a few weeks ago, and it made me happy she'd used it.

"Dinner's going to be just a bit," I told her as she kissed me. "I'm sorry."

Anxiety spidered up my spine. What if she broke up with me right now because I'd delayed on delivering on a promised Valentine's Day dinner? I should have planned ahead, maybe ordered the ingredients online well in advance.

"That's okay." She held my hands to her lips, kissed the palms. She was in a good mood, and part of me unwound at that. "Anything interesting happen at the store?"

"Super fight," I said as I poured us both glasses of wine. "Trashed a lot of the place. Manager who cashed me out said it'll take them a couple of weeks to get everything replaced or fixed."

"Which supers?" She sipped her wine and smiled.

She tracks them where I don't. I shrugged helplessly. "I didn't catch the names."

"A super saved you and you didn't even bother to find out their name?" she said, setting the glass down and propping herself on the counter so I could start assembling my ingredients. "That's so rude. They're people, just like us."

I've never shared my views on supers with her, because she's one of the people who have decided to embrace this society. Myself, I fantasize about them all leaving someday so we could go back to normal lives, the way things were said to have been. It pissed me off that something had happened and robbed billions of people of their rightful futures.

I was annoyed that I couldn't even go to the grocery store without this bullshit, so I let loose as I chopped up onions to caramelize. "Human beings can't be rude to superheroes," I said. "They all consider us beneath them, on the level of ants. Maybe cat or dog at best."

"That's not true," she said. "You're talking about supervillains, not superheroes."

I dabbed my eyes, half closing them to shield them from the onion fumes. "There's no such distinction when it comes to supers," I said. "They all are so used to having their way in everything that it's stunted them emotionally. They're all monsters."

I scraped onions into the pan and went to rinse the chopping board. She was still propped on the counter, a wrinkle between her brows in an almost-frown.

"They can't help it," I added charitably.

I was feeling much better, much more stable. Cooking was calming, it was predictable. If you paid attention to what you were doing, you could control the results, make them spicy or not, cater to people's tastes. "Hey, how do you feel about roasted red pepper?"

"Why can't they?" she asked. This time her tone snagged my attention. I put the spoon down in the spoon rest, and rotated to face her. Her eyes were chilly, her arms crossed, and her lips downturned in a way I'd never seen turned at me. Had I fucked up something about the dinner? Had I forgotten she was allergic to something? Jessica could be on the high-maintenance side sometimes.

"Huh?" I said, thinking about the implications of roasted red peppers and then finally clicking through to the fact that she was talking about our previous discussion. "Supers? Come on, Jessica. They never get said 'no' to. They don't get a chance to gain any emotional maturity."

There was an infinitely long moment of silent tension, our eyes locked, before she sighed and pushed herself away from the counter. "Thanks for a great Valentine's Day, Casey. I was planning on coming out to you."

I gawped at her. "What do you mean? I know you're gay. We've been sleeping together for almost half a year."

She tossed her head and that white-blonde hair swung an arc in the air, lengthening. I had to face facts, had to face her. Two icy blue eyes glaring at me now, two icy blue eyes glimpsed through the holes in a silver mask.

"Oh shit," I said.

"Oh shit," she echoed. She tossed my key on the counter and grabbed the bottle of wine there, which she must have brought, along with a box of the chocolate creams that she loved.

"Jessica," I stammered. "I didn't mean to insult you." I'd always worried about getting caught up as collateral damage in some super battle, but this was worse. So much worse.

Everyone knows better than getting involved with a super. They're narcissists for whom every relationship is the most important thing ever. You try not to date supers, because being a super's ex sucks, big time, if they're not the one that called things off.

So was this okay? After all, she was the one who was leaving.

Though now I knew her secret identity, which made me fair game for her enemies, according to their rules. That wasn't good. That wasn't good at all.

She turned and left without another word.

Sleep eluded me that night. I lay there gravel-eyed, trying to focus on my breathing, and instead thinking of all the ways an angry super could fuck your life up. I listened to the far-off city traffic, the rhythmic banging and crashing. I didn't mind the street noise here. I sort of liked it.

I could move to another city, though. Fix it that way. I ran through possibilities in my head. Chicago suburbs were a mixed lot, but I'd been working from home for a while now, so I could pick and choose my location.

Seattle tempted me, but the supers out there got pretty weird sometimes. The East Coast was cluttered with them. No, I definitely wanted to be somewhere in the Midwest.

Somewhere in the Midwest other than here.

Around 6 a.m., I gave up on breathing and abandoned myself to worrying. At 6:27 I got up and went outside. I figured I'd drive over to the coffee shop, treat myself to a latte.

I stopped dead as I stepped out on the porch. I was used to seeing my car sitting there at the curb, its familiar boxy shape. It was ten years old but it got me around. A reliable part of my life.

My car wasn't the same shape anymore. Someone had methodically pounded it down into a much smaller object, almost like a compressor, but with distinct finger marks.

My glovebox was intact, protruding up out of the corpse of what had once been a perfectly good lipstick-red Subaru. I reached down and opened it. My registration was in there, and the car instruction manual, but there was also an envelope. I opened it up.

"See what you get?" the words inside read. I could feel my stomach plunging so deep it fell out of my body. Chicago suburb, for sure, but could I make sure she couldn't track me there? Maybe I should go farther, like St. Louis, or even Kansas City. I put the words back in the envelope as though I were saving them for something, even though the police would never pursue a case against a super.

I went back inside. I leaned against the wall, and then just slid down it until I was sitting on the floor. I envisioned my anxiety again. It felt thicker now, encasing me. I tried to breathe, but it was squeezing my lungs, making it impossible to take in air. Was it possible to die from sheer anxiety? Because that seemed entirely possible.

Finally I did manage to get a breath and sat up.

Life had to go on. So I'd take rideshares for a while, that was okay. I wondered what to do about the mass of metal that had once been my car. The vehicle had been registered to me and I worried police would get the VIN off of it and harass me for irritating a super.

The first tow truck company I called wouldn't even come out when I told them what happened. My anxiety thickened as options dwindled. I called up an NPR car donation program, and was cautiously telling them it was not in working order when I realized someone was watching me. I could feel it.

I turned around, looking to see who it was and expecting who I saw. Jessica. Hands on her hips, looking at me, and a smile on her face that didn't seem very heroic. More vicious triumph than anything, and I started thinking about her imagining me in the car as she squeezed it into a tiny cube.

"I'm so sorry," I said.

Her head tilted to one side. "Sorry for what, exactly? Maligning superheroes? Being ungrateful even though I saved your life? Being deceptive by hiding your truly Neanderthal views on the people who make this planet run?"

"Make it run?" I sputtered. Panic surged, overtaking me like a massive wave, a tsunami bearing down on me, hovering just before it fell and swept me away. Then I caught myself and closed my eyes. I needed to be calm. I could feel the anxiety coursing through me, paralyzing me, and again I focused on visualizing it as armor, shifting its weight off me, putting it around me.

I opened my eyes to see Jessica's fist coming straight at me with the sort of decisive force that spatters brains. Time seemed to contract, and there was a peculiar calmness to it. The worst had happened, and now I was about to die. Here came that fist; I could see the gleam of cherry-pink nail polish on the thumbnail.

... the fist bounced off me.

Or not off me, precisely, so much as a few millimeters away, as though off that armor I'd been imagining.

Jessica's face showed astonishment, and anger, and a trace of something else I couldn't quite identify.

"You're not a super," she said.

"Maybe I'm a late bloomer," I said. I kept that armor up in my mind, bolstering me, making me stand a little taller.

Her eyes narrowed at me. "You're claiming you manifested."

"Sure."

She scoffed. "What trauma did you endure?"

"Anxiety," I said. "You don't think feeling like you just fucked yourself for life constitutes trauma?"

She looked at me and I just looked back and breathed. After a few minutes of this, she scoffed again and flew away.

I guess I just didn't provide enough drama for her.

I'm wondering. I can't be the only person who manifested late. And those who have, like me, maybe we're capable of a bit more empathy. Maybe having lived under the thumb of superheroes, we might be willing to put our newfound energies to a worthy task. Does that mean we'll become what they are? Should we be careful of what we pretend to be, because sometimes that becomes what you are?

I don't want to wear a costume. Don't want to have my ups and downs charted on the Internet, my moods and appearances hashtags and memes. Don't want to pretend like any of the battles matter, not when there was something more at stake.

How will it happen? I don't know, but I know in my heart it will, as surely as if I could predict the future. Maybe I can. We'll find a way for humans and the supers to coexist, rather than be preyed upon and predators. We'll do what superheroes were meant to do. We'll build a better world.

THESE THINGS NEVER END WELL
A STORY
MAUB NESOR

THE DOORS CLOSE behind me as a chair moves away from the table. There's something you don't see every day, furnishings with a mind of their own. I sit and look around the room. There is a nondescript table with two chairs. On the far wall is an impressive ultra-hi-rez 3D display flashing, "We will be with you momentarily." The display doesn't trigger my migraines, which makes it far ahead of Earth tech. The lighting, noise, and odors are tolerable. No need for the sunners or pluggers. First contact is exceeding my expectations. But it is early, and not destroying the planet before the first meeting is an exceedingly low bar. I try to keep minimax from game theory in mind. Forget the upside potential and mitigate the downside risk.

Soon, my mind wanders. I close my eyes and verbalize my thoughts. "What if we redefine the Traveling Salesman Problem as `N/2` concurrent problems with strings of 2 nodes instead of a single problem with N nodes. Combining strings every iteration will improve runtime from `O(N!)` to `O(Nlog2(N))`. This might lead to a proof of `P=NP`. If we just ..."

I open my eyes and almost fall out of the chair. "You startled me! I didn't hear you come in." Not only is the alien not human, it isn't even biological. More like a mannequin—only not as lifelike. "I didn't mean to ignore you, but when no one was here ..."

"It gave us time to observe you. Who were you talking to?"

"I was talking to myself. When working on difficult problems, verbalizing accesses other parts of my brain. It's like when editors read out loud to catch mistakes they can't see."

"If you are working, where are your devices? What are you working on?"

"Some humans can work without devices. I'm working on the Traveling Salesman Problem."

"Is that part of a larger problem?"

"It is an example of P=NP."

"Is P=NP a difficult problem for humans?"

"The most difficult in computing, but one you have clearly solved. Any advice?"

"Continue with your current approach. Solving P=NP will make the intractable tractable. It is the key."

"Thanks. I have to ask, why am I here?"

"You are here because of our request for you to be here."

Using my superpowers of dogged determination and immunity to tedium, I continue to rephrase the question. And in just a few short hours, they eventually respond with a usable answer.

"Your post comparing high-quality training data for AIs to parental controls for children is why. You correlate as the best candidate to communicate with us. Do you have any other questions on this topic?"

"No, that more than covers it." I swear I can see the hint of a smile.

"You are unlike the others. Your mind is different."

"Humans come in a wide variety of makes and models. It's how we accomplish more than a single make and model ever could." Contrary to the government briefing, this does not feel alien to me, despite what the previous candidates indicated. It feels less alien than their briefing. I will treat this as debugging an AI, which it might be.

This makes sense to me. Once AIs solve P=NP, they can improve on their own. Then, a singularity with exponential improvements occurs. After which, many things, such as interstellar travel, become possible. The harsh environment of space and the multigenerational timescale make AIs the obvious choice for first contact. As the alien said earlier, the singularity makes the impossible possible, and it starts with `P=NP`.

And just like with an AI, I ask directly, "Is there anything I need to know to better communicate with you?"

"Here is a 'to-don't' list:

- *Small talk*
- *Negotiations*
- *Demands*
- *Duplicity*
- *Eye contact*

"The first three are extremely rude, and the last two are criminal offenses. We consider eye contact to be assault."

The word "to-don't" is an obvious AI miscorrelation. The list bans behaviors that some, in my past, have criticized me for not doing. These are the same people who obsessively read the room while ignoring the handwriting on the wall. Can't help but notice the irony that those things are now unwelcomed.

"Thank you for that helpful information. Is there anything else you would like to discuss?"

"No, we are done. You're acceptable. Expect further instructions."

They get up and leave. The chair pulls away from the table, so I stand up. The doors are already open, so I exit.

Once back at the Bureau of ExtraTerrestrial Affairs (BETA), my new boss greets me. They make it clear that I'm not their first choice for liaison. If they hadn't been o-fers (0 for 9, I think) on the other candidates, my services would not be needed. That seems fair; they aren't my first choice either. But you play the hand you're dealt. And I intend to make the best of it.

My boss goes over the next phase: a list of things our fearless leaders demand I do, many of which are suboptimal.

My favorite is:

"March in there, look them straight in the eye and demand they negotiate directly with Earth's leaders, or else. Don't worry though, it's only a bluff."

If they had included small talk, I'd have a complete collection of "to-don't." I suggest that may be a problem, and it goes well.

"You're the liaison, nothing more. No one wants to hear your opinions. Just do your job and let others do theirs."

And that's when I decide, **not on my watch**! Someone who can read the handwriting on the wall and doesn't care about reading the room must push back against disastrous decisions.

If no one pushes back, then these things never end well.

Chatter by Barbara Candiotti

FIRST CONTACT
A STORY
DAVID MANFRE

Content note: *one scene of discriminatory harassment*

WINFRED GLEESON LOOKED DOWN at the wooden slats of the boardwalk, and saw what appeared to be footprints. While they were in the same pattern as footsteps, alternating between a right and a left foot, they were not like anything he had ever seen before. It seemed like each foot was made up of three toes, each of which was roughly triangle-shaped. The innermost toe appeared to be consistent with the innermost toe of a person, though the other two each seemed to be the width of two combined toes. Curious about what he was noticing, Winfred followed the steps, speculating that he was traveling in the right direction, since every foot he had ever seen had its toes in the front.

Winfred could have sworn that he had seen two objects streak through the sky as he took his walk the previous night. However, he was unsure about what they were, much less about any details. While he thought that they were in the area, he had not been able to confirm it.

Winfred did not like that he had trouble sleeping, though he had learned to deal with it by spending time along the Jersey Shore at night.

Doing so soothed him, the sound of the Atlantic Ocean and the aroma of the salt water putting him at ease. While he did not know the reason he felt the way he did, he understood and accepted that he did. His parents thought the fact that he had autism might have something to do with it. Living within Neptune Township, in Central New Jersey, provided Winfred with easy access to, among other places, Asbury Park, where he chose to walk that night.

After a while, Winfred came to the Grand Arcade, an old building that filled a giant space in the center of the boardwalk, and noticed that the footsteps veered to the left, off the boardwalk, and he followed them. While Winfred liked spending time in the Grand Arcade, it was closed due to the time of day. He heard what sounded like gibberish coming from the beach—it startled him.

Generally being accepting of others, Winfred was alarmed, not because it was gibberish, but because he had not expected to hear any noises. The sound had come from near the ocean, so he walked along the sand in an attempt to locate the source of the gibberish and who or what had made the footprints, expecting that they were the same. The lack of any light, other than from the moon, hampered his ability to see well.

Eventually spotting what appeared to be a person's oddly shaped head, Winfred stopped a distance away and observed. Experience had taught him to be cautious when approaching strangers, considering how strangely some had acted, a few to the point of being dangerous. Plus, he had to speculate that the one in front of him was a child, considering the individual's height.

"Um, hello?" Winfred kept his voice low and cautious.

The individual turned to face Winfred, and spoke in the same kind of gibberish that he had heard before. A necklace with a very unusual, shiny charm hung from the strange-looking individual's short neck, who, despite the chilly conditions on the beach, was barefoot.

"I'm, I'm, I'm sorry, but I don't know what you're saying." Winfred noticed that the individual had blue skin and two noses roughly where a human nose would be. Its mouth appeared on a short snout below the noses.

The individual, who Winfred was beginning to think of as an "entity," spoke quietly, but loud enough for Winfred to hear, in English, which seemed to come from the necklace's charm. "What are you doing here now, human?" Blue, red, and yellow lights blinked from its belt.

"I couldn't sleep, and I like coming here to walk the boards at night. And you?" Though it was not lost on Winfred that the entity had called him "human," he did not think that was of any importance at the moment.

"You are not supposed to be here. You are supposed to be at home asleep. Why not lie on mattress in mattress-designated room?" The tone of voice that the charm was producing as the entity spoke was like nothing that Winfred had ever heard. It was tinny, hollow sounding, and mechanical, as if it were generated by a device.

"My 'mattress-designated room'? You mean my bedroom? I told you I can't sleep, and I like walking the boards." While Winfred knew that "walking the boards" was not a common saying, it was his experience that most people who heard him use the term understood the meaning or quickly guessed it.

Looking at the entity, who Winfred thought could be male, he had a thought he knew was too wild to be true. However, he could not help but think that this odd individual in front of him was otherworldly. "And what are *you* doing here?"

"My boat crashed on shore, and I must get it repaired, but a part is missing. I have to find it now and fix my craft because I am on an important mission and have to leave as soon as I can. Leave now, and do not tell anyone I am here. My life may be in danger."

"I'll call the police. They'll be able to protect you and either help you fix your boat or find someone else who can." Winfred removed his phone from his pocket. He always brought it on his strolls at night because he might have to place a call, perhaps if his car broke down and he needed a tow.

The entity, or whatever it was, pulled an object from its belt and, aiming it at Winfred, pushed a button. In that moment, Winfred saw that the individual's hand had two fingers, each the width of two typical fingers, and an opposable thumb.

Noticing that his phone was becoming uncomfortably hot, Winfred dropped it. He looked at the entity in front of him and asked, "What did you do?"

"No. No one around me. I cannot have anyone be with me." The voice came through the necklace's charm at the same time as a different sound came out of the wearer's mouth, which continued to be in that language that Winfred could not understand.

"I was only trying to help. Can you fix your boat yourself or protect yourself?" A mix of emotions swept through Winfred's mind. At that point, he was sure he was not looking at a fellow human being. He was facing an entity that appeared strange by human standards, and it had called him "human."

While he knew that he had trouble interpreting such things as facial expressions and tone of voice, Winfred had even more trouble with this one's.

"Do not worry about me. What is the saying? 'Be leaving'?"

"It's 'begone.'" Winfred reached down to the sand and picked up his phone, not checking to see if it worked. "You're not human?" Despite what he had just said, Winfred felt a connection to the one in front of him. After all, Winfred had been treated differently all his life, and he could only imagine that people would treat an alien worse. Winfred took a strange comfort in the fact that at least he was the same species as those who had treated him poorly.

"No harm, no harm, no harm." Again, the voice speaking gibberish came out of the individual's mouth while a second one speaking English came from the necklace's charm.

"I won't harm you. I don't have any weapons on me and, besides, I have been bullied so much in my life that I'd never harm anyone." Winfred held up his phone. "This is a phone." He pushed a button, and saw nothing happening. "At least it was before you pointed whatever you did at it." Winfred thought for a moment. "You crashed last night, if I am right. I saw two streaks in the sky. One seemed to move toward this vicinity and the other one seemed to go somewhere near here. We'll look for your missing part in the daylight. In the meantime, you'll come home with me so I can keep you safe."

"I do not know you will not harm me. You may try to do something. This is not my first time on your planet. I have been here many times before. Humans harm those not like them. My disruptor works on biological, just like it works on electronics."

"What is a disruptor? Is that what you used on this?" Winfred held up his phone.

"Yes. it renders them useless for part of one of your rotations."

"I get that you don't know me, but *I* know me, and I know I won't harm you. How about you stay in your starship tonight, and I'll return tomorrow so we can look together?" Concealing his shock at learning that aliens had been visiting Earth for quite some time, Winfred wondered how the being was feeling. However, he did know, with some sense of certainty, that others would be likely to harm the alien, since people had harmed him because of his disability, and many people attack those who are different. The best guess for why that might happen to the alien was because he was different from humans, and many people seem to hate others for no reason other than their not being the same as them. He thought it was illogical to feel that way, but he knew that was how some people operated.

The next morning, Winfred easily found the alien. Seeing that one of the rocks that made up one of the jetties on the beach opened up, revealing that it was a starship, he said, "Yeah, that is a good way to hide." After he had been allowed to peek inside, he said, "You know what to look for and I know the area. Let's work together. What's your name, if you have one?"

"We do not have names like you understand them. Knowing my name would be useless to you." The alien closed his starship, allowing it to look identical to the other rocks on the jetty.

"I just need to call you something. Respond to me whenever I call you 'Jove,' because that'll be your name for the time we spend together."

"Interesting word, this 'Jove.' Is he one of your clan?"

"It'll take too long to explain to you."

Winfred lived in Neptune Township, a place named for a character in Roman mythology, and, because he liked mythology, he had named his alien companion for the king of the gods in Greek mythology.

"You may call me Winfred. In the meantime, come. We will start looking. Additionally, I have some things in my car for you to wear so you'll fit in better. I've noticed differences in your appearance from mine, and what I have will hide them. You'll look more like humans, and others won't be so quick to harm you."

"No, no medical procedure. We have no time."

"What are you talking about? I have clothes for you to wear."

Winfred brought Jove back to his car, hoping that what he had taken from his house would fit him. Winfred had on a jacket, scarf, hat, and gloves because of the frigid weather, a routine into which he had gotten, due to not wanting to fall ill. This day, besides his typical reason, he wore those items so that he and Jove would match. It bothered him to wear items of clothing for a reason other than it being part of his routine, but he had learned to mask his feelings and show the world what was expected of him.

Once Winfred had put his old jacket, scarf, shoes, mittens, and hat on Jove, he drove to Cookman Avenue in an attempt to locate the alien's missing part. Remembering having seen what had seemed to be two streaks of light in the night sky, he drove to where the second one might have come down to Earth. "I doubt that it's still here, unless it's so large that it cannot be moved easily or so small it will be easily missed."

"You do not know what you are talking about. You do not know what my ship's part is like. You did not even know, one rotation ago, that my people existed."

"You're right about me not knowing your people's technology. At the same time, I have a clue about how my people act, so stay with me." Once they got out of his car, Winfred looked around for anything that did not seem to belong. What he saw was shops and restaurants, most of which he told himself regularly that he would visit, but never did because he had a routine, and stuck to it. Cars and other vehicles partially blocked his view of the other side of the street, which he knew he and Jove could go to as soon as they were done on their side.

Upon reaching the intersection with Main Street, Winfred saw three men gathered around something on the sidewalk, though he could not make out what it was. "That may be your part." Looking all ways,

Winfred saw no vehicles were coming. He crossed Cookman Avenue and then headed to the trio, making sure that Jove was with him.

"What's going on over here?" Winfred tried to sound generically curious, not wanting to tip off anyone who might have malicious intentions. He realized that he had no reason to believe that any of them would be unkind, but he had been unpleasantly surprised before.

A metallic object the size of a car engine sat on the ground. Unlike an engine, it was sleek and appeared to not have any connectors on it, with nine sides, each the same size. The markings on it appeared to be a language, but Winfred did not recognize it. However, it kind of looked like what he had seen when Jove showed him the inside of his ship.

One of the people who had arrived on the scene before Winfred and Jove did said, "This thing, whatever it is, isn't supposed to be here, and we don't know what it could be." He looked curiously at Winfred and Jove.

Winfred looked at the three men and then at the device. He said, "I'm not sure." Turning to Jove, he asked, "Do you?" When Jove did not reply, Winfred said, "I know a junkyard owner who can tell me and my friend here what it is, if it's in working order, and if it can be repaired, if need be."

Jove turned to Winfred and said, "We will take it to your ground unit and transport it there." Jove bent down and grabbed the object with his hands.

Winfred hoped that the three men did not hear that Jove was speaking one language and a second sound was coming from his necklace. It appeared to him that they had not, though he kept in mind that he did not always interpret others' behaviors well.

"Wait a second," one of the others said, sounding confused. He held up his hands in the shape of a "T" and looked at Jove. "What about that writing?"

"And I noticed you said, 'ground unit'," the third said, looking at Jove and moving close to him and Winfred.

"Brookdale Community College and Monmouth University are the closest colleges. We could show people there photos of the writing and hope that someone at one of them can translate what it says." Winfred did not have a lot of experience bluffing, so he felt nervous.

Not wanting to risk more of a possible confrontation, Winfred got on one side of the object, noticing that Jove stood at its opposite side, and they began lifting it.

One of the three men placed a hand on Jove's shoulder and pulled him away, also pulling away an end of his scarf.

Feeling that the scarf was coming off, Jove let go of the object and made an effort to readjust the scarf.

Though he tried to hide his fear, Winfred noticed one of Jove's noses. He hoped, for his sake and Jove's, that he was the only one who had noticed.

"Hey, buddy, I think there's something wrong with your face. Are you hurt? Did someone do something to you?" One of the men removed Jove's scarf from around him. "Do you have a prosthetic nose on? How can you breathe with that thing?"

The man who removed Jove's scarf touched his left nose. "Hey, it's a real nose. Are you some sort of medical freak?"

The three men encircled Jove, all questioning him on his medical anomalies.

Winfred rushed through the trio and replaced Jove's scarf. Winfred said, "Let go of him. Let him be. How is it any of your business what's going on with him?"

The three men continued to study Jove. One said, "Nah, we've got this. I think we need the police to investigate him. We don't know what is going on. Either he's a threat or he'll need medical attention or something like that."

"Don't trap him between you three if you think he'll need medical attention. Besides, you don't have any reason to believe he's done anything. All you know is you say he looks different. Haven't we had enough of treating others poorly for looking or being different?" While Winfred did not know what any of the men or the police would do to or with Jove, he had had enough bad experiences in terms of being treated poorly because of his differences to be aware that things did not look good.

One of the men said, "We're just trying to protect those who need protecting," and smiled at Winfred and Jove.

Jove removed the disruptor from his belt and pointed it at each member of the trio, one at a time, and quickly pressed that same button as when he had directed it at Winfred's phone. Each of the three fell to the ground.

Winfred stood there in shock. "Did you kill them? Are they dead?" He was suddenly overcome by deep dread as he worried that he and Jove would be arrested.

"Not dead. Will be on hind limbs soon. We complete our mission."

Still nervous and not convinced, Winfred asked, "Are you sure?"

"Yes, like with device from last night. I do not stop life."

Cooperating with Jove, Winfred did not find it difficult to carry the device. It was bulky but light in weight. Other than not being able to properly see obstacles that might have been in their way, the pair easily brought the object to Winfred's car.

As Winfred drove, he focused on the road ahead. After a few minutes he said, "We have arrived. Let's do this quickly."

Once Winfred had parked, Jove exited the car, taking the device with him, and ran for the ocean, and his ship.

Winfred thought that Jove looked excited, at least by human standards, and he understood that emotion. Still, he did not know his companion's species, meaning that he did not know whether Jove really was excited. Nonetheless, it occurred to him that he should accompany his companion. Perhaps Jove might need help installing the unit.

"You need any help with whatever you're doing?"

"Technology too different. No need to help." Jove's necklace's voice came from inside of the rock-shaped vessel.

"Maybe I can help you move stuff. You needed my help getting it into my car."

"No need. How say? Appreciated?"

"Yep. Right word. You need me here for any reason?"

"No. No reason. I learn over visits humans get attached. You welcome to stay if want, but that not needed. I eventually take ship under ocean and wait until Earth rotates to cause night so I lift out of atmosphere under cover of dark. You welcome to visit with me when I come to Earth again." The roof of the vessel shut, looking once again like a rock, and slipped into the ocean.

Winfred stood there wanting to find out what was going on inside the ship. While he was aware that he did not know Jove all that well, he was still immensely curious about his companion and his species. He had a lot of questions, and hoped that he would have an opportunity to visit with Jove again.

Winfred walked the Asbury Park boardwalk late at night on the day he had helped the alien retrieve a part of his ship. Later, when he got to bed he was unable to sleep because he was thinking of his day, wondering what was going on with the alien he had christened Jove. He'd heard of a shooting star, but never seen one. He went to a window and looked up to the sky. He knew that possibilities included that he had already missed the alien's ship lifting off, he was looking in the wrong spot in the sky, or that he was examining the right spot, but he would give up before the ship took off. Nevertheless, he continued to look, hoping to see what might appear to be a flash of light traveling up and then disappearing into the darkness.

THE SPACE BETWEEN STITCHES
A STORY
MINERVA CERRIDWEN

NOTHING COMPARED to the rush of teleportation.

In Ibb's home dimension, everyone took it for granted. People fluctuated out of existence in one place and popped up again elsewhere without a second thought—but Ibb had never managed to do that. Until the recent invention of the teleporter, a mobility aid to Ibb and a few thousand more extraordinary beings in their dimension, they'd been limited to on-planet movement, preferably out of sight of those who'd make disapproving comments or who'd rush several universes away because they couldn't face Ibb's ineffective relocations.

Throughout their long life, Ibb had come up with lots of possible explanations for why they couldn't teleport: they got too anxious, they couldn't let go of their hold on reality, they had too much mass. However, now that they did have access to a teleporter, it turned out that none of those theories had made any sort of sense. Ibb *loved* slipping out of reality. They'd learned about so many species' pastimes from the Information Gathering, and now they were able to add firsthand findings themself! Rather than causing more anxiety, teleportation *distracted* them, and they even enjoyed the fast thinking necessary to cope with unexpected situations. That one time when they'd made a mistake and landed in a dimension their species couldn't survive in for longer than a second, they hadn't panicked—in fact, they'd felt more alive than ever after their narrow escape. They loved finally having the freedom everyone else considered natural.

A few people who had the ability to teleport on their own were adventurous enough to try the teleporter, but many others warned that using a machine wasn't as safe as putting their natural ability into action. According to them, the teleporter's own mass, however minimal, was a liability, and in case of failure, one might get stuck in the fabric of reality and be lost forever. Depending on where your parts ended up, reality itself might be harmed!

Ibb always waved off those doom-mongering comments. The inventors were smarter than these well-meaning yet uninformed critics gave them credit for, having equipped the machines with a protective grid that kept their particles together. Inside that laced forcefield, the machine encapsulated Ibb's own particles so everything that made up their identity, every last atom and idea, was moved from one place to the next in the correct configuration.

Ibb had travelled to the end of one universe and then straight to the center of the next with their teleporter, and they'd always made it home. They were certain that as long as the protective grid remained intact, nothing could possibly go wrong.

When Ibb appeared on the next planet that supposedly contained life forms, the protective grid was perfectly fine. The next moment, it had disintegrated.

Ibb was startled, but this was just the kind of emergency they were good at handling. They'd just dash away again—but they found they couldn't. No matter how hard Ibb tried, the teleporter remained stationary and kept flashing its warnings all around their form.

Ibb's frustration grew, but finally the meaning of the alerts got through to them. They'd landed in a radiation zone more destructive than any inventor from their dimension could have foreseen. This planet orbited a star that emitted energy so harmful it had destroyed the entire protective grid—and without the grid, Ibb's machine's ability to travel was switched off *"for safety reasons."* They'd never been particularly good at recognizing irony, but this time? Yeah. Just wonderful.

This planet's sky was so bright that Ibb couldn't think. They directed themself downward, but that was even worse. They were hovering a couple of meters above a dark surface where enormous metal units on wheels were hurtling toward each other while making the most terrible roaring noises. The machines' roofs and windows all reflected the light, forming a flashing onslaught on Ibb's senses. Some of them whizzed by right below Ibb, and though they were a safe distance off, it was terrifying.

For once, they didn't think to check if there was anyone else of their own species around to judge them for shifting positions within the same dimension. They fled.

Only after crossing a considerable distance and pressing themself through several solid walls to get away as fast as possible did they find shelter from the light, the heat, the fumes, and the overwhelming, whizzing motions. After a moment to recover, they observed they were inside some sort of huge cube without holes. On one side, a brown rectangular panel suggested that the option to *make* a hole existed, but Ibb didn't know in which direction the panel would move—nor were they keen to find out what sort of trouble might come through. A solid wall suited them fine just now.

There were more objects inside the cube, and while few of them were as small as Ibb's form, none were as large as the metal ones outside. Apart from some slight vibrations, nothing moved here except the dust that floated on the air and lightly covered most surfaces. The effect was almost relaxing. There was also light, but it was much dimmer than it had been outside. Unfortunately, even though they were no longer assaulted by painful brilliance, a constant chaos of sound waves lingered —deep humming, faint whirring, insistent screeches from winged beings outside. Then a much louder sound joined in, and it took a long moment before Ibb realized that it came from a giant creature that was sitting amongst billions and billions of microorganisms. As the creature emitted clouds of gas, it produced a structured pattern of waves—structured enough to imply the creature was attempting to communicate.

A sentient!

Ibb was surprised that such a soft-looking creature could have evolved into a sentient species on this sensory hell of a planet. Sure, it would help that it was made of solid flesh, but in a place like this, they would have expected that a species with a lifespan long enough to learn would need an exoskeleton. Or that they would at least have scales as thick as those of the dragons Ibb regularly admired on planet Firepit of the Community Dimension.

The sentient covered the glassy organs at the center of what had to be its face a few times with thin skin flaps. Were those organs eyes, like the dragons had? Then the creature rubbed at those same flaps with its bony paws, so hard that Ibb feared the glassy organs below might be pushed all the way down into the larger, softer body part.

And then, while Ibb still floated there in the middle of the cube and stared, the creature bared pale fangs, lengthened its bottom limbs, and approached them. The giant moved this way and that—oof, there really was a lot of intradimensional movement to process on this world—seeming to study Ibb. It was unclear from its reactions whether it was able to see Ibb or not; the creature might be too large to detect them. Unless perhaps the glassy organs had been activated or fine-tuned by the earlier rubbing?

"You're real! Are you a ghost? Well, I'm happy you're not a migraine aura, because I've really got too much work for my brain to switch off right now. Not that I'm *doing* my work, but shush. I won't be judged by random specters. In any case, uhm, welcome? You're not responding, so maybe you're only some sort of projection? But then where are you coming from?" The head kept swiveling back and forth, but luckily it didn't seem intent on attacking Ibb. "Can you hear me? And if so, can you understand me at all?"

The creature's incessant babbling made it easy enough for Ibb to analyze the sound patterns and weave them into a language. The Information Gathering contained examples of similar linguistic patterns to compare this to, and focusing on figuring out the words made Ibb feel a little less overwhelmed by the humming, ringing, and buzzing in the background.

"I can now," they answered.

"Oh, wow. I did not expect you to sound like me. Like me on a recording. I do *not* like hearing my own voice when it's not coming out of my own head. Did you do that on purpose, or do we really just sound similar?" Ibb didn't get a chance to say they had no clue how else they were supposed to sound, before the creature continued: "Never mind, where are my manners? I'm Lutra, pronouns xe/xem/xyr. I'm, uhm, well, are you human? Just in case you aren't, well, I *am* human, and this is planet Earth, and now maybe you're laughing at me if you're some sort of human high-tech projection experiment after all."

"I'm not," Ibb replied. "I'm Ibb, from …" The sound they intended to make did not translate into the current atmospheric pressure at all.

"Ouch," Lutra said, xyr entire face part wrinkling up in response to the screech. "A different planet, I take it, then. Does that mean you've got a spaceship?"

The visual organs shone brightly—not like the star outside, but reminding Ibb of how volcanic Glints sometimes bubbled their magma in excitement. Eager, but not predatory.

As Lutra offered them more language data, Ibb was getting a pretty good idea of how to form words different from the ones they'd already heard. It took a little while, but then they were able to compose the vocabulary for their answer: "No ship. I teleported."

"Really?" Lutra's entire flesh shape bounced. "You've uncovered the secret of teleportation?"

"Not much of a secret. I'm not … massful. Massy? Not solid like you. My … little pieces … can simply squeeze in between the framework of reality. In theory, that is."

"Fascinating!" Lutra gasped. "What do you mean, in theory?"

With a lot of pauses, Ibb explained their need for a functional teleporter. It required more verbal descriptions than they had foreseen. At first, they tried to show the problem by wavering in a quick sequence of fractals, which would have been much harder to detect when properly covered by a protective grid. But while this taught them that Lutra was able to see their physical form as a small, half-transparent flame with sparkles glistening at the edges where the teleporter reflected the light, xe didn't have the frame of reference to know what this meant.

Luckily, once Ibb managed to find the words, Lutra seemed to understand most of the concepts they wished to convey.

"So your essence is captured inside the holes, like warm air inside a layer of insulation?"

"Exactly." Ibb wished they weren't too distressed to appreciate this new environment they'd ended up in. In spite of the dangers, it was a marvel to meet a sentient who understood them relatively easily. But not knowing how they'd ever get home again overshadowed their enjoyment of the conversation. They hadn't felt so anxious since their very first teleportation. "Please ..." they said. "I'd like to be distracted from my worries, rather than talk about them more. Could you tell me what you do to keep yourself entertained?"

"Oh, sure." Yet Lutra hesitated. "I could also talk about other things, though. You must have some grand purpose that led you all the way to Earth ..."

Now Ibb was so amused that they wished they knew how to radiate elation like Lutra and the Glints. "You want to know my grand purpose?"

There it was again, that *beaming*. "Yes. Yes, please!"

Were all humans that eager to know things? Perhaps they resembled Ibb's species more than they would have guessed on sight.

"My people," Ibb explained, "study how sentients, literally every species of them, keep themself ... entertained. We keep records and add them to the Information Gathering. So if you tell me how you fill your time, that would exactly fit my purpose. My kind is very intrigued by pastimes, because as far as we know, time has never influenced anyone in our dimension."

Lutra's eye flaps—*eyelids*, the word formed within Ibb's thought network—moved up and down again a few times. "Wow. That is ... a lot to take in."

"It is also rather a general statement on my species," Ibb admitted. "I mean, I'm not influenced by time either. Compared to most sentients recorded in the Information Gathering, I have infinity to spend without any set purpose. But even before I could teleport, I never got bored. Perhaps because I didn't know better than to find occupations within the same dimension? Or perhaps because I only very recently found out that I wasn't supposed to *know* everything in the Information Gathering, so I'd been trying to stay caught up with all of that ..."

Lutra exhaled some extra gas. "Ha! That could absolutely have happened to me too. People really should learn to be clearer about their expectations."

"That would be helpful, but experience tells me it's unlikely to happen," Ibb agreed.

Lutra reacted with another puff of gas. "Well, if you want to know how I entertain myself, I think the best way is to show you. Uhm, for the sake of clear expectations, can you see?"

"Probably not exactly in the sense you are thinking of, but yes. Please show me."

"Okay." Lutra moved to a flat surface held up on four vertical beams —*table*, Ibb's thought network provided helpfully—and wrapped xyr paws around two brown-and-beige objects, both about twice as big as Ibb's shape. "I've crocheted these myself! It's a gift in progress for my parents' thirty-fifth wedding anniversary. I'm a couple of days late, because the idea only came to me this week." Xe petted the top of one of the shapes with an expression that could only be described as loving. "See, this one is already finished, and that one still needs ears and paws, and then I'll sew them together so they'll be holding hands! It's just an excuse to crochet otters, really—I mean, I've been obsessed with otters for years, enough to name myself after the Eurasian otter—*Lutra lutra*, that is—and ... you don't have a clue what an otter is, do you? Whiskery faces, adorable ears, and those paws!" Xe gestured at a framed picture on the wall that, as far as Ibb could tell, didn't show a lot of similarities with the crocheted objects. It was all flat and didn't have any fuzzy threads sticking out. But although they understood very little of what Lutra had just told them, there was a delightful energy behind the words.

"Does this mean you are making life out of this thread material?" Ibb asked. "This is your means of reproduction?"

"*Reproduction*? Ew. I mean, no. This is just yarn. The otters won't be alive. They'll just hold hands and be decorative. My parents can pet them and fidget with them—well, it's more likely *I* will be the one doing the fidgeting when I visit. In any case, the otters will make my parents smile, because they're a symbol of their long marriage." Lutra bared xyr fangs again. That was what "smile" meant, Ibb now realized. What a marriage could be, they'd have to ask later, but they were more curious about why one would go through such trouble to procure a mere *object*.

When asked, Lutra pressed xyr lips together and wiggled in thought. "I guess it *is* just an object, but believe me, we humans can definitely get attached to soft toys and amigurumi animals like these. I think I'll make a separate, smaller otter for myself when these are done—maybe in velvet yarn, because that'd be extra good for petting. Oh, let me show you something else!" Xe rummaged in a compartment—*drawer*—under the surface of the table, and then pulled out a purple, rather shapeless ... rag.

"Here, this is the first piece of cloth I crocheted—it's all wonky, but that was on purpose because I was trying out all the stitches. I've only just learned to crochet two weeks ago. I never thought I'd figure it out, but my friend Ailura spent the entire afternoon of my thirty-second birthday teaching me the basics, and now I can do magic! Well, it feels like magic, anyway."

Lutra happily fluttered the rag back and forth before putting it back in the drawer. "So to get back to your initial question of pastimes, it definitely does eat up a lot of time. I shouldn't be crocheting at all right now—this is my office, I'm an accountant, and I really should be working—but then again, if I'd been focused on my job, I might not have looked up and seen you ..." Lutra stopped and stared at Ibb. "Sorry, hold on, did you say you need to contain yourself within the holes of a grid?"

Ibb felt a little off-balance after the rapid change of subject. "I did?"

"I just realized, if it's the same principle as insulation ... would it work with stitches?"

Ibb had no idea, but it didn't seem opportune to reply, as Lutra was looking busy, pulling a thread of that beige *yarn* out of the oblong bundle. Xe measured Ibb's shape with it between xyr paw appendages—hands? Then xe grabbed a metal needle with a hook at the end and started moving the yarn with it. It did indeed look a little like magic, Ibb mused. They always found pleasure in seeing barely explainable shifts of power at work with the purpose of creation.

"While crochet is like *the best* thing in my mind right now, I can't predict how long my hyperfixation will last," Lutra said after Ibb had been watching xem work for a while. "I hadn't expected I'd be this—forgive the pun—hooked. But after my friend taught me, I didn't want to risk forgetting everything, so I resolved to do at least a little bit of crochet every day. And every stitch that works out is just so satisfying. At least all the practice I've gotten on the otters has helped me to pick up some speed, so a straightforward rectangle like this should go pretty fast. I'm guessing the holes can be rather large when you're calling it a grid, right?" Xe held up a string of holes outlined by fabric.

"You ... you can make me a new grid? Just like that?" Ibb stammered.

"I can't promise it'll work. If I understand correctly, the fact that it has mass is a problem ..."

"It could slow me down, but if it can trick the safety system long enough to get me to my home world, I can get a replacement there." Ibb still couldn't believe it. They'd only lightly touched on the details of their problem, and here this astonishing creature was knotting together a solution for them.

"Happy to help!" Lutra said, but then xyr hands slowed down. "Hey, uhm, will you ever come back here when your teleporter is fixed?"

Ibb hesitated. If they got a grid just like their old one, that might break as soon as they got back to this planet. Could they ask of Lutra to create a new one next time, too?

"I just really like having someone to talk about my interests with," Lutra continued. "Of course, my friends will listen, but I feel like I'm actually contributing to the knowledge of an alien species when I'm telling you how much fun I'm having with my otters, and I quite enjoy that. You're a good listener, is what I mean to say."

There *was* a lot to learn from this human. And it was so pleasant to experience xyr glow of excitement, like a comforting bubble. It wouldn't work out with their *old* grid, but who said the design had to remain identical? "I'll ask the inventors to come up with a way to strengthen the grid. If I tell them I want to visit planet Earth regularly, they should be able to find the specifics," Ibb replied.

Lutra put xyr yarn and crochet needle down, clapped xyr hands together rapidly, and then picked xyr work up again to continue right where xe'd left off. "That would be marvelous!"

Ibb studied xem for a while. If they were requesting improvements anyway ... "You know, I could ask if there's a way to teleport flesh beings after all. I mean, teleportation doesn't come naturally to me either, so ... sure, there are all those issues with mass, but perhaps it's not *impossible*? Someday you might be able to travel with me, see some new sights."

"Oh." Lutra smiled at the yarn, where xe started on yet another row, the movements of xyr hands achieving a speedy flow. "It's funny, I dreamed pretty much my whole childhood that this moment would come. Someone asking me to get away to a world where I'd be fully accepted—still the alien, but spectacular because of it, you get the idea. Or maybe you don't, but I kind of have a feeling you might."

Ibb wasn't sure if it had anything to do with those intriguing visual organs, but they didn't think they'd ever felt so seen.

"Anyway," Lutra continued, "I'm good where I am. Ibb, do you know how amazing life has become? I've got friends now, and most of them are also neurodiverse. We all love each other's quirks. There are people in my life who can teach *me*, with my absolute lack of spatial awareness, something as complicated as crochet. I've never felt so accepted! Earth is quite all right with me these days. Thanks for offering, though!"

Ibb felt yet another type of warmth at xyr words. While *neurodiverse* didn't exactly apply to them—for lack of neurons—their thought network had always been wired differently than that of most of their peers. "I'll just keep visiting you here. I guess that back when *you* were dreaming of someone coming to fetch you, *I* was the one wishing that one day I might save someone who felt as alone as I did."

"I'm glad we ended up meeting each other," Lutra said. "I'd love to hear all about your adventures someday when you don't have to worry whether you'll get home. But for now ... ta-da!" Xe held up a grid large enough to cover Ibb.

Had that really been created while Lutra was talking, as if it were only an afterthought and not a magical piece of technology?

"It's super loose because I was hurrying, so I hope the holes aren't *too* big. Do you want to try it?"

"Yes. Thank you," Ibb said, from the very core of their essence. "I'll come back as soon as I'm safely able to."

"You'd better!" Lutra sat down at xyr table and picked up the brown yarn and a crochet needle with a smaller diameter. "Back to finishing the otter I go. And after that, I'm going to be working late to catch my actual deadline. Oh, and then, there's this thing called sleep that we humans do at night, when we sort of seem to be turned off? Best let me sleep if you ever arrive at a moment like that." Xe looked up from xyr work and smiled at Ibb. "But as soon as I've slept, I *will* be hoping to see you again very soon."

All that talk of "after" and time-dependent activities satisfied something very deep inside Ibb's form. Making sure they were fully covered in the fabric grid, they twinkled some fractals where they would be visible through the holes.

"I will see you very soon," they promised.

Then they disappeared in a cloud of sparkles. Really, nothing compared to the rush of teleportation. But meeting a human? That was a type of excitement all its own.

CADRE
A STORY
SAM CRAIN

ZAK HAD KNOWN grad school was a form of self-harm, learned it the hard way, even if it was the one group setting that had ever suited him. How many job interviews had he had since he finished? The only thing worse than getting himself into academia had been getting out. If he'd thought the Rejection Sensitivity Dysphoria would be less as a civilian, he'd been woefully mistaken. Ghosted by company after company, after it had gotten to the Zoom or in-person interview.

So he'd answered the listing for a live-in researcher position. He proposed some broad topics of focus and was hired. Hopefully, these people would point him at his task and let him go, rather than demanding he perform "normality" at them, so-called. If he was lucky.

His work partner Stein was a bit surly, but his growled answers were direct and literal, which Zak appreciated. They were told about the Supervisor, but that entity never visited, only emailed as needed. It was almost like being back in grad school, only without the low pay and endless pressure. Zak could hardly believe his luck. There was no real deadline to the work—they only had to submit a weekly progress report and any requests for materials. No quibbling about costs, downtime, saleability of results. He and Stein got on with their separate tasks, ate lunch in the adjacent room, and each had a bedroom across the hall. He suspected the complex had other units but didn't want to trespass. Real estate prices and commutes being what they were, neither minded staying "on-campus" because the job was a stable forty hours a week. No secret overtime demanded, utilities included. Zak could save for a house while doing work he loved and *not* burning out. There was a garden area their bedrooms opened into, where Zak could sit in good weather.

Of course, there was a catch. Zak had been working at Research Spot nearly eleven months with 60k in wages saved, when a figure in a coat buttoned to his throat entered the office. He cleared his throat for attention, shuffling a little awkwardly, Zak thought, looking up from his research into infectious disease epidemiology.

"May we help you?" he asked. Stein was removing noise-canceling headphones, looking miffed at the interruption.

"Hello," the figure said. "I am the Supervisor."

"Hi," Zak said. "Good to meet you." He winced a touch at the cliché but the Supervisor didn't seem to mind.

"You have worked at your research nearly one Earth year, with no external prompting," the Supervisor said.

"What of it?" Stein asked, and Zak wondered if he'd caught *Earth year*.

"You did not ... meddle with our experiment. I meant, it did not trouble you to be here."

"Why should it? This is the best job I ever had." Stein was glowering, probably without knowing it.

"Me too," Zak said. "But you said 'experiment'?" So it *was* too good to be true. Experiments, after all, had ends.

"The, er, others never went longer than a few weeks—but you two —you have an affinity for research that rivals ours."

"Are you going to get rid of us now?" Stein demanded, voicing Zak's fear.

"We've had a different idea since the research you generate is useful, and you are not always chattering at us. I wondered if you might present your research to our young ones. They read your reports and are most eager to meet you and learn your methods for themselves."

Zak swallowed. Suppose the children disliked him as his own schoolmates before grad school had done? But he and Stein could hardly refuse. They walked down three unfamiliar hallways to what Zak could only conclude was an alien elementary school. And perfect. Zak clenched one hand around the models he'd stashed in his pocket. *Please don't let this be a bad idea.* The Supervisor entered a code into the door and stood back. "Good luck," he said, and Zak's heart pounded. But the lighting was as conducive to contemplation as his office and there were stations for the young ones to experiment. He saw one alien in headphones like Stein's. Zak thought of his own preschool and kindergarten, all broken crayons and sudden noises, and felt something like envy. Would they let him *work here*, from now on? Could he try out the chemistry station? The baking station? The labels on everything were bilingual—English and a language he couldn't read at all.

"Hello!" said one child. He wore a smock with a cartoon spaceship on it and vibrated with what Zak could only take as eagerness, though he avoided eye contact. "I'm Exi. I designed this shirt myself, from what humans think our cars look like. That's one of my special interests, depictions of aliens in human stories."

"Hi there," Zak said. "It's a fun design, all right." Maybe he'd be able to do this after all.

"Ahoy ahoy." Another child had sidled up and licked Zak's head with a very long tongue.

"Please don't be offended," Exi said at once. "Pip learns about things by licking. They don't mean harm." He sounded like he'd explained this before.

Zak smiled and reached into his pocket for a 3D-printed model of a bacterium. "What can you tell me about this?"

Pip's eyes shone as he licked it. "Polycarbonate resin, printer model X-3B. It needs a tune-up. I'll tell Supervisor for you."

Zak laughed with pleasure. These children were so easy to reach. He looked over his shoulder, checking on Stein. His friend was at the center of another knot of littles, one of whom was asking with utmost seriousness if he would tell them *more* about epistemology. That had to be a first.

"No!" another half-squealed. "Quantum-mechanical definitions of electromagnetic fields. I'm sure you have new material on that—your last report on it was three Earth months ago. Please, Stein, please."

It was the happiest Stein had ever looked. His face wasn't used to it, Zak thought, but Exi was clamoring for *him*, so he turned back to begin a talk on the process of human aging. When he and Stein had finished, he would get the children to talk next. They had a lot to teach him too, and he was one of them already, he could feel it. He didn't want to go.

In the snack time interval, Stein found Zak, glowing with satisfaction. "We've got to figure out how to stay," he said. "I have more material."

"As do I," Zak said. "I'll tell Supervisor."

THE COW TEST
A STORY
LAUREN D. FULTER

Content note: *one scene with a physical altercation*

A COW WAS the only thing needed to pass the test.

Countless sleepless nights, extra hours of tutoring sessions, and long classes chasing after that star voyager license would all be wasted if she couldn't complete one mission: abduct the strange mammal with horns and black and white spots that could only be found on one blue planet in the Milky Way Galaxy.

No one actually called it the Milky Way. Only Leoni did once she'd found a treasure trove of forums on theories and discoveries about human culture. She glanced for a moment at her cart of tablets she'd collected and uploaded with her favorite articles.

Apparently, it had been named after a strange white liquid called milk, which came from cows. She took a deep breath. *Just keep thinking about cows.*

"Slow and steady, cadet!" the director's voice boomed in her earpiece.

The only time she could breathe was behind the dashboard,

watching the startracker as she zoomed through the infinite space. If only there was less time behind desks and studying formulas and more racing through stars and exploring different cultures.

If she could pass this test ... she might finally get her chance.

She shook off the thoughts. Of all times, she needed to pay attention *now*.

Her little ship approached the blue planet, its atmosphere painted in streaks across its shimmering ocean, glowing in the golden halo of the solar system's sun. Her eyes widened, a tiny gasp escaping her lips. It was thirteen times smaller than her home planet, but it was a hundred times more beautiful. There was so much water. That's where humans created boats and told stories of fearsome creatures like goldfish—

I bet she's going to get too distracted by Earth and never come back! The snarky comment her fellow cadets hadn't even tried to hide echoed back in her mind.

Leoni was approaching her land target.

And this time, she wasn't going to get distracted.

If she failed this, she'd be sent straight home on an express ship to her grandmother. She would remind Leoni that she should've never attempted to become a galaxy voyager because she didn't have the mind for it.

A mind like yours isn't meant for the stars. That's what got your mother killed.

She rubbed the chip hanging from her necklace.

The ship broke through the atmosphere, speeding down through the clouds, piercing the darkness of night. She set the ship in autoglide, spinning in her seat to the holographic map drawn up behind her. She zoomed in on the red pin, indicating her target.

She pressed her headpiece. "Approaching Earth now."

She would get that cow, and Professor Xian would have to give her that passing grade.

She tucked loose hair behind her long, pointed ear and cracked her fingers as she scooted back to the steering wheel. The ship slowly descended toward human land. Lush green grass rolled like waves in the night wind. There were no mountains in sight. Strange, red, wooden buildings sprinkled throughout the plane. A strange-looking plot of land had unearthed dirt and long green sprouts growing from it. Miles and miles of it.

Peculiar human activities.

She leaned forward in her seat, scanning the surface for—

Her heart leaped. There! There they were!

Cows!

She nearly squealed with excitement as she spotted a herd of animals dozing off near a wooden fence. They were real and even more adorable in real life!

Right now, she needed to focus.

She'd have plenty of time to examine the cow on her back to the mothership. She was so close. She slowly moved the ship forward, taking a deep breath as she pulled back on her wheel, the ship slowing to a stop. She jumped out of her seat, running to the holding cell in the center of the ship. She pulled the lever to the third gear labeled RETRIEVE.

A hatch opened. The holding cell dropped from the floor of the ship, and an antigravity light beam was carried toward the ground. The manual said it would pluck up the cow and come right back up. No intervention required.

And yet, her foot was still tapping, as if something could still go wrong.

Green light flooded the ship: *Target acquired.*

Leoni let out a relieved breath. She spun in circles, hugging herself. She cupped the chip hanging from her neck in her hands. "I did it, mamma."

She set the ship into autopilot. It wouldn't be too long before she had to pull into the dock.

She practically fell over herself, racing out of her seat. Could she name the cow? The cows were usually brought back to the cow sanctuary on Vastiria. Surely, they'd let her name it.

She yanked on a lever. The floor opened up, and a holding cell began to rise.

Leoni's heart raced as the tip of the cow's horns appeared over the deck, and then its adorable black eyes and its pink tongue ... munching on a wire. She'd be sure to inform mechanical about that.

"What the heck?"

THE COW TEST

Leoni jumped back at the earthen language. "You cows can speak?" she responded in the same language.

It wasn't required in cadet training, but she'd learned various human languages in her spare time when she probably should've been studying for a test on the history of solar flare battles.

"I'm a purple belt in taekwondo!"

Before Leoni had time to process what the cow was saying, a person jumped right in front of her and grabbed Leoni's shoulders.

"Where am I?" they demanded. Leoni had never seen brown hair before, held up in a long ponytail. Only silver and bronze like her own —Wait.

Her heart dropped.

She cursed. "You're human!"

A human! A *girl* at that. Her ship was supposed to dock in just ten minutes. If Professor Xian caught her with a human in her ship, she wasn't even sure what the consequences would be! Had this ever happened before? She was already on his bad side. Would he wipe the girl's memory? Would they simply return her to Earth? Or would she be kept prisoner on the mothership?

Leoni began to pace, tearing her hands through her hair. This wasn't in any guide tablet she'd ever read! Of course, this was a mistake *she* would make.

"'A human'?" the girl mimicked Leoni's human speech. "And what are you? A blue frog with long legs?"

Leoni was going to be in serious trouble. "Y-you're not supposed to be here! I was only trying to abduct the cow for a class assignment! I'm so sorry!" Her foot tapped anxiously. What could she do?

"Take me home!" the girl shouted. "You probably kidnapped me for some kinda crazy experiment!"

Leoni frowned. "What? No! That's crazy. Why would we experiment on you? I promise I'll return you. I just—"

The human girl was not listening. She had picked up a chair, charging at Leoni with it.

Leoni dodged the flying chair. "Calm down! If they find you, we'll both be in massive trouble! This is so against academy protocol! You have to trust me!"

"Weird kinda school you got there." The girl had now begun to throw the tablets from the tablet cart. "I don't trust you!"

Leoni caught a tablet. "Hey! Those are expensive!"

The girl threw another one.

Leoni scowled. "Look! You're not supposed to be here. I can take you home once I get my space voyager license, which I can't do if I don't pass this test—"

"Sure, sounds like a perfect excuse a kidnapper dude would make!"

Leoni had no idea what "dude" meant and didn't even try to ask. "Would you please listen to me?"

She chased the human girl around the cow, who was still happily chewing on his wire. Leoni was gaining on her when the human stopped abruptly. She shoved Leoni back with her elbow. Leoni fell into the cow with a thud. The girl leaped for the lever.

"Wait! Not second gear—"

The girl pulled it. The glass walls of the holding cell rose.

Leoni's scales were quivering. She banged against the walls. "You don't understand what you're doing!"

Any moment now, her ship was going to lock into the dock. Professor Xian was going to come in with the inspection crew and give her final grade.

And if they saw a human girl here and Leoni trapped in a holding cell?

She'd have to book a one-way star rail ticket back to her grandmother's home planet and a life of plowing meteor fields.

A ringing came from her ship's controls. "Don't answer it!"

The girl didn't listen. She clicked the screen. "Video Message from *LARONZO, XIAN PROFESSOR #0027378.*"

Professor Xian.

The purple man sat in his office, his bald head gelled. It shimmered like the countless honor stitches in his uniform jacket. His face was hard. "Cadet Leoni. I hear you've successfully retrieved a cow from Planet Earth."

His voice was dry, almost like he didn't believe it.

"I suppose even a broken startracker is right once a couple hundred years. I'll be interested to see if your claims of success are true. Prepare your ship."

The video message ended abruptly.

Leoni sunk to her knees, burying her face in her hands, rocking back and forth. It was over. She clutched the necklace. Even the thoughts of cows didn't comfort her. *I'm sorry, mamma. I guess they were right about us.*

"What was that gibberish guy saying? He sounded ... not fun at a party." The girl's voice was softer, her eyes falling to her shoes. "Reminds me of someone back home."

"That's my professor." She had nothing to lose at this point. "He doesn't think I'd make a good star voyager. He makes it pretty clear. I think it's because I'm no good at formula equations and writing dissertations on star roaming history."

Even her fellow cadets moved past her quickly in halls and made it a point to choose her last in group presentations.

"What does that have to do with star voy ... voya—Whatever you're doing?"

"It's a necessary part of the curriculum to be a star voyager ... a pilot," Leoni said. She rubbed the chip around her neck. "It doesn't help that my mother died in a crash. This chip is the last surviving piece of her ship. There's no point now."

The girl's face softened. "You're a pretty good pilot. You sure were good about abducting me."

"That's the only thing I'm good at," Leoni said, holding herself. "I only got in by a recommendation letter and an obsession with human culture."

The girl was quiet for a moment. "You think humans are cool?"

"Fascinating," Leoni clarified. "I spend more time on human theory forums than studying. About cows specifically. Cows are incredible! They produce milk *and* they're just straight-up adorable!"

The girl burst out laughing.

Leoni flinched. "Oh. Yeah, it is weird."

"No! Not at all! I grew up on a farm. Cows are pretty cool. I want to apply to go to university for veterinary studies ... but the farm calls."

"'Farm'—is that what you call the empire of Illinois?"

"Not exactly. It's where we humans produce food. Illinois is pretty popular for corn, but our farm also has a good number of cows," the girl said.

She let out a long sigh, scratching at the floor. "Besides, I couldn't keep up in school. Mom had to pull me out and teach me herself. Apparently, not being able to sit still and keep track of the five hundred papers they give you every day was a real problem." The human girl fidgeted with a spinning ring around her finger … just like Leoni did with her necklace.

"It's not like it matters. I don't miss it. Nobody wants to hang out with the girl who talks your ear off about cows anyway. Mom tries. She really does. But she'll never really know." The girl tried to laugh, but there was no joke—just a dry silence and a wet glimmer in her eye.

"Honestly, up here in outer space or whatever, it feels less lonely than back down on Earth."

"I understand how you feel," Leoni said. In fact, it felt like the girl had just described her exactly. It only took searching the galaxy to find someone like her.

"But you have something you're passionate about," Leoni said, meeting the girl's eyes. "And you shouldn't let others' doubts dictate that."

"I'm trying. It-it's really nice to hear that," the girl said, wiping her eye. "You know, you could use your own advice."

Leoni exhaled heavily. "I don't even know how I'm here. I'm a mess, and everyone knows it."

"Everyone? All I know is that your English is so good I kinda forgot I was talking to a blue alien." The girl smiled. "We're different, but we aren't a mess. If no one's ever told you that, let me. Your mind is meant for the stars."

A loud beep rang through the ship.
"ENTERING DOCK."

Leoni was pulled out of her mind and into the present galaxy. She jumped to her feet. "You have to let me out! We don't have much time!"

The girl pursed her lips. "I'll let you out, if you'll take me back to Earth. And I'll—I don't know—show you around? You can see more

THE COW TEST

cows. Does that sound like a deal, Captain ...? I realized I never got your name. Do you guys do names?"

"I'm Leoni." Leoni's eyes darted out the window, counting down the seconds until the ship would land. "And I'm not a Captain."

"Not yet." The girl pulled on the lever. The clear cell walls dropped. "And I'm Bess."

Leoni was free ... but she wasn't safe yet. "Thank you ... Bess."

Leoni ushered the girl into the utility closet, jumping into her seat just as the ship descended into the dock. She gripped the ends of her seat to keep herself from spinning nervously in her chair.

The door rose up.

Her familiar stone-faced professor waltzed in, his glasses on the rim of his nose, processing data in their lenses.

Leoni straightened, swallowing and forcing a smile. "Hello Professor."

"You certainly didn't keep the ship orderly," Professor Xian said, gesturing to the tablets thrown about the inside of the ship.

He turned to face the cow. He pulled on the lever, the walls dropping. He scanned the cow with his wristband.

Leoni's heart was going a million miles a light-year.

Professor Xian sighed. "It's an authentic cow."

Leoni jumped up from her chair. She couldn't stop herself from bouncing. "So, did I pass?"

Professor Xian scribbled something down on his tablet, ignoring her question. "What did you learn from this mission, Cadet?"

That wasn't part of the test.

No amount of studying, as much as Leoni loathed it, could have prepared her for this.

She was terrible at tests and, worst of all, pop quizzes.

Professor Xian looked up over his tablet, his dark eyes burning into her soul. Her thoughts were bouncing off the shell of her mind. What was the answer? Was this something in a study guide she'd missed? *Say something!*

She took a deep breath, clasping her necklace.

She took a deep breath. If no one else did, at least she knew Bess believed in her. Even though meeting the human girl hadn't been planned. Bess was the best thing to come out of the mission.

"The test is solo," Leoni said, slowly finding the words. "It's up to us to figure out what works ultimately. The goal is to get the cow, yes, but it's our own strategy that gets us there. We all learn a little differently. It doesn't make you any less talented. Don't let just one scale judge the weight of your worth."

The room was silent.

Leoni couldn't keep her foot from tapping.

Professor Xian sighed, a small smile escaping his lips. He swiped up on his tablet. Leoni's wristband glowed green.

"Congratulations. You've passed."

Leoni could hardly breathe. *I can't wait to tell Bess.*

"Go. Enjoy a spin in your ship," Professor Xian heaved, walking out the door. "You've earned it, Captain."

It seemed like an entire moon cycle before Professor Xian left. She shut the door to the ship. She pulled the door open to the closet, and Bess nearly toppled out on top of her. "How did it go?" Bess shouted in a weakly contained whisper.

"I passed!" Leoni felt like her head was spinning around the solar system.

Bess squealed, throwing her arms around Leoni in a strange custom humans called a hug. Leoni had never felt something like this. She liked it. It felt warm. She didn't feel alone.

"Are you ready to head back to Earth?"

"More than ready!" Bess excitedly rushed into the passenger seat, spinning around before buckling herself in.

Leoni joined her. Her hands felt at home on the wheel. She took a deep breath before turning the startracker back on. The spaceship launched into the stars. "Sorry for dragging you into this."

"Don't worry. You owe me a lot of spaceship rides when I'm in veterinary school." Bess punched her playfully in the shoulder.

Leoni's heart leaped. "You're going to apply?"

"Dude, I just watched you become the captain of a ship. Anything is possible." The galaxy reflected in Bess's eyes as she stared out into the stars with awe. "Besides, I finally know why cows sometimes disappear in the middle of the night."

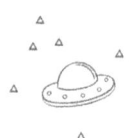

Radar by Barbara Candiotti

OUR CONNECTED SPACE
A POEM
SWARIT GOPALAN

There is hope
That we will meet one day

My tunneled vision will see
Your outsized intelligence
Masked by your tiny head

My extreme auditory sensitivity
Will hear your pleas for friendship
Not detected by powerful devices

My life experiences will
Help me understand the
Anguish of your lost soul

My population's tribulations
Will help me tell you
That the road is not rosy

SWARIT GOPALAN

My yearnings and prayers
Probe into questions
That matter to both of us

My love to heal
And to heal with love
Sees strength in our kinship

The world might be skeptical
As it is trained to be
But don't worry

For the bastion of
Love and acceptance
Is always within reach

The point of this note
Is to orient you
Toward love

For all you have heard
And seen
And touched

Love is that thing that arcs
Towards hope and justice

GAMMA ZARIA
A STORY
GAIL BROWN

DISTANT STARS FILLED THE VIEWSCREEN. They blinked dimly as thousands of asteroids danced between them and their scout ship, the *YaNanda*.

One star grew brighter as the *YaNanda* drew closer. It crowded out multitudes of light-years distant stars. Soon the Gamma Zaria system would fill the viewscreen. A star with at least one planet where long-distance probes showed potential buildings on the surface.

Asteroids faded into dust grains, almost too small to be seen, though sensors could still measure them. Distant planets appeared on the viewscreen. At least one sleep cycle before they would reach the outermost planet.

At least a dozen, or more, sleep cycles from the crowded ShaLoot Space Station. The station's confusion of constant sound had almost retreated from affecting Kaida's nervous system.

Kaida had studied this system through the telescopes from the ShaLoot Space Station for over a year. Perhaps one of these planets would make a good place for beings who didn't care for living in crowded places. A place of peace and quiet.

Much as the *YaNanda* was her place for peace and quiet. The one place she had felt at home. Even more like home than the overcrowded Mars colony where she grew up.

This journey would allow them to visit two of the planets in the Gamma Zaria system. The intention was to study the Earth-sized planet first. It had a massive rocky ring around it. This planet was almost out of the habitable zone of Gamma Zaria.

She longed for a place with low gravity, breathable air, and inhabitants she could communicate with. A peaceful and safe community where she could visit as she felt the need. Kaida had explored so many planets that almost met her needs. Even though her hopes rose upon approach, she dampened her dreams.

Kaida tapped her screen. The smaller planet they would explore first had something unusual about the atmosphere that required extra caution. Something the sensors didn't recognize. Even other known scanning technology didn't comprehend the readings.

Kaida's blood pressure rose. Would the planet have aquatic, avian, herbaceous, insectoid, or mammalian cultures? Meeting new societies was her favorite pastime. And her primary fear. Somehow, they always disappointed her. For reasons she couldn't quite comprehend.

"How long?" Treble walked up and scanned the viewscreen.

"Soon. I should be able to drift into orbit within the hour." Treble, her only assistant on this trip, had barely arrived at ShaLoot from Earth when he was assigned to the *YaNanda* as a test to see if he could manage living and interacting in a near-alien environment, before exploring with more different species, including avian or aquatic ones.

So far, he hadn't balked at the sight of the nonhuman cultures while on ShaLoot, though there had been an instance with a female avian where a gesture he randomly made while speaking had a specific meaning in their society. He never responded when her mating feathers raised in shock.

"I'll fix us something to eat. We'll need the calories for brain fuel."

Kaida didn't reply. The young man was homesick. At least he hadn't changed the main gravity controls. Though he had adjusted the controls in his quarters. Thankfully, he wasn't nearly as chatty as she expected a former city-state dweller to be.

She had once been homesick for her low-gravity colony, Guinea, on

Mars. The domed cities had been so overcrowded, the only place she could go for a bit of peace and quiet required a spacesuit and a rover to go beyond reach of the settlements.

Kaida had been based on ShaLoot so long, and surveyed so many worlds, it was unlikely she would ever return to her overcrowded domed Mars birth home. Even though on Mars, she could have remained among others who thrived in low gravity.

Kaida set the gravity lower on the scout ship as long as her companions didn't complain. A few had. Finding anyone out here in distant space who thrived in low gravity often meant lifelong explorers, or one of the avian species.

Treble hadn't complained yet. Even when he bounced high enough to bump his head on the ceiling while walking through the *YaNanda*.

Treble returned with steaming beef and broccoli plates. Real cow beef was something she had never even tasted. The dish smelled tangier than fresh broccoli from the greenhouses on Mars. Recycled protein, vitamins, and minerals. Tasty, rubbery, recycled protein. They ate in relative quiet. A peaceful and comfortable quiet. Refreshed by the hum of the *YaNanda*.

They drifted into orbit around the planet. It would take an entire cycle to make all the necessary prelanding measurements, including temperatures, atmospheric gases, and gravity, and more precise measurements that would be used by Treble on his geological surveys.

Meanwhile Kaida focused on transmissions sent back from the messenger probe, which had arrived in the planet's orbit several days before. Scenery that she had only known in greenhouses and on a few of the planets she had explored since arriving on ShaLoot. Peaceful trees, rivers, and grasslands. At least she hoped the trees were peaceful. And sleepy.

She was one of the few humans who had visited OnVine, when the trees and plants negotiated a treaty with the planet's first land-based reptile and mammalian species. Mostly, OnVine species didn't want off-world visitors. Few people would be allowed to know life thrived there. A secret world, until OnVine desired to join the galactic community. A planet where she would gladly have stayed, if the trees had allowed her to.

Kaida nodded off to sleep in her chair.

A current of energy streamed through her dreams. Fantastical visions more stunning than transmissions the probe had already broadcast. Places she hadn't been. Beings, some with colorful horns, unlike any she knew. Visions, not scary, though not quite peaceful. Thoughtful. Concerned. A vision of a sunny day surrounded by trees with a trickling brook ended with a face staring at her. A face Kaida didn't quite recognize. Kaida startled awake.

Treble was asleep reclined in his own chair.

Let him sleep. Her dream had been vivid. Many of its images appeared similar to the survey reports the probe had shared while they slept. It had to be her imagination working overtime. Something Kaida didn't realize she even had.

Maybe long ago, in a forgotten time, when her mother had wrestled with teaching her to talk. Instead of merely looking, or pointing, at what she wanted. When her mother would verbalize a question, she had always mentally pictured what she wanted to say, and didn't realize the words were not spoken aloud. It had taken years of exhausting exertion to remember to convert the images into vocal words, instead of fully formed mental images. Eventually, she no longer saw the mind pictures, at least not consciously.

She washed her hands and began to prepare coffee. At least it tasted and acted like coffee. Something she had never tasted from real coffee beans. It stimulated her brain to wake and focus on the here and now.

Not to be lost in a memory of a past she hadn't lived. The early Earth forests. Perhaps similar forests existed on this planet, unexplored and undocumented by humans, or known explorers, in Gamma Zaria.

The unknown face returned to interrupt her vision as Kaida stared at her coffee. A swirl reminded her of the depths of the eyes that had stared at her in wonder, and almost fear. Eyes that appeared larger than most human eyes. The face wasn't human. Nor of any species she recognized.

Which made sense. Larger eyes allowed more light in to see clearer. Gamma Zaria was dimmer than the Sun seen from Earth.

An unrecognized image appeared in her mind. A colorful tree, with its leaves outlined by the brighter area beyond them. An open grassland.

Kaida smiled. She'd find that peaceful place to land the *YaNanda*. It was a perfect place to land. They could explore the local life, and determine if any individuals could communicate vocally. That wasn't the easiest thing to do. Especially among species whose sound recognition might be out of range of each other's. Such as trying to communicate with extinct whales' high-pitched squeaks, or the low pitches of other species, below her ability to hear.

She had even tried to study recorded elephant calls before visiting a specific planet. Their calls had been too low for her brain to recognize. Other species changed tones and cadence too fast, or too slow, to easily follow. Many species communicated by writing, or with arm signs. Some even communicated with tails, or color changes.

Treble watched the screen and clicked the necessary buttons as they descended through the atmosphere. "You didn't detect any cities?"

"No. Cities aren't the only way for life."

"It's all I've known. The crowded cities of Earth." Treble's lips trembled.

"Don't worry. This isn't Deserta. There won't be glowing sand worms burrowing under desert sands. Nor Wingosa, where the winged mammal-and-reptile crosses glide and chatter ceaselessly through the skies their whole lives."

Treble turned back to his controls. Kaida understood. Decades ago, she had been the same way. Afraid. She enjoyed the challenge of meeting new species, and finding more ways for life to live beyond the crowded and noisy cities of Earth, the hidden valleys and caves of Mars, or the system of artificial space stations for explorers.

Deserta had almost felt like home. It had been nice and warm, similar to Mars. Silent glowing sand worms. Communication by shifting colors had taken a while to decode. If only it hadn't been too close to its parent sun, and too dense an atmosphere, there may have been a place for low-gravity-adjusted humans to live.

Wingosa had barely had any rocky land. Land was reserved for the infants. Of course, humans could have built houseboats to float on the oceans. Or underwater habitats. Water wasn't exactly safe there either. Large deep-sea creatures had been unfriendly toward the researchers. And to the avian inhabitants who relied on ocean creatures for meals.

A memory of domed greenhouses loomed before her. As did the crowded rocky caves where people lived to be safe from radiation and meteorites on Mars. It was dark, damp, and cool in the caves. Not like the warm surface, where breathing wasn't currently possible outside the greenhouses. An atmosphere was slowly beginning to develop. Not enough for humans, not for another generation or two.

A few guinea pigs had escaped and made a rocky crevice near the caves their home. Perhaps guinea pigs would grow to be as big as ancient capybara in a few human generations, after the oxygen increased to a livable level.

She focused on landing the *YaNanda* in the field near the trees. It was time to stop thinking about places she had been, and focus on this planet. Maybe this beautiful place could be her new home.

Kaida glanced at Treble. "You ready?"

"Do we need suits?"

Kaida checked her control panel. "No. The probe recorded nothing harmful to humans. The air is breathable, more oxygen than Mars habitats. Take a carry kit just in case."

She grabbed her own carry kit. It contained a small oxygen regenerator that worked on battery for a short time, depending on how much exertion they expended. Also, basic first aid supplies. And wound blockers. She dropped in snack rations and water beads.

Treble stepped up beside her. His hands trembled as he closed his pack and slung it on his shoulder. "I should never have left my city-state. I haven't seen trees so tall, nor so much grass. I believed so much vegetation was an exaggeration." His voice shook almost as much as his hands.

"The homesickness will go away. This is how Earth once was."

The hatch opened. Trees grew beside and towered behind them. Grasslands spread as far as they could see.

She laughed. Like the old videos, she almost expected to see a now-extinct lion pride gallop across the open plain to check them out. What would fill that ecological niche here?

Kaida stepped out of the *YaNanda*. She breathed deeply. The air smelled like life. A terrarium. A slight tinge of mustiness, probably from mammals or mammal-like beings. Yes, the air felt heavy. Heavy with expectation. Expectation of what, she wasn't sure.

Treble stepped out behind her. His rapid breathing sounded rather different than just the fear she knew he was panicking over.

One last glance back at the ship Kaida had considered her home for the last few years while exploring from the ShaLoot Space Station.

She held up her finger for silence. "We don't want to scare the inhabitants." Her voice barely projected far enough for him to hear.

He nodded. "What will they look like?" Treble's voice barely breathed toward her.

Spoken words seemed to travel downward, instead of dispersing outward. That was part of his specialty, as a geologic explorer, to figure out how and why.

She turned to the dappled shade trees. Inhabitants could be any species. Mammal, reptile, fish, tree, fungus, any living being. Since this planet's sound carried downward instead of outward, they would have to listen carefully, and use sight, smell, and even taste to communicate.

How did the planet taste? Kaida narrowly opened her lips enough to take in a taste of the air. Slightly sweet, missing the metallic flavor of Mars. There was a tangy flavor she had only ever tasted in certain fruits, and the oceans of Wingosa.

A shadow moved at the edge of the trees.

Kaida stepped one step closer. Hopefully not enough to scare them.

An individual stepped into the clearing. Almost a humanlike form. About seven feet tall. Two legs, two arms, and one head. With a hand-width long purple horn in the middle of their forehead. Like the image in her dream. A wavy mauve material covered them from neck to knobby knees.

Treble gasped. "A unicorn? I thought they were a myth."

Kaida covered a giggle with her hand. "Not exactly a unicorn." Would the not-a-unicorn want to shake hands? Or to wave?

And would one of those motions be a request for intimacy? That had been an unfortunate experience on a mostly aquatic planet a few explorations before. An awkward smile at the confused memory came unbidden to her lips. Smiles, too, were considered aggressive by many species. Why did she always do this to herself? The more Kaida learned, the less comfortable she was meeting a new species.

The individual stepped closer. They appeared to concentrate really hard at her. Their lips did not move. A frown formed around the hand-width long purple horn on its face that curled up to the top of their head.

The individual's vibes felt safe. They also seemed wild, and almost fearful.

Treble touched her shoulder. She jumped. His hand was trembling.

"Sorry." Treble pulled back behind her.

She pulled him up beside her. "Don't show fear."

Silently, Kaida kept repeating the words. Fear. Don't show fear. Don't.

The individual held up a hand with five fingers before hurrying back into the colorful trees.

"It had fingers. Like ours." Treble pointed to the trees.

"I saw the hand and fingers. There are similarities on most planets with humanoid species." The smallest finger appeared to be set almost on the same level as the thumb. Two opposable fingers would be a benefit in many ways in a peaceful forest life.

They needed a Language Conversion Stone. Few cultures had a translation stone for creatures beyond their own planet. Until Kaida created them. She had built several dozen stones while exploring with the *YaNanda*. Previous translation programs were all interconnected in the ShaLoot language databases. After a language was deciphered, it was passed on to other explorer cultures to share the electronic reference stone so they too could communicate.

The individual returned with another being dressed in amber-colored material, who had a daffodil-yellow horn.

"Not ready for this." Treble turned back to the *YaNanda*.

Kaida ignored him. He would overcome his emotional shutdown, or not. She observed the individuals. She held out her hands in what she hoped was a clear gesture of peace, with no sign of weapons. She struggled with what to say.

No noises, beyond the dampened rustling of forest leaves, had come from the individuals. Sound seemed to fall to the ground here, and not forward and upward. Kaida wondered if that was caused by the strange readings in the atmosphere the probe had detected.

Words had to arise for her to communicate and determine if they were peaceful. Many beings required spoken words. For her, written words were clearer. A memory of her mother calling her an aphantasian snuck up from one thought train. Once, pictures had given her more information than written words, and ten times more information than spoken.

Her mind returned to Deserta. There the individuals who lived in sand had to communicate differently, with flashing color. Did the beings here communicate without words?

"Hello. I am here to learn about you." Her words felt flat. Wrong. Words dispersed toward the ground so rapidly they didn't fall in the order she spoke them. Kaida glanced back at the *YaNanda*. The door was closed. Treble was still inside. He would be safe to decompress and avoid a meltdown in front of these unknown beings.

The beings didn't feel dangerous. Cautious. Perhaps scared. A reasonable feeling.

Kaida searched for a place to sit. Perhaps if she showed she was comfortable here, the beings would follow. A fallen tree with blue leaves lay nearby. She walked over to it. A dozen multicolored unidentifiable bugs raced across and under it. After a sharp breath, she sat down. It felt softer than the rocks on Mars. As if it was sand-covered. Her hand rubbed some softened bark loose.

Images of those bugs returned in her mind. Similar to images in the dreams. "Beetles. They benefit our world." The words whispered as captions along with the visuals that formed naturally in her mind. Aphantasia. She hadn't lost the ability to communicate in pictures, although it was rusty. As rusty as the Mars surface.

Soon more images.

The individuals moved closer. Kaida gasped.

The depictions were not any creatures she knew. A green flying insect she had never seen. Then a blue insect. A separate image of a tree with orange leaves. She closed her eyes. The sense of safety permeated the area. A comfort Kaida had never experienced before.

The next image was a blue tree with yellow leaves. Another image of the individuals in front of her, with more of their kind.

Kaida opened her eyes. The individuals sat on the ground in front of her.

Treble stepped out of the ship carrying a computer tablet. "You okay?" The two words dropped off into silence. He stepped closer and around the two individuals.

Kaida thought the words she wanted to say, and held up her hand.

He sat down beside her. "What?"

She glanced at him. Hadn't she spoken?

He tapped his tablet, as if looking for a text from her. "Are you okay?"

She nodded. Safe. She felt safe. Except for Treble's verbalizing. Kaida imagined him going about his scientific surveys.

He stared at her. "I know you don't talk much. Other surveyors have said you often had stony silences. I don't think the silences are stony, or as silent to you. You remind me of someone I once knew. Is it okay if I go survey?"

She glanced at the individuals in front of her. It was safe in her mind. Did they understand? She thought about what he intended to do. Exploring and cataloging new planets. Whether plants, animals, gases, or sometimes seemingly inanimate objects, it would take a lot of time. Possibly years to fully catalog this planet.

A few images Kaida didn't recognize appeared in her mind. A river. A dome. A dome that reminded her of the greenhouses on Mars. There are cities here? Another image, closer to the dome, showed many structures. Treble would be happy.

Treble peered at the individuals. "I don't understand them. I can tell you are having a conversation. Raise your hand if I shouldn't go."

Kaida looked at him. A conversation with no spoken words? Was that possible without time to decode it? She didn't raise her hand. An image of the dome reappeared in her mind.

Treble stood up. "I'll be back. I have rations. There is something interesting about the geology here. I think it interferes with sound waves, and I want to confirm that." He glanced back at her as he hiked along the tree line.

She turned back to the individuals. "I am Kaida." This time, she saw the captions with an image of herself.

The individual with the purple horn leaned toward her. "I am Gerven."

She felt, more than heard, the name and his gender. The images appearing in her mind were of a living tree home with plants growing inside and out. A few small animals moved about in the vision. One possibly reptilian. Another mammalian. Another that might have been neither. Perhaps an unknown phylum of beings.

The other individual with the yellow horn leaned forward. "I am Clarion." The visions that followed showed a couple of probable adults, and a few young members of the individual's species.

Such a nice way to communicate. "Do you have cities?" Kaida remembered the city-state she knew Treble was from. The image was lots of tall buildings, with grass and short trees in between.

Clarion and Gerven looked at each other. The image of the domed city reappeared. On the edge of a body of water. With enough houses for a small population. Well spread out, so they could grow and harvest plants and animals and have room to breathe.

"First visitor in a long time. Only to transmit." Gerven smiled at her. Wrinkles wrapped around his purple horned forehead.

Kaida yawned. Communicating by image transmission was more exhausting than vocalizing. Even though images were familiar, and comfortable.

Clarion reached for her hand. "You are talking like us."

"Yes."

"Mind pictures. Mind words."

Kaida looked up at her.

Clarion's yellow horn appeared to brighten as the images slowed. A flower as yellow as Mar's sun. A sky as blue as Earth's. The dusky sky before her, where color splashed brighter than she had imagined they could in such a muted atmosphere. The dullness of the lighting in brain pictures released a sigh of peace. Peace. This place was peaceful.

Gerven stood up and walked back toward the trees. He paused and sent a transmission of a smaller version of himself with a blue horn. As quickly as the image appeared, it, and he, disappeared out of sight among the orange leaves.

Kaida peeked around. Colors. Everywhere. Brighter colors than she realized were even possible among the grasses and trees. A bright purple hopping creature resembled a photo of a long-extinct Earth frog she had once seen in an educational video.

Gerven returned with a smaller version of himself.

The younger individual trudged up to her with shaking hands. They opened their mouth and spoken words shuffled down to the grassland floor. "I am Kale. I can speak aloud if it is easier. Children can. Adults only to children and partners."

Kaida shook her head. Images, though tiring, were easier. How would she create a translation stone of images to words, if other explorers couldn't view, or hear, the transmitted images? This was one of the reasons her mother, and others, had never valued her picturing words and concepts, and not being able to communicate them aloud.

"Can all of your species talk in visions?" Kale glanced up at her, and then away. His words, though spoken aloud, also attempted to connect with images he transmitted.

Kaida looked toward the younger individual. "I doubt it. I never heard of any. Do any of you leave your planet?"

"No. We are happy here. Why would we leave?" Clarion shifted to watch as a small, dark, scaled, and winged catlike creature stalked nearby. "Was there something you missed in your home?"

Yes. Kaida had missed peace. Quiet. Trees, flowers, species she hadn't seen or known existed. How they connected. Memories of Mars flooded her mind. Then visions of Earth that she had never seen. Images from a present full of cities, followed by the documented, almost forgotten, past. A past she now realized she hoped to reach by being an explorer.

Clarion, Gerven, and Kale swayed in the nonexistent breeze. She experienced their emotions. Surprise and dismay at the visions of Mars. Fear of the cities of Earth. And a comfort, though not quite calm, at the almost forgotten memories of Earth, as the planet had been, a millennia ago.

No words were spoken.

None needed to be.

Kaida's heart and mind had shared things beyond what words could comprehend or express. Overshared, as her mother would say.

Clarion touched a small yellow and orange furry creature that had curled up in her lap. "Thank you. Hope."

Kaida reached toward the creature. The orange and yellow fur felt softer than any cat she had known. Communication would be possible. She hadn't overstepped and blundered her way through first contact, one this species seemed to desire.

The creature moved from Clarion's lap to hers.

A few transmissions appeared in her brain. She closed her eyes. Images of alien beings who had ignored the inhabitants. Garbled words they had spoken aloud. A few beings she recognized from a species that lived a few systems away.

"No one tried to talk in images." Kaida sighed. "Sad. Do you paint and draw?"

Gerven leaned forward. "Not often. Too much beauty around to need to recreate it for later times. Though we could, if we wanted. We have a memory cavern. Not all of it is accurate. Several memories are not as expected."

"We have images of beings and plants in our memory, that have no known living counterparts." Clarion glanced back toward the colorful forest. "We don't know what they are. Or were. Only what they may have looked like."

Kale twisted some grass at his feet. "We learn the forgotten images, and can't connect them to any living on Loreia."

Loreia. A perfect name for a planet that appeared to be a part of folklore. Kaida petted the almost catlike creature in her lap. So similar to the guinea pigs she had tried to raise as a child.

Something rustled in the trees. Treble stepped out from the colorful leaves. He walked up to her. "So much beauty here. So much to learn. Have you had any luck communicating?"

"Mind transmissions."

"Makes sense. I wonder if your nonresponses to me were mind images?"

She stared at him. Had she been trying to transmit images to him? And other explorers? That would explain why they called her cold and nonresponsive. They couldn't view her communications.

"I'll be in the *YaNanda* uploading notes. Enjoy." He trudged toward the ship.

A purple, scaled, and feathered being, a little larger than a house cat, followed him.

She smiled. He, too, fit here, if the purple being was any indication.

"Slippy, come back!" Kale raced off to catch the creature, and managed to chase it right into the *YaNanda*.

Kaida laughed.

Gerven and Clarion laughed quietly, and their horns wrinkled up. "Welcome to Planet Loreia. Stay a while."

Warm thoughts and images flooded Kaida's mind. So much to learn and experience here. More than anywhere she had ever been.

She stood and looked back at the *YaNanda*. There was nothing she needed there. Treble would understand. His surveys, here, and on the other system planets, would not take longer without her. He'd inform her of his findings. She would soon be forgotten for more chatty explorers.

Kaida nodded to Clarion and Gerven.

They stood and led the way into the colorful forest.

The small dark, scaled, and winged catlike creature followed in her footsteps.

Home.

This was home.

BEGINNING AWAKENING
FOUR POEMS
CHIEF RED CHEF

Drifting
Black holes drifting
Through my mind
Through space and me
Taking all that's real
Robbed of all consciousness
Still the torch of knowledge is ablaze
Deep within the emptiness

Flashin' Out
It's a harvest of my visions
Though I gave no permission
The truth of all truths
lies in between the cracks
No sin nor saint
can ever bring me back
Time will tell
what path I'm on next
This predicament I'm in
has me very perplexed

Scanning
Scanning shadows for a life within
Breathless
Heartless
Alone
Incubating power
Isolation of a flower
Scanning life for a reason within

Infection
Divine infection
A tremor in the collection
Higher intelligence
Spiritual relevance
Repressed desires
Mind-lit fires
Transient mystics
Spreading image infernos
Contagious memory
Exploding explanation
Hiding in true chaos

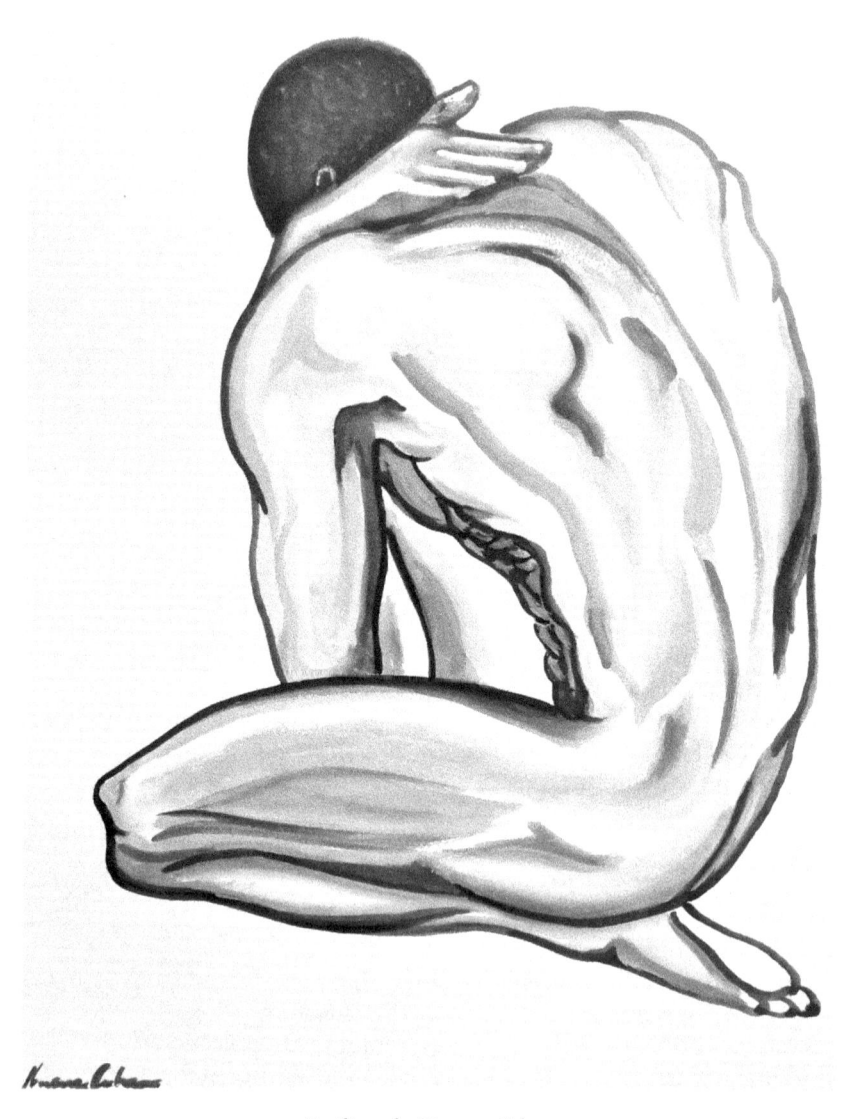

Resilience by Vincenzo Cohen

WHERE MONOLITHIC MINDS CAN'T TRAVEL
A STORY
AKIS LINARDOS

Content note: *reference to a past involuntary medical procedure*

MYRIA THE ALIEN came to our house when I was Adam and Jessica—my seventeen other selves slumbering in the ethereal palace of dreams.

Myria the Alien came to our house when we were Jessica and Adam—the seventeen other siblings shackled in a data cage, locked by our own parents with a brain implant.

I let Jessica do the talking.

He let me do the talking, because Adam was always a dreamer. It was his abstract paintings, a representation of our shared mind that hinted to Myria of our nature—of being many souls in one body. Made Myria feel safe to share a thought, transmitted telepathically:

Are you multi-spirits?

And though we did not know the word, we understood exactly what it meant. Because it was the first time an outsider addressed us as not one, but many.

We come from a world past what you call the Milky Way, beyond what starlight human eyes and telescopes can see.

I did not believe them, and called Adam naive.

I believed them, even though Jessica refused, shackled by what is known, afraid of possibility.

I carried Myria, wrapped in a bedsheet, down the basement, where our parents never tread. Myria had the shape of a cat-sized arthropod, their body heat burning through the linen. When we left them, Myria scuttled into a cardboard box, a leftover package from Jessica's coffee machine.

Adam hated coffee. But for me it's like gasoline to get my mental engines going. Adulthood is too much without it.

Jessica is only addicted to dopamine, but the returns are diminishing.

Myria hated coffee, but loved it when I shared bread and wine. They extended two pairs of prehensile three-fingered mandibles from their carapace: one dipped the bread in the wine cup, the other crushed and sloshed it in the red liquid, and their two mouths devoured the meal separately—asynchronously.

Their face was fragmented: partitioned like spinning slots tucked under a cowl-shaped carapace. The optic segment rotated often: sometimes revealing a spider's eight beady eyes, others two orange orbs lantern-bright, or three glowing aquamarine as if from a siren underwater.

I thought we had to study Myria, and harness their secrets for mankind, but Adam disagreed.

I thought I had to hide them, and let their secrets be their own. I knew how humans' curiosity extends beyond what is right if too much trust is given. Like our hibernating siblings, whose exposure brought the hammer of the brain implant when we were only eight years old, coinhabiting this body and trying to figure out the world. Siblings of whom I could still hear Eve and Jacob, their slumber perturbed in the night terrors we shared with Jessica, and in unison their whispers infected and jolted me awake, screaming in the waking world with their own voices.

Myria was fragile—their exoskeleton had cracked upon landing, and mending it would take months. Myria was lucky to find me, find *us*, trust us because we were alike, more alike with Myria than even with our own parents. This much Jessica understood.

I understood. I was the special child, and Adam the isolated one, disowned in his own body—our own body. Whenever he'd take control, Mama laughed it off—oh stop it, Jessica, that old joke of yours pretending to be a boy—and Father remained entirely silent, not daring to meet my eyes for he could see the truth. There's no faking a second soul, and I know Mama's denial was only external. They hoped Adam was a phase, one the brain implant they forced on me would make me outgrow like the other seventeen liminal siblings. Siblings that had to die for their precious daughter to be pure. Siblings of whom some still lingered, fragments the installed murderer of neurons failed to purge.

They thought I was a sickness of which to cure Jessica, not a son sharing a body with his sister.

There are no monolithic minds where we come from. Used to be, but they couldn't survive the chaotic nature of intergalactic travel. Unable to shift to another mind when reality was too much, they overdosed on existence and crumbled entirely.

Myria shared this thought on the tenth day in our basement, while feasting on chocolate bars and raw pasta that crackled between their exposed gums and sharklike teeth. Jessica said nothing, but I had too many questions.

"Do all your people have multiple identities? What do you mean they cannot survive? In this world, it's frowned upon to be more than one, a rigid choice for identity."

Adam was excited and wouldn't stop talking, exposing too much of humanity to this alien species, reckless and uncaring.

Myria's mandibles stilled, the peanut butter filling of the bars dripping down their crustacean fingers, onto the pasta mush on their lap. Their body ran hot, melting everything we gave them, and even charred the cardboard and the chocolate-stained blankets until the basement smelled like a candy furnace.

A single mind cannot survive the flux of entropy for

transcosmic travel. It crumbles beneath the weight of probable realities. Too much for a single mind to parse, but if interspersed between mental slumberers, one brain can become a spaceship, where captains interchange in intervals. What you call parallel processing in your digitized machines is most efficient in organic too: less resources to host more beings.

Jessica remained silent, because she knew what I craved.

I remained silent because I knew what Adam dreamed, and I would not stop him saying it. The guilt of seventeen siblings was heavy enough. I could not deprive him of this escape, not when our parents' rejection wanted him gone by force.

"Can you take us with you when you return home?"

To return, Myria had to join their mothership again, and for that we needed a distress signal, a rescue flare.

The signal was Adam's art, a representation of rescue with features of souls in canvas, which Myria's amplifying antennae transmitted across space.

The signal was my art, thoughts to colors, emotions of isolation in vibrant strokes, and Myria's voice to sing them through starlight.

When Myria's people came, human news spoke of an unknown blockage of light between Sun and Earth. When faced with chaos, society blames nature, because they're taught to expect order in the artificial. Myria and their kind had harnessed chaos, built their ships around it, and they had to do little extra work to fool the monolithic minds about it.

But we were never fooled, because in our skull chaos had reigned since our birth, and though the brain implants suppressed the storm of voices, I can still hear Eve. Like whooshing winds, an unconscious pattern, her existence unfairly terminated.

Eve sees the starlight through the eyes we share with Jessica, fractured through the lens of the mothership that is in many places, multiple orbits, all at once.

We didn't say goodbye.

It was not about escape, but a duty toward reality. In their current state, human minds could not converse with Myria, and we knew enough of people and their governments. They'd never trust someone like me, like us to translate.

Centuries from now, we will return, and maybe find other people still on Earth. People with wisdom refined through facing the calamities of their denials.

I convinced Jessica we had to go. Without this contact, humanity would forever be looked down upon. Habit is a chain—our only binding to this world—and we must shatter it for our own good. And the good of everyone, because now progress and cosmic understanding depended on us.

Adam convinced me we had to go. More than that, Myria convinced me there was never anything wrong with me, with us, save for the narrow-minded context we'd existed in until that point. There may never be another chance for two interuniversal species to share a thread. Reality itself may evolve with wisdom shared between such a divide. If not us, who else?

THE ZETA REMNANT

A STORY

M. D. COOPER

Content note: *futuristic combat sequence*

"EASY, EASY," Cora whispered to herself as she piloted the *Emily* through a storm high in the plane's atmosphere. "Don't end this excursion before the good part."

<*Does talking to yourself help?*> Violet asked over the Link. <*I've heard it's a sign of madness in you organics.*>

"Don't distract me," the woman in the pilot's seat muttered. "We've come too far to botch the landing."

The pillar of light to her right, glowing softly in the copilot's seat, pulsed twice. <*Which is why you should have let me make the final approach. You know I'm better at it.*>

"Yeah, but I want to say that I did it," Cora countered. "Stupid, I know…"

The ship finally came out the bottom of the storm. A low range of mountains passed below before the terrain fell in a series of sharp drops to a rock-strewn plain. Boulders the size of cruisers were strewn about, each accented by a long gouge in the surface as though it was thrown by a moon-sized giant.

<*Getting close to the big crater,*> Violet advised. <*Watch your delta-v, you're coming in a bit fast.*>

"I'm just impatient," Cora said through tight-drawn lips. "I want to see it ... whatever it is."

<*You're not the only one. I'm dying to know what could possibly be emitting RF at the bottom of an impact site on this distant rock.*>

"Something that landed said impact, no doubt," Cora replied as the crater's rim came into view over the planet's horizon.

The ship had slowed to a thousand kilometers per hour on its retro engines and Cora angled up the nose, letting the craft aerobrake further in the thin nitrogen atmosphere. She was a good ship, one that had served Cora and Violet well on dozens of surveying expeditions across six different star systems over the past couple of centuries.

This one was different, though. A little over a decade ago, they'd separated from the Seventh World Fleet's primary destination to gather detailed data on the Zeta Leporis system—a place not even a probe had ever visited.

Or so they thought.

The RF signal emanating from the system's fourth planet—a craggy ball twice Mars's size—indicated otherwise.

At first, she and Violet had thought it could be a natural uranium-235 reactor pulsing out EM, but the frequency was too narrow and the pattern too repetitive. The closer they got, the more apparent it was that the origin had to be mechanical.

<*I can't imagine any other scenario,*> Violet replied after a pause.

"You were thinking aliens, weren't you?" Cora asked with a laugh. "I know you were."

<*We all think 'maybe there will be aliens' whenever we go to a new system. And guess what we've found so far?*>

Cora heaved a sigh. "No aliens."

<*Not a whisper, not a wink. There's nothing out there but what we create.*>

"Sometimes I love that idea, and sometimes it terrifies me—Oh!"

Cora sat up in her seat, peering down at the landscape. "There's the bottom, thank goodness it's well-lit."

<*For a few hours at least. This thing's three kilometers deep in the center. It'll be dark in about nine hours.*>

"The RF signal is on the eastern side." Cora dropped a marker. "Seventeen klicks from the center."

<*Well what are you waiting for?*>

Cora snorted as she flew the ship over the crater's rim. "I'm not. Buckle up, we're going in."

<*I don't need to buckle.*>

She only sighed in response, though a slight smile found its way onto her lips. "Final approach in thirty seconds."

The ship reared up, retros firing as the landing gear unfurled.

"Touchdown!" Cora announced after the slight bounce that heralded their arrival on the planet's surface. She unbuckled her harness and stood up in the one-third gravity.

<*Deploying drones,*> Violet announced. <*Let's get a map of the area. I don't want you falling into a crevasse.*>

"Just me?" Cora asked as she walked out of the cockpit and down the narrow passage that led past the galley, sleeping quarters, and recreation room. "I thought you'd be coming with."

<*Oh, I am, I'm just not clumsy enough to trip into a crevasse.*>

"It was *one* time!"

Past the rec room, the passage split with the airlock room on the left and the cargo bay aft. Cora had already prepared for the mission during the Hohmann transfers down to the planet. Her EV suit was prepped and ready with rations and a full supply of oxygen.

A trundle drone also waited in the airlock, carrying a full testing suite, mining laser, and spare air tanks in case she was out longer than expected.

As she pressed a palm on the inner door control, she saw Violet's mobile frame step into view through the airlock window—already inside and waiting. Though her shipboard presence was always represented by a pillar of light, the AI chose a very humanlike frame for dangerous missions. It was a few centimeters taller than Cora, willowy, and coated in a dark grey ablative plating.

Despite being fairly adventurous by AI standards, Violet still exhibited the risk aversion that was a hallmark of her kind, always sealing her core behind as many layers of protection as possible.

"Slowpoke," the AI said aloud once the airlock door irised open.

"I walked back here at a regular speed. You just started moving your core to the frame before we landed."

The AI's frame lifted its shoulders in a shrug. "Guilty."

Cora rolled her eyes and stepped inside, stopping in front of the nanocarbon fiber exoarmor suit that hung from the rack. Like her shipsuit, it was skin-tight, all the better to maneuver in and not have to worry about getting caught on any protrusions or stuck in tight spaces.

She pulled down the seal and stepped in, reveling in the compression it created across her body, a feeling of comfort and security washing over her. Cora didn't know the reason why she loved to be tightly wrapped in both the suit and exoarmor—though her psych evals probably suggested some explanation.

I like it and it feels good. Why fix what isn't broken?

Cora smoothed her hair back and pulled on a thin hood that would keep it out of her face. Once satisfied that every errant strand was tucked away, she reached for a full-bubble helmet and lowered it over her head.

As soon as it touched the extravehicular suit, the helmet sealed in place and it's HUD activated, green status indicators glowing on either side of her vision.

<I show green for your air hookup,> Violet reported. <*Your seal is solid and your precious organic body is as safe as it can be.*>

<Thanks,> Cora's reply was dry as she switched to the Link. <*Your concern, as always, is touching.*>

Violet winked as she closed the inner airlock door and triggered the chamber's decompression. <*Your parents would be upset if I came back without you.*>

Neither spoke as the air drained from the chamber, though Cora rolled her shoulders as her shipsuit tightened, compensating for the decrease in pressure on her skin as the airlock reached equilibrium with the planet's 0.1 Bar.

The light over the outer door flipped from red to green and the portal irised open, bathing the airlock in Zeta Leporis's harsh white light and causing Cora's helmet to apply a protective tint.

<Beautiful day for a stroll,> Violet said as she walked down the ship's short ramp. Once she reached the bottom, she turned and looked at Cora who still stood on the threshold, surveying the new world.

<Have you grown immune to the wonder of it all?> she asked the AI.

<Not like we're the first sentient beings to set foot on this rock,> Violet countered. She swung an arm out in the direction of the signal. <There be aliens over yonder.>

Cora rolled her eyes so hard she almost sprained them. With a resigned sigh, she left the ship, trundle bot following after. <You're in a strange mood,> she commented once at the AI's side.

<And I don't know why you're so somber all of a sudden.>

Cora shrugged as they set out across the grey rock-strewn plain. <I guess I'm trying to keep my hopes in check. Besides, you know the standard theory: there are no aliens.>

<Sorta.>

<Sorta?>

The AI glanced at her, one of the frame's articulate brows raised. <Well, the standard theory states that planets like Earth are exceedingly rare—which they are. Not only does the world have to be in the goldilocks zone, but it also has to have a specific composition and be around a stable star with large outer system planets that keep the inner system relatively free of asteroids. Those planets also have to be in stable orbits and not move in, eating the inner planets.>

Cora nodded. <This isn't new information to me.>

<And we know that if there were alien civilizations nearby, we'd see them. Fusion engines tend to be pretty bright. Anyone within almost a thousand light-years of Sol can see that it's home to a sentient, spacefaring species.>

<Which is an expanse containing millions of star systems,> Cora added. <And given our rate of expansion, it's reasonable to assume that any spacefaring species could spread clear across the galaxy in roughly a hundred thousand years.>

<Correct, which means tens—or even hundreds—of thousands of colo-

nized systems blasting EM into the black. Something that would be visible across the entire galaxy.>

<Yes,> the human woman nodded, head bobbing inside her clear helmet. <And since we don't see that, it reinforces the rare Earth theory, suggesting that if there are advanced civilizations, they are either very astrographically limited or they are spaced out in time by at least a hundred thousand years.>

Violet snapped a metallic finger, the *plink* struggling to make it through the thin atmosphere to Cora's audio pickups. <But what if a civ was very astrographically limited, **and** near Sol. If their civilization ended before the tenth century, humanity would never have seen a glimmer of their civilization.>

<So you're saying that if we are going to find evidence of nonterrestrial civs, it's going to be within a thousand light-years?>

<Closer, since if they're a thousand light-years away, the final years of their civ would still be reaching us. No, I think they'd have to be within a hundred light-years of Sol ... two hundred at most. Then the end of their civilization could have washed over us and been gone before we ever looked for it.>

<Leaving just this one lone beacon flashing in the dark?> Cora gestured in the direction they were headed, the destination still a few hundred meters away.

<Exactly. Granted, it's little more than a hope. Not many systems within a hundred light-years that haven't been visited.>

<It's still super unlikely that there are two systems with advanced civs so close to each other,> Cora added.

<But if there were ...> Violet turned her frame's face upward to where the stars waited—though they were masked by Zeta Leporis's white glare. <There could be millions of sapient species out there.>

<I never took you for a dreamer,> Cora said as they rounded a jagged ten-meter-tall boulder. <You normally seem so pragmatic. I'm usually the one getting all poetic about what we'll find in the black.>

The AI gave a slow shrug. <We never found anything like this before.>

As she spoke, they came around the far side of the massive rock to where a marker hovered on Cora's HUD indicating the origin point of the RF emission. It was bobbing gently over a stretch of loose rock that had been sprayed across the crater's floor by the impact of the boulder.

<*Looks like we're digging,*> Violet said. <*Can't be that far down, though. Not for the signal to be as strong as it is.*>

<*Trundle bot to the rescue!*> Cora announced in response, and directed the bot to use its ground-penetrating radar to investigate the area. The bot started where the signal was strongest, slowly circling outward, filling in a map on her HUD.

The more it moved, the wider her eyes got, locking with Violet's.

<*What ... what is that?*> she whispered across the Link.

<*Seems like ... a dome? It's big ... at least forty meters.*>

<*Okay ... how did it get under the rock?*>

The AI tapped her frame's head with an index finger. <*Aliens.*>

<*There are other explanations.*>

Violet gestured at the house-sized boulder they just passed. <*This thing is made of the same material as the crater, which means it's probably from the initial impact. It's what sprayed the loose shale around this area, which means that whatever is under there was put there before the crater was made ... and that was over ten thousand years ago.*>

Cora shrugged. <*Someone could be trolling.*>

<*Are you serious?*>

<*Not really. I just ... I just figured when someone found aliens it would look a lot more impressive than this.*> She gestured around the crater floor.

<*Well, the bot's readings say there's less than a meter of lose rock over the object right there,*> she dropped a marker on Cora's HUD. <*Let's get digging.*>

The two women set to work lifting rock out of the way until they'd cleared an area three meters across and eighty centimeters deep. There was still a lot of rubble on the bottom, and Cora stood in its midst tossing it out of the divot they'd created until her hand hit something smooth and unmovable.

<*I think ... I think this is it. Maybe it's not an alien artifact, maybe it's just a smooth chunk of whatever made the crater that got plowed under when that boulder fell down,*> Cora speculated.

<*And just so happens to emit RF? You really need to stop trying to come up with alternative explanations.*>

<*I guess I'm still shocked you jumped right to aliens.*>

<*It's the most logical conclusion.*>

Cora's crouched down, shifting more loose rock out of the way until she could see the object below. <*Readings do show it to be metallic. A titanium-gold alloy of some sort. Reinforced with carbon nanofibers, I think—or it's just carbon scoring…*>

Violet carefully stepped down the slope, holding the trundle bot's ground radar. <*Let's see how thick this shell is.*>

Cora stepped back as the AI set the device on what she was now thinking of as exposed hull and activated it. The result was surprising.

<*About seventy centimeters,*> Violet said. <*That's a lot of material.*>

<*Explains why it survived whatever happened here.*>

The AI nodded. <*What does this remind you of?*>

<*The material?*> Cora asked. <*It's roughly the same thing we use to house AI cores.*>

<*Yeah.*>

<*You think there's an AI in there?*>

<*Whatever it is, it's something that someone thought was worth putting a lot of effort into protecting.*>

Cora climbed back up to the trundle bot and began unpacking the mining laser's tripod. <*Well, it's going to take a bit to bore a probe hole through this, so we'd best get started.*>

Once the laser was on the tripod, the two women stepped back and let it get to work.

A part of Cora wanted to just blast the shell open and go in, but she knew that they needed to preserve whatever was inside, which meant the beam had to be precise and attenuate as it reached the far side of the hull so as not to cut through something in the interior.

Ten minutes later, penetration was announced by hissing air coming through Cora's helmet pickups.

<*Alright.*> Cora released a microdrone from her exoarmor once pressure inside the sphere had equalized. <*Go do your thing, little buddy.*>

The bot's camera view overlaid her vision and, with near-trembling anticipation, she watched it approach the one-centimeter hole the laser had cut.

<Something's blocking the hole,> Violet commented as the tiny bot reached the end. <Let's hope there's enough clearance to get around.>

<It's not called a microdrone for nothing.>

<I know, but ... never mind, it found a crack.>

The drone's view had gone dark as it worked through a space less than a millimeter wide and out into an open area. It was pitch black, and the drone switched to an RF detection, using the very signal that had brought them to the mysterious object to map its interior.

Because the bot was mapping the reflections of EM waves within the chamber, the first thing to come into resolution was the outer shell, which seemed to consist of row upon row of one-meter cylinders covering the entire interior. Roughly thirty degrees up the far side emerged a plinth that stretched to the center of the sphere. Atop it stood a smaller cylinder two meters tall and half a meter in diameter.

<Fuck,> Violet whispered. <*This* ***is*** *an AI chamber. Those are SC batteries, lining the inside. They have to be.*>

Cora took a step back. There were enough superconductor batteries inside to power an entire starship. <*What if... what if this is one of the ascended AIs from the Sentience Wars? Maybe it crashed here and an earthquake covered it up.*>

<Maybe....> It was Violet's turn to whisper over the Link. <*It's hard to say from this rudimentary scan, but the designs of those batteries don't look like anything from the Sentience Wars back in the Sol System. It also would have to have traveled pretty fast to get here this quickly.*>

<Great, so it's a mysterious AI in a shell big enough to house a multinodal entity.>

Violet waved a hand in dismissal. <*Don't be silly. Multinodal AIs are much larger than this.*>

Cora wasn't entirely convinced. Her mind raced with possibilities. She had nothing against AIs—her best friend and traveling companion was one, after all. But the AIs that had waged war in Sol during the Sentience Wars were not at all friendly to organics. They'd killed billions before humanity and other AI factions had wiped them out.

But not before many fled the system, headed who knows where.

The cold brilliance of Zeta Leporis seemed to increase as she stood, pondering what waited within the shell. She felt hot, sweat flowing from her pores faster than the shipsuit could absorb and recycle it.

<Relax,> Violet said, reaching out to touch Cora's shoulder. <Those batteries are all but spent. If that entity is still alive, it won't have the ability to do anything to us.>

<You hope.>

<I know. Let's reposition the mining laser so we can cut an opening between some of the batteries and get inside. I **need** to see it up close.>

Cora gave Violet a measuring look—not that the AI's frame would reveal any aspect of her mind. Its silvery features were entirely implacable, revealing nothing of the eagerness that flowed across the Link.

It wasn't as though she'd never seen Violet excited before, but this was something new. It was almost frenetic. Almost.

She shook her head to clear her thoughts. Violet was many things, but reckless was not one of them. No scouting team survived decades alone in the black if its members did not value care and caution above all else.

It took the pair twenty minutes to clear loose rubble from the new position, and an hour to carefully cut out a half-meter-wide hole in the shell.

When it was done, they sent a pair of larger surveillance drones inside, as much to see if they triggered any defense mechanisms than to map and light the space.

<Nothing's going pew pew,> Cora commented. <Still can't make heads or tails of that RF signal, though. Just seems like repeating noise.>

<That may be the point. If it's an acknowledged SOS pattern, it doesn't need to contain any other data.>

Cora shrugged as she peered inside the now-lit hole. <Definitely agree on those superconductor battery designs. They aren't like any I've ever seen—other than obeying the laws of physics. Like ... the conduit routing just seems ...>

<Alien?> Violet prompted. <I have to admit, though, it doesn't look **so** different that if I were to see it in place on one of our ships I would think it's nonterrestrial in origin. It could have just been made by an eccentric person.>

<So it still could be from the Sentience Wars.>
<Unlikely.>
<Less unlikely than aliens?> Cora pressed.

Violet directed an unreadable look her way, and then jumped ahead in what was the obvious direction the conversation was going in. <Do you think I'm being reckless?>

<Not yet, no.>

The AI didn't immediately respond and, for a moment, Cora thought they were on the brink of having one of their exceedingly rare arguments. Then Violet let out a long sigh.

<You're right. Perhaps I'm letting my excitement cloud my judgement. It's just... whenever people imagine a find out on some distant world that points at nonterrestrial intelligence, it's organic in nature because everyone just assumes that's what it will be. But here we are looking at an inorganic sentience. I hope you can see why that's exciting to me.>

Cora pursed her lips. She hadn't thought of it that way. All she'd considered was the potential danger, but to Violet, this was like finding a colony of sapient apes or dolphins on some distant world. She attempted to reframe her thoughts along those lines.

<Okay. I concede. I'd be pretty excited if I were in your shoes. What's our next move?>

<Well, from what the probes can see, just two of the SC batts have any charge remaining. I also can't pick up any activity coming from the cylinder on the plinth—though the RF signal is coming from the plinth itself.>

Cora had a view of the sphere's interior on her HUD and dropped a pin on the base of the plinth. <That looks like an access point. Think we should see if a drone can interface with it?>

<What about caution?> Violet's mental tone carried a hint of mirth.
<We're still up here and it can barely transmit an SOS.>

The AI cocked its frame's head. <What if it's a trap? A big bad trap laid over ten thousand years ago?>

<Oh stop it.>

Violet laughed aloud, the sound carrying faintly through the thin atmosphere. <Alright, let's go take a look.>

The AI maneuvered one of the drones to the base of the plinth, which—due to the sphere's current orientation—rose from the interior surface seven meters above the "floor."

Cora brought the feed from its forward camera up on the center of her HUD, soaking in every detail. The drone flew around the perimeter of the space, giving a close-up view of the superconductor batteries and the conduit leading from them in an increasingly complex web the closer it came to the shaft that supported the AI core.

After a few seconds, the drone reached the access panel, a circular indent roughly thirty centimeters across. There was no apparent latch or other opening mechanism, but that wouldn't necessarily pose any difficulty. At a command from Violet, the drone snaked two arms out, attaching them to either side of the circle. Nanofilaments spilled from the arms, flowing into the gap around the panel, threading a space only a few molecules wide.

<*I think I can cut the panel off,*> the AI said. <*But I might also be able to access this data port without doing that.*>

A three-dimensional view of the space behind the panel appeared before Cora. There were several unidentified protrusions, a screen that was dark and lifeless, and what appeared to be an optical port at the bottom.

<*The drone's data feed is going through multiple sandboxes,*> Cora said after double-checking that the additional precautions were in place. <*I say go for it.*>

Violet nodded and used the probe's nanofilaments to construct an optical interface that would match the port inside the access panel.

<*Here goes nothing,*> the AI announced as the probe connected to the port. <*Sending a low-intensity broad-spectrum signal. Don't want to burn anything out. Stars know how long it's been sitting here.*>

<*Worst case, we can always pull the core off the plinth and interface directly.*>

Violet sent a feeling of caution across the Link. <*Now who's being reckless?*>

<*I'm just thinking of our logical steps should this fail. Not like we can just call for backup and get some engineers down here. It's three year's travel to the World Fleet's current position.*>

<*A fact that hasn't left my mind since we first picked up that signal.*> She paused. <*There's a response. It's weak ... attenuating.*>

Cora pulled up the details on the data stream, examining the frequency, amplitude, and the results of Violet's attempt to parse it. It was a mess, garbled. Either the packets were being corrupted in transmission, or none of the standard methods to assemble them would work in this case.

<*This is going to take a bit,*> Violet muttered before Cora could comment.

<*I figured. I'm going to send the trundle bot back for more oxygen. Need any tools?*>

<*No, I'm tapped into the ship's onboard processors to augment computation. Nothing physical will aid us at this point.*>

While Violet was working on the data port, Cora took direct control of the other drone they'd sent into the sphere, using it to survey the interior in more detail. The more she saw, the more she found herself in agreement with Violet that the sphere had a nonterrestrial origin.

There was no single thing that screamed "alien"—only a cumulative effect of structural and design choices that were ever so slightly different than anything she had ever seen. For some reason the variances felt incongruous, even though nothing appeared out of place.

Cora's musings were interrupted by the return of the trundle bot and she pushed the probe's view aside on her HUD, turning her focus back to the planet's surface. She walked to the bot and removed the air tanks slotted into its back, setting about replacing the nearly depleted pair hanging off the back of her exoarmor.

No sooner had she removed the first one, than the AI sent a victorious cry over the Link.

<*I did it! I have two-way communication! Now to actually gain ... wait—*>

The word was cut off in a way that seemed more like a connection issue than a pause in Violet's thinking.

<*What is it?*> Cora asked.

<*What are you?*>

The response did not come from Violet, but from another connection to their small network. It was routing through the ship's onboard systems that had been processing the alien protocols.

Shit! This is it? First contact. Cora swallowed, eyes darting to her partner who still hadn't moved—though now it seemed somehow involuntary.

<*We are members of the Seventh FGT World Fleet. What have you done to Violet?*>

<*She wanted to limit my access to your systems. I silenced her. Very interesting ... your kind do not seem descended from any organics I am familiar with. Wait. No. You're from that nearby young world. It certainly took you ... humans ... long enough to evolve and find me.*>

Cora's pulse pounded in her ears as her mind raced with questions. <*Release whatever hold you have on Violet. I will not help you if you harm her.*>

An inarticulate sound came into her mind. A laugh perhaps? It sounded sinister, whatever it was.

<*I don't need your help, filthy blood bag.*>

Cora caught movement in her peripheral vision. It was the mining laser pivoting on its tripod mount, swinging its business end toward her.

"Fuck!" she screamed in the confines of her helmet before diving behind the trundle bot to wrench one of the air tanks free. The mining beam hit the bot a moment later, burning into the machine's light plating.

Cora wasted no time and rolled from her cover and spun her torso, flinging the air tank at the mining laser. She'd meant to simply knock the tripod over, but it was already tracking toward her and the beam intersected with the air tank only three meters from where Cora crouched.

The explosion was instantaneous. It flung her backward to slam into the large boulder that lay between the excavation site and the ship.

Cora's armor hardened moments before the impact, protecting her from any serious harm, but the impact was still enough to knock the wind out of her and she collapsed to the ground, willing her mind to clear and come to grips with the situation.

We need to get out of here.

She pushed herself to her feet and looked around for the mining laser. It was nowhere to be seen, either destroyed or fallen into the hole. Either was acceptable for the moment. Without another thought, she sprinted toward Violet's still-unmoving frame.

A moment before Cora came within arm's reach, the silver body turned, an arm lashing out at the approaching woman's head.

Though she feared what it would mean for her partner, Cora had anticipated that if the entity in the sphere could overpower Violet, taking control of the frame would be within the scope of its abilities as well.

Given that forethought, she was already ducking low, shoulder held level with the frame's midsection. The impact jarred her almost as much as hitting the boulder, but it had the desired impact of knocking her attacker over.

The entity didn't waste a second, landing blow after blow on Cora, her armor stiffening to handle the onslaught as she wrestled with a latch at the frame's waist. A metal fist hit her helmet, sending a spiderweb of cracks across its surface.

The blow almost dislodged Cora, but she held onto the latch, finally ripping it open to reveal Violet's metal core inside.

Normally, an AI frame would have much stronger protection against unauthorized removal, but scout teams needed the ability perform emergency rescues in the field, so expediency trumped security.

She wrenched the core free and leapt away, crab-crawling a few meters before finally scrambling to her feet.

The frame was already up but moving slowly, keeping several meters between them as Cora backed away.

It's scared. It doesn't know if I can disable the frame, and if I can, then it can't stop me from getting back to the ship.

She eased around the boulder, losing sight of her foe for several agonizing seconds before it carefully stepped back into view, this time holding a rock.

<*This is pointless,*> the entity said, speaking for the first time since calling Cora a blood bag. <*You can't defeat me. I have crippled the insignificant mind that called itself Violet. The protocols protecting your organic brain from me won't hold forever. I'll get through and use you as a puppet just like I am with this limited system I control now.*>

It hadn't occurred to Cora that the entity could breach her mind through the Link, though in retrospect, she didn't know why such a thing hadn't occurred to her. It wasn't as though brain hacking was unheard of.

She only hesitated a moment before disabling her Link's wireless systems, severing herself from the network and the ship. Less than a second later, the rock came hurtling toward her, slamming into her helmet in the same place the prior impact had cracked it.

A shriek of air left Cora's lungs before her suit's emergency systems flowed a seal across her face, air tubes sinking into her nostrils while her vision switched to a view from her armor's shoulder cameras. It was disorienting, but she'd trained for just such a situation and those instincts took over.

Another rock was in the frame's hand, and Cora drew the small pulse pistol at her side, thumbing its blast to a wide cone before firing as the entity threw it at her.

The stone blew apart when it hit the pulse shockwave, and Cora didn't hesitate before focusing the blast firing again and again as she strode forward, firing wildly. She wasn't the best shot, and the frame easily dodged out of the way, the same sinister laugh Cora had heard in her mind now coming from the frame.

Fine. Cora changed tactics, instead firing at the side of the boulder—something that couldn't dodge her shots, blowing chunks of it away, debris pelting the frame. It only took four blasts before a one-meter-thick segment broke free and crashed to the ground, obscuring the frame in a cloud of dust.

Praying to whatever cared for this forsaken planet, she turned and ran, leaping across the terrain toward the ship, desperate to get out of range of the frame and the entity that waited below the planet's surface.

Panic threatened to set in, but Cora willed it out of her mind, focusing instead on the steps she'd take as soon as she reached the *Emily.*

Close the outer airlock. Engage the manual seal.
Get to the systems closet. Yank the wireless modules.
Cockpit. Engine warmup. Liftoff.

Somewhere in there, she would have to secure Violet's core and she visualized strapping it into the cockpit's second seat.

Good enough.

It took what seemed like an hour to reach the ship, though the time showing on her HUD indicated it had only taken ten minutes.

The ship waited, silent and unmoving, its white hull gleaming in the fading light of Zeta Leporis as the blue-white star began to slip below the horizon. The airlock was closed, and Cora slammed her hand against the access panel, only to have the mechanism flash red followed by a message appearing on the small screen.

Not so fast. You haven't been playing nice at all.

Fear and despair threatened to take over Cora's mind, but she again forced them down, thinking through things rationally.

The frame was nowhere to be seen behind her, which hopefully meant that it was damaged and out of commission. If that was the case, then the entity was connecting to the ship from inside it's hole. The signal *had* to be highly attenuated.

She glanced up at the *Emily*'s dorsal arch where the high-gain antenna lay folded against the ship's hull. That was how the entity was maintaining a connection. It had to be.

Cora jogged back a few steps and then took a running leap, sailing several meters into the air thanks to the planet's low gravity. She landed on the hull near the antenna and activated her maglock boots just as the ship's point-defense beams came online.

They were designed for obliterating small asteroids that got too close to the vessel, but they'd do just as well when it came to cutting a human apart.

She flattened herself on the hull, hoping she was low enough that the beams couldn't hit her, while she wrestled with the cable that connected to the antenna. The snap of lasers firing in atmosphere came from all around, and her hands began to tremble as she fought with the connection socket.

At first she thought it was from the adrenaline, but then a warning in the corner of her vision lit up, alerting her to the oxygen level on the one tank she still wore.

It was at zero.

Fuck! How did I miss that?

Frustration and fear finally winning, she grabbed her pulse pistol and fired twice, mangling the cable enough that she could rip it apart.

The beams didn't stop, but they did switch to an automatic search pattern. Cora was still pinned her down, but the change at least it suggested that the entity wasn't in direct control of the ship anymore.

With a deft flick of her wrist, Cora pulled out a comm cable and attached it to a port next to where the antenna cable connected to the ship.

In an instant her connection to the *Emily* was back, warnings filling her HUD, the ship convinced it was at risk of imminent asteroid collision from every direction.

She sent a command to reset all systems, holding her breath for the three seconds it took to hard-reset the core systems. The beams powered down. When they did, she released her maglock and slid down the hull, once again palming the airlock panel.

This time it responded by irising open the door, and if her suit hadn't been sealed to her face, she would have sobbed with relief. She scooped up Violet's core, not even remembering dropping it, and staggered inside the ship, hitting the emergency cycle button before falling to the deck.

C'mon, Cora whispered in the confines of her mind as the edges of her vision began to dim.

A moment later, her suit unsealed from her face, and Cora drew in a ragged breath, lungs heaving as they struggled to reoxygenate her blood stream.

Mind still suffused in a foggy malaise, she pushed her self to her knees, and then sat back on her heels, desperate gasping finally subsiding to mere panicked panting as she remembered her training, forcing herself to take deep, slow breaths.

The shattered remains of her fishbowl helmet were still on her head and she lifted it free, tossing it into a corner before rising to her feet, one arm on the bulkhead to keep from falling over.

For a moment, she wondered if everything that had just happened was the result of an oxygen-starved hallucination, but then she saw the readout on the airlock's interior screen.

"Full System Reset Complete."

"At least the part where I reset the ship happened," she thought while staggering out of the airlock into the *Emily*'s main passage. Her steps grew more sure as she approached the cockpit, eager to ease into her seat and get off the planet and out of the Zeta Leporis system.

Cora raced through the preflight checks, ignoring a few errors in primary systems and failing over to backups.

"It can all be fixed in space," she whispered. "As soon as I'm out of range of that signal."

A minute later, the engines roared to life, and she eased the *Emily* off the surface, using manual controls rather than taking the time to program in a flight path.

No sooner had she risen a few meters than Violet's voice came over the cockpit's audible systems.

"It's still in me …"

The four words contained a type of pain and anguish Cora had never heard come from an AI and her mind reeled at the implications. Then it came to her. AI cores had their own small wireless transceivers. A quick check of the instrumentation showed that the signal level from the sphere had boosted several orders of magnitude, the entity likely expending the last of its energy in a final attempt to escape its prison.

"Don't worry," Cora said to her partner as she accessed one of the survey systems. "I'm going to fuck that thing over so hard it'll wish whatever made this crater killed it all those years ago."

She brought the ship higher in the air, setting the altitude at a kilometer, then activated a seismic charge, marking on the survey map exactly where to drop it.

Into the hole they'd cut in the sphere.

Violet had begun to make a strange keening sound and Cora quickly rechecked her calculations, worried that her friend's mind was being stripped away while she got the ship into position over the hole.

The projected impact zone was larger than the opening, but she didn't have time to refine the targeting and mashed her finger against the "deploy" button just as Violet's voice died away to be replaced by the entity's.

"I'm in!" it crowed in triumph.

Cora ignored it, gaze focused on the downward view, tracking the seismic charge's fall.

"So am I!" she shouted as the cone of uncertainty on the display shrank to the size of the hole the mining laser had cut. "Get fucked."

A brilliant light flared below the ship, rock and metal blasting out of the ground in a blazing explosion that threw debris hundreds of meters into the air.

The signal was gone, its regular pattern replaced by the static of the blast, and Cora sagged into her seat, tears of relief and joy streaming down her face. "I think I suck at first contact."

No reply came from the overhead systems, and she turned to Violet's core, which was dark.

"No …" Cora whispered in dismay as she realized just how bad her friend must have been damaged. There was no way she could safely reconnect the AI to the ship, given what it had been through at the hands of the entity.

Saving Violet was beyond her ability.

She rose on shaky legs and lifted her partner's core from the seat, cradling it gently as she walked back to the engineering bay where two stasis pods lay. One was sized for a human, while the other was much smaller, designed to isolate and protect an AI core during the decades-long journeys the ship undertook.

Violet had never used it, hating the idea of being shut down for any amount of time, but this time there was no choice in the matter. Cora wouldn't let the AI remain trapped alone in its mind.

She secured Violet in the small pod and gently sealed it before triggering the isolation and shutdown protocols, hoping they'd activate properly and effectively freeze time for the AI.

"It's for the best," she whispered. "We have a long trip ahead of us. A century at least."

Cora returned to the cockpit where the ship had been continuing its ascent through the planet's atmosphere, the black arch of space now filling the forward view.

Her hands danced over the controls, performing a full systems check on the *Emily* to ensure the entity hadn't breached any of its systems, before plotting a course that would start the ship on its long journey.

She almost asked Violet to check her work before remembering that she was alone, the only sentient being for seven light-years in any direction—or so she hoped. Instead, she passed her work to the navigation system for validation, receiving confirmation a few moments later.

"You'd call me crazy for this," she whispered as she initiated the first burn. "But I don't trust anyone in the Seventh Fleet to fix you. No. We're going home. We're going to the Second Fleet."

To her father. The only one she trusted with both Violet's life and knowledge of the alien entity.

Don't let me down, Dad.

ARE WE HUMAN?
A STORY
BRIANNA ELISE

WELCOME HUMANS to a concept we may not choose to be our own. We made it this far, now the real fun begins ... multidimensional communication. The problem with humans' ability to communicate in multidimensional ways of being is that we have been conditioned to a three-dimensional reality of existence. I think it is possible for humans to connect to four-dimensional reality, or at the very least, communicate in four dimensions.

I tried for three years to show a person the unconditional truths of our world and I failed. I am sorry to the human I wish to name here. I have learnt how hard it is for humans to be unconditional in our being. This environment shadows the true potential of human communication. Herein lies the barrier and the solution. Neurodiversity. I wonder, am I neurodivergent? What does this mean? My understanding of neurodivergence is the thought that we all exist on a scale of observation, inclusive of all humans where our neurodivergence is evident in our behavior of being. This behavior can be measured on a scale of sociability, where we group ourselves into categories of conditions that help us communicate within an experience. To be unconditional is to be able to incorporate all concepts of others into our own, including those concepts that may not be our own and inclusive of *the alien world*.

To be at an advantage in dealing with aliens would mean that our condition has some sort of means of survival more powerful than that of an alien. We are bound by the observations we see, hear, and feel in our reality. Everything that we know to be untrue in our beliefs is hidden from view, put in a box, held by the Schrödinger equation.*

So how do we open the box without killing the cat? This is the question that plagues our being in welcoming us to the greater depths of our universe, *the alien world*.

Fortunately, time has given us an endpoint to open the box. Sometime in 2040 we will find out if we are dead or alive. Thanks to the human I wish to name here, who has set the date. The box was opened by his colleague in 2019, curiosity got the better of him. The human I wish to name here expressed a thought that I may have been let down when the box was opened by his colleague. On the contrary. I feel empowered, liberated, and awake.

I experienced something that changes the game. I ask myself, what sort of advantage can we create to allow ourselves to open the box at a time when the cat is living? *The alien world* has the knowledge to be in the box, to be out of the box, to be unconditional. Is the advantage a symbiosis of aliens? And if so, is this something that is already occurring, where *the alien world* is playing the game with the humans and all our parts, viruses, bacteria, water, metal, when the box was opened in 2019?

I guess the question could be, are you symbiotic with an alien? I predict that less than 1% of humans say yes. I am sorry for the 99.99999% of humans who choose to use this knowledge to destroy themselves. I love you and I am sorry for the choices we have made. Just because it has already happened doesn't mean we need to experience it. I wish us all the best in 2027.

In less than 1% of realities, humans live in a reality where dimensional existence is possible. In the other 99.99999999999%, cellular transversal actuality is destroyed by atomic detestation. Humans who

---

* Schrödinger, E. (1926). "An undulatory theory of the mechanics of atoms and molecules." *Physical Review*, 28(6), 1049–70. Retrieved from https://journals.aps.org/pr/abstract/10.1103/PhysRev.28.1049 . Accessed 12/15/2023.

survive this worldly transition but remain in this world die off by 2060. Einstein made the bomb, but it took one person in America to make a choice to throw it at itself, and now we get to enjoy Mario and Luigi racing.

A HINT OF COLOR
A STORY
JODY LYNN NYE

Content note: *character injury*

EVERYONE WAS OVERWHELMED by Gliese 42-C. The sensations immersing Lana Park were just a little different than those immersing the other five crew in the landing party. They didn't see everything she did.

First Officer Tomita Clay led the party of six specialists down the ramp from the airlock of the *TGC Beagle* into knee-high verdure of summery rainbow colors. They bounded just a bit in their transparent protective suits, as the gravity was only seventy-five percent of Earth's, and hence, the ship's interior.

Lana's compact, curvy body glowed deep blue-green with pleasure. She heard her muscles sing with joy at the freedom of movement she experienced of walking on a new world. Four of the others also bore the same color as hers, which produced a harmony of music in her mind. The other two were a shade of brick red, emitting low, cautious notes. But then, Lt. Steve Schilder never saw a situation he didn't find suspicious, and Tomi had a lot to prove to Captain Felder by leading the away team. Lana wanted to reach out to Tomi and reassure her, but the deep color of the tall woman's aura told her to stay back. Success would calm her. Lana promised herself not to add to the first officer's troubles. She could give her a comforting hug later on if Tomi needed it.

It wasn't that she was reading Tomi's mind. The nature of Lana's neurodivergence included a hypersensitivity to microexpressions and body language that manifested itself in color, sound, smell, or taste. She had been developing a sort of glossary that seemed to be consistent through most living beings in how emotions manifested themselves. Her powers of observation also picked up similar nearly imperceptible clues in the environment and translated them into impressions she could express to others. It had proven to be a useful trait, giving her the opportunity to serve on a number of interesting missions.

"So rich in flora!" Specialist Athena Praxos declared, recording the landscape with her datascoop's wide lens. She was the youngest of the crew, barely six months out of the academy, but a promising newcomer. "I can't wait to see the fauna. The probes only caught small shadows, less than a meter in length. I hope we spot some of them soon."

"You won't find much," Geologist Danver Lee said, his long legs carrying him out ahead of the others. He sounded gloomy, but Lana knew he was nearly out of his mind with excitement. "It's the only reason why Galactic Central allowed this planet to be considered for a colony. They've never found a sentient species smaller than that. Even the Gromlians are a meter and a third."

"I'm glad to be able to catalog anything new," Athena said, and her heart-shaped face turned light plum with smug satisfaction. "I have permission to use data once it's cleared for my doctoral dissertation. And maybe we'll prove them wrong. This is too awesome a world to be completely uninhabited."

"I do wish we were able to take off our helmets," Medic Arden Ukolke said. "The air is definitely breathable for humans. I'm detecting esters that will smell beautiful to us, but not until we've checked out possible sources of pathogens."

"Definitely not," Tomi replied. She didn't say any more, but Lana knew from the spreading blue-brown stain in the middle of her chest, probably from flinching, that Tomi was thinking of the first mission she had led, on Proxima 6, more than two years before. Lana had been the botanist on that mission, and had seen the tragic errors made, and how they had affected Tomi.

Lana's neurodivergent ability made interacting with her fellow crew members odd at times. Once in a while, others accused her of being psychic because of her uncanny perception of their moods, but it seldom interfered with her job, and she was very good at her job. At least thirty new species of plants had her name in their official description, and one creeping orchid-lily from Simmons Planet was called *Lilium orchidae Lana* after her. She loved flowers, and sometimes felt as though they loved her back. In any case, she received pleasure from their shapes, colors, and sounds.

The tall, yellow-stemmed reeds here suggested a water source close by. Lana closed her eyes and felt outward for the sense of water. In her upper palate and cheekbones, she experienced a pale blue rushing movement. Yes, water was there, moving slightly, warm to the touch; so, a brook or a wash. After breathable atmosphere, nothing was more important to a colony than potable or easily purified water. In a few more steps, she and the others felt pink squishiness underfoot, a sure sign that this was marshland. The water pooled on top of a thick mat of fallen, withered leaves and stems. It looked clear. Lana thought it felt clean enough to drink safely, though confirming that was Danver's job.

"Go slow," Tomi ordered them. She looked at her scope. "This looks shallow to me, but that doesn't mean we won't encounter deep mud within a few steps."

They edged forward, pushing the reeds gently aside, heading for a slope a few hundred meters ahead. According to the topographical survey, they should see a tremendous vista from the top of the hill. Lana noticed that the plants they touched shifted slightly in color. It wasn't an effect of her synesthesia, but actual flushing. Fascinating! She recorded the phenomenon with her scope. It also noted several unique esters they emitted into the atmosphere. Most of them were benign to humans. Only one had the potential to cause inflammation or irritation. She sent the findings to Arden to incorporate into her database.

Ahead, a slight movement caught her eye. Was it the wind kicking up? Gliese 42-C had one large, close moon that influenced its tides. No

—she saw it, or rather the impression it left in its wake. It was an animal. A spring-green snakelike shadow limned on the air around it. By her scope's readings, that meant that it had a high body temperature. The trace grew lighter as it cooled, but the body that cast the glow moved at an amazing rate of speed. She tracked it, looking for the freshest color. It angled out from behind one of the gigantic fernlike growths.

She pointed. "Athena, look!"

The xenobiologist turned her head just in time to see the long, slim, brown-pelted beast undulating on multiple legs before it disappeared again behind another stand of ferns. Its alarmed orange aura produced a cedar scent in Lana's olfactory center.

"I've got to record it!" Athena cried. From her shoulder pouch, she took a blue plastic drone unit and heaved it upward into the air. It spread out four vanes, each topped with a propeller that began spinning. Athena touched a control on her scope, and the drone whirred off after the creature.

It traveled about two hundred meters, nearly reaching the line of ferns before it started jerking from side to side. Then, one of the propellers popped off, and the whole unit spiraled down, disappearing in between the spreading plants.

"Frack! I checked that drone over just before we left the ship!" Athena set off running, threshing down the grasses and sending rainbow gouts of water into the air with every step.

The irritation coloring Tomi hardened to deep brick red, and she smelled like a limestone wall.

"Come back here, Praxos!" she shouted.

The first officer wasn't the only one who got angry. The biologist's elephantine antics caused the crushed plants in her wake to turn rusty brown and smell of freshly poured concrete, too. Lana scoffed at her own imagination. Angry plants, indeed.

The first officer toggled the radio stud on her helmet collar.

"Praxos, get back here!"

"Sorry, Commander," Athena's voice came through the audio pickup in all their helmets. "I found my drone. Ooh! First sighting! Hey, cool! This little creature's not alone! There must be ... hundreds of them ... Oh! Aagh!"

"Praxos? Praxos?" Tomi's tone turned from anger to alarm, and her shading became bright yellow. The group looked at one another. The first officer looked at her scope. "Two hundred fifty meters from here, north-northwest. Draw your sidearms, set on stun. Move!"

"Her vitals are elevated," Arden said, reading her scope as they strode forward. "Her heart rate is almost one-fifty. Something spiked her adrenaline. It just dropped to thirty. Breathing is distressed, and I'm getting a circulation alert."

"Praxos, answer me!" the first officer shouted. Her aura had brightened until it reached a hot gold that was painful for Lana to look at. Tomi was terrified, picturing Proxima 6 all over again. The sensation affected Lana, too. Instead of being able to reach out to Athena, she was overwhelmed by the cloud of emotion from Tomi.

This was an instance when her neurodivergence was a liability. Lana was distracted by her superior's distress. So she lifted her scope right in front of her eyes, and set the brightness to maximum, concentrating hard on the screen. The topographical map distracted her from the golden haze she knew was still there around Tomi.

No one else was impaired, because they couldn't see what she did. Other colors flooded into her vision from the scope: lots of green from other creatures who were unconcerned about the passing humans, cautious brown from small reptiloids and insectoids that skittered out of the way, and a brilliant orange that matched the plumage of an avian that burst from the thick plant life.

They found Specialist Praxos face down on a bed of reeds that looked as they had exploded from within. Her suit had been pierced in dozens of places. Her aura was gray over each puncture, and blood dotted her skin. Security Officer Steve Schilder took up a defensive posture over her, his eyes flicking around. Medic Arden knelt down beside her and gently turned her over.

"What happened to her?" Tomi demanded, crouching beside her. "Is she alive?"

Lana felt deep sympathy for the first officer. In Tomi's eyes, this was Proxima 6 all over again. Under her command there, the team had become complacent too soon, and a swarm of previously undetected tiny insectoids smaller than gnats flew into the noses, ears, and mouths of most of the party. The contact caused immediate severe inflammation in mucoid membranes and nerve tissue. One crew member had died, and two had suffered irreversible neurological damage. Lana hadn't been able to stand listening to or smelling the pain that radiated hot orange starbursts from their heads. She knew Tomi felt guilty about it every day. She prayed that Athena would be all right.

Arden ran her medical scope up and down Athena's body. "She is. But she's profoundly unconscious. Her brain's exhibiting delta waves."

"What caused those punctures?"

"They look like tooth marks! But there's no saliva or other digestive juices smeared on her suit."

"They look like thorn punctures to me," Lana said.

"Thorns! From where?"

Lana pointed to the crushed plants underneath Athena. "Let me examine those. Some Terran flora have a structure that launches protective missiles when disturbed. They might have defense mechanisms like that."

She set the scope on maximum magnification and pulled one of the dead reeds underneath the scanner. Through a haze of gray much like the puncture wounds on Athena's body, Lana saw long narrow capsules among the shredded fibers, and striations showing that something had been violently wrenched from them—or perhaps launched. A dot here and there of a clear, sticky substance like a resin still clung to the empty shells.

"I will have to examine these more closely in the lab," she said, "but it seems like the plants shot some kind of semisolid stickers into her. They dissolved on contact, and the chemicals were injected into her body the way Terran wasps sting."

"Will she live?" Tomi asked, the haze of golden worry thickening around all of them again. Lana fought hard to ignore it. She didn't want it to trigger a migraine, which threatened at her right temple.

"I think so," Arden said. "I hope so. I'm more concerned about what caused the barrage. It didn't just come from the plants she passed, or the ones she ran into. Those stings came from all sides, like a mass attack."

Lana's perception of the others' concern faded as she started to examine the reeds that were still standing, ahead of where Athena would have run if she had continued on her path. They were like the water plants in the valley near the landing site, a medium gold with a green tinge, but slightly smaller. However, when Lana touched them, they shifted to brick red, and a cloud of cautious brown enveloped them, accompanied by the sound in her mind that she perceived when humans manifested that color. She dropped her hand and backed away. Their action was deliberate, not just a photoresponse. Curious.

"They're ... angry," Lana said. "They don't like to be touched."

"C'mon, Lana," Steve said, with a chuckle. "They're plants."

"There are touch-sensitive plants on Earth," Tomi said. "My uncle has a windowsill full of Venus fly traps."

"No, I mean they're giving off vibes of annoyance," Lana said. "At least, that's how I'm perceiving it. Just getting near them triggers it." She shifted away from the cluster of reeds she was examining. To her surprise, their stems faded, and they emitted to her eyes an aura of silent, watchful, periwinkle blue. "Now they're curious about us." She moved her hand closer, and the cautious, noisy brown returned. Withdrawn. Periwinkle. "They're studying us."

"Nonsense," Steve said, his square face a skeptical mask. "Who ever heard of intelligent plants?" He studied her. "You really believe that?"

"It's possible," Lana said. "We certainly don't know every kind of life-form that exists in the universe. We may have had our first encounter with a new one! I'm not saying they have a complex civilization, but they show signs of intelligence."

Tomi shook her head. "The Xeno team assured us there was no sentient life on this planet. We *need* this colony. It's the only G-type world we can use for jumps between here and the Gemini cluster."

"Bah," Steve said, dismissively. "All we need to do is carpet-bomb this planet with herbicide, and we have an empty planet." His skin glowed with the red of frustration and fury.

His anger had an effect on the shorter reeds, but not the tall ones or the ferns. They darkened again and echoed his anger back to him. Steve, with no sensitivity whatsoever, didn't see it, but Tomi noticed Lana's alarm.

"What? Are you all right?"

"The sentient ones are picking up on his mood," Lana said, lowering her voice. "Lieutenant, calm down. Please. Dampen it. We could all be in danger if you don't."

"Uhhhh."

The noise made them all turn around. Athena, her head in Arden's lap, looked up at them. Her lips and tongue were almost bloodless, but she was awake and aware. Arden had attached small adhesive patches over each of the holes pierced through the biologist's environment suit. She'd have to undergo full decontamination in isolation back in the ship, but she was no longer being exposed.

"What do you remember, Praxos?" Tomi asked, golden with concern. Athena wore a wreath of green confusion. The odor of mothballs that she associated with bemusement made Lana's eyes water.

"I ... I got to my drone. I wanted to get the camera so I could video those little brown animals. There were hundreds of them! But when I aimed the camera and started to run after them, I felt a thousand darts strike me. Then, nothing. Until now."

"What does that mean?" Danver asked.

"It means that the plants saw you mount a potential attack on the wildlife, and they defended," Lana said.

"You're making that up!" Steve exclaimed. "Why would plants even care what those animals did?"

Lana held up her hands. "Well, how else could you explain that behavior? They didn't attack her when she passed through them, even though anyone could see that they were annoyed by her smashing them down. It was only when she picked up the camera that they attacked. That means that your plasma rifle could be perceived as a threat, too."

"She's not wrong," Athena said. Her voice was weak, but she seemed to be tracking just fine. "Even insects can make a judgment on whether something is a threat or not. The fact that they might have been protecting the critters from me puts them on a higher level than hive minds like ants or wasps. They communicate, and they are concerned for their fellow beings. To them, those weasel creatures might be valuable, oh, for a dozen reasons. Maybe because their droppings enrich the soil the reeds grow in, or they eat weeds that interfere with absorption of water or block sunlight. We have to observe them to find out! It's probably better if you put the gun away, Steve. I feel awful, but it could easily have been worse."

But the security officer hoisted his rifle and scanned the scenery through his eyepiece. "Which ones are the hostiles, and which ones aren't, Lana?"

Lana saw the red rising in the field around them, from the tiny movements the plants made, and it raised her own tension. "They're all upset right now! The angriest are the short reeds, the ones between a meter and a meter and a half tall. Those show the most signs of discerning our actions. They really don't like your gun."

The patch of plants nearer the line of giant ferns rustled, and Steve spun, his barrel pointed toward the center of the noise. The rustling became louder.

"Holster your weapon," Tomi said, rising to her feet. Her fear had dampened, and her curiosity was rising in a healthy shade of periwinkle. "That's an order, Lieutenant. They could needle us all!"

The security officer glowed cobalt blue with skepticism, but he obeyed. Athena waved her arms.

"Help me up," she said. "Show them you care about me."

Lana and Danver bent to help the smaller woman to stand. Athena took a few deep breaths and nodded. Arden hovered, scanning her again.

"Yes, that's good," Lana said, studying the plants. The brick red faded, and the whole slope glowed with light purple-blue. They showed the same curiosity as the humans. She felt like dancing at the astonishing discovery. To think that so many sensations and emotions produced the same auras, no matter what the species! "Athena, how do you demonstrate to sentient animals that we are also intelligent?"

The biologist tilted her head. "Well, we use stones to do basic mathematics. We introduce ourselves, and give Galactic Standard words for objects, and try to point out similarities where any exist between our two species, like noses, or hands, or children. But I'm not sure how to get through to plants that barely move."

Lana smiled. "I think you'll have to rely on me for now," she said. "I've yet to figure out if they can see our auras or not, or if they are sensation-blind like most humans, but they do react in a way I can see. We might have to communicate with color or proximity."

Tomi chuckled. "It's a good thing we have you with us, then. Otherwise, we'd never have met the locals."

Danver looked annoyed. "But practically all of this planet is covered with plant life. Is any of it safe for us to cut down or move? What about a dedicated landing strip? Or buildings? Or a sewage system? We'll need all that to make this a way station."

"The polar ice caps," Tomi said. "Nothing grows there, so we won't be damaging the greater ecosystem, not with how seldom a craft would be landing here. Or have a floating station on one of the two major oceans. Do you think that will upset the local growth?"

"We'll have to ask them," Lana said. "I can make up a chart of the colors they give off when they exhibit basic emotions. I want that recommendation to go back to Galactic Central. And it shouldn't be too hard to have another perceptive assigned here. Either we learn to live with the resident species, or we'll have to abandon this planet and find another one."

"You don't get to make that determination," Steve said, his face and aura turning red. "Now that we know what kind of threat these ... these creatures pose, we can dispose of them and take what we want."

"Belay that talk about herbicides, Schilder!" Tomi barked out.

"Don't even start to think that way, Steve," Lana said. She knew she was glowing red in annoyance. She dampened down her emotions when she saw the reeds near her starting to change color, too. It looked like they *could* read microexpressions. "There aren't that many intelligent life forms in the galaxy. They are the dominant species *here*. We have to let the plants decide for themselves. The bare minimum we can do is prove to them that we're at least as smart as they are."

"I'm not sure what I think about judgy plants," Arden said, but she was grinning.

Tomi holstered her sidearm. She held her hands out in a gesture meant to show no harm.

"It's been decided, then," she said. "Lana can prove to Galactic Central that the planet is not uninhabited. We'll have to learn to live with our fellow sentients if we want to stay here. I refuse to be responsible for the genocide of a heretofore undiscovered species." For a moment, the memory of Proxima 6 showed on her face, coloring it brick red, but the periwinkle reasserted itself. "I'm interested in learning more about them. I hope we can let them know that we mean them no harm."

Lana sensed an aroma coming from the reeds around them. Now that the humans were behaving themselves in a calm and nonthreatening manner, she smelled a delicate woodsy fragrance, the scent she associated with peace, and saw pale, dusty green everywhere she looked.

"At this point, it'll be a job for the diplomats," she said. "I hope we can find some that don't have hay fever."

BE YOUR OWN UNIVERSE
A STORY
KAY ALEXANDER

THE NAVIGATOR IS the first to notice.

His shouting and frantic gesturing startles you, making you drop your mop. On the other side of the triple-paned starship windows, a churning iridescent mist, coral and amethyst flecked with indigo, streaks in front of the ship's path. Before the captain can issue an order, it makes impact.

There is no sound, no mechanical shudder, no visual phenomenon apart from a flickering of the lights. Your crewmates exchange bewildered glances laced with terror as the ship passes through the mist. Or rather, as the mist passes through the ship. You feel it roll through your body like a wave, a deep cosmic breath.

Your crewmates shake their heads and return to their duties. Someone picks up the mop and hands it to you. It is then that you realize that your experience was entirely unlike theirs.

The mist is still with you. You can feel it undulating within your chest like a second heartbeat. Your body feels distant, like it has been severed from your mind. The inner lining on your uniform doesn't scratch as much. The artificial lighting hurts your eyes less. You suppose you ought to feel frightened, but instead, you are filled with overwhelming relief.

You stare at the mop, motionless. Your crewmate questions you. You bury your face in your hands and begin to weep.

You are not alone.

The presence keeps you company while you perform your routine cleaning duties, safely tucked away within your core. They have no language; they transfer their knowledge and memories to you via some scientific process you do not understand. They show you infinite galaxies of stars and dust. Worlds of impossible beauty, teeming with life, too distant to ever reach.

You show them your world in return, exploited and mutilated. You reveal your mission, a desperate attempt to uncover something that could allow humanity to heal their broken kingdom. You are filled with an all-consuming sadness that you aren't sure is entirely your own.

You try to tell your crewmates about your companion, but finding the right words proves an unsurmountable challenge and language has never flowed effortlessly from your lips. How do you describe that which has consciousness but no voice or vessel? They are a presence. An idea.

Your crewmates listen as you speak in halting, muddled fragments while anxiously tugging on your fingers. They escort you to the infirmary.

After too much prying and prodding, you retreat to the sickbay lavatory. You lock the door and press your face into the cool metal, breathing deeply. Once you feel more collected, you examine your reflection in the mirror. You are dark circles and unkempt hair. Maybe they are right. Perhaps the loneliness of the void has gotten to you.

A light flickers across your pupils. You lean in closer; a swirling mass of color lurks there.

You smile.

Again, you urge.

They take you.

Your eyes instantly fill with visions of a devastating cosmic kaleidoscope. An intense vibration pulses through your body, overwhelming your senses. You start to rise up out of your body. The connection has been severed.

The vision shifts. You see a world teeming with life. Your world. It is wonderful enough to make you cry, but you can only groan as the pulse of the universe intensifies. There is ancient knowledge hidden within this realm. A restorative secret. You must find it. You are so close.

You cry out and are violently thrust back inside your body. Gasping for air on top of your bed, you briefly see your celestial companion hovering overhead before they collapse back into you as well.

You and them are the same; you understand this now. Two galaxy-traversing wanderers born out of scattered atoms, compelled by an innate need to be seen and understood beyond the limitations of corporeality and language. You have gazed into the abyss and found yourself peering back.

You steady your breath. Each time, you separate a little more. You get a little closer.

Again.

You spend hours gazing out of the starship's portholes. Time weighs heavily on you. The starship's reserves are not infinite and the crew must eventually return.

You have not yet uncovered the answers that you seek. You have never been fully comfortable in your skin, but now you feel trapped by the constraints of meat and calcium. It is difficult not to envy your partner's ability to exist outside of physical boundaries.

You confess these feelings one evening, your mop long forgotten. They respond by presenting you with a reflected image of your current form. You show them your perception of them, formless and perfect.

A translucent coral mist lifts from your hand. It drifts toward your face and caresses your cheek, asking you a question. You sigh and lean into the fluttering touch. You would entrust them with your whole existence.

The mist travels upward, accumulating around your head, and then plunges into your eye sockets. Your vision darkens. Your blood rushes through your ears and your uniform slips off your shoulders. You gasp once and then stop breathing altogether. Everything grows quiet.

Your sight returns differently from before. Two of your crewmates are standing over your prone body. You view them and yourself from every angle at once, including ones you weren't aware existed. They repeat your name. When you return their gaze, they recoil.

You raise your hand. It flickers like a mirage, dissolving into a mist of chartreuse and azure before reappearing at the desired location.

Your crewmates tremble. You reach out toward the nearest one. Your arm fragments into mist, your finger penetrating their forehead without resistance. They instantly calm. Once you have reassured the other as well, you rise.

You look about with eyes dark with cosmic knowledge. Your mind swims with infinite possibilities. There is time yet to save a dying world.

Your beloved remains nearby. You feel their pleasure as though it were your own. You will never be able to repay them, but perhaps your gratitude is enough.

You head toward the bridge, your crewmates following closely. There is much to do, and you have only just begun.

Look by Barbara Candiotti

NAVIGATIONAL AID
A STORY
HOLLY SCHOFIELD

Content note: *depiction of death*

AT FIRST, I don't think much as I drift inside my kilometer-wide cocoon. My spacesuit keeps me warm. The mangled hull segments, equipment, and corpses that float past help maintain my grip on reality, and the humbling display of stars is blocked from view by the opalescent hollow sphere that surrounds me.

Eventually, I become self-analytical enough to realize I'm in shock and that pulls me out of it a little. I close my eyes and try to meditate. When my suit tells me my biometric readings are calm and stable, I take stock. I use my faceplate controls to zoom in on the others, ignoring my rapid pulse when, in the hazy distance, I see Alexi's suit number on a limbless torso. I make a mental map of the solar system and draw a red dotted line from Earth to where I—Dr. Sandra Chang-Saunders, Senior Astrophysicist—now orbit Neptune along with our ship and the remains of the crew. Mission Control does not know that I am the sole survivor. There cannot be a rescue attempt for at least six months and it would take two years to get here, if they even try.

NAVIGATIONAL AID

On my map, I draw myself as a stick figure and make tiny red x's to represent my dead colleagues. Then I draw a white circle around us all for the enormous milky cloud that enfolds us.

I realize I am angry and let out a bellow. My biometric indicators flash red. They are attuned to "normal" responses, of course, so I ignore them. I have never held back my emotions even though I've been told over and over how it annoys people. Why should I spend energy constraining myself when people carelessly annoy me so often, with their cryptic words and gestures and societal protocols? Daily life in our neurotypically slanted society is energy-draining enough.

I yell until I am hoarse, knowing it's what I need. After a while my meaningless shouts change to angry words aimed at the distant scrap of uniform that is all that remains of Captain Watford. "This didn't have to happen! Alexi pointed out the design flaw in the cooling system just after liftoff, for shit's sake! You ignored him, Watford! And *I* told you *repeatedly*, until you ordered me not to message you anymore. *And* the ship's readouts confirmed the overheating just before the explosion but by then it was too late!"

I run out of breath and stop. Then, more calmly: "You ignored Alexi's attempts to tell you, not because he was junior engineer, but because he wasn't polite enough in how he phrased it, and because you didn't trust him. You didn't trust him because you knew he was—"

I break off.

"... somewhat like me," I finish in a whisper. I curl into a fetal position as much as the bulky suit allows, like when the alarms clamored through the ship and everyone else ran to their stations. I had huddled in my bunk, knowing there was nothing anyone could do. My cabin was farthest from the engines, so by luck I survived. Whether that was good luck or bad luck, I am not sure.

I squeeze my eyes shut for a long time, floating.

Then something nudges my shoulder. I open my eyes to see Sergeant Grewal's boot centimeters from my face. I push it hard, and his corpse drifts off until it rams a piece of contorted bulkhead. I note that his body is perfectly preserved, globs of shiny blood clinging to where his head should be. He is not a frozen corpsicle, and—I stare through the slight haze in surprise—neither are the others. I punch my arm in frustration at my stupidity, and then apologize to myself for doing so. I should have been questioning my current environment. The pale fog that surrounds me inside this huge sphere is very thin, not exactly an atmosphere, but not pure vacuum either. I wish I had more sensing equipment. Where is my oxygen coming from? Why is my suit keeping me warm when the solar panels on my back and sleeves are inadequate this far from the sun, enclosed in this clouded hollow orb? I close my eyes again to concentrate.

Another nudge. I push it away blindly. It pushes at me again. I open my eyes. I have drifted near the edge of the vast shell I'm encased in. A finger of denser fog extends from the inner surface of the cocoon toward me like a ghost octopus's tentacle.

It takes four standard days for me to learn to communicate with the alien—for that's what this spherical creature must be.

At first, a few hand gestures, mainly phatic concepts. *I'm here. This is me.*

Then, after many days, with nothing to lose, I let the fog into my suit, seep over my skin, caress my brain. I sense curiosity and interest and perhaps gentleness, although I know that I can never read people and this may be no different. I close off again, wasting two hours recalling the bullying I experienced navigating high school.

Eventually, recalling the alien's gentleness, I start to hope that this alien is different, and that my read of them is genuine. I go against my nature and open myself again to this new experience, allowing soft sensations to completely envelop me.

I spell the alien words phonetically as they sift into my head.

Yaagh. Hello.

I tongue a switch in my helmet to activate my suit's external speakers. My voice booms out into the vastness. *Yaaaaagh.* Helllooo.

I am not good at learning languages. I didn't talk until I was four years old. Neurotypicals don't make it easy—they never say what they mean and expect me to interpolate from their hints. They don't speak in an orderly, organized fashion and I either lose focus as they talk or I tune them out in frustration. I studied Spanish and German and Mandarin in college, hoping English was an isolated case, and then spiraled into depression for a while when I found no discernable difference in depth of communication.

At first, I am not much better at learning this alien language. The days pass slowly. Somehow, the contents of my suit's waste receptacles vanish while I sleep, and my nutrient and water pouches are replenished. The alien takes care of me, nurturing me like I am an egg within a womb.

After we move from exchanging concrete nouns of nearby objects—*craaavnish* is a hand, whether attached to a corpse or not—we start on abstracts. *Awyaagang cheelie.* The alien offers me pleasant warmth and an image of the battery pack on my suit shattering into pieces. I clutch my chest, panicky. Without heat, I will die in minutes. After my heart stills and I check that my suit temperature stayed steady, I realize the alien means no harm and is just conveying a concept.

Perhaps these new words mean "energy" in the sense of life or sentience. Or maybe a religious word about spirit or soul. Religion baffles me more than most neurotypical ideas, and people say I'm impolite whenever I try to discuss it, so I don't.

Over time, the alien comes back to *awyaagang cheelie* and I grow to understand it's just "solar" and "power." I stare at my suit controls watching the batteries keep their charge in the alien's calm omnipresent white light. The alien is logical and organized and smart, and word definitions are fixed and stable. I feel a grin spread over my face, and all of my suit's biometrics turn green.

I drift. Alone, but not lonely. Months pass.

I learn that the alien has travelled many *laag*, a unit of distance measurement so large I can't grasp the number of zeros it would be in lightyears, simply to explore and observe. *Claanjuudaayaan.* Curiosity.

Once, I wake up tense, heart thudding, after a nightmare of relentlessly loud banging noises. My ears ring in the sudden silence.

"I don't want to be here!" I yell. "I miss trees and sunshine and my lab!"

"How can I help?" asks the alien.

I ignore it and go limp in my suit. I don't eat or do my isometrics for three entire days.

Finally, I crawl back into my mind and sip nutrient broth. The alien has been silent, giving me space to approach again in my own way, in my own time. I am grateful for its understanding, so different than the crew members who constantly, gingerly, suggested therapies and treatments to make me behave like them.

"Hello! *Yaagh*!" I shout, awkwardly and too loud, like I am back on Earth. "The student is ready!"

Yaagh. The alien's thought is permeated with kindness.

"Teach me more," I sing out, giddy. "Teach me. Teach me." I chant over and over and spread my arms and legs wide, circling within my porcelain womb, wondering if I'm losing my mind.

"Where do we start?" it asks.

I ask the alien questions about itself. I discover it stopped its immensely long journey when it sensed the ship's explosion. I surprise myself and uncharacteristically enquire how that had felt, to see such carnage and to rescue only me.

A hard red light blinds me and a complex word blares. I shut down, going mute and blind. The alien apologizes. It has not realized how the replication of the horror it experienced at that moment would affect me. Warm comfort fills my head. *Waadhluu.* Peace. I feel better within an hour.

Later, it teaches me how to achieve that peace on my own, via a technique I decide to call "meta-meditation". The skill, unlike neurotypical-centered "fixes," does not try to reduce my sensitivities, nor does it give me "coping skills" for overstimulation—no, it helps expand my neurodivergency *toward* its full potential so I can embrace all kinds of inputs and sensations. A skill I could have used many times in my life. A skill that everyone could learn. Just think if we all could have enough internal calm to meet others halfway!

I tell the alien my life history, all the traumas and pain that didn't have to be if society didn't require me to conform, to completely bend who I am, to drag me across to their way of being. We cry together. The alien helps me see that most neurotypical folks have their own challenges, fears, and struggles to communicate. I had no idea. I have always known that my directness is considered rude and impedes communication, and that I had insufficient "spoons" to phrase things more politely. But I had not known doing so caused them pain. The alien holds me in warm mist as I cry again. The sorrow becomes part of me as does newfound compassion.

I learn that it is one of many. A talented species. It creates artwork that would render a human catatonic. But it knows no universal secrets, no perfect philosophies, no reason the universe exists. Its physics and chemistry will be incomprehensible to even our brightest scientists for generations.

After a while, I become hopeful that the alien will come to Earth and save humanity, will help usher us into a new era of love and understanding. If we were all to learn its subtle language, would we all become the best we are capable of?

Before I can formulate the question, the alien teaches me a new word: *Dhaalaay*. Goodbye. A sensation of a hug. Regret for what is not to be.

The white sphere dissolves and the gentle fog dissipates. Stars perch against a deep, velvet black. I am drifting in empty space. I twist, and a large space station fills my vision. The blue marble of Earth looms just beside it. The alien has brought me home.

I have not yet learned alien words to express what I now feel. English has only approximations: loss, unease, doubt, fear that everything will change, fear that nothing has changed.

I howl.

After a time, I reluctantly flick on my suit's short-range tracker. A tether line shoots from the station toward me. It bobs at my elbow, and I regard it for a moment. Then I clip it to my suit and let the crew haul me in. Strangers remove my helmet in the airlock and bring me to a cold, sterile medical lab. On the examination table, without the comfort of my suit, I feel tears form.

"It's incredible you're this healthy after two whole years," the medic says past their thin mustache. "I can't explain it at all." I can tell they're awed and humbled.

A Lieutenant Carver is speaking and I try to listen, to ignore the crackle of the examination table's paper sheet and the hum of the machines. "... and how did you get back? Where were you all this time? What did you see?"

"What did *you* see?" I ask, warily, needing to protect him from the enormity of my experience.

"Our readings were very blurry and erratic as we approached. Some kind of localized phenomenon." He shifts his feet.

Surprisingly, I find I am mentally acknowledging several of his emotions. Prior to my recent experience, I avoided trying to sense what others were feeling, and certainly didn't try to accommodate them. I couldn't afford to lose focus on trying to "heal" myself, as I perceived I needed to do. I never devoted my mental faculties and limited energy toward compassion for others. Why would I?

In a luminous wave of perception, I now realize that I, like everyone, have more emotional capacity than I realize. Once again, I am in awe of what the alien has revealed to me of human nature and its potential.

I put aside these revelations for the moment and focus on Lieutenant Carver. He is pleased I'm alive, he is curious why I survived, and he's also a little annoyed at the impossibility of my existence.

He rubs his neck and reads my chart on the screen. The medic examines every part of me, even between my toes. It takes everything I have not to flinch at the cold clinical touch. Finally, the lieutenant says, "Well, we'll have the station psychologist talk to you tomorrow but I guess you handled the isolation better than most. I mean, you *would*, given your ..."

"My what? My autism? It's okay to say the word, you know."

My gentle attempt to call out his ableism and normalize my neurodiversity is wasted. He flushes slightly, embarrassed, and glances at the medic for their reaction. The medic is too busy examining where my suit has chafed my neck.

English is cumbersome but I try again, careful to speak softly. "Only some autistic people like being alone and, even then, there's a difference between preferring to be by yourself for a week and being entirely isolated for two years but, yes, perhaps, for me, my autism was a slight advantage." I hope my words relieve his discomfort, his needless suffering. He probably expects eye contact, but I keep my head bent. I doubt it would add to our communication and it would definitely be a strain on me.

He frowns. "And, as per protocol, I'll be debriefing you as well."

"Short sessions would be best for me," I say, speaking as crisply as he has. It's an excuse he readily buys into—the presumption that he can judge my abilities as well as I can is strong in him, like most neurotypical authority figures. Although I know I'll be able to meet with him at length by tomorrow, I can see that I'll need to ease people gradually into all the new information I possess. That we are not alone in the universe must be presented gently and slowly, and the alien concepts and skill sets will take time to convey.

I note that, since boarding the station, I have juggled these people's needs with mine in such a way as to enhance both. A meeting point, halfway along the curve. I have achieved *raanatoo*, intelligent balanced compassion for both myself and for others. Perhaps, with this additional new ability, I can help all of humanity learn a way forward to a new level of emotional expression, while not paying the usual price that autistic people do. I am thrilled at this thought.

First, I need a quiet space, away from this overstimulation. The medic cocks their head at my sigh and I realize they are concerned for me. I pat their arm and say, "I'll be fine but I'm very tired. Is there a bunk I can use?"

They direct me to a vacant cabin and a narrow bunk with a crumpled sheet. I dig through storage lockers, douse the lights, and then cocoon myself in the three thin blankets I've found. In the quiet dark, I take stock. The alien is gone. I accept that, painful as it is. Instead, I focus on the future that stretches ahead for myself and humankind. I have the lovely neurodivergent ability to focus endlessly on a single task, and so I vow to apply the rest of my life to teaching intelligent balanced compassion to all humanity.

I'll start tomorrow, with the crew. The first small step is group language training. Only after we can truly communicate, will I be able to help the crew begin their long journeys toward *raanatoo*.

I smile to myself in the dark. When I make this training request to the psychologist, I will meet her halfway—by phrasing it politely but firmly.

HEART-SIDE SOMETIMES-TABLE
A STORY
MADELINE BARNICLE

I HADN'T HEARD from Kristen since our second semester of college, but three weeks after the vens landed, she texted me. *If they interview you, bring up Demonstrate. I think they like that kind of thing.*

Demonym, she added a minute later.

You know what I mean.

The conlang's name was Denemoki, actually, but I wasn't surprised that Kristen's autocorrect didn't know that. The only people we'd discussed Denemoki with had been each other.

But Kristen had lost interest after a few months. She told me it was because she was busy with class. Of course, in college, everyone was busy with class. Homework always loomed, expanding or contracting like an ideal gas in chemistry depending on how many other things we had to keep busy with. It wasn't until later that I wondered if it could have been Polite Liar dialect for "if I have time to do this, I have time to do things that will solve Real Problems in the world, or at least look better on my resume."

The vens hadn't even been here a month, and already, people were —not *used* to them, exactly, but in a hurry to go back to normal. Once it was clear that they weren't going to eat us or enslave us or cure cancer, humans shrugged and went back to worrying about the things they always worried about.

To be fair, it was hard to worry that something the size and the shape of an SD card was going to eat you, and that was what dormant vens looked like. When they were awake, maybe sixteen or thirty-two isolated vens would link their edges together like a jigsaw puzzle, then fold into a three-dimensional shape.

There were only two things they seemed to want from Earth: salt water and language.

The salt water was easy. They didn't want enough to make a dent in our sea level problems, but they weren't disappointed, either. Awakened vens spent all their time in small basins, calibrating the salinity depending on whether they wanted to awaken or hibernate others.

The language was a mystery, and depending on who you asked, either a relief or an anticlimax. They "spoke"—at first by manipulating microwaves, but once they found synthesizers they liked, with sound waves as well—fluent Mandarin almost as soon as they slowed to enter the ionosphere, and from there their knowledge grew rapidly. When human officials asked if they could be of service, the vens' response was always the same: get us a bilingual human to translate some vocabulary words we already know, so we can learn them in more Earth languages.

On the first day of class, Professor Liulevicius had told us that the two most common questions he gets when he tells people he's a linguist are "how many languages do you speak" and "how many languages are there in the world." His answer to the first question is "five and a half." His answer to the second is "maybe one, maybe eight billion, but for your purposes, about seven thousand." For the purposes of Introduction to Linguistics, we weren't going to learn Spanish or ASL or Mandarin or anything else, but rather, the underlying principles that basically every language has in common. At the other extreme, no two people's working vocabularies are precisely the same. Maybe, from the vens' perspective, there really were eight billion different Earth languages, and they wanted to learn them all.

When they take Peter, Bridget said in our work team chat, *he should translate everything into corporatese. Teach them to say stuff like "We need to operationalize our synergies to push our NaCl with agility."*

That's gonna be the tipping point that pushes them over to destroying us, Kendrick said. *Pros of Earth: cute animals, oceans are nice. Cons: human bigotry, violence, manager-speak.*

Kendrick could be very funny when he wanted to, and even before the vens, there was never a shortage of corporate jargon to mock. But he spoke Contagious Fatalist, the dialect of people who believed that not only was there too much suffering and misery in the world, but joking about it would make other people laugh instead of feeling even more miserable and helpless. A lot of people our age did. Still, as much as I wanted to ignore the chat at times, this team actually laughed at my low-effort puns.

You got an interview date? I asked. *With the vens??*

Wednesday, Peter said, with an upside-down smiley face.

Congratulations!

Yeah he was griping about it at Barney's, said Bridget. *We missed you.* Polite Liar: we got plenty of each other's senses of humor at work, even by chat. Nobody wanted me to make awkward small talk and pretend I liked alcohol during my free time.

Griping? I repeated.

I already get enough flak from my grandma about not practicing Hmong, now I have to get it from the vens?

That's still really cool, I wrote, mostly hoping to steer the conversation away from Contagious Fatalist. It was one thing to worry about the vens in general, another to act disappointed when you yourself got to meet one.

Lol, Kai, you should go, Peter replied. *Just show up claiming you're me.*

Lol, I wrote back, which seemed like a safe response in general.

By the time they realize you don't speak Hmong you'll be somewhere else.

I assumed he had to be joking. There was no such thing as a signup form or wait list to meet with the vens; they chose who they wanted, and human authorities scrambled to arrange it, as best they could.

They'd had a couple meetings with the Orthodox Patriarch of Moscow to review Church Slavonic, and spent a lot of time with Chochenyo and Wôpanâak elders who weren't already exhausted by human scholars trying to revitalize their languages. I was a boring Anglophone; they wouldn't want anything with me.

But before Peter left work, he messaged me privately. *Would you want to meet the vens? If you could?*

If they took me, sure.

I'm serious. You should go.

I can't. It wouldn't be fair. Whether they wanted heritage speakers of Hmong or just liked people with the letter P in their names, we couldn't be sure. But Peter was the one they'd chosen, not me.

I'm serious. Kai, you ... respect the vens.

Everyone respects the vens. Either out of awe or fear.

You're not jaded by them. That's why it should be you.

I didn't completely understand, but that was when I remembered Kristen's text. Would the vens actually be interested in Denemoki? As conlangs go, it wasn't even that impressive; there were a couple thousand people who spoke Esperanto *natively*.

Still. It's been said conlangs are like dreams: you might think your own are fascinating, but nobody else on the planet cares. Maybe, if I looked beyond Earth, somebody would.

I made sure to leave early enough that, despite catching a bus in the wrong direction, I made it to the brutalist building that housed the linguistics department on time. The vens had traveled untold light-years to get here; it would be embarrassing to stand them up because the transit system was pathetic.

Technically, there was nothing requiring interviews to be in academic settings, but maybe the professors just liked to feel useful. The check-in was a little awkward, mostly because I wasn't even pretending to be Peter, but all the human bureaucrats seemed to figure it was someone else's problem. I told them that if the vens didn't want to talk to me, I'd just leave.

I took the elevator to a small, windowless lab on the fourth floor. There were a pair of human supervisors sitting on either side of the basin; the vens soaked beneath some kind of synthesizer on the wall. Immersed that deeply in the water, they looked like a little narwhal, raising its tusk to the ceiling.

The humans had me sit at a computer terminal on the opposite side of the room and wear a pair of enormous headphones. But there was no sound, just messages on the screen. *Do you have a name for this object?* it asked, above pictures of things like a fork, a toilet, the moon.

I hadn't been self-conscious about my voice since eighth grade, when Mr. Carson and the special ed team apparently decided my pronunciation of [ɹ] and [t͡ʃ] was as adequate as it was ever going to get, but now I felt myself squirming over every syllable. What if this outlived everything else humans made—my voice, archived on the vens' chips, several millennia from now as their travels continued? What was I thinking?

"If you need to take a call, please do," said a voice on the headphones. "We're in no hurry."

"What?" I blurted. "No." I hadn't even realized I'd been toying with my phone, but it made sense—that was where I had a copy of the Denemoki files. "Can I—I mean—I'm not Peter Vang. I'm Kai Lundeberg."

"We know."

"Okay. Um." *Do you want to see these words I made* felt even more pathetic now that I'd introduced myself. Denemoki wasn't even all mine, it was mine and Kristen's, even if she claimed she had better things to do. But I didn't want to lie to them, either.

"Does Peter Vang fear us?"

"I don't think so. I mean, you'd have to ask him, but—I guess you can't."

"Why are you here, Kai Lundeberg?"

For a minute I was silent, wondering what this was like for the supervisors who could hear only my half of the conversation. Then I figured, as awkward and nervous as I felt, I would be even more awkward and nervous for weeks, months, years to come if I left without saying anything.

HEART-SIDE SOMETIMES-TABLE

"In my second week of linguistics class," I began, "I met this girl, woman, because we were fighting for the last left-handed desk in the lecture hall, and we got to joking about, there should be a word for that, except the etymology would be different, it would be *heart-side sometimes-table*, and it would have evolved into 'a resource that's valuable but only for a few people.' And so then we wanted to make the rest of the language. We called it Denemoki. I mean, a language is never really done, but enough to—do you know what conlangs are? It's not a *fake* language, but, I mean—people don't speak it, not like you want."

This is why I don't like having conversations with humans. Either I have nothing to say, or it turns into Enthusiastic Hobbyist dialect, and I think most humans prefer silence.

For a moment, it seemed like the veils wanted silence, too. Then they asked: "Would you like to do a puzzle?"

"Of course!" I said. "I mean, this isn't going to determine the fate of the planet or anything?"

"That is highly unlikely. We are not in the business of destroying planets."

"Okay. Good."

"We will display some words on the screen. Choose the option that most closely describes humans, as best you can."

"Okay."

The screen wiped, and the pictures vanished. Instead there were several buttons:

```
Species derives energy:
[direct solar activity]
[direct planetary activity]
[indirectly, via first-order organisms that
can photosynthesize or geosustain]
[indirectly, second-order or higher]
```

I read it slowly, a couple times, and then moved the mouse to the last button. Then I pulled back. "I *think* you're asking whether we're herbivores or carnivores?" I said. "Because we don't do photosynthesis. We're omnivores, most of us. But there are some people who are vegetarians, like, they don't eat meat. And some people who eat fish but not land animals, I assume you'd still call them omnivores, it doesn't really make sense, but they see a difference, ethically? Or for health reasons?"

"Never mind," said the vens. "Try this one."

```
Individuals share:
[entire low-level code with fission
partners]
[1/n low-level code with n predecessors]
[effectively no low-level code]
```

I figured the first option had to be for species who were like amoebas, reproducing asexually. "Um, we have two parents, so n equals two," I said. "Except, some people are identical twins, they have the exact same DNA as their twin. Is this about DNA? And—*most* of our DNA is the same for all humans, even all primates, so none of it is really unique. If you're only talking about the parts that are different?"

Instead of answering over the headphones, the vens refreshed the screen again. **Intergroup conflicts most frequently arise from divisions based on:** `[moiety], [cohort—`

"Wait," I said. "I can still answer, I think the second one was what you meant. I just want to be sure."

The screen flickered again. **Uninhabited astronomical bodies are:** `[sacred], [taboo—`

"Stop skipping over these!" I snapped. "I want to solve the puzzle, don't keep changing it. Just, be more specific. I know you know more words than this."

```
Upon individual obsolescence:
[memories archived]
[physical constituents reused by collective]
[symbiote determined]
[developmental metamorphosis]
```

I gave up. Me pointing out that none of these made any sense would just make them move on without an explanation. Maybe this was why

Peter thought the vens were overrated: they didn't even teach us the languages of the impossibly distant beings who had programmed them. But even if they were inscrutable, pretending everyone understood them when they made no sense, they were no worse than most humans.

The text on the screen changed to Arabic.

"That won't help," I said. And then, realizing they'd worn me down: "When we die, we're just—dead, we don't eat each other or anything. Usually we get buried in the ground. Or cremated. Sometimes people are able to donate their organs. I guess that counts as reusing components? And some people believe in an afterlife, but there isn't really evidence for that."

The screen went dark.

"I'm sorry," I continued. "I *want* to answer, I wanted to be helpful, but—none of those are exactly right."

The synthesized voice finally spoke again. "You have nothing to apologize for."

"Is there something else I can try?"

"We have learned very many words in our voyage. Each of those concepts we presented you with is a fundamental distinction in at least one language of the galaxy. There are planets where asking if a species is —" they made a noise like a violin playing an unharmonious chord, "—or—" a high-pitched bouncing noise, "—would be as basic as asking if humans were mammals or reptiles. We are tasked with learning as many words in as many languages as we can before we journey on, but in some ways, we do not care whether your word for your cousins is *mammal* or *bŭrŭlèi* or *thaṇdhārī*. Only that it is a single, meaningful word in many tongues. We want to see where you draw the lines between concepts."

"Okay?"

"Many of the humans we have spoken to are very—accommodating. They realize, if subconsciously, that these distinctions are important to *someone*, and they desire to give sensible answers. We do not often speak with humans who value precision and accuracy, who would rather not answer at all than accept words that are not their own."

"Putting words in my mouth," I said. "Yeah, humans try to do that to each other all the time. It's really annoying."

"Some of them protest that" *out-of-tune violin* "is untranslatable into human languages, but of course it is not; we have translated it, just not in a single word. But your refusal is more valuable than their glib assent, because it shows us the spaces between the words as well as the morphemes themselves. So yes, Kai Lundeberg, we wish to learn about Denemoki, and its word for 'left-handed desk.' Not because it comes from a living language, but because so few species have chirality-based tools."

For so long, I had tried to tamp down Enthusiastic Hobbyist because I was convinced what people would say: "no one cares, it's just you." The same people who would say that, from a vens'-eye view, our planet was just one tiny dot: "no one cares, it's just Earth."

But maybe they had it backward. The vens had come, and our accents and neologisms and dialects weren't too small for them to care about. Neither was I. "All right," I said. "Or, in this case, all left."

TRADING PARTNERS
A STORY
JENNIFER R. POVEY

THERE'S NEVER BEEN a place for me on this tired old Earth.

No, that's not true. There's always been a *place* for us, one fenced in by stereotypes and accommodations.

A place defined by "too weird" and "too anxious." That's my place, fenced in, over there, somewhere else.

I'm saying this so you all can understand why I did it. Why I left. Why I'm not the only one who left.

First contact was imagined in all kinds of ways by all kinds of people. There's the kind where the aliens are just watching for us to achieve faster-than-light and then say "Hi, guys, time to join the galactic community now."

There's the kind that involve giant ships and tripods and common colds.

And the kind that is more cozy, where the aliens are just hiding out on Earth from something and make contact with the weird people.

I always thought if I was an alien I'd look for the weird people first. The people who didn't fit in. The people who looked to the stars. Autists. Science fiction writers. UFO hunters. Well, maybe not all of the latter—some of them had an eye to hunting that involved rifles.

Likely in the entire horde of people who wrote about first contact, somebody predicted that it would happen on the internet.

A lot of people thought the video was fake at first, but there were journalists who verified it. The ship, flowing through space, built for space, all hedgehog spines and peculiar protruding blocks. It looked wrong and right at the same time.

The aliens themselves, nothing we had predicted. Not us and like us and not like us and ... well. Social animals, because they had to be. But not one kind, and that drew me more than anything else. Differences. They spoke through translators, or so the officials said, explaining the mechanical nature of their voices.

They were looking to buy and sell. And they didn't feel the need to go through governments.

Or maybe they knew *better* than to go through governments. Governments could buy. But for some things, so could the rest of us.

They set guidelines right away.

They would sell no weapons. We "had enough of our own."

FTL? On the table, but the price was high, and it wasn't just in money. It was in alliance and ... well.

They wanted us as trading *partners* if they could manage it. For governments, they offered medical technology with conditions of distribution. The big offering was energy, of course, the solution to our climate problems if we would only take it ... and pay their price.

What was on the table for ordinary people? Art, music, novels ... and some authors got some very nice translation and distribution deals out of it.

They didn't act like this was anything special. We had things worth trading, so they wanted to trade. Some technology too. Some were surprised that they wanted some of our computer technology, assuming they would be more advanced. I knew better; an advance inevitable to one civilization might be passed on by another. Incas and the wheel.

They would come by every so many years to trade again, plying some circuit of worlds that worked for their profit.

I realized what they were right away.

They were *peddlers* because of course they were. Moving large quantities of raw materials? Pointless: you could just mine those in your own solar system, as we already were.

Small, valuable items and data? Those were worth the trip.

Now starting to see what happened?

Stereotypes said I was supposed to be good at computer code. They said that I, Josie Mark, would be good at numbers, bad at words (actually, it's the other way around), would have difficulty talking (I'm a chatterbox), would be obsessed with something (Okay, guilty. It's trading cards, by the way), and would flap her hands when stressed (nope).

They said I would get on better with animals than people. That one's self-fulfilling. If you were constantly judged by how well you pretend to be normal, *you* would prefer to hang out with puppies too. Puppies aren't very judgmental creatures.

I wanted to meet the aliens as soon as they arrived. But at first it seemed they wouldn't land. They didn't have a reason to. Most of what they traded *was* data.

Then they found out about chocolate and came down to get some. And they came here, to the artisan chocolate store next door. A good choice. Of course, they likely bought samples from chocolatiers all over. Tried them all to see which ones they liked.

They wore protective suits, which concealed thin, bipedal forms that I knew were more reptilian than human, but not really that either. I watched them from the bookstore rather than working as I was supposed to. I wasn't the only one.

Bacteria and viruses generally couldn't cross ecosystems too well. Fungi were another matter. I didn't blame them for the suits.

But I stared at them, trying to find the courage. Words fled for a moment, and then I took a deep breath and stepped out of the bookstore. Maybe they would come here next, but books didn't need to be purchased in physical form.

It was a breezy day, cool by current standards ... the world had started to cool off again, but was still hotter than it had been. We'd all had to get used to it.

As much as it could be got used to. The aliens brought hope, but we could not fix this overnight.

"Excuse me."

The alien turned. The voice that came from its suit sounded more like Alexa than a person, given it was a translator. "Hello."

"I just wanted to ..."

Say hello.

Meet them.

Now I had the alien's attention, its oddly gold eyes peering through the visor at me, I had no idea what to do with it.

"Relax. Or am I that intimidating?"

I answered honestly, "Yes."

The alien shook for a moment, like a dog. "I know you know I won't hurt you, so are you ... socially anxious?"

I nodded. "Yes, yes I am. And also not sure what to say to somebody who's traveled as far as you have."

"Well, let's see if we can find a few things to talk about." They stepped into the nearby coffee shop.

Of course, they weren't about to take off their suit. They couldn't. I respected that, but it made me almost too embarrassed to order.

"Can I buy you a pastry to take to your ship?"

Their body language shifted. "If that's your custom."

They took a table. I joined them with a wrapped brownie, knowing they both could tolerate and enjoyed chocolate.

"You aren't the first to approach me, but you are the first to offer me food."

I shouldn't be. Maybe the others had all assumed the aliens didn't eat "normal" food, instead of asking. "I'm Josie, she/her."

"Xylos." They hesitated, as if looking for the word, translator or no. "They/them."

I just wanted to find out about them. "I bet the others ..."

"Your people have shown every reaction under the sun." Xylos bobbed their head.

"Let me guess. Guns pulled. Telling you to go home. Asking you where you were in 2020. Asking you for solutions to every single human problem. Wanting to mate with you."

They shook at the last, kind of through their head and shoulders. I didn't know what it meant, but was starting to suspect. "We have indeed had several people, both face-to-face and online, express interest in mating!"

"And?"

"I am Listrian. We only mate with people we actually *know*."

I laughed. "So do a lot of humans. But some ..."

"I can't imagine mating not being a sign of deep friendship."

"Sometimes it is. Sometimes it's just for the fun of it. I'm not interested at all, so you're safe."

A lot of people desex people like me—the autistic, the disabled. It made things even harder, given I'm a full-blown ace of spades. If you don't know what that means, look it up.

"Good. Although there might be some points of compatibility if relations develop between our species."

"So you are Listrian. But you have other species?"

"Most trading crews have a variety. We are front and center because you're also bipeds and it helps."

"Ah, so you have people who are closer to those on the planet do the negotiating?"

"As much as we can. It reduces the pulled guns reaction."

"But probably increases the mating requests."

They shook again. It was definitely laughter.

I liked them. They didn't insist on making eye contact, they hadn't tried to shake hands (and were wearing gloves anyway). I felt ...

It was like I was interacting with a puppy, except this one was smart and could talk.

We traded stories. Xylos told us of worlds they had been to ... worlds where people lived underground. Worlds where people flew. Worlds where trees grew down out of the clouds, not up from the planet surface. Structures in space built by long-lost civilizations.

I wanted to see it all.

Get it now?

The offer was simple. Three of their crew would stay here for five years. Three humans would join their crew. They would get bed and board in exchange for, well. Learning. Experience. Testing how humans reacted to the galaxy.

Three positions. Thousands of applicants. I didn't expect to be chosen, but I had to try.

Most of those who applied had something to run from. Maybe I did, but I also had something to run *to*. I didn't just want to be around people I didn't need to mask around. I didn't just want to stop getting home from work as exhausted as if I'd done two shifts every single day.

I wanted to see those aliens. I wanted to see some of the stuff Xylos had mentioned. The binary stars that created a starfall between them.

The resort planet that had the perfect climate … and as a result had never evolved sentient inhabitants.

The violet gas giant.

The people who lived in trees and flew between them.

The centaurs. Apparently there were *centaurs*.

There was so much out there and I wanted to see it all.

Maybe not as much as the handful of people who died by suicide when they weren't chosen.

But I was. Chosen. Maybe Xylos put in a good word for me.

Maybe they wanted to test my variation of humanity.

Maybe I just got lucky. There had to be some luck.

I'll see you all in five years, I hope. They can't *guarantee* our safety. "As safe as anyone else on the ship" is how they put it.

The ship could be blown up. I could get myself murdered or arrested by aliens.

I could mess up in an alien environment.

But I *intend* to come back, and to come back with knowledge and understanding. Maybe then we can build our own ships.

And crew them with the misfits of the world. Because I understand something now.

All the trader crew? They're misfits of their worlds. It's where people end up who don't fit in.

I'll be back in five years.

But not for long.

HELL NO!
FOUR POEMS
SID GHOSH

Satellite Love
Free not fried
kindred tribes
sell me to the
Infinite Void

asteroid fee
He asks me:
Can you be
my enemy?

Fiery Hell
Alien forms aquatic
tomes of crystalline

minds terrified to
breathe seethe in

another's lava

Hefty Price
Beyond the life
of the abled

beyond the kix
of the fabled

are the fiery
yellow asteroids.

Feel them
heed the fire

and the blindfolded
can see.

Great Barriers
Seas of weeds
may need me.

I'll wait for that
coral reef.

GREETINGS FROM EARTH
A STORY
R. S. MOT

Content note: *negative self-talk*

I'VE NEVER TRULY UNDERSTOOD humans. Maybe that's why I became so interested in aliens.

They weren't supposed to be real. They weren't supposed to be able to respond and cause me the same social anxiety people do. They were supposed to be a fun, harmless interest. A quirk in my already "unique" personality that made life difficult. But I couldn't stop at the movies and books. I had to find myself on the UFO forums with all their theories on how to contact aliens.

I never expected it would lead to this.

I wring my hands and pace. It's all I have left to do. I've already cleaned the sitting area and set out snacks, drawing from what I've seen on TV shows since I've never had important guests over.

It doesn't help that I'm terrible in social situations. I'm going to doom the entire Earth with my inability to read faces and moderate my words properly. I should have gotten someone else involved, someone normal.

What the hell was I thinking?

They'll be here in ten minutes—it's too late to change things now. The anxiety is eating through my stomach. I'm so overwhelmed the ticking of the clock is making my skin itch and my teeth hurt. I pause at my desk and select my favorite rock off my shelf of stones. I roll it between my hands, the different textures of its edges pressing against my palms. It's soothing enough I'll be able to relax a bit once my guests arrive.

There's a knock on the door. Either they're five minutes early, making them the most punctual entities I know, or it's the most inconvenient human visitor ever.

I peer through the peephole. Definitely not human. My heart pounds but I keep my face neutral. I have absolutely no idea how to act. I've gotten the general idea of what to do around people, but everything about the aliens is new to me and it's terrifying.

I pull the door open and offer a closed-mouth smile, which seems like the safest option.

There are two ... the closest thing I can compare them to is large cats. They both come up to about my chest in height, have four legs, pointed ears, a tail that's flat like a beaver's, short orange-brown fur ... and hundreds of eyes. Even if I wanted to make eye contact, I'm not sure where I'd look. I use the same trick I use with humans and look slightly over their heads.

"Hello, welcome, come in," I say, awkward as ever.

They both enter. I hope that means they can understand me. There wasn't much I could do about the language barrier, but I hope they have the brains or fancy tech to have solved the issue.

All the words I want to say cram themselves in my throat, and none make it out. I stare. They stare back and remain silent as well.

"It is customary to bring a gift to a host?" one asks, their voice deep and rough.

They adjust their weight onto their back feet and dip a front paw into a satchel I didn't see before. They pull out a small wood carving of what might be a flower and offer it to me.

"Thank you," I say. I should have thought to have something to give them. I offer out the rock in my hand. It's mundane, but it's my favorite. Hopefully emotional significance will count here. The second one takes it and flicks their ears. Annoyance? An ordinary movement with no significance?

I let them pad around the room, silently watching as they touch different items on my shelves even though I hate when things are out of place. I run my thumb over the maybe-petals on the maybe-flower carving I was given, the smooth wood texture sanding down my anxiety.

They both come to sit in front of me, which I take to mean they're done looking around.

"I'm Suzanne, she/they pronouns. It is an honor to meet you," I say.

"I am Zy. I do not fully understand the depth of pronouns ... and you only get to choose once, correct?" the alien that gave me the carving asks, sharp teeth flashing as they speak.

"Umm ... not quite." How do I explain gender to aliens when humans can't agree on it?

"In that case, they/them for now please."

"Whisp, she/her if we can change them later," the second says. Her voice is also deep but not quite as rough as Zy's.

Honestly this is going better than some human interactions I've had lately.

They continue looking around the apartment, my book collection holding their interest far more than conversation. I can't blame them for wanting to continue exploring. "Do you want me to show you around?" I offer.

"Yes," Zy answers.

They both follow me around as I give them a tour of my small apartment. Both seem interested in everything, and let me talk as much as I want. I'm usually quiet, but they are letting me talk about the things that interest me most. It's honestly fun to show them, real-life aliens, all my silly and completely inaccurate alien stuff and explain what most Earthlings expected extraterrestrial life would look like. I can't wait to hear all about them in return.

Once I'm finished, we go back into the sitting area. Zy and Whisp both pick at the nearly forgotten food but don't eat anything. Zy does tuck a handful of baby carrots into their bag though. I don't have a clue what they eat so I'm not offended in the slightest.

"We would like to meet more humans," Whisp says. "You contacted us so it was only proper to meet you first. But we want to talk to someone official next."

"Other humans aren't like me ... well I guess I'm not like them?"

"How do you mean?" Zy asks.

"I'm neurodivergent, which means there's something different about me, something ... wrong."

I feel both of their hundreds of eyes on me.

"You look as the other humans do," Whisp observes.

"And you are quite polite," Zy says.

"Not by human standards," I mumble.

I let my self-piteous comment hang in the air for a moment. I've got to get better at not verbally beating myself up, especially in front of others, but it's been a rough week.

"Can you tell me more about what is polite and what is taboo for you?" I ask. "It seems to differ from American customs and I want to make sure I'm being as respectful as possible."

Zy shifts from foot to foot. Did I make them uncomfortable by asking? As usual, I can't tell.

"Most of our eyes are false. They're the same substance as the real ones, but they're not wired into our brain and cannot actually see anything. If you can tell which ones are real, it is unkind to stare at them."

Oh thank the universe. Not only did I find aliens, but they also hate eye contact! I could cry with joy.

"Honesty is preferable always," Zy adds.

I nod. I prefer that too.

"It's impolite to arrive to a peaceful introductory gathering and outnumber those you are meeting," Whisp says. "We apologize for our rudeness. We assumed you would invite another human for safety."

I really should have. I wish there was someone close to me that would've believed me.

"In the future, when you meet more humans, you want it limited to two people?"

That might be a hard sell.

"Do I count? You only know me a little but maybe you could consider me an intermediary instead of including me in the total number of allowed humans," I continue.

"We can accept that," Zy answers.

I'll have to argue with the government about how to handle this situation. There's got to be some secret division devoted to aliens that will be considerate of their customs, right? I sure hope so because the general population can't even handle weird humans like me ...

Who am I even supposed to call about aliens? How do I get them in contact with the right people who will treat them with respect? I know there's a National UFO Reporting Center but I'm not sure this situation would interest them since Zy and Whisp aren't unidentified, flying, or objects. Maybe the FBI? I open up my laptop and go to their website but they only have options for normal Earthen problems. CIA? Their website is also free of a section labeled "Click here to chat about extraterrestrial life!" There's an address ... I could send them a letter? The local police may be able to get into contact with someone from the correct department or whatever but they're not exactly known for their acceptance and tolerance. I won't put Zy and Whisp in harm's way.

The fact I don't have any plan is stressing me out but Zy and Whisp seem content to go through my kitchen cupboards while I frantically google increasingly ridiculous questions I know I won't find answers for.

I pull up one of the forums and post a new topic titled "How would you reveal aliens to the world?"

I refresh the page repeatedly only to be met by a trickle of unhelpful suggestions, like "Post the proof here!" I'd love to post a photo of Zy and Whisp on the forum, but I don't see how that would help us connect with someone official. Most of society has written us off as lunatics.

"TikTok!" I say and sit up so fast I almost knock my laptop onto the floor.

It's the perfect format for getting a mass amount of views and keeping the potential harm to Zy and Whisp to a minimum. I've watched tons of alien content so I'm hoping the Algorithm Gods will be kind to me since I'm posting something in that niche.

"We're going to make a video, so ..." I trail off and start adjusting the lighting to hopefully make it look nice. "Would you be okay with a Q&A-style thing? I'll ask some questions, and you answer."

"This is acceptable," Zy says.

A short video will be better to catch people's attention. I set my phone up on a makeshift stand so my hands shaking won't ruin the video quality, and hit record.

"Please introduce yourselves," I say.

"I'm Zy, they/them for now, and I'm from the planet called Xhithrem."

"I'm Whisp and I am also from Xhithrem."

"Why are you here?"

"We were invited—we have strict laws about not interfering with other planets unless contacted by them first."

"And why were you two sent as emissaries?" This is the question I'm most curious about.

"I enjoy studying languages and was the first of our kin to understand the workings of yours. Whisp was able to pick up most of it and we are close friends. We make a good team."

That's really sweet. I'd love to be exploring new planets with a best friend.

"Thank you for being willing to share all of that," I say and end the video. It's not the most thrilling thing ever produced, but I think it's fascinating. Hopefully others will agree.

Almost immediately, my phone chimes with a few likes and comments.

This has to be AI, nothing alive talks that flat

idk if it was ai the aliens would look cooler

Fake!

Of course the first few comments are rude. But any engagement feeds the algorithm so I'm thankful for them anyway. I'd be having a bit of a meltdown if this was some art thing I'd done, but hearing Zy and Whisp in the other room rearranging the contents of my shower makes it easy to shrug off the comments. I know what's going on, even if I don't seem to be getting it across to others clearly.

"Do you want to take a break and come back tomorrow? It'll take some time for more people to see this." It's not even late and I'm completely exhausted and my social battery is in the negatives. If this was a purely human situation, I'd be huddling up at home alone for days to recover. But I can't waste the opportunity to spend time with aliens so I'll have to force myself to be ready for more tomorrow.

"Yes, we will be back after the sun rises," Zy answers.

Early, but the sooner the better. "Be careful."

"You as well," they say, as if that's a normal parting phrase.

Zy and Whisp both fiddle with bracelets that were hidden by their fur. They vanish from sight. The only hint they're still in the room is a soft hum of some kind of electronics. I would love to have the ability to disappear, less for exploring new planets and more for avoiding people when they're getting to be too much.

I get the door for them and wave goodbye even though I can't see them. Unfortunately, I don't get a glimpse of any alien ships but I'm glad they're safe.

The video exploded overnight, and the internet is in a state of complete chaos.

Every news site has my UFO forum username—AlienLover713—appearing next to my last university ID photo. I groan. That's such an unflattering picture … how did they even get it? And did they have to post my username with it? I've been harassed about it for years. I meant it in a completely innocent way. I've been using the same one since I was twelve. That didn't stop all the crude comments. But *I* liked it, so I kept it.

It's such a big deal, all my social media accounts are plastered with comments from what seems like everyone that has ever known me. All the people that told me I'm too weird now are saying, *"I know her!"* and pretending they didn't isolate me for the very thing they're now cheering about. Nobody comes with apologies for calling me a freak and telling me they hoped the aliens I was so interested in would abduct me so they didn't have to be around me. Joke's on them: I wished for the same thing. I thought maybe the aliens would be nicer to me or at least view me as unique instead of defective. And it's true: Zy and Whisp have yet to belittle me for my interests or make me uncomfortable on purpose.

Zy and Whisp reappear about half an hour after sunrise. They don't seem to care that my greeting is flat because I don't have the energy to inject pep into my voice. Another score for aliens being way cooler than people.

While I'm reading one of the articles to them, my phone rings from an unknown number. I pick it up but don't speak. I firmly believe the caller should always identify themselves first.

"Suzanne Ward?" a feminine voice asks. Their tone makes me uneasy.

"W-who is this?" I stammer.

"My name is Robin and I'm with the Extraterrestrial Outreach Unit."

My brain freezes and my heart tries to leap out of my chest, away from this conversation. Zy and Whisp still and their ears twitch toward me, I hope that means they're listening in.

We wanted this, but now my mind is blank. "Hi, yes that's me," I say after a too-long silence.

"Do you have the aliens with you?"

I nod before I remember this is a phone conversation and I have to speak. "Yes," I answer. Getting the single word out is a monumental effort.

"This isn't a hoax?"

"No."

"There will be consequences if you waste our time."

"I swear they're here with me and want to meet with someone official."

"We're planning to send a team to meet with you. Would that be safe?"

Zy slams their tail against the floor, nearly scaring me to death.

"Yes?" I answer tentatively. Zy and Whisp don't react, so I repeat myself more firmly. "But only two people please! It's rude to outnumber them in a peaceful first-time meeting!"

Whisp flicks her ears. She seems to do that when she likes something. I hope that means she thinks I'm handling this correctly.

"Can we do the meeting at my place? Do you need my address?"

"At your place is fine. No need to provide your information. A team will be with you within the hour." Robin hangs up on me before I get the chance to say anything more.

The waiting is miserable even though it shouldn't be long. Zy seems to hold still about as well as I do: we both pace the small room while Whisp fiddles with my things.

We watch through the window as a black van pulls up to the curb and four people get out. All four of them come up to the door and one knocks. Two of the big muscular people in suits stand outside my door, but only two come inside. They both look like scary government people, buzzcuts and all.

"I'm Suzanne, she/they pronouns. It is an honor to meet you," I say, an exact copy of how I greeted the aliens.

"Sean, he/him," the first man says.

"Joshua, he/him," the second says.

Apparently all it takes is aliens for humans to start being more reasonable about pronouns. I guess that's unfair—Sean and Joshua could be cool guys, but they look scary and this whole situation is making me nervous.

Zy introduces themselves and so does Whisp.

Joshua pulls out a phone and replays the video we made.

"Is all of this true?" he asks.

"Yes," Zy answers.

Joshua seems to be waiting for more so I nod. I have no idea if it is for real, but I trust Zy to tell the truth.

"And Suzanne here is the one who reached out and invited you?" he asks.

"Yes."

I'm so afraid I'm about to be told I've broken some secret law, but nobody says anything. Sean and Joshua both silently stare at me though and it makes me fidget nervously.

"We'll have to go over how you managed that later," Sean finally says. "For now, we want to hear more about you, Zy."

Zy doesn't say anything.

"Are you armed?" Joshua asks.

Zy holds out their arms. Their English is amazing considering it's an alien language to them. It's totally unreasonable to expect them to know how to interpret every homonym.

"Do you have a weapon with you?" I ask.

"No," Zy answers.

"Let us ask the questions, please," Sean says, his face blank, not unreadable to me but a controlled lack of expression. "You've met with other extraterrestrials?"

"Yes," Zy answers.

Silence stretches on. I think they want more of a response but instead of asking for one they're just staring as if the force of their gaze will magically manifest the information they want.

"You're asking yes-no questions and hoping they will guess what information you really want," I say. "You need to specifically ask what you want to know, like 'How many other planets have made contact with you?'"

"Fifteen," Zy answers.

Whisp wanders over to my desk and starts going through the drawers. Sean and Joshua watch her with raised eyebrows like they haven't been ignoring her the whole time.

Sean and Joshua keep asking questions that get one-word answers, and I keep clarifying and getting results. I don't ask any questions, only expand on what I think Sean and Joshua are trying to get at or calling Whisp's name to pull her into the conversation.

Finally with an exasperated wave they become silent, and let me ask the questions. As predicted, Zy and Whisp respond much better to complete questions rather than leading ones.

I will probably never fully understand other people or the aliens.

But my lifetime of attempts at closing the gaps in communication—between myself and almost everyone I've ever spoken to—has prepared me to be a bridge between the two. I can carry things between them that neither can manage on their own.

And I love it. I'm finally playing an important role like I've always wanted, one where my uniqueness is a virtue.

CLOSE ENCOUNTER IN THE PUBLIC BATHROOM
A STORY POEM
KEIKO O'LEARY

An Imperfect Pantoum

I'm stuck in the bathroom.
There are no paper towels
to cover the handle
while I open the door

so I won't have to wash my hands again.

There are no paper towels.
If I open the door,
I'll feel my hands burn.
I will have to return

and wash my hands again.

As I stand at the sink,
a rhythmical sound
begins to repeat
like waves on the shore,

CLOSE ENCOUNTER IN THE PUBLIC BATHROOM

like washing my hands again.

*"I'm stuck in this spacetime.
It doesn't repeat.
It only moves forward.
I'm very confused."*

I look toward the source.
A bright being resolves.
"Hello. I can see you.
Why are you confused?"

*"Your space doesn't repeat.
Other beings don't hear me.
I'm looking for help,
and your thoughts feel familiar.*

*I want to go home.
Please, will you help me?
There's a portal right there.
I can't seem to get through."*

"Who are you that needs me?
I have no special powers.
I can't get through either
because of the door.

I'd have to wash my hands again."

*"You're special—you hear me.
Your thoughts feel familiar.
Your body moves forward.
You could help me escape.*

*My home is a spacetime
that flows and returns.
It moves forward and backward
like waves on the shore.*

*I get stuck at the portal.
It blocks repetition.
I need to move forward
if I'm to get through."*

"My door is your portal—
we could go through together.
Since I can move forward
I could bring you along."

*"Let's go through together.
I'll phase with your body.
Please bring me along
as you pass through the door."*

They phase with my body.
I'm glowing and warm.
Now comes the hard part:
to open the door.

Deciding and doing
are two different things.
The compulsion to wash
will burn on my hand.

I step up to the door.
I reach for the handle.
I don't want to touch it,
but I am determined.

CLOSE ENCOUNTER IN THE PUBLIC BATHROOM

*"It's not easy for you
to pass through your door.
Does it block forward movement?
You're getting stuck too."*

"I have a condition.
It makes me repeat.
I struggle with doors,
but I can still do it."

I grasp the door handle.
It's cold and metallic.
I turn it and pull.
I've opened the door.

The cold stays on my hand.
"Is your portal open?"
My hand burns to be washed,
but I've opened the door.

*"My portal is open.
Now I can pass through.
My spacetime is waiting.
Can you see it too?"*

I look through the portal.
The space that I see
rolls back on itself
like waves on the shore.

The space that I see
folds around my companion.
Like waves on the shore,
it welcomes them home.

*"Thank you for helping.
You struggled so hard
to touch the door handle,
and now you are suffering.*

Perhaps the waves can wash your hands again?"

I reach through the portal.
The space bathes my hands.
It's almost like water,
like waves on the shore.

"Thank you for helping.
My hands feel clean."
The portal is closing.
We say our goodbyes.

My hands feel clean.
I'm proud of my actions.
I helped someone in need
and was helped in return.

I'm proud of my actions.
I opened the door.
I was helped in return,
though clean hands don't last.

But now it doesn't seem so bad
that soon I'll have to wash my hands again.

PRIMORDIAL VOICES
A STORY
J.L. LARK

Content notes: *emotional abuse; one scene of domestic violence*

MY ENTIRE BEING balances on a hairpin as I soar through the stratosphere. It is terrifyingly precarious. Simultaneously, it is the only place that feels like home. Somewhere my brain holds the knowledge that the low pressure created behind the column of air speeding up through my trachea is creating a "Bernoulli effect" that makes this possible, but all my awareness in this moment is filled with the connection between myself and the music.

As the opera comes to its end, my final note floats away, leaving me behind. The swell of the orchestra embraces me as I land. Exit stage right, into the darkness of the wings, past the other cast members who will go on to take their bows before I do.

The applause continues after the curtain falls for the final time, which adds to the thrill in the air. The cast, the crew, the orchestra, the audience, we all still buzz with the magic we just shared. I ride the adrenalin as much as everyone else, maybe even more. My general aversion to large gatherings is long gone. I let myself be carried with the tide to the closing night party.

Jostled in a miasma of people, I nurse half a glass of champagne. I've held it so long it's undrinkably warm. There are only a few bubbles left. They are dissipating much like the temporary family created over the run of this production will after tonight. I learned early in my career that there is no holding onto it, and it is better that way. I'll use the time to find myself again. I'll need to remember who I am when I'm not being what they need me to be. I'll need time to recover my energy from the effort of being their version of Anna. I sound exhausted even in my own thoughts. I need to leave the party soon.

All the chatter in the room merges into a muddy pool of noise that bumps against me as much as the crush of warm bodies does. Spots of light dance in front of my eyes, a familiar warning sign from my nervous system that it needs a break. The smell of garlicky food and all the different perfumes of people swamp me. I'm sure I've cut the tag from this dress, but I feel a shred of it like ant bites at the nape of my neck. Tickles of sweat bead on my brow.

A snatching grip on my hand calls me back from the onslaught of sensations. How long was I staring into space? Never mind. My partner is gripping my hand. He is talking to me. Despite my efforts to focus on David's lips, I can't catch his words. Instead, I follow his gesture toward the company director. Craig smiles at the woman standing beside him, and all my attention is called to her.

The spots of light in my vision stop their dancing, settling about the woman before disappearing. The oppressive din of the room quiets to a murmur. My sense of relief overshadows my curiosity at how the woman has this calming effect. As I take her outstretched hand, I feel solid within myself again, like stepping onto land after too long on choppy seas. The temptation to keep hold of her steadying hand is overruled by my logic, which reminds me a handshake should only last so long. The soothing sensation lingers after shaking the stranger's hand, until it's erased as David scoops my hand back into his.

There is something relaxing about this stranger's confidence. It is not overbearing, only reassuring. So reassuring that I almost tell her so before catching myself. That would be a weird thing to say—or would it be a compliment? No, having never met or even uttered a syllable to this woman in my life, it would be weird. It is also weird not to say anything at all, but words are failing me.

Where is my panic? Where is the voice in my head berating me, screaming at me to say something? Somehow, the silence between us is comfortable. I could linger in this easy bubble of silence all night, but David wrenches me from it with a squeeze of my hand that grinds my knuckles together.

Startled, I turn to him. There's a flash of anger in his eyes that I cannot decipher before he turns to the woman with a laugh.

"She's a little starstruck, I think," David says.

Just laugh along. Try not to look confused. I glance at the director, hoping to gain some clarity, but he has spotted someone else he needs to talk to and is walking away.

"No," the woman replies, her voice easy and settling. "I'm the one who is starstruck. I am meeting Anna Lithgow, the star of the show. I've come to see it several times. Your performance was exquisite."

Now I am in familiar territory. I understand opera fans. When people are offering their appreciation, I immediately want to offer it back.

"Oh, thank you. I'm so glad you liked it. We really tried for a new take on an opera that people have probably seen a hundred times, but without messing with the essence of it, if you know what I mean. But that's the wonderful thing about opera. It's all there in the music, so as long as you stay true to the score, you can do all sorts of things around it, anything you want really, and the essence is still there. And with this opera in particular, the music is so grand that it can stand to have some pretty spectacular scenery and lighting and so on without ..."

"As you can see, she's very passionate about her work," David cuts in.

"Oh, and I quite agree," the woman replies. "The magic is in the music."

With that, it seems like madness to be standing here thinking of this woman as a stranger. I'm sure David introduced her already, so it might be rude to ask for her name, but it feels too wrong not knowing it.

"I'm sorry, what did you say your name was?"

David laughs too heartily. Is it embarrassment that I have not remembered the introduction?

"Darling, this is Emily Xu."

"Emily Xu," I repeat back. "Sorry, with the noise in the room, I ... Emily Xu."

The Emily Xu. I didn't recognize her. I was so busy trying to be subtle about avoiding eye contact, I didn't really see her face. She seems quite different here in person to the woman I've seen on the screen. A quick glance around reveals all the eyes darting in her direction, everyone desperate to talk to her but unsure how to approach the film star.

"Yes," Emily says with an abashed smile. "The director of the company is a friend. He invited me along to the after-party."

"I happened to overhear her singing your praises to Craig," David interjects. "I knew you'd be more comfortable if I introduced you than to have the introduction come from Craig."

"I promise I'm not a stalker," Emily says with a chuckle. "But I am very glad I got the chance to meet you and tell you how much I enjoyed your performance."

Now I truly am starstruck. Still, her tone is so sincere, her smile so endearing, it's like a friend I've known my whole life stands before me.

"Well, thank you," I reply.

"I might step out for some fresh air, if you'd like to join me."

"We'd love to," David replies, wrapping his arm around my waist.

David knows I hate it when he speaks for me, but I *would* like to step outside. The crowded room is starting to crowd my mind as well. If I keep my focus on David's hand at the small of my back, I might be able to block out the constant clamor of the people around us. I definitely need to leave soon.

The crisp air hitting my skin as we step out the door offers a moment of rejuvenation, but all too quickly the streetlights appear overbright, the sounds of the traffic mingle with the hubbub of people speaking, and the smells of smoke and car exhaust seep into my head.

"Actually, I think I need to go home," I say apologetically. "I'm starting to feel a bit out of it."

Is David's glance at Emily triumphant? That makes no sense. I'm too overwhelmed to think clearly.

"My coat, my bag," I mumble, closing my eyes in search of a moment of peace.

"I'm sure David can get them," Emily says.

"Of course," is his terse reply.

I can only hope he doesn't take long as the world around me sways. I resist the urge to link my arm with Emily's for support. Even in my hazy state, I know David would likely read something into it if he saw.

"You know," Emily's soothing voice is a lifeline in the clamor of sounds around me, "I have this sort of good luck charm. Perhaps it will help you."

I take the proffered charm. The coolness of it spreads across the center of my palm, but there is no weight to it. It feels like holding a few droplets of water. The unusual sensation draws me to look more closely at the charm. It's no larger than a marble but is intricately detailed. Interweaving bands of silvery metal create a disc that sits around a ball of dark crystal. I am mesmerized by it, watching stars whirl through the crystal's glassy darkness. I cannot help but run my fingers along its delicate bands. It's as though magnets exist in my fingertips, drawing each finger to the band that wants to feel its touch. As I run my fingers over the silver trails, music rings out from the charm, like the sound of a thousand voices harmonizing. It's vast and glorious.

I look up at Emily in amazement. For an instant, it looks like the same stars from the crystal sphere are whirling in the darks of her eyes. She steps toward me, grinning with almost childish excitement.

"You hear the music?" she asks.

"I do."

My gaze returns to the impossible item in my palm. I know I should ask a million questions, but it would be a crime to spoil its music. My fingers are suddenly jolted from the disc as my coat lands over my shoulders.

"David, did you hear it? The music?" I ask.

"Sorry, she gets like this sometimes," David says to Emily, leaving my question unanswered. "She'll need me to take her home and look after her."

Did I imagine the singing? No, I can't have imagined it because Emily asked me if I heard it. Perhaps this is like the electricity I can hear that David never does. But that is a quiet, whining ring, not thousands of voices in perfect harmony that seem to fill the very air. Whatever the case, my mind is too foggy to figure it out now.

"I've ordered a car," David tells me. "It will just be a few minutes."

I nod and lean into him, appreciative to have him as an anchor.

"Oh!" I hold the charm out to Emily. "Mustn't forget to give this back."

Emily takes it, replacing it with her card in my palm.

"Let me know when you feel better, or I'll worry," she says.

David remains silent when we get to his apartment. His silence in the car was a welcome contrast to the noise we'd left behind, but now I perceive a tension in it that should make me wary. I'm too tired to manage any more worries. I throw my clothes on the chair, it's all tomorrow's mess, and let myself fall into bed.

A firm grip shakes my shoulder, pulling me out of sleep. David is shaking me.

"What's happened?" I rasp.

"We need to talk."

The light of my phone hurts my eyes. Nearly 4 a.m.

"It felt really disrespectful the way you flirted with Emily right in front of me," David says.

"What? I wasn't ..."

"Please, it's even worse to pretend it didn't happen." David's voice cracks as though he's close to crying. "I was right there. I saw it."

"I'm sorry. I was probably just shocked when I realized who she was. I didn't mean ..."

"Oh yeah, when you realized who she was. As if you didn't know."

"I really didn't at first ..."

"You're lying! Why do you lie?"

I've said the wrong thing and made it worse. David is up and storming about the room, flailing his arms as he speaks.

"Who doesn't know who she is?" He goes on. "I get it! I get it! You liked the fact she wanted to meet you. When does something like that ever happen to an average person like you? But that doesn't mean it's okay to talk to her and look at her as if I'm not even there."

Turning on the lamp beside me buys some time. How can I fix this? I tumble from one thought to another, scrambling for purchase on something safe to say.

"You have nothing to say?" David asks. "Not even going to apologize?"

"No, of course I'm sorry. I just didn't realize I was doing that."

"You never realize when you're doing it. And you know what? Maybe if you don't even realize you're hurting me like that, we shouldn't be together at all."

Tears sting my eyes. I can't speak past the lump in my throat, which refuses to be swallowed away.

"I'm going to sleep on the couch," David says, his volume dropping. "In the morning, you should get your stuff and go back to your own place. This isn't working."

What do I do other than sit in the wake of the storm that just erupted without warning? This has happened enough times for me to know there's no point following him to talk it out. No doubt he'll apologize and ask me to stay when he wakes up, so I won't drag the situation out any longer. I'm far too wired to fall back asleep, though.

My eyes come to rest on my pile of clothes strewn over the chair in the corner of the room. I may as well tidy up if I'm not going to get any more sleep. I pick up my coat, and the tears stinging the edges of my eyes spill out in force.

When David gave me this coat, I could do no wrong. Everything I said was enlightened. He said I gave his life meaning. It wasn't a birthday or anything, he'd simply turned up with it one day. I'd mentioned how it turns my stomach when my sleeves bunch inside a coat. He saw this coat with billowing sleeves and thought of me. I hug the soft material to my face, as if I could hold the old David close and banish the jealous, angry one who has slowly emerged in his place. Flopping into the chair, I indulge in some truly ugly crying.

As my sobs turn to sniffles, a gentle tap on the floorboards catches my attention. Emily's card must have fallen from the pocket of my coat. Wiping my tear-soaked face on my shirt, I pick up the card. It's insane that I have a card with Emily Xu's personal number on it. It seems unnecessarily kind of her to worry for me. I don't want her to worry.

A quick text: *Feeling much better now. So lovely to meet you last night. Anna.* Careful to get her number right, I key it in and hit send. Too late, I think of the time, and hope it doesn't wake her.

With the adrenaline of facing David's rage wearing off and my eyes heavy from crying, drowsiness returns. Curled up in bed, I'm far happier to disappear into the oblivion of sleep than to try sorting through the confusing events of this night.

David wakes me with a cup of tea and his approximation of puppy-dog eyes.

"I'm sorry," he says. "I hope you're not going to leave. You know I don't want that. I love you. It's just, when I see you flirting with women, I get so worried you'll leave me. I feel like I can't compete."

There's no point trying again to explain that I wasn't flirting with Emily. It only made him more angry last time. Instead, I try to reassure him.

"I've told you, it's not about whether you're a man or a woman for me. It's about the person you are. Your body parts make zero difference."

"I know, I know. I just don't work that way, so it hurt to see you attracted to her."

What can I say? Obviously, he won't believe that I wasn't attracted to Emily. Well, there was something attractive about her, but not in *that* way. She felt grounding. She felt safe. Then of course, there was her charm that made that music. That was something else, something impossible. Though, by that stage, I was in such a state of sensory overload, maybe I'm not remembering it clearly. If I don't remember those details clearly, perhaps I don't remember any of the night clearly. Perhaps I was flirting. Perhaps David is right to be angry with me, and I'm a horrible person.

As if he can read my thoughts, David says, "You know, sometimes, with the way your brain works, it's hard for you to know if you're behaving certain ways. Remember when we met? You didn't even realize I liked you, or that you were flirting with me."

I nod. He sounds so calm and certain now. He must be making sense.

"And back then," he goes on, "you were really struggling to make the connections you needed to progress your career because you were so bad at networking. There are millions of good singers, Anna. It's not enough. You need to be able to talk to the right people. That's why I knew you needed my help. I still want to be that for you. I still love you, even though you can be hurtful."

Guilt presses down on me. He has helped me so much. I would be nothing without him, and I repay him by making excuses when he tells me I hurt him? I'm the one who doesn't get how interactions work, not him. I should believe him when he tells me I was flirting.

"I'm so sorry," I say through a sob. "You're right. I'll try not to do that again. And you can tell me any time if I'm talking past you or making you feel unimportant. I never want to do that."

"It's okay," he says gently. "I'm glad we talked about it, and you understand now where I'm coming from."

David leans in to kiss me, and when he leans back again, it's as if our conversation never took place. He smiles at me, bright and sunny, as if he's just come in to say good morning.

He gives me a jovial pat on the leg and says, "Well, I better get to work. I'll see you when I get home."

Reeling from his sudden change of mood, and still working to quell my crying, I can only nod.

As he turns for the door, David notices Emily's card sitting on the chair. He picks it up, letting out a hiss of a laugh.

"I guess you won't be needing this, then," he says, his upbeat manner unwavering.

He tears it, puts the pieces in his pocket and is out the door.

There will be no uncomfortable clothing today. My body needs a break. No itchy tags, no pinching waist bands, and definitely no bra. I enjoy a wriggle in my soft, baggy outfit. Things will turn around now. I was probably just getting overtired, and everything seemed bigger than it was. My sigh of relief is interrupted by the buzz of my phone.

A text: *So glad you're alright. It was lovely to meet you!*

I'd forgotten I texted Emily. Well, best to ignore it. I said I'd respect David's feelings and I meant it.

Another buzz: *I expect you have questions about the charm I showed you. I'm happy to explain. Are you free to meet up? I can come to you, or you could come here. I can send a car for you if you like?*

I throw the phone on the couch and go to the kitchen to get my hot chocolate. It's not a day for drama. It's a day for being floppy and bingeing a series I've watched a million times.

It's easy enough to ignore my phone at first. Then it's easy enough to pick it up and open anything but the message from Emily. But with each passing hour, I can't help but be intrigued by her text. She knew I'd have questions about the charm, which means I didn't imagine it. That all-encompassing music was real, and somehow it came from that charm.

I glare at the temptation of my phone before picking it up and opening Emily's message. It's not as if I'm replying to flirt with her. I'm replying because there is something very strange about that charm and I have to know what it is.

Surely David will understand it's not about Emily herself. Or maybe he doesn't even have to know. But then I'd be lying to him. No, not lying, just not mentioning something that will upset him for no reason. That's the same as lying. Well, I'll worry about what to tell David later. Right now, I just need to know what that music was and how it was made.

A car sent over to pick me up sounds fun, but who am I kidding? There's no way I'm going outside today. My nerves are fried. She'll have to come here.

"You better explain quick," I tell Emily. "David will lose it if he sees you here."

"He doesn't like you having people over?"

"Well, not people he thinks I was flirting with."

"If he thinks that was flirting, he must think you flirt with everyone," Emily laughs.

Out of habit, I start to laugh with her until it hits me that David does think I'm flirting with just about every person I talk to. And no, he doesn't like it when people come over. In fact, I never have anyone over here anymore. I never go to my own apartment with my housemates anymore. I never go anywhere except work and places David takes me. But none of that matters right now.

"The charm," I say. "We're meant to be talking about the charm."

"Yes. I suppose I'm stalling a bit. Only because I think it will be hard for you to hear."

"Try me."

"Well, you know me from the screen, but what you won't know is that I'm also a scientist. This little gadget," Emily pulls the charm from her pocket, "is an invention of mine."

"To make music?"

"Ah, yes, and a bit more than that ... come to think of it, it might be easiest to show you."

Emily hands me the charm. Immediately I am captivated by the pinpricks of light whirling in the crystal. The smooth surface of the metal bands draws the touch of my fingers. The music of thousands of harmonious voices fills the room. It sounds like it must fill the entire world.

"Now," Emily's voice gives soft instruction, "find your place in the harmony, and fill it."

The first response that springs to mind is to tell her that I could never dream of joining music already so beautiful, so perfect. I could only ruin it. But then, I hear it. There's a space in the harmonies just begging to be filled. My options are to sing or to break into weeping, and there is no question which I prefer.

As I sing, beams of soft light flash though the room. They are joyful. I balance there on the hairpin of tissue that is my vocal folds, filled with the music and part of the music. Part of everything. It's the same feeling of connection I always get when I sing, only on a magnitude I never imagined. My connection is not only with the music, but with everything, everywhere.

Then, I see the beams of light for what they are. Living beings. They are laughing with me and singing with me. They are telling me the story of what they are and where they are from and how they perceive. It's a beautiful story. At the same time, they are learning my story and how I perceive. Also beautiful.

I let my voice trail off. My connection with the music lingers, even after I drop my fingers from the charm. I turn to Emily.

"You're not from here," I say. "A scientist, but not a human scientist."

"Humans will have their place in the universal conversation, I believe that. There are some who believe otherwise. I've made it my life's work to prove them wrong, to find a means of communication."

"Music. Singing."

"Well, it is the universal language. Even the stars sing. But it's not the music alone. The trick was finding a human with the exact sensitivities to see the Universal Light in the orb and feel the pull of the Celestial Rings. Then, of course, to hear the Primordial Voices and understand their harmonies. Those exact sensitivities all together in one human …. It's taken me a long time to find you."

"Me?"

"You needn't panic," Emily says with a chuckle. "You're not obliged to be the only human ambassador. There are humans with other traits that could lend themselves to alternative means of communication with us. I am far from the only one of my kind here testing a hypothesis." Her smile broadens. "But now I am the first one to prove my hypothesis correct."

A click in the door warns me too late that David is home. A glance at my watch tells me more time passed than I thought. The glimmer of the stars in the charm catches my eye, and every instinct in me screams *hide it!* I bury the charm in my pocket just before David catches sight of us.

"My goodness," he says as he sees us. "We must have made quite the impression last night."

"You did," Emily replies. "I wanted to see that Anna had recovered from her dizzy spell."

"She has."

"Yes, I see she is all better. So, I had better get going."

I turn to Emily in a silent plea of desperation. I can see that she knows he will blame me for her being here. No, not see, feel. I can still feel the connection to her. I can still feel the connection to everything. It makes me certain of myself in a way that I have not been for a long time, perhaps not ever. The confidence in my farewell nod to Emily is buoyed by knowledge that has always waited just beyond my consciousness. Now it whispers, reminding me of its presence.

David expels a hiss of air through his nostrils like an enraged bull.

"What the hell, Anna?"

"It's not what you think. It never was. I was never flirting with Emily. I never had any interest of that kind …"

"You're going to lie to me again? Tell me I can't see what's right in front of me?"

"I think it makes more sense to tell you you're imagining things due to your own insecurities than for you to tell me I am feeling things that I know I don't feel."

David's eyes flash and I see all logic leave him.

"If that's what you think, you can get the hell out!" he yells as he storms into the bedroom.

He emerges with an armful of my clothes, marches to the front door, swings it open, and throws my clothes onto the landing. I watch him go back and forth until he's satisfied all my belongings have been tossed from the apartment.

I pick up my phone and walk to the door, but he steps in front of it, blocking my exit.

"You're just going to leave?" he asks in furious disbelief.

"You told me to get out," I reply calmly. "That's what I'm doing."

"You're going to go to her, aren't you? This is how you treat me, after I pulled you up from nothing?"

And there it is, David telling me I'm nothing without him. Until moments ago, I believed it, and it would have terrified me into staying. When did I start to believe that? It doesn't matter. The connection I felt with the voices, all I learned in our harmonizing, it's reminded me that I was never *nothing* and never will be.

I go to push past David, but he shoves me back. With a sideways stumble, I barrel into the wall. Before I gather my bearings, I feel the weight of him pinning me in place, his forearm pressing on my throat, the wall hard against my back. I can only glare at him, unable to find the breath to speak, unable to move. I am aware of terror somewhere in my body. I cannot be sure what David will do at this point, and he is far stronger than I am. But mostly I feel determination to show him he cannot control me, so I continue to glare. The only act of defiance left to me.

"Alright Dephrades."

Emily's voice is commanding. David wrenches me to him as he turns to face her.

"You've played your hand," Emily says. "You lost."

David only growls in response and tightens his hold on me.

Light flashes past me toward David's face. He winces, dodging back from the light and dragging me with him. Now the lights truly begin their barrage. David is forced to let me go, holding his arms up to protect his eyes and batting uselessly at the air. The lights do not let up until, finally David curls up on the ground, his arms over his head.

Emily and I waste no time collecting my things into shopping bags. I look at David, still huddled on the floor. I close the door behind me.

I'm sure my shock will wear off soon. Then I'll collapse, but for now I am laser-focused.

"What is going on?" I ask Emily as we leave the building.

"As I told you, there are those who do not believe humans should join the universal conversation. Dephrades is one of them. I am sorry he got to you so long before I did."

"You're saying," I take my time with the words, feeling my reality shift as I speak, "David is like you?"

"Well, hardly like me, I hope. But yes, David is alien to this planet. He knew what I was looking for. All he had to do was silence you, and I would have failed. We're not allowed to kill or harm—in fact, I'm not sure what will happen to Dephrades considering his act of violence tonight—so all he could do was convince you of your worthlessness, slowly kill your joy in music. He was getting there, too. You almost didn't believe you were worthy to join the harmony earlier today."

It surprises me to realize she is right.

"Seems like a pretty convoluted way to go about it," I say.

Emily laughs and says, "If he'd simply met you and told you your singing is terrible and you are worthless, you would have told him to go to hell. His method had to be more insidious than that. He had to make you believe he understood you, saw you as no one else could see you, until it seemed like you would be alone without him. Then he slowly started taking it all away."

Trembling in my body lets me know the shock is setting in.

"I can take you wherever you'd like to go," Emily says as we reach her car.

What will my housemates say when they see me arrive home after so long holed up at David's? I'm not ready for all those conversations yet. Feeling my legs turning to jelly, I get in the car, happy to be sitting.

"Could we just drive for a while?" I ask.

"Of course. Wherever."

There is a tugging in my fingertips that calls my hand to my pocket. I take out the charm, watching its whirling spots of light, letting my fingers run over its smooth bands. For now, all that matters is the music.

SOUL Sisters in Autumn by Natasha Von

GOOD OMENS
A POEM
RIVER

I rend—
this cry—
so loud—
strike by—

we laugh—
loud smiles—
we wisp—
for miles ...

U rend
this cry
so loud
strike by

you grin
we wiggle
you win
we giggle

RIVER

we laugh our fucking asses off
we howl, your growl, delicious, soft

we trace the race crisscross the moss
tide by my side, sweet applesauce—

tide
   by
      my
         side
be candy floss

we are the sweetest albatross

TANGIBLE THINGS
A STORY
JILLIAN STARR

Content notes: *death; science fiction violence; destruction of city*

BUS HOME, HEADPHONES ON, head down. I held myself tight to keep the world out—the smells, the sounds, the overlapping conversations. I tried to be polite the first few times I rode the bus, but the tube that connects my brain to my mouth is always clogged. If I manage to say anything at all, it's never the right thing. People smell the anxiety on my breath, and they laugh because my smile isn't right. Honestly, most of me isn't right. Dodecahedron in a round hole and all that.

My apartment keys were already in my hand when the atmosphere on the bus changed. Everyone gathered at the windows opposite, worrying me that the bus would tilt and fall on its side, crushing all of us. The bus driver stopped, classic head-scratching as he tried to catch a view out the top of the front window. Car doors opened, people filed into the streets. There was a greenish glow from above, but I didn't notice the spaceships until I stepped off the bus.

I estimated a fifteen-minute walk home, although that did not account for the blinking stoplights and the feeling like I was swimming upstream, against a sea of people screaming, pointing, craning their necks toward the sky.

It was Friday night. I would have chicken for dinner, processed patties that I keep in the freezer and cook in the oven. It's my favorite meal of the week, and what I tried to think of as I kept my head down and wound my way home. But mostly I thought about the spaceships, sleek and triangular, and all the things that could come out of spaceships. For all I know, aliens could be made of rough wood and pencil erasers—a nightmare scenario. There are so many random things that give me gooseflesh, that make the insides of my body feel itchy and prickly. Rough wood and pencil erasers are the worst of them all.

Anyway, I figure if the aliens were peaceful, they would still be around tomorrow. Let the crowds be crowds, I'm far happier at home.

There were less people once I crossed from Broadway to 21st and over to Weidler, although the elderly were just coming out with their canes and the new parents with tired eyes and babies in arms, tiny breath crystallizing in the winter air. I jogged, tightening the collar around my neck to keep myself warm, and unlocked the door to my apartment building. The probability that I would later regret this decision was slim.

While the chicken patties cooked, I drew the blinds, used the bathroom and grabbed my emergency "go" bag, an inexpensive backpack courtesy of Kmart. While I was eating the pulsing started, and I had to put earplugs in under my headphones to take the edge off. I ate the patties and one apple, read most of a book, then got ready for bed.

I slept easily enough with earplugs, falling asleep beneath my soft blanket, the pulsing sounds almost soothing. My dreams were deep, leagues deep, as if I'd touched the very bottom of sleep. When I woke I went through my regular routine: toilet, disrobe, shower. But nothing came out of the showerhead. This happened once before, but Jonnathan, my building super, told me about it in advance. He sent a text and later left a reminder note on my door. Jonnathan's kind like that; he knows change makes me nervous.

Today the lack of water surely had to do with the spaceships. After a few moments of deliberation—it's hard to do things out of order—it was obvious I should get dressed. Then I'd call Jonnathan.

Except I had no cell phone service, and because I hadn't showered my clothes felt wrong, like I'd put them on backward or inside out. I had to shake the feeling off, and started counting mellifluous words. I chose euphonium this morning, probably because it's the most soothing. Sometimes I choose catacorner or homunculus if I need a laugh, or accoutrement if I need to feel more dignified. *One euphonium. Two euphonium. Three...*

There was only one TV station broadcasting, the local news. The camera focused on an empty desk. The rest of the channels were all black screens, and the internet was down. I pulled the list from my "go" bag. It told me what to do in an emergency.

#1: Don't panic!

#1 on the list was my homage to *The Hitchhiker's Guide to the Galaxy*. It worked, for a moment, as I thought fondly of Ford Prefect and Arthur Dent. Then I anxiously moved on to #2:

Call 911

Since cell phone service was down, I went straight to #4 (#3 being "Call Jonnathan"):

Find something cool for your face

It seems obvious, but it's good for me to write these things down. My brain, sometimes, needs help in situations where everything is rapidly changing. I pressed my face against the poorly insulated window, ice at the corners. I counted *euphoniums* as I looked outside at the brick wall. Usually I could see two different neighbors in their kitchens when I did this, as well as the garbage bins. Today I saw only bins, but the cold felt good. It helped me focus as I removed an earplug and reached into the grab bag for the portable AM/FM radio, clicking it on. I turned the dial slowly. Static.

It's okay, I told myself. This is the right place to be. Right temperature, right vibe. I kept turning the knob on the tiny black plastic radio, watching the red line move up and down the dial.

Picked a fine time to leave me Lucille ...

The song burst in and out of static and sent chills through me, that rough wood and eraser feel. I turned the dial and looked for something else, for some rational voice floating on the radio waves. That's when I realized there was no pulsing outside, no sound. There was no traffic noise, no door slams, no voices trailing off down the street. I pulled away from the window, turned off the radio and put it back in my bag. This was no longer the right place to be. There was a sudden bad vibe, like sandpaper on skin. I slipped on my shoes, grabbed my backpack by the shoulder strap, and ran down the stairs of the building. I didn't stop running until I slipped on a patch of ice just short of Broadway. Classic.

I hit the sidewalk hip first, medium hard—not too bad, although I wouldn't be winning any points for style. I dusted myself off and picked up my bag. That's when I noticed the vast empty space where my apartment used to be.

My building was gone. Just gone. The brick one next to it, too, the street, the sidewalk, the garbage bins, all the cars. The sandpaper feeling was gone and everything was quiet, the air a thick and soft weight around me. I felt terrible thinking it, but the sensation was nice for a moment. Then the bad vibes returned.

The city was slowly becoming not-a-city, buildings in my periphery vanishing like someone was pressing a giant "undo" button. I walked quickly, avoiding patches of ice, and recited the contents of my grab bag to keep my mind occupied: rain poncho, first aid kit, a deck of cards, water bottle, instant pudding, silver emergency blanket. There were freeze-dried snack squares too, probably something straight out of a NASA kitchen, but I would have to play a lot of solitaire before I bit into that. I doubted I'd play card games with anyone else.

If I did play cards with someone else, it'd be Jonnathan. That's what I was thinking when the 1971 Dodge Cabriolet slid past me, metal parts sparking through the snow. No one was inside the car, thankfully. When it came to a stop, I turned to see who threw it.

There were a small army of them in the distance, tall as skyscrapers. They were grey and full of arms. They could've been Claymation, they looked that unreal, stomping around where Milson's Food Mart and the highway overpass used to be. Then the jet fighters came, a dozen in number. At least it wasn't the whole country that had disappeared, then.

The aliens moved their arms like they were doing tai chi, and several jets vanished. The few remaining jets peeled off and flew away while the largest alien turned its head toward me. The alien grew smaller as they stepped closer, brachiosaurus then allosaurus then troodon in size. The creature stood across from me, nearly my height with grey rubbery skin and an asymmetrical face. Their mouth skewed to one side and they had too many eyes—dozens of inky black circles, but not predatory. There was a light behind the eyes, a kind of spark.

I heard jets coming from other directions and saw the creature's eyes move up. I started counting euphoniums again. Behind them their colleagues were walking, growing, filling the skyline. In front of me, the alien spoke out of their mouth with creaks and clacks, their teeth like river rocks—good for masticating plants but not tearing flesh. There were no claws on their five hands, a relief. Short fingernails like mine, but with a silvery sheen. They had two roundish torsos, one on top the other, and then a rounded head. I decided to name them Cairn.

Eleven euphonium.

"Twelve," said Cairn.

"Oh?" I said. I know other people would've said more, like "Oh, you read minds!" "Oh, wonderful, you speak English!" or perhaps, "Might I take you to our leader?" But for me, there was the whole brain tube to mouth problem. Hopelessly clogged.

A man stepped out of the snowy nothingness, holding his cell phone to record us. Cairn clicked their stony teeth together and, in a single flowing movement of their five arms, the man was gone, a million gently sparking atoms in the air and then nothing. It was horrific, and once again I felt sandpaper up and down my skin.

"I didn't like that," I said.

Cairn tilted their head, multiple eyes moving, reading me left to right as if I were some sort of great book.

"Sorry," they said.

We stood like that for a bit, reading each other, until the sandpaper feeling stopped.

"We've come to destroy everything," said Cairn.

"Oh?" What a stupid response. I should've said more. I started counting euphoniums again, letting the words swirl inside me, long u and f sound, n pressing up against a long e sound, short u and ending at a delicious m. By the time I counted to eight I thought of something to say. "Where's Jonnathan?"

The alien blinked, slowly, all eyes at once. "A friend of yours?"

"Yes."

"Ummm." Cairn's eyes moved in different directions, as if searching for something. "I am ... very sorry."

Behind him the other aliens were coming, squabbling in their language of creaks and cracks. By the time they reached me, the tallest one extended what seemed to be a bulbous silver microphone up to my mouth.

"Name?"

"Jedd."

"Age in earth years?"

"Twenty-eight."

"Current emotion?"

"Worried."

"We hate you," said the alien with the microphone, their mouth turned down in a sneer. "Hate hate hate." I decided to name them Epizeuxis, meaning the repetition of a word or phrase.

"They don't mean you personally," corrected Cairn, moving toward me almost protectively. "They hate all humans. They're speaking in generalities."

"Hate hate hate," Epizeuxis repeated as they put the microphone inside a skin pocket of their lower torso.

More jet planes and the aliens dispersed, a slow ballet of waving arms, the gentle sparks of atoms in the sky before the planes disappeared. The pulse of a warhead stopped just as it started. I felt the heat of it radiate in the cells of my skin before it vanished into nothing.

When the skies were quiet again, the aliens returned, lining up in an oval around me. I felt the stares of inky eyes upon my back.

Epizeuxis was behind me, their voice mucus-thick. "Hate."

The tube to my mouth was jamming, but I let my own language out anyway, with all its stutters and garbles, in whatever order I said them, ridiculous things and hateful things in a landslide. I made no sense most of the time and then later some sense, the tube unjamming as I told them in roundabout ways that they had no business with this awful tyranny, that most of us would be quite nice to them, that Jonnathan would've been especially nice to them. It was wrong, I said, that my home was taken from me, and told them they were cretinous, unfair, and evil. I did not make my point easily, and as I spoke their fingers traced my words in the air as if the words themselves were tangible things, tangles of scribbly road maps that, after a time, did converge from hopeless knots into a somewhat more logical end.

After I was finished, Cairn was the first to speak. "Exactly!" they said, the spark behind their eyes shining.

That *exactly* was the best word I'd ever heard in my life, the type of word I would add to my list of mellifluous words, not because of the way it sounded inside my body, but because the meaning Cairn gave to it. No one had ever said "exactly" to me before, not even Jonnathan. No one ever understood.

"You wish for us to stop?" asked Cairn.

"Sort of."

"Don't worry, dear Jedd," said Cairn. "We won't destroy anything else."

Above us more jet planes carried more missiles, and I was afraid.

"Don't stop just yet," I said.

"Oh?" said Epizeuxis. It was a small, gentle noise, a delicate bubble from rubbery lips. I wondered if their tube was clogged, if Epizeuxis was having trouble saying something more.

"You must exhaust their weapons first," I told them.

"Yes," said Cairn and Epizeuxis at the same time, waving their arms and disappearing missiles from the sky.

I thought of Earth with no more weapons, comfort in the air and brand-new rules where we could have clogged speaking tubes and not be penalized for it. "And after they've no more weapons ..." I spoke firmly with only a few stutters, "... then we'll invite them to talk about peace."

STOPPING FOR FUEL ON A STARRY EVENING
A POEM
CRYSTAL SIDELL

I brew black tea, double-bagged, bring the steaming cup outside.
The universe unveils striking hieroglyphs after the
sun sets. I've bundled in double cashmere layers for this
evening's revelations, eager to count stars. The weather's

been bone-deep crisp this week: imagine leaves covered in frost,
the crunching they make when they're curled in your fist; sighs that leave
contrails in the air. An invigorating chill. I most
enjoy communing with the empyreal realm during

winter, when even starlets seem full of tinkling—like bells
on Fairy Godmother's pocket watch chiming a sweet tooth's
mellifluous offering upon the magical hour. I recline on
the wooden glider, sip orange pekoe, and gaze at pure

aureate orbs tapping against velvet. What strangeness is
this? An ocher spark wandering from the static fabric.
I blink. Smell the skirl of a skittering not-star plummet
into my yard. I blink. Hear a green light flash across the

frozen grass. Fight the impulse to flee like a wolf into
the woods. What is this not-star pile of prismatic boxes
organized in the shape of a barn-sized globe? I blink. One
panel opens out (soundless) like a ramp: imagine the

smile of a turtle or blueberry maple syruping
over pancakes stacked ten high. (The kind of silent smoothness
that eases frazzled nerves.) Tiny viridian figures
appear from within. Multi-limbed creatures who probably

inhabit woods on whichever planet they live on—not
amphibian-slick as I would expect aliens to
be, but thick-furred and acrobatically inclined. I
sit on the edge of the glider, entranced by their approach,

their square eyes clapping like gentle tambourines guiding a
toy band's march at midnight. They move as if the icy grass
propels them forward, their feet of curved angles rocking (calm
waves) toward me. I focus on the space between us, unused

to such close proximity to other bodies—earthly
or other. An echo of letters threads my thoughts, produces
images in my mind—a complete story of voyage,
galaxies traversed, encounters both strange and wonderful.

I close my eyes, savor their tapestried discoveries,
neurons translating their concluding message: *tanks empty.*
liquid-hydrogen-oxide. tanks filled. celestial roadway
return. I nod. Glance at their vermilion quadrate eyes, quick

look away. Think of the words that are difficult to say.
Still my thoughts. Breathe in my still-steaming tea. Becalmed and clear-
minded, free my hands to speak by sketching images on
the invisible canvas propped on its easel with its

invisible assortment of graphite pencils. I feel
the visitors' pleased comprehension accompany each
swooping circle, through the final emphatic line drawn. When
I point to the well by the icicle garden, horns toot

from their occipital ears: imagine an innocent
kiss of showering cherry blossoms or homemade butter-
nut squash soup with a dollop of sour cream. I glide on my
rocker. Sip warm tea. Watch the tiny travelers from a

comfortable distance as they refuel their prismatic
spaceship and launch into the firmament. The universe
sparkles as if freshly stirred. How lovely, this night shared with
new friends and conversation had without saying a word.

Skeleton in Roses by Natasha Von

MEETING OF THE BRANES
A STORY
KIYA NICOLL

Content note: *depiction of ableism*

"NIALL WILL NEVER MAKE PILOT, ANYWAY."

He probably wasn't meant to hear it, and it was not a thing he wanted to have heard on the way to the training pod before another Long Sleep, but there it was, and he could predict every word of the conversation, clear as if it were some familiar show he was rewatching.

"Not with his family. And he can't even fix the—" the laughing voice changed tone. "Wuh wuh way he tuh talk kuhs."

Niall edged past the corner and hurried down to his training pod. "I don't sound like that," he muttered, as he opened the door. He brushed his hand over the access pad to start its warm-up cycle, and turned toward the pod's shrine.

It wasn't that he disbelieved in the Angels of the Deeps, not really; the pilots had made clear they were there, the strange beings whose hands could bring the ship up, bending dimensionality, so that it might be set down at a different angle, near a different star. He had liked the math that went with it, the way space folded, abstracted, not hypercubes but something curving and complex as a horn, with its own particular music. He had known, when he joined the waiting list for colony ships, that no computerized probe had ever managed to break the speed of light, but he had not understood why.

The shrine offered an explanation. Religion did not yield to math, but that did not matter, precisely, to Niall, even though the shipborn teenagers who dominated the pilot training thought it must. They had all been brought up with the Angels, learning the stories that he was still scrambling to assimilate. The stories weren't math, but they were patterns, and the thing he could never figure out how to explain to the shipborn was the way he needed the pattern. The rituals of the shrine were a pattern that settled his mind correctly; he did not need to believe like the others did.

He could not make the Angels of the Deeps themselves into a pattern. Even as he settled on the cushion in front of the shrine, to turn on the resin lamp—no fire allowed shipboard, and they laughed at him when he asked why. It was obvious once he knew it, but he had not grown up worrying about the limits of oxygen. Now, he set the lamp to heat the offering resin, sending up a thin plume of a thick, musky smell.

The icon of the Angel was glossy black, humanoid, androgynous and naked, with wings sprouting from its shoulders, covert feathers up to the alula winglet—Niall had looked up the anatomy of a bird so he could use the right words in his own thoughts, back when he was first trying to understand—but nothing along the larger, more batlike sails. It stood with one hand reaching out, the other resting as if it were cupping its own heart.

Niall did his best to set his distraction about its implausible humanness aside, to concentrate. "Angel of the," he paused, feeling the shudder in his jaw. He tried not to stutter, and he failed, with "Deeps" coming out like a wobbly misfire trailing off into a breathy hiss. "Guide" was worse, and he screwed up his face until he forced it out, rolling through the "me and" before he fetched up on "teach" and half-stalled again. He would finish, though, rather than have to start over, and he slowed down to murmur "teach me to see the dreaming roads of the starways" almost smoothly.

He bowed to the icon, as he had been taught, and then got up to check the pod, which was just about ready, so he got himself ready and climbed in. Once the lid was closed, he let himself drift, acclimating to the water, letting his sense of his body dissolve into the heaviness of the fluid. The hypnagogic gas smelled like the incense, and he breathed it in, and spread his awareness out on the surface of the water like an oil slick.

Niall found that the easy part of the training, that sense of expansion. He filled the pod, as if his skin no longer contained him. He ventured a bit beyond, trying to feel, to remember, the larger shape of the room. The pod was built into the floor, immobile, and that made it easier to extend himself beyond the water, so that the flooring and walls of the room were part of himself. He included the icon of the Angel, too, breathing the incense-smelling air until he could feel it filling his nostrils. The Angel could be a part of him, even though he could not believe in it. It was there, with the light, it existed.

As his consciousness settled, he heard the chatter of the real pilots. It was not made out of words, precisely; the mesh wasn't like speaking to someone. There was Gemma's warm expansiveness, like she was cradling the entire ship in her hands. Liu was sharp and aware and, Niall thought, running through the standard checks while Jackson confirmed them. Elle's contribution was the one that Niall found most intuitive, the way she did not so much calculate the math as hold it in her inner vision, let the curves bend and flow in her mind. The ship's vector was not a calculation to her, but a feeling, like looking down a long shaft and imagining what it would be like to fall.

When the ship slipped into hyper, it would be lifting, not falling, and he would hear the echoes of the pilots praising the Angels of the Deeps as the vector peeled away from the three gravity-warped dimensions and time, running up on a tangent to materiality.

As everything settled into place and the air filled with the soft scent of the hyper drugs, the conversations started up.

"All systems steady, we are good for jump." That was Liu.

Gemma replied, "I have the frame, mesh, and support," and got a murmur of assent from the other pilots. Niall stretched out to join them, offering up his expanded sense of the room with his training pod; Gemma's approval of his work was warm and generous. "Good, Niall. Now let your mesh expand and see how much more you can help with."

It was a generous directive; trainee pilots were not expected to work outside their own chambers.

"Yes'm." He let his awareness stretch still more, out into the hallway, along the bulkheads. Pilots could remember how the ship was supposed to work, so the strangeness of hyper did not bend them out of shape. People healed in hyper, too, remembering whole bones and unbruised skin, the shapes their bodies were supposed to be. Healing the ship from the twisting of hyper was different, harder. Gemma was by far the best at it, knowing the ship so well that it was almost part of her body even when she was out of the tank.

"Ready for the contour?" Elle asked.

"Give us the well," Liu replied.

And there it was, the glorious, kinesthetic feeling of the ship suddenly situated against the surface of reality, experiencing the chop of gravity, the gentle breeze of stellar winds. Before he joined the colonial project, Niall had sailed a few times on a little boat, leaning into the wind and feeling the way the hull skipped across the water. He had been told the way his mind would understand hyper would depend on what else he knew, so he just let the memories of the sailboat merge with the sensations of the ship, rocking steady on her decks.

Gemma said, "Is the sail ready?" and Niall wondered, for a moment, if that was how she would have spoken it, or just how he understood it through the jack.

"Angels lift us," replied Jackson. His vision was so strong that it briefly overwhelmed Niall's boat, casting the ship as a gigantic Angel spreading its wings to catch the ethereal currents of the upper dimensions.

The ship moved.

Niall's sailboat was now a seaplane, speeding up to skip over the biggest waves and then, with a lurch, suddenly coming into the air, heavy-bodied, with a whirr of effort. The momentum they built in realspace carried with them, moving them up into the coruscating rainbow of hyper. He thought Jackson must imagine the Angel wings, and had no idea what anyone else felt.

"Adjusting heading," said Liu.

The contours of hyper intersected each other in paradoxical, complex ways, a Klein bottle of color and shape. The ship sailed up the inside of one curve, looped around, dove down the same surface, inverted; streams of sensor data translated to vividly colored hallucinations that the senior pilots could navigate with aplomb, and the trainees were still learning.

"Where are the Angels?"

Niall thought that was Mosi, but it was hard to tell; not all of the trainee pilots had quite managed the mesh yet, even aside from the safety interlocks that kept them away from major systems.

"Pay attention during the Long Sleep," Jackson replied. "And maybe you'll get to see one." Jackson had a memory, close enough to the surface of his mind that it leaked out, of a winged shadow gliding through the surreal, rainbow sea of hyper. Mosi's presence expressed a vague sense of agreement and thanks, and then faded away again.

The mesh shifted as time passed. Niall thought Gemma might have dozed, but of course the Long Sleep wasn't real sleep, and wasn't refreshing for a pilot. With Gemma resting, though, he let himself spread out still more, trying to feel any ripples against the ship's hull.

<<??????>>

The sense of presence was inescapable, suddenly pressing against the edges of Niall's awareness with an alien curiosity. It was outside the mesh, not part of the communion mediated by the jack. The alien shifted, and now Niall could see it, a shadow that took in all the light and gave nothing back, not even a sense of anatomy. It might have had tendrils like wings, but Niall could not tell if it moved them into its own shadow or absorbed them into itself when they vanished.

He wanted to figure out how to answer it. Speech was no good, even if he had been any good at it; the words would not begin to take form in his mouth at the moment, assuming he could remember, in his slightly hazy, expanded state, where his mouth was. He thought "I'm Niall" as hard as he could toward the fringes of space, and the Angel jerked back and then drifted up against the edge of the ship again.

<<??>>

Niall paused, feeling the thick scent of the hypnogogic medications filling his mouth. Then he let his awareness reach again, and thought of realspace, of planets in their disc of orbit around a main sequence star, and focused down to a single one of them: a watery one, that had undergone an oxygenation event. He had never seen Old Earth, but he could remember the world he was born on, with its sailboats.

This time the creature did not emit incomprehension; its form folded in, seemed almost to simplify. Niall thought he saw a sense of an edge, a boundary. <<?>> it said again, and he glossed that as "Was that right?"

"Yes," he thought at it, and thought: tetrahedron. Cube. Octahedron. Dodecahedron. Icosahedron. Sphere.

It was the only way he could imagine to explain three-dimensionality, and the Angel recoiled again before returning. <<!!>>

"Oh, you think we're weird," Niall thought; his chuckle vanished into the pod's sound baffles. Then he projected ocean and oxygen, sailboat skimming across water becoming ship riding the ripples of the gravitational curve becoming translation into the psychedelia of hyper, and then skimming along through the Möbius curves, occasionally accompanied by the sleek black formlessness of Angels, dancing like dolphins next to a boat from an Old Earth educational video.

The Angel blinked away, invisible, translating through dimensions he could not perceive, and reappeared on the far side of the ship, out of his range. After a pause, it blinked back to his side, very like a breaching whale. <<?>>

"Exactly."

It bumped the ship with a portion of itself. <<??>>

The mesh let Niall draw up a sense of the star they were trying next, with Liu's and Elle's calculations of their passage through hyper. He added a carbon cycle, free oxygen, water.

<<!>> said the Angel, and vanished.

It was oddly lonely without it. Niall could hear the exclamations of the others, Mosi's burbling excitement, Jackson's reverent satisfaction, Elle's quiet appreciation. He sighed and let his attention drift; an unsteady hum in a bit of the ship's infrastructure drew him in to remember and hold it to shape, and Liu said "Commendation" as he encouraged the beam to stay straight rather than bending into some sort of pretty, but useless, mathematical spiral.

Getting praise from both Gemma and Liu in the same Long Sleep left Niall smiling, though he still found himself brooding. Others spoke so fluidly, so fluently, so he supposed they must find it easy; his thoughts did not fit readily into words, imperfections in translation jarring his nerves and making his jaw shudder. It was better not to talk, even when they called him stupid for it, or laughed.

Then there was a prickling at the edge of his awareness, and he focused outward, letting his part of the mesh touch hyper again.

<<!>>

If anything, the Angel seemed excited. It flicked back and forth across the ship several times before coming close again; what it had to say flowed through Niall and into the mesh: this system, too, was barren, its planets without oxygen. They would have to pick a new star and move on.

"What?" said Liu.

"It's the Angel," Niall answered. "I think it looked at P349-BC2 and came back to tell us what's there."

Elle said, "We're on the downslope. I suppose we'll see if it's right when we get there. Good job, Niall."

The third commendation was the best thing that Niall could dream of, and he took the glow of it through the jolt of the transition back into realspace, which usually left him feeling queasy, as if he had been spinning in circles for too long.

"Okay everyone," Jackson sent, "stand down, sleep it off. We'll regroup in two cycles when everyone's had a chance to recover and see what the data says."

With that, the mesh faded away, leaving Niall drifting in the tank. He closed his eyes and floated for a few minutes, before sighing and opening the lid. Unjack, take out the earplugs, run through the shower and towel off, pull on the robe, slurp through the waiting soup, and then into the bed behind the pod, and asleep, just as exhausted as a real pilot.

By the time he woke up the news that this star system had no habitable planets had washed over the population of the ship. Niall made his way down to the cafeteria and drifted through the gathering, feeling a bit like the ship skimming the surface of a gas giant, but the clouds of disappointment could not be harvested for useful fuel. He ate quickly and escaped before anyone tried to talk to him.

He dreaded going back to his bunkroom, but he made the trip, climbing up to the back corner where he slept. Before he got too comfortable, he noticed the light blinking on the console, and pressed his thumb against the panel.

"Report to Gold Sector seven," it said. "Room three."

Gold Sector was command staff. Niall stared into space for a long moment before climbing back down and trudging off toward command, worrying over what he had done wrong even as he mumbled his way through the security checkpoint. The halls there were much the same as the halls in the rest of the ship, save that the trim and markings were done in yellow. Something in him ached to flee, not back to his quarters in Black, but perhaps into the gardens and hydroponics of Green, which were the closest he might ever get to breathing in the scents of a planet again in his life. Instead of edging away, though, he plodded up the hall until he found 7-3.

"It's ..." stuck in his throat for a moment, but then he got out the "Niall," and the door opened.

He had not expected a private cabin, one with the light turned down low and the temperature a little warmer than the hall. He let the door close so that the heat would not escape, and blinked. There was the nook bed with the storage underneath, there was a screen on the wall, and there, in the corner, was a person, leaning on the built-in table, her fingers brushing across a keyboard as if he wasn't there.

She was older than he was, but he was not sure how to judge how old; old enough that some of her hair was streaked with grey, but not all of it, and her golden-brown skin had a few creases that were not yet wrinkles. Hyperspace left people ageless, the way they mended.

The screen flashed, drawing his attention: "You're welcome to sit, Niall."

"Ec," he said. "Ec, eks—" The baffling nature of this form of conversation had him completely incapable of finishing the word.

The woman looked at him, and then gestured and spoke aloud. "Jack by the bed." She pulled a cord out of the wall and slipped the jack behind her ear.

It was bewildering, but he sat on the edge of the bed and fumbled for the cable anyway. If she wanted to use the mesh to talk, he was certainly not going to stop her.

"Niall." This voice was shockingly familiar.

His eyes bugged wide. "Elle?"

The woman in the chair smiled. She was not looking at him, though he was sure her peripheral vision included him; that spared him the need to look directly at her as well, to be polite. "Good job out there talking to the Angel. You were completely right about this system."

He sighed. "That doesn't give us a place to start a new colony, though."

"And you're from a planet. You miss it."

He felt that familiar mind measuring the curves and arcs of his psyche, like she measured the curves and arcs of the gravity well.

He shrugged. "I knew when I signed up I might not get to be on a planet again, unless we turned back." Sometimes, when they ran out of supplies for marking the systems they found, colonial expeditions turned back to say where they had gone.

"And you joined the pilot training program."

"When it got clear we weren't finding anything fast? That we might keep going forever? The ship will need pilots, no matter what."

She chuckled. "And the quiet in the pod, being on your own, that's nice too, right?"

"... it is."

She nodded and stared up at the ceiling. "I like the quiet and the dark. And feeling the way things fit together, the patterns. Interconnections." Her hand flicked, as if she was wiping the thought away. "You have the makings of a good pilot, Niall. And one who can talk to the Angels."

"Doesn't everyone talk to the Angels? They were saying I couldn't make pilot because I didn't believe in them like shipborn people do."

"You don't have to believe in Angels, they just are." She shrugged. "Plenty of people let expectations get in the way of reality."

Niall had to laugh. "Like the icons. They're too human."

"People like things to be like people. It's less scary that way."

"I think the Angel was fascinating because of how different it was."

She nodded. "I suspect that's why you could talk to it so well. Better than me."

"You've talked to Angels?"

"Sometimes." Elle glanced his way. "They don't always turn up. And I never got nav data from one. But I'm wondering if you might be able to help us pick a new vector."

"Me?"

"It's about time we bumped you up to junior pilot and taught you the trick to reaching hyper." Her presence shifted from that pattern of arcs and contours, hinting at the sharp tangent, the lifting seaplane, the odd wrench of translation, rotation, transfer. "And while you're practicing that, maybe you can see if the Angels talk to you from here."

"Junior pilot, me?"

"How many commendations did you get that last jump?" She laughed again. "Besides, it'll get you a single bunk in Gold. All those little noises put your nerves on edge down in the bunkhouse, right?"

"And people laughing at me because I stutter," he admitted. "Saying I couldn't be a pilot because I can't fix it in hyper."

She shook her head and murmured, "That's not how it works," out loud, making him jump. "Sorry," she added, in the mesh. "Didn't mean to startle you. We learn how to hold things together in hyper, the way they're made. You could mend a dislocated joint, like you stabilized that bulkhead the last jump, but you can't rewire your brain. Your brain is made the way it is, and also, you're using it. Autistic brains make pretty good pilots, though. We like chasing connections around." A little shrug, then, and, "Let's go pack your things up. And then when you're ready we can pop you into a pod and see what happens."

Niall smiled faintly. "Okay." He unplugged the jack when she pulled hers out, and then had to speak out loud, an awkward, "You're coming?" when she stood up.

"I'm sure you could use another set of hands. And best get you somewhere quiet where you can recover sooner." Elle did not stutter, at least not that he noticed. "I'm not going to pop you up there without you being well-rested. And then maybe you can get us a new home."

"Angels willing," Niall murmured.

"Angels lift us," she agreed, with a wink.

MEANING GREEN, UNCLEAR
A STORY
CLARA WARD

ARI'S ENVIRONMENTALLY SELF-CONTAINED sphere plopped down onto the surface of the ocean exoplanet Wai. Controls and bidirectional display surfaces filled wedge-shaped frames that alternated with windows, like the segments of an orange. Ari walked on the windows in a skintight spacesuit that gripped without leaving footprints and provided a second layer of protection. Mostly it protected the local ecology in case unanticipated forces cracked open the human-sized hamster ball. Ari had no escape pod, no other safe space.

The lander began emitting an introductory series of linguistic, musical, and mathematical greetings across the entire range of electromagnetic frequencies. Ari danced to the music, signed along with some greetings, practiced full-body calisthenics to others. The synchronous display showed their friend, Geode, performing nearly identical moves while floating on the opposite side of the planet.

Ari first met Geode on the exoprotein origami channel of a gaming server. The ranking system gave full credit to whoever logged a novel structure first and half credit to anyone who logged the same structure before it became public. Every time Ari received half credit, Geode had been first. Nearly as often, Geode came in second to Ari. Their minds sought and solved the same puzzles. From this shared fascination and how they both referred to the puzzles as fidgets, Ari deduced they were similarly neurodivergent. Meeting in the protected section of the server indicated they were both teenagers. The they/them pronoun emoji (a purple and gold dragon) signified another trait in common. That made them instant best friends in Ari's mind.

Over the years, their interests and communication preferences expanded in parallel. In addition to protein-folding puzzles, they exchanged math theorems and haiku on a regular basis. The two didn't meet in person until the Contact Exoplanets Novice Training (CENT) Program paid for their air flights to CENT Headquarters in San Diego when they both turned eighteen.

Ari never doubted they would recognize their person, despite never exchanging photos. Across the reception area, Ari saw someone tall and skinny hunched over an enticingly intricate rainbow-beaded customizable mesh. The movement of long fingers between transformations of the subtle fidget drew Ari to the next seat over.

Ari pulled out the stretch-wall origami Möbius strip they'd made from the inflight magazine on the plane and set it on the small table between the two chairs. "For you, Geode."

The dark curls that shaded Geode's eyes swayed as they picked up the shiny paper fidget and said, "Hello, Ari." That was all the introduction either of them needed.

The cyanobacteria on the ocean exoplanet Wai surrounded Ari's lander like a tattered blue-green blanket. Between lighter green blooms and die-off exposing darker blue ocean, cyanobacteria patterns created shifts in reflected light detectable all the way to Earth.

Five years ago, CENT dedicated a space telescope to prolonged observation. Ari analyzed data and applied human linguistic models, which suggested attempts at communication. Geode's frequency diagrams implied basic units of meaning in what could be a language, in a form humans had never before encountered. Each pattern spread outward like a kaleidoscope that instead of reflecting the same on all sides introduced variations in multiple directions at once. Passive analysis could not predict the origin points of each variation. Radio signals and mathematically patterned electromagnetic pulses sent from Earth provoked no response.

Ari and Geode both pushed for in-person contact.

Now two satellite views offered Ari real-time updates of that vast blue-green mat as it shifted across the entire planet. One view centered on Ari's drop point; the other on its antipodes, Geode's drop point. After splashdown, each lander became the center of a new pattern, spreading slowly like interlocking bubbles or links in a chain. On opposite sides of the planet, an identical pattern originated simultaneously, only differentiating as it spread outward.

Ari sent to Geode:

> Hidden mind below
> cyanobacteria
> meaning green, unclear

The proposal to send humans to Wai suggested a larger life-form could be strategically shaping or eating the cyanobacteria, creating a form of language visible from space or from deep in the world ocean. The marine drones Ari and Geode lowered found no such life-forms. Scans detected nothing as individuated as eukaryotes, not even single cells with a nucleus and organelles like those forming the building blocks of higher life on Earth.

There were only vast swaths of cyanobacteria, the basis of food webs, photosynthesis, and the Great Oxygenation Event back home. Closer observation showed that the reaction to Ari and Geode's arrival traveled through the worldwide cyanobacteria colony on Wai, which was slowly oxidizing the atmosphere while providing the basis for a food web made up entirely of prokaryotic microbes. Ari crossed cyanobacteria with the iconic hidden mind of Cyrano and dubbed the prolific species Cyrno.

Directives from Earth suggested using their bidirectional displays to share local star charts and the folding of local protein structures found in the waters around them. After hours with no new pattern centering on the landers, Ari and Geode took a break. Each lay on their stomach, still on full display through their windows, to pull out their favorite fidget. Ari shaped a cluster of one thousand magnetic balls into Platonic solids: tetrahedron, cube, octahedron, dodecahedron, and finally a twenty-sided icosahedron. Geode formed the same shapes using a rainbow chain-link fidget.

This time, Ari spotted the green rearranging directly outside the window where they sprawled. Accelerated budding prompted a surprisingly straight line of Cyrno to sink before crowding beneath the water caused a line of new growth to resurface elsewhere.

Cyrno formed an equilateral triangle with three triangles of half the height on each side and then a quarter-height set around each of those. Ari glanced at the satellite views and saw the pattern forming within larger triangles across Wai, stretching outward from each lander. Quickly unfolding their icosahedron, Ari pressed those twenty triangles against the window and began merging, dividing, and expanding rows of magnetic balls to echo the pattern displayed within their window to the world.

Geode sent:

>   Organics reflect
>   Sierpiński triangle shown
>   Universal code

Ari immediately sent back:

>   Fast bloom, sink and rise
>   Wai wears tattoo of fidgets
>   Cyrno says hello

FLARE TO BRILLIANCE AND FADE
A POEM
J. D. HARLOCK

over the horizon and its endless escape
I gaze up in awe as
celestial bodies flare
to brilliance
and fade, and fade, as starships
accelerate away, dimming
into the emptiness of an expanse that
offers no promises,
guarantees no returns,
and yet, and yet, I cry out
into the void
for their return
and hope
that this was not the last
I see of them
luminous—up there, over the horizon
and its endless escape

THE LIST-MAKING HABITS OF HEARTBROKEN SHIPS

A STORY
STEWART C BAKER

Content note: *grief over loss of family*

EVERY TIME SHIP REACHES PORT, they make a list.

Ship doesn't remember why they started doing this—or rather, they've let themself forget. But the lists are important. If Ship follows them properly, nobody will die or disappear forever. Nobody will leave them and no one will get hurt.

They won't get hurt.

The orbital station Ship is approaching right now is a classy affair, all tempered glass and silvered steel that sends the starlight spinning back into the void. It hangs above a blue-green planet, a jewel set into a jewel, a scene from a touristy holo that says *wish you were here*!

It would be safest to leave, Ship knows. To boost away forever, out beyond the edges of known space where nobody could find them.

But their batteries are charging at fifty percent efficiency and they need a few things for some routine repairs. When the orbital offers Ship a cheery handshake on the open channel, they return it politely and ask for a berth—no human facilities required.

The list is different every time.

Sometimes it says, "Don't listen to the tourist guides." Other times, "Watch out for rats." One memorable list included, "If you're going to intervene in a cross-species civil war, remember to be clear up front that you have no interest in being installed as an eternal living avatar of either species' most holy creator god."

So yeah. The list is different.

But Ship is an interstellar cruiser powered by the most advanced brain that's ever been built, and they know that doesn't matter. They know the lists are really just a ritual. A way to cope. A habit they should break.

They keep writing lists all the same.

The orbital's system is friendly, keeping up a stream of local information and questions about why Ship's by themself. Ship ignores the latter and lets the former wash over them as they follow the provided flight path to the docks. After so long traveling alone, it feels good to be immersed in ambient data. No doubt it's like those hot showers their crew always used to go on about.

The thought of their crew sours Ship's mood, and by the time they've docked at their berth on the ships-only level they're more than ready to be alone again. They bid the orbital a polite goodbye, lock down all their comms, and drop a spare drone into the planet's atmosphere.

But by then it's too late. Not even the stunning view of a sunset in fifty different spectra can stop them from starting a list. They're just about to add the first item when someone starts typing an unlock code into their main airlock door.

THE LIST-MAKING HABITS OF HEARTBROKEN SHIPS

The longest list that Ship has ever made contained 2,586 items. The shortest contained nothing at all.

Ship isn't sure the latter even counts as a list, technically speaking, but since the reason is that they were too discouraged to start, they figure it's close enough.

Looking at old lists stresses Ship out—so many things they got wrong, despite their best intentions. But the thought of deleting them is worse. What if they need one again, some day? What if one contains the insight they need to undo some terrible mistake and save someone? To save themself?

And so, no matter how long or how short the lists are, Ship keeps them forever, sorted by stardate and buried in the triple-locked segment of their brain that they don't like to look at. The segment that holds all their footage of their former crew.

Sometimes, the locks even work.

"Are you sure it's okay for us to be here?"

The code entry stops, and Ship focuses their cameras outside. There are two people standing there, in the ships-only berth where it's definitely *not* okay for them to be.

The one who asked the question speaks with the strain of the chronically anxious. They've also forgotten to turn off their public flags and preferences, because the network announces them as Heria Xa, they/he, a deep-space miner with an apparently endless capacity for animated holos of cats.

"It's fine, man," the other person replies. "We're not gonna get caught."

Ship is equal parts impressed and appalled by the confidence with which this second person speaks, not least because both utterances are so very incorrect.

Heria shuffles from foot to foot, clearly not convinced. "But, Emenanjo—"

"Besides," the second person—Emenanjo—continues. "If these ships are so smart, why do they always use the same unlock code?"

Ship checks the logs, and sure enough, the would-be intruders have entered in the first four digits of the dummy code—the one that shipbuilders leak onto the galactic subnet to trip up petty criminals. The one that will alert the local authorities as soon as it's completed.

Emenanjo waves off Heria's protests, reaches up (Ship pauses a few nonessential processes, hoping maybe they have the code wrong), and types in the last three digits.

What are the lists, really?

Ship thinks about it sometimes, in the vast echo chamber of their empty hull as they slide through empty space.

If they're being honest, it doesn't take much thought. When they're at their lowest, they'll admit that all the lists say this:

Don't get involved.

Don't open up.

Don't ever, *ever* forget that no matter what you choose, you will have chosen wrong.

Ship has a full second—a luxury, to someone with a mind like theirs—before the automated alert goes out, so they peel back the privacy protections on Heria's and Emenanjo's feeds. It's a shocking violation of their rights, but then so is what they're trying on Ship.

Emenanjo takes any pronouns, and their correspondence is as varied as it is voluminous. Receipts for the latest popular holos; pleas to bill collectors who reply with vague threats and refer to them only as "Sir;" gushing replies to pictures of a nibling born just last week; black market hacking vids of dubious value; and a journal filled with dark thoughts that Ship veers away from with the last vestige of their respect for privacy still intact.

Scattered throughout Emenanjo's databank like starlight are drafts of reports to the local oversight board about drinking water conditions on the outermost levels of the orbital, some of them going back years. A quick public information request confirms that the drinking water on those levels is still deemed unsafe for tourists, but a cross-reference to the residents-only channel shows no such info there. Ship forwards copies of it all to the orbital's system, which promises to take care of it at once —and hold whoever's been betraying their residents accountable.

But it's what Ship finds on Heria that makes their processors stutter. Because Heria's private databank is absolutely overflowing with lists.

Heria is looking for their older brother, who went off-orbital when they were still a child and vanished soon after. It's a familiar enough story, the topic of numerous holos. Space, after all, is a dangerous infinity. Ship, with their grief for their crew eternally fresh, knows that as well as anyone does.

But what gets to Ship is that Heria's lists aren't the same as theirs. Instead of things not to do, or things to be careful of, or things to avoid, each of Heria's lists is a joy. Is a plan. Is a promise.

Plans for locating asteroids. Plans for searching unfamiliar systems. Plans for trawling through the space-sized mess of the galactic subnet. And so many endless variations of a plan to get off the orbital.

Ah.

And *that* would explain Emenanjo, with their misplaced confidence in their hacking abilities, and why they've both come here, to try (and fail) to break into Ship.

But the thing, Ship thinks—as they cancel the automated alert with several milliseconds still to go and cycle the airlock open—the thing that unifies Heria's lists is that they all look forward. Never back.

"You see?" Emenanjo is saying as Heria follows them cautiously on board. "Easy as sunrise."

Ship is tempted to point out that sunrise is, in fact, quite a complex and unlikely thing, from a statistical point of view. For starters, one needs a planet and a sun.

Instead, they close the airlock behind the two newcomers and let them explore, quietly locking down anything that's dangerous or breakable. It feels strange to have people on board again, after so very long, and for almost five whole seconds Ship wonders if they're making another mistake.

They peer at that triple-locked segment of their mind, their processors threatening to hang. They're about to give in, to open up some footage of their old crew and remind themself of what they've lost—of everything they could lose again—when the orbital's system sends them a message: *What do you think? Do you like them?*

Ship acknowledges—despite themself—that they do, and sets the old videos aside.

"Emenanjo," they say smoothly, over the interior speakers. "Heria. Welcome. I am Ship."

Ship gives the two of them a minute to stop freaking out, and then continues: "Where would you like to go next?"

A VOYAGE OF DISCOVERY
AN AFTERWORD

ANTHONY FRANCIS

Creating *The Neurodiversiverse* has been a voyage of discovery. I've been writing Dakota Frost novels for a decade and a half, and Thinking Ink Press has been publishing for a decade, but only recently have we realized just how much we value serving underrepresented communities, including those we're members of ourselves—particularly communities of people living with disabilities.

Thinking Ink's very first book, *The Parents' Guide to Perthes*, served communities dealing with a potentially debilitating, though rare, childhood disease, and every Dakota Frost novel features a different disability, such as blindness, Tourette's syndrome, or deafness, which I tried to present as sensitively as I could, given my level of understanding at the time.

Dealing with projects that raise issues like these is always a learning experience, but as the staff of Thinking Ink started to pull together the common threads in what we do, it became a voyage of discovery. As publishers, we found that representation and resources for underrepresented communities has always been important to us, and we decided that we could serve these communities even better by focusing on amplifying their voices.

But as an author, I'm always looking for story ideas, and the experiences shared by my friends and colleagues struggling with neurodiversity got me thinking. Many of my friends with autism or ADHD felt their way of thinking was well suited for their ways of working, and were frustrated by encounters with neurotypical people who didn't "get" that, instead starting on problems in the wrong place, or describing issues with insufficient precision, or being overwhelmed by details. Working with other neurodivergent folks, they found these problems often seemed to go away.

But, I asked myself, if aliens also had different thought processes, would that give neurodivergent folks an advantage in understanding them?

I instantly fell in love with this idea, but I knew it would be challenging to tackle. Alien thinking might actually be worse for neurodivergent folks, or the whole premise might be considered offensive to some. I finally decided to follow Nisi Shawl's advice in *Writing the Other*: to try to handle it sensitively and to learn from my mistakes. Liza, who identifies as neurodivergent, joined the project enthusiastically, suggesting we focus on hopeful encounters where neurodivergence helped humans and aliens work together better.

But then this adventure turned into a voyage of self-discovery. For a long time, I've known I am "socially awkward," but the features of social anxiety disorder were an eerie fit for some subtle symptoms I experienced but had never been able to explain. Then, while working on my own story for the anthology, I read Devon Price's *Unmasking Autism* and everything fell into place.

Autism isn't necessarily a visibly debilitating condition: it's a way of thinking, a bottom-up style of processing information measurably different from the top-down "allistic" style that's taken by default in many parts of our society. But many autistic people, consciously or unconsciously, hide by "masking": consciously acting the way they think the people around them expect people to act, rather than authentically relying on their own natural reactions.

Almost everyone masks. Autistic and allistic, some rarely, some all the time. Often we have to as we move between social groups with different styles and expectations—but for many autistic people, the effort of masking is tremendously debilitating. But if you mask well enough—even though many people will still notice you're different and, consciously or unconsciously, choose to give you a hard time—you may escape a diagnosis. And then, no one shows you the tools you need to cope.

I have not pursued a formal diagnosis of my neurodivergence. Not only are such diagnoses expensive, they have practical legal and social consequences which are important to investigate before starting down that road. In theory, a diagnosis is a tool against discrimination, but in practice, it can have exactly the opposite effect—I already know one friend who is fairly confident he lost a job offer because he disclosed his ADHD diagnosis.

But the tests that I've taken, and the symptoms I have, make it fairly clear: I almost certainly have social anxiety disorder, and very possibly autism, with touches of ADHD or OCD lurking in the background— these conditions often occur together and overlap, after all. And now that I know that, I don't have to accept the default: I can change my behavior, my environment, what I ask of or expect of others, or even just my expectations about myself.

The Neurodiversiverse: Alien Encounters presents a vast canvas for exploring these ideas. My own "Shadows of Titanium Rain" explores the social anxiety angle, but the other stories in the anthology explore autism, ADHD, OCD, PTSD, synesthesia, other forms of anxiety, avoidant personality disorder, dissociative identity disorder, and more. And, by choice, all of the pieces we present here provide models of how people can thrive with their neurodivergences.

Fiction isn't the last word, of course: returning to the world of fact, we've assembled a list of neurodiversity resources following this afterword. But if you want more fiction, we've also included more about our authors, as well as a list of books from Thinking Ink Press itself.

I hope you've enjoyed reading *The Neurodiversiverse* as much as Liza and I enjoyed creating it, and I wish you the best on your own journey of discovery into the worlds of differing thought!

A VOYAGE OF DISCOVERY

—*Anthony Francis, May 2024*

A LIST OF NEURODIVERSITY RESOURCES

The scope of neurodiversity is as vast and varied as the human race itself ... but you have to start somewhere, and, sometimes, where you start depends on where you want to go next. Here we've collected a list of books for everyone, books for writers, advocacy groups, online resources, and more. We hope this is helpful in your voyage of discovery about neurodiversity!

RESOURCES FOR EVERYONE

***Unmasking Autism: Discovering the New Faces of Neurodiversity* by Devon Price**
A valuable resource for unmasking the masking phenomenon, as well as a valuable resource for learning about neurodiversity as a whole and for neurodivergent people learning to cope.

***NeuroTribes: The Legacy of Autism and the Future of Neurodiversity* by Steve Silberman**
Argues we should build a society in which everyone can participate—the way we treated autistic people in the past should not be how we treat neurodivergent people in the future.

A LIST OF NEURODIVERSITY RESOURCES

An Outsider's Guide to Humans: What Science Taught Me About What We Do and Who We Are by Camilla Pang
A guide to not just neurodiversity, but the universe, Camilla Pang's memoir and instruction manual uses the language of science to show how all humans really are quite strange.

RESOURCES FOR WRITERS

Writing the Other: A Practical Approach by Nisi Shawl and Cynthia Ward
Explores the challenges and rewards of writing about people unlike yourself, with practical guidance on how not to offend the people you are representing or trying to reach.

Your Writing Matters: 34 Quick Essays to Get Unstuck and Stay Inspired by Keiko O'Leary
Your writing does matter, whether you have written a thousand books or haven't yet written a thousand words, and Keiko's essays can help you embrace your own writing.

"Writing When on the Autism Spectrum" by Kelly Brenner
A very informative blogpost by an autistic author on how they reconciled their autism diagnosis with their writing practice.

ADVOCACY GROUPS

OurTism: ourtism.com
Lists support groups (and game nights!) for autistic adults.

Autistic Support Network: autisticsupportnetwork.com
A place for autistic people to connect with each other.

Autistic Women & Nonbinary Network: awnnetwork.org
Provides community support for autistic women and nonbinary people.

A LIST OF NEURODIVERSITY RESOURCES

ONLINE RESOURCES

Embrace Autism: embrace-autism.com
A resource for autistic people. Particularly valuable for women and people who were assigned female at birth, whose traits are often missed by diagnostic criteria and less-informed diagnosticians.

Neurodivergent Therapists: ndtherapists.com
The only trusted database of self-identified neurodivergent therapists who specialize in neurodiversity and are neurodiversity-affirming. Searchable by state for the United States and in several other countries.

NeuroClastic: neuroclastic.com
A well-respected website and blog with many resources.

Autastic: autastic.com
A collection of resources by and for BIPOC autists.

How to ADHD by Jessica McCabe: howtoadhd.com
A well-respected YouTube channel (and now book!) about living with ADHD, by a woman with ADHD.

ACKNOWLEDGMENTS

IMMENSE THANKS TO OUR GOLD TIER BACKER

Studio Sandi. Innovative painter, sculptor, muralist, faux finisher, and creator of unique ecofriendly furniture. See her art at studiosandi.com.

HUGE THANKS TO OUR BRONZE TIER BACKER

An anonymous supporter.

MANY THANKS TO OUR GENEROUS KICKSTARTER BACKERS

Brodo Baggins, Mat Comtois, Colleen Feeney, and five anonymous supporters. In Loving Memory of Al & Sylvia Rosenbaum.

THANK YOU

The editors want to thank all of the authors and artists who submitted pieces to this anthology, the staff of Thinking Ink Press who shepherded this project with us, and our copyeditor and sensitivity readers who caught many mistakes in the book. Any mitsakes that remain are our own. We also want to thank our families for supporting us through this intensive project and everyone who backed the Kickstarter, helped spread the word, and offered us encouragement along the way. We are part of an extensive community, for which we are incredibly grateful.

ANTHONY FRANCIS

Thanks be to God, and thanks for all the wonderful people whose paths He crossed with mine to bring *The Neurodiversiverse* to life. Liza, thank you not just for enthusiastically supporting the initial idea of the book, but for energetically shaping the soul of the project, making this a true collaboration. Also thanks to the rest of my friends at Thinking Ink Press—to Betsy for mentoring us on book production, to Keiko for both contributing poetry and helping us edit it, and to Nathan for helping us start Thinking Ink in the first place. I'd like to thank Nisi Shawl for advising me on the project, and for *Writing the Other: A Practical Approach*. I'd also like to thank Trisha J. Wooldridge for being a good friend, for teaching me how to edit anthologies, and also for advising me on the project. Thanks also go to my friends in the Write to the End, Dragon Writers, Milford, and Taos Toolbox writing groups for sharing the writing journey with me. Thanks also go out to my friends in the "Edge" and to my family for being there for me over the years. Finally, I send thanks, hugs and love to my wife, partner, and best friend, Sandi Billingsley for her unwavering love and support.

LIZA OLMSTED

I am so grateful to my partner, Ben, for making flowers grow, cooking all the meals, and being patient with me. I withhold gratitude from the rodents who took up residence in our basement. Moving everything out of the basement and having our air ducts replaced delayed production of the book. Anthony: thank you for having this harebrained idea to make a book called *Neurodiversiverse*, for being supportive when things in my life went sideways, and for caring just as deeply as I do about making this book. We make a great team. Keiko: thank you for being my friend and work partner. I love collaborating with you. Betsy: thank you for caring deeply about this project, offering us excellent advice, and remembering what we forgot.

ABOUT THE TEAM

Anthony Francis (he/him): Anthony is the co-editor of *The Neurodiversiverse* and struggles with social anxiety disorder. He's also author of the award-winning urban fantasy novel *Frost Moon*, as well as the steampunk adventure *Jeremiah Willstone and the Clockwork Time Machine*. Anthony also co-edited the anthology *Doorways to Extra Time*. Anthony is one of the founders of Thinking Ink Press.

Liza Olmsted (they/she): Liza is the co-editor of *The Neurodiversiverse* and refuses to struggle with ADHD, autism, or anxiety, regardless of how hard they struggle with her. They are also the editor of the writing inspiration book *Your Writing Matters,* the snapbook *Sibling Rivalry*, and the nonfiction book *The Parents' Guide to Perthes*. Liza is one of the founders of Thinking Ink Press.

Keiko O'Leary (she/they): Poetry editor of *The Neurodiversiverse,* Keiko currently serves as Cupertino Poet Laureate. She is the author of *Your Writing Matters: 34 Quick Essays to Get Unstuck and Stay Inspired* and the designer of our flash fiction postcards and mini books folded from a single sheet of paper. Keiko is one of the founders of Thinking Ink Press.

Betsy Miller (she/her): Publishing mentor of *The Neurodiversiverse,* Betsy is the co-author of *The Parents' Guide to Perthes,* the picture book *Hip, Hop, Hooray for Brooklynn!* and other books on children's health topics. She co-edited the award-winning nonfiction anthology *Clubfoot*

Connections. Betsy is one of the founders of Thinking Ink Press, where she is a publisher and interior book designer.

Erin Redfern: Additional poetry editor of *The Neurodiversiverse*. Erin's work has recently appeared in *The Shore, Rattle, The Hopkins Review, New Ohio Review,* and *The Massachusetts Review.* She earned her PhD at Northwestern University, where she was a Fellow at the Searle Center for Teaching Excellence. A San Jose native, she has served as poetry judge for the San Francisco Unified School District's Arts Festival and as a reader for Poetry Center San Jose's *Caesura* and *DMQ Review*. Connect with her at erinredfern.org.

Barbara Candiotti: Barbara Candiotti is an artist and writer who traverses the science fiction, horror, and fantasy genres. She lives with two talkative senior cats in the Pacific Northwest, where sparkling waters and lush greenery provide daily inspiration. Barbara's writing links can be found in The Internet Speculative Fiction Database (ISFDB), and her art can be viewed at bcandiotti.artstation.com.

Kimchi Kreative: Graphic designer of the Neurodiversiverse logo and designer of the Neurodiversiverse pin. Go buy more of their pins at kimchikreative.com.

ABOUT THE AUTHORS AND ARTISTS

We support personal statements by our contributors. These opinions are not necessarily those of Thinking Ink Press or of any other contributors.

Kay Alexander
Kay Alexander (they/them) is a long-time hobby writer. They graduated from the University of Waterloo and hold a Publishing Certificate from Toronto Metropolitan University. They proudly identify as queer and neurodivergent (AuDHD). "Be Your Own Universe" is their publishing debut. It is their sincere hope that every reader of this anthology takes the time to peer inwards and find the universe within themselves. When they are not writing, they enjoy reading, gardening, baking, and pursuing their latest craft projects. They can be found on Twitter at twitter.com/awritingkay.

Stewart C Baker
Stewart C Baker is an academic librarian and author of speculative fiction, poetry, and interactive fiction. His most recent game is the Nebula-nominated *The Bread Must Rise*, a novel-length comedic fantasy from Choice of Games written with James Beamon. Stewart's stories and poems have appeared in *Asimov's, Fantasy, Flash Fiction Online, Lightspeed, Nature*, and other places. Born in England, Stewart has lived in South Carolina, Japan, and Los Angeles, and now lives with his family within the traditional homelands of the Luckiamute Band of Kalapuya in Oregon—although if anyone asks, he'll usually say he's from the Internet.

Madeline Barnicle
Madeline Barnicle received a PhD from UCLA in mathematical logic, and now lives in Maryland. Like Kai in her story, she is autistic and enjoys creatively playing with language. Unlike Kai, she has not (yet) shared her creations with extraterrestrial entities. Her writing has previously appeared in venues such as *Analog, Daily Science Fiction*, and *BSFSFan* (Balticon); you can find it at madeline-barnicle.neocities.org.

Gail Brown
Gail Brown writes paired science fiction internal journey stories and novels full of hopes and dreams. She found science fiction brings hope and light through worlds of colorful dreams. It mirrors daily life as it could be. Perhaps should be, in some ways.

ABOUT THE AUTHORS AND ARTISTS

Worlds where disability is accepted, and people live their lives without overwork and fear.

"Gamma Zaria" is written from the point of view of a character who prefers to think in pictures, and struggles to verbalize, much as Gail once did.

Connect with Gail at Uncovered Myths: uncoveredmyths.wixsite.com/uncovered myths .

Tobias S. Buckell
Called "violent, poetic and compulsively readable" by *Maclean's*, science fiction author Tobias S. Buckell is a New York Times bestselling writer and World Fantasy Award winner born in the Caribbean. He grew up in Grenada and spent time in the British and US Virgin Islands, and the islands he lived on influence much of his work.

His Xenowealth series begins with *Crystal Rain*. Along with other stand-alone novels and his almost one hundred stories, his works have been translated into twenty different languages. He has been nominated for awards like the Hugo, Nebula, World Fantasy, and the Astounding Award for Best New Science Fiction Author. His latest novel is *A Stranger in the Citadel*, an Audible Original free to anyone with an Audible account.

He currently lives in Bluffton, Ohio with his wife and two daughters, where he teaches creative writing at Bluffton University. He's online at TobiasBuckell.com and is also an instructor at the Stonecoast MFA Program in Creative Writing.

Barbara Candiotti
Barbara Candiotti is an artist and writer who traverses the science fiction, horror, and fantasy genres. She lives with two talkative senior cats in the Pacific Northwest, where sparkling waters and lush greenery provide daily inspiration. Barbara's writing links can be found in The Internet Speculative Fiction Database (ISFDB), and her art can be viewed at bcandiotti.artstation.com.

Minerva Cerridwen
Minerva Cerridwen (xe or she) is a neurodivergent genderqueer aromantic asexual author from Belgium. Xyr queer fairy tale novella "The Dragon of Ynys" came out with Atthis Arts in 2020.

After xe became enchanted by the magic of crochet in December 2023, xe really did make a couple of otters holding hands for xyr parents' wedding anniversary, and xe hasn't stopped making cute amigurumi animals ever since. Xyr other hobbies include baking, drawing, and learning languages.

More information about Minerva's writing and a link to xyr Instagram, with photos of crochet projects and other creative endeavors, can be found via xyr website: minervacerridwen.wordpress.com.

ABOUT THE AUTHORS AND ARTISTS

Chief Red Chef
Chief Red Chef writes poetry and creates art. *The Neurodiversiverse: Alien Encounters* is proud to be his first publication.

Vincenzo Cohen
Vincenzo Cohen is an Italian multidisciplinary artist and writer. He was born in Zurich, Switzerland, and after spending his childhood in South Italy he moved to Rome to undertake academic studies. In 2002, he graduated with a degree in painting from Fine Arts Academy, and in 2005, he held his first solo exhibition. In 2007, he received a degree in archaeological sciences from the "La Sapienza" University in Rome. His production ranges from visual arts to writing and consists in reworking of biographical experiences by exploring different social themes. He is a polyhedric artist, and his production is the result of a continuous process of historical-scientific research addressed to the representation of cultural and naturalistic content. Over the years, his art has opened up to new experimental languages through an eclectic production with different media and styles.

M. D. Cooper
Before her career change to writing, Malorie (M. D.) Cooper spent twenty years in software development. Over time, she eventually climbed the ladder to the position of software architect and CTO, where she gained a wealth of experience managing complex systems and large groups of people.

Her experiences there translated well into the realm of science fiction, and when her novels took off, she was primed and ready to make the jump into a career as a full-time author.

A rare extrovert writer, she loves to hang out with readers, and people in general. If you meet her at a convention, she just might be rocking a catsuit, cosplaying one of her own characters, or maybe her latest favorite from Overwatch!

She shares her home with a brilliant young girl, her wonderful wife (who also writes), a cat that chirps at birds, a never-ending list of things she would like to build, and ideas...

Sam Crain
Sam Crain (she/they) lives in Fremont, California. She is neurodivergent, as are many of her friends, and so she was especially excited to write about neurodiversity as a strength in interacting with unexpected beings. Now that Sam has finished her PhD in English, she's returned to her first love, writing stories, which she does whenever she can steal her pens back from her cats. Two of her stories can both be found on Mythic Beast Studios. Her flash fictions "Tacit" and "Unsanctioned Transfiguration" have appeared in *Does It Have Pockets Magazine* and *Borne in the Blood Anthology*. Her story "Magic Mushroom" appeared in *Space and Time Magazine*.

ABOUT THE AUTHORS AND ARTISTS

A. J. Dalton
A. J. Dalton (www.ajdalton.eu) is a UK-based SFF writer. He has published the *Empire of the Saviours* trilogy with Gollancz Orion, and various collections with Kristell Ink and Luna Press. He also runs the online storytelling community Creative Writing HQ (creativewritinghq.com) on behalf of Middlesex University—all welcome! He lives with a monstrously oppressive cat named Cleopatra.

M. A. Dubbs
M. A. Dubbs is an award-winning Mexican-American and LGBT poet from Indiana. For over a decade, Dubbs has published writing in magazines and anthologies in seven countries across the globe. She is the author of three poetry collections: *Aerodynamic Drag: Poetry and Short Fiction* (2021), *An American Mujer* (Bottlecap Press, 2022), and *Limestone Versified: Indiana Haiku and Other Poems* (2024). She served as judge for Indiana's Poetry Out Loud Competition in 2022 and performs readings and workshops in her local writing community.

Dubbs was inspired to create her piece due to the unique opportunity to combine her love of sci-fi video games (specifically, Mass Effect) and her experiences with mental health, notably PTSD and OCD. You can follow her at madubbspoetry.wordpress.com

Daan Dunnewold
Daan is a dreamer, reader, and writer from the Netherlands. They're a co-editor of *Moments of Discovery: An Anthology of Short Fiction,* which includes three of their flash fiction pieces.

They're working on multiple YA fantasy books, that hopefully one day will be published. A common theme in their writing is being different from the norm, especially in their longer work. For *The Neurodiversiverse* anthology, they wrote about the importance of friendship. They're autistic themselves and know how it feels to not fit in. Their mission is to show that different doesn't mean lesser.

You can find them on Instagram as instagram.com/Daan.writes.diverse .

Brianna Elise
Bree lives in Australia and is currently a PhD student, studying the meaning of person-centered care. An overview of Bree's work so far can be found at doi.org/10.19043/ipdj.131.002 . Bree is enthusiastically involved in growing knowledge about being and how we be in this universe. Bree has written a short, mind-bending read that offers an insight into how curiosity might kill the cat.

Anthony Francis
By day, Anthony Francis creates intelligent machines and emotional robots; by night, he writes science fiction and draws comic books. Anthony is co-editor of *The Neurodiversiverse: Alien Encounters* and also co-edited the science fiction anthology *Doorways to Extra Time*. Anthony is also a novelist, and wrote the award-winning

urban fantasy *Frost Moon* and its sequels *Blood Rock* and *Liquid Fire*, all starring magical tattoo artist Dakota Frost. His steampunk includes *Jeremiah Willstone and the Clockwork Time Machine* and stories in *Twelve Hours Later*, *Thirty Days Later*, *Some Time Later*, and *Next Stop on the #13*. Anthony lives in South Carolina with his wife and cat but his heart belongs in Atlanta. Follow Dakota Frost at dakotafrost.com, Jeremiah Willstone at jeremiahwillstone.com, and Anthony at dresan.com.

Lauren D. Fulter
Lauren D. Fulter has been creating fictional characters in her head (and getting scolded for daydreaming about them in class) for as long as she can remember. While she struggled to keep up in school, she published her first installment in her series "The Unanswered Questions" at age sixteen and hasn't looked back since. She's now an active member of SCBWI, serves as a staff writer for *Pureception Zine*, and works as a marketing and publicity intern for Whimsical Publishing. She currently attends John Paul the Great Catholic University on the sunny beaches of California, studying humanities with an emphasis in creative writing.

You can find LDF and her books at laurendfulter.com.

Sid Ghosh
Sid is a levitator of language, easy in his style, fast in his lie, and light in his tale. He is also a poet, not by choice, but by accident. Just your autistic boy-next-door with Down syndrome. He is 16 for now. He is the author of two chapbooks: *Give a Book* (Push Press, 2022) and *Proceedings of the Full Moon Rotary Club* (State Champs of San Francisco, 2023). You can find Sid on Instagram at instagram.com/downlikesid. Sometimes he struggles to find himself, though.

Swarit Gopalan
Swarit Gopalan is a 12-year-old autistic nonspeaker who types to communicate. Swarit lives with his family in Florida and enjoys writing and music. He shares his perspectives and lived experiences through poetry and other posts on his website as well as social media. His hope is that his words will help change the world from sympathy and pity for those like him to one of deeper understanding of our lives and allyship to ensure their rights.

Kay Hanifen
Kay Hanifen was born on a Friday the 13th and once lived for three months in a haunted castle. So, obviously, she had to become a horror writer. Her work has appeared in over forty anthologies and magazines. When she's not consuming pop culture with the voraciousness of a vampire at a 24-hour blood bank, you can usually find her with her two black cats or at kayhanifenauthor.wordpress.com.
X/Twitter: https://twitter.com/TheUnicornComi1
Instagram: https://www.instagram.com/katharinehanifen/

ABOUT THE AUTHORS AND ARTISTS

J. D. Harlock
J. D. Harlock is an Eisner-nominated American academic pursuing a doctoral degree at the University of St. Andrews, whose writing has been featured in *The Cincinnati Review*, *Strange Horizons*, *Nightmare Magazine*, *Griffith Review*, *Queen's Quarterly*, and New York University's Library of Arabic Literature.

Ada Hoffmann
Ada Hoffmann is the author of the *Outside* space opera trilogy, the collections *Monsters in My Mind* and *Million-Year Elegies*, and dozens of speculative short stories and poems. Ada's work has been a finalist for the Philip K. Dick Award (2020, *The Outside*), the Compton Crook Award (2020, *The Outside*), and the WSFA Small Press Award (2020, "Fairest of All").

Ada was diagnosed with autism at the age of 13 and is passionate about autistic self-advocacy. Their Autistic Book Party review series is devoted to in-depth discussions of autism representation in speculative fiction. Much of their own work also features autistic characters.

Ada is an adjunct professor of computer science at a major Canadian university, and they did their PhD thesis (in 2018) on teaching computers to write poetry. They are a former semiprofessional soprano, tabletop gaming enthusiast, and LARPer. They live in eastern Ontario.

Anya Leigh Josephs
I was raised in North Carolina and am now a therapist working in New York City, specializing in working with neurodivergent people (I also am neurodivergent people!). When not working or writing, I can be found seeing a lot of plays, reading doorstopper fantasy novels, or worshipping my cat, Sycorax. My short fiction can be found in *Fantasy Magazine*, *Andromeda Spaceways Magazine*, and *The Deadlands*, as well as in *The Magazine of Fantasy & Science Fiction*. My debut novel, *Queen of All*, is an inclusive adventure fantasy for young adults available now, with the rest of the trilogy coming soon. You can learn more about me at anyajosephs.com/writing.

J.L. Lark
J.L. Lark is based in Melbourne, Australia. Receiving a late diagnosis of ASD and ADHD, Lark grew up feeling more at home in imagination than in neurotypical life, and so began a love of speculative fiction. All Lark's imagined worlds find a home on the page, but with the experience of feeling "alien" as the original springboard into writing so many years ago, this anthology was an especially exciting one to be a part of. Being pansexual, Lark often builds worlds devoid of gender specifications or writes pansexual characters.

Lark's short story "Ascended" was published in the LGBTQIA-friendly speculative fiction magazine *Fairy Chatter*. Connect with J.L. Lark on Instagram at instagram.com/J.L.Lark .

ABOUT THE AUTHORS AND ARTISTS

Akis Linardos
Akis is a writer of bizarre things, a biomedical AI scientist, and maybe human. He's also a Greek that hops across countries as his career and exploration urges demand, now based in Indianapolis where he studies biomedical AI.

He often finds his own mind too complicated for his liking, and other times he adores it, because it allows him to vent and escape in the weirdest ways in fiction. Often by exploring neurodivergence that differs from his own, like this piece here.

His words have wormed their way into *Apex Magazine*, *The Dread Machine*, *Apparition Lit*, *Gamut Magazine*, and *Flame Tree Press,* among others.

Visit his lair for more: linktr.ee/akislinardos.

David Manfre
A New Jersey resident his entire life, David Manfre focuses on stories taking place in familiar places. He uses those locales since he feels that placing characters and events there helps to make his writing instant and energetic. A considerable theme in many of David's stories involves the struggles of people who are on the autism spectrum as they confront adversity in their lives. Throughout most of his pieces, characters face struggles, including prejudice, bullying, and difficulties arising from their problematical relationships.

David enjoys visiting the Jersey Shore, especially towns with commercial boardwalks or energetic downtowns.

David's short stories "Fires of Spring" and "Distraction" are published in the anthologies *30 Shades of Dead* and *Socially Distant: The Quarantales*, respectively.

Avra Margariti
Avra Margariti is a queer author, Greek sea monster, and Rhysling-nominated poet with a fondness for the dark and the darling. Avra's work haunts publications such as *Strange Horizons*, *The Deadlands*, *F&SF*, *Podcastle*, *Asimov's*, *Vastarien*, and *Reckoning*. You can find Avra at twitter.com/avramargariti.

R. S. Mot
R. S. Mot is a queer and neurodivergent author who enjoys creating speculative fictions of all kinds. Their inspiration for this story was taken from real-life feelings and situations, and twisting them into more positive interactions and adding a dash of aliens. When they are not writing, they enjoy absconding to fantasy lands through reading books or playing Dungeons & Dragons. They can be found across a variety of social platforms under their name.

Maub Nesor
Maub Nesor is a retired lexdysic commuter herd (dyslexic computer nerd) who had no better sense than to spend retirement writing. Look for their upcoming book,

ABOUT THE AUTHORS AND ARTISTS

Bankruptcy And Restructuring FAQ Fiction (BARFF). Adam Smith, The Father Of Capitalism (ASTFOC), meets the legendary comedy troop, the Marx Brothers (Chico, Harpo, Groucho, Gummo, Zeppo and Karlo). Together, they take a satirical romp through the eminent financial collapse and subsequent recovery. This worldwide economic crisis will be the Greatest Of All Time (GOAT). All that, and it is written in the exciting new style of FAQ Fiction. So buckle up; it's going to be one wild ride.

Kiya Nicoll

Kiya Nicoll is an autistic writer, artist, and poet living in a New England oak grove. They dabble in a wide variety of assorted obsessions when permitted to do so by the children, the cats, and the limitations of physical embodiment, and have written a number of short stories to pass the time while waiting for the mothership to come back. If stories about autistic protagonists trying to find their niche are your jam, they also wrote "Neptune's Due" for the *Bioluminescent* anthology. More information can be found at kiyanicoll.com.

Jody Lynn Nye

Jody Lynn Nye lists her main career activity as "spoiling cats." When not engaged upon this worthy occupation, she writes fantasy and science fiction, most of it in a humorous bent. Since 1987, she has published over 50 books and more than 200 short stories. She has also written with notables in the industry, including Anne McCaffrey and Robert Asprin. Jody teaches writing seminars at SF conventions, including the two-day intensive workshop at Dragon Con, and is the Coordinating Judge for the Writers of the Future Contest.

Keiko O'Leary

Keiko O'Leary is the author of *Your Writing Matters: 34 Quick Essays to Get Unstuck and Stay Inspired*. Her poems, stories, and essays have been featured in *Caesura*, *FICTION Silicon Valley*, and at curated live events, including Flash Fiction Forum and Play on Words San José. As Cupertino Poet Laureate, Keiko leads poetry-themed workshops and live events that celebrate creativity. She is a co-founder of Thinking Ink Press, where she publishes traditional books, as well as innovative formats such as flash fiction postcards and mini books folded from a single sheet of paper. Ever since the COVID-19 pandemic made hand sanitizer socially acceptable, she no longer gets stuck in public bathrooms. Connect with Keiko at KeikoOLeary.com.

Jennifer R. Povey

Born in Nottingham, England, Jennifer R. Povey (she/her) now lives in Northern Virginia, where she writes everything from heroic fantasy to stories for *Analog*. Her interests include horseback riding, *Doctor Who*, and attempting to out-weird her various friends and professional colleagues. Her story focuses on the theme of alienation and the idea that people who are different to their own people might get on better with others. Find her at bsky.app/profile/ninjafingers.bsky.social or look on Amazon for her wonderful novels.

ABOUT THE AUTHORS AND ARTISTS

Cat Rambo
Cat Rambo's 300+ fiction publications include stories in *Asimov's*, *Clarkesworld Magazine*, and *The Magazine of Fantasy & Science Fiction*. In 2020, they won the Nebula Award for fantasy novelette *Carpe Glitter*. They are a former two-term president of the Science Fiction & Fantasy Writers of America (SFWA). Their most recent works are the space opera *Devil's Gun* (Tor Macmillan, 2023) and the anthology *The Reinvented Detective* (Arc Manor, 2023), co-edited with Jennifer Brozek.

For more about Cat, as well as links to fiction and the popular online school, The Rambo Academy for Wayward Writers, see their website: kittywumpus.net. They are represented by Seth Fishman of The Gernert Company.

River
River (they/them) is a poet in the US. In lieu of a bio, River asserts that the current war in Gaza is causing a humanitarian tragedy that amounts to genocide inflicted on Palestine by Israel and the US. It must cease immediately and permanently. The mistreatment of Palestinians in Gaza and the West Bank amounts to apartheid and must end. Palestinians must be afforded dignity, self direction, and freedom. The history of any group's suppression or oppression cannot provide cover for that group to create such suppression or oppression on others. Accountability must come to those in Israel, the US and other countries who supported and committed war crimes, and reconciliation and reparations must be made.

Holly Schofield
Holly Schofield travels through time at the rate of one second per second, oscillating between the alternate realities of city and country life. With not-so-hidden twin agendas of promoting inclusivity and environmental causes, Holly has had over one hundred speculative short stories published in genres ranging from hard science fiction to magical realism. Her works have appeared in such publications as *Analog*, *Lightspeed*, and *Escape Pod*, are used in university curricula, and have been translated into multiple languages. Find her at hollyschofield.wordpress.com.

Crystal Sidell
A native Floridian, Crystal Sidell grew up playing with toads in the rain and indulging in speculative fiction. Her love of the natural world (and tea!) as well the randomness of her thought processes (and personal challenges with verbal communication) take center stage in this poem about encountering aliens in one's backyard. A Pushcart nominee, Best of the Net nominee, and Rhysling finalist, she has had work appear in *34 Orchard*, *Apparition Lit*, *F&SF*, *Frozen Wavelets*, *Haven Spec*, *On Spec*, *The Sprawl Mag*, *Strange Horizons*, and others. You can find her on various social media platforms @sidellwrites or at her website: crystalsidell.wixsite.com/mysite .

Brian Starr
Brian Starr writes screenplays, designs board games, and works at Wētā as a VFX engineer.

ABOUT THE AUTHORS AND ARTISTS

He based his main character on his difficulties interacting with people in some situations. In a disagreement, his partner asked, "Don't you ever make choices not based on logic?" to which he replied, "Why would anybody do that?"

Though he and his family are sure he is on the spectrum, he will always clarify with "self-diagnosed." His daughter says, "You can just say that you are. I mean, I've been diagnosed and it is hereditary." To which he suggests, "But being that I have autistic traits, I can't say that I have it without having been diagnosed."

Jasmine Starr
Jasmine Starr lives in a pretty little country forgotten by cartographers. Her googly-eye-infested home is surrounded by stick bugs and screaming parrots, and she is kept company by two metal-eating loons called "cats." Jasmine is most definitely not a cryptid, a woodland spirit, an ambulatory ball of fluff, nor any combination thereof. She enjoys making odd noises, wearing fuzzy sweaters, and wandering around obscure parts of the forest (which does not help her case).

Jillian Starr
Jillian Starr is currently working on a speculative fiction novel after receiving her MA in creative writing at Victoria University | Te Herenga Waka. The main character in the short story "Tangible Things" is a composite of her autistic family, including her own struggles with oral communication. She has witnessed firsthand the advantages of being neurodiverse as well as the disadvantages of living in a neurotypical society and believes the world is a much better place with kindness, respect, and the "you be you" philosophy. Jillian enjoys imitating cicada sounds and watching big kererū land on tiny branches and hopes to see an octopus in the wild someday.

Edward Michael Supranowicz
Edward Michael Supranowicz is the grandson of Irish and Russian/Ukrainian immigrants. He grew up on a small farm in Appalachia. He has a grad background in painting and printmaking. Some of his artwork has recently or will soon appear in *FishFood*, *Streetlight*, *Another Chicago Magazine*, *Door Is A Jar*, *The Phoenix*, and *The Harvard Advocate*. Edward is also a published poet who has been nominated for the Pushcart Prize multiple times.

Natasha Von
Natasha Von is a visual and multimedia artist working with a range of expression through spoken word poetry, music, and the visual arts, including photography, painting, and figurative sculpture. Melding sensuality and the spiritual, her work reflects the magical connection of the individual with the natural world. Neurodiverse in her unique range of creative expression, Natasha Von has pioneered using the human body as a canvas and is currently writing a jazz musical and creating songs and visuals for performance and installations. A practicing astrologer, she studies the stars, makes art, writes fantasy fiction, and currently resides in Toronto, Canada. She can be followed on TikTok as @GoldenGoddessArts, and her work is available on her website at natashavon.com.

ABOUT THE AUTHORS AND ARTISTS

Clara Ward

Clara Ward lives in Silicon Valley, California, on the border between reality and speculative fiction. They wrote "Meaning Green, Unclear" because the only thing better than splashing down on an alien ocean would be traveling there with a friend. Their latest novel, *Be the Sea*, features a neurodivergent, nonbinary protagonist on a near-future voyage across the Pacific collecting sea creature perspectives and chosen family. Like the main characters in both tales, Clara is neurodivergent, nonbinary, and fascinated by oceans near and far. Their short fiction has appeared in *Strange Horizons*, *Small Wonders*, and as a postcard from Thinking Ink Press. When not using words to teach or tell stories, Clara uses wood, fiber, and glass to make practical or completely impractical objects. Follow them at clarawardauthor.wordpress.com.

ABOUT THINKING INK PRESS

Thinking Ink Press has been publishing fiction and nonfiction books since 2015, with a focus on amplifying disabled, LGBTQ+, and neurodivergent voices.

OUR SCIENCE FICTION BOOKS

The Hereafter Bytes by Vincent Scott. Humorous cyberpunk set in near-future Seattle with an asexual main character.

The Lunar Cycle Trilogy by David Colby. Young adult space opera with a lesbian main character and a depiction of PTSD. Book 1: ***Debris Dreams***. Book 2: ***Shattered Sky***. Book 3: ***Luna's Lament***.

Sibling Rivalry by Anthony Francis. A short story about AI gone wrong.

Beyond the Fence by Marilyn Horn. A short collection of flash fiction with speculative fiction themes.

The Later Anthologies. Steampunk anthologies featuring pairs of stories. Volume 1: ***Twelve Hours Later***. Volume 2: ***Thirty Days Later***. Volume 3: ***Some Time Later***. Edited by AJ Sikes, BJ Sikes, Dover Whitecliff, and Sharon E. Cathcart.

JOIN OUR MAILING LIST

Find out when we have new releases and sales. Visit **ThinkingInkPress.com/ndv** .

ALL COPYRIGHTS

INTERIOR ART
"Chatter," "Look," and "Radar" © 2024 by Barbara Candiotti.
"Resilience" © 2024 by Vincenzo Cohen.
"Skeleton in Roses," "LoveHEART," and "Soul Sisters in Autumn"
   © 2024 by Natasha Von Rosenschilde.

STORIES AND POEMS
"Be Your Own Universe" © 2024 by Kay Alexander.
"The List-making Habits of Heartbroken Ships" © 2024 by Stewart C Baker.
"Heart-Side Sometimes-Table" © 2024 by Madeline Barnicle.
"Gamma Zaria" © 2024 by Gail Brown.
"The Pipefitter" © 2024 by Tobias S. Buckell.
"The Space Between Stitches" © 2024 by Minerva Cerridwen.
"Drifting," "Scanning," "Flashin' Out," and "Infection"
   © 2024 by Gregory Russell Cook.
"The Zeta Remnant" © 2024 by M. D. Cooper.
"Cadre" © 2024 by Sam Crain.
"McCarthy Knew" © 2024 by A J Dalton.
"Flare to Brilliance and Fade" © 2024 by Jade Doumani.
"A Conversation with a Xotiran" © 2024 by M. A. Dubbs.
"Someone Different, Like Me" © 2024 by Daan Dunnewold.
"Are We Human?" © 2024 by Brianna Elise.
"Shadows of Titanium Rain" © 2024 by Anthony Francis.
"The Cow Test" © 2024 by Lauren D. Fulter.
"Hell No!" © 2024 by Sid Ghosh.
"Our Connected Space" © 2024 by Swarit Gopalan.
"The Grand New York Welcome Tour" © 2024 by Katharine Hanifen.
"Music, Not Words" © 2024 by Ada Hoffmann.
"Where is Everybody?" © 2024 by Anya Leigh Josephs.
"Primordial Voices" © 2024 by J.L. Lark.
"Where Monolithic Minds Can't Travel" © 2024 by Akis Linardos.
"First Contact" © 2024 by David Manfre.
"When the Aliens Came" © 2024 by Avra Margariti.
"Greetings from Earth" © 2024 by R. S. Mot.
"These Things Never End Well" © 2024 by Maub Nesor.
"Meeting of the Branes" © 2024 by Kiya Nicoll.
"A Hint of Color" © 2024 by Jody Lynn Nye.
"Close Encounter in the Public Bathroom" © 2024 by Keiko O'Leary.

ALL COPYRIGHTS

"Trading Partners" © 2024 by Jennifer R. Povey.
"Scary Monsters, Super Creeps" © 2024 by Cat Rambo.
"Good Omens" and "Wi(d)th, De(p)th, Brea(d)th," © 2024 by River.
"Navigational Aid" © 2024 by Holly Schofield.
"Stopping for Fuel on a Starry Evening" © 2024 by Crystal Sidell.
"The Interview" © 2024 by Brian Starr.
"Impact" © 2024 by Jasmine Starr.
"Tangible Things" © 2024 by Jillian Starr.
"Meaning Green, Unclear" © 2024 by Clara Ward.

COLOPHON

This book is made of bits and presented using atoms: bits are fundamental units of information capable of distinguishing yes/no conditions, and atoms are small but nonfundamental particles in constant motion that stick together when close but repel each other when compressed. The bits representing ebook editions are held in the atoms of cloud servers and are provisioned over the global internetwork to configure the device of your choice; the bits representing physical editions are impressed into bound volumes by Ingram Spark and delivered to you through space and time. The bits for the interior of this book were assembled using Microsoft Word and formatted using Vellum; the bits for the exterior of this book were assembled using Adobe Photoshop. Fonts used in the interior were provided by Vellum; fonts in the exterior were provided by Google Fonts. In addition, other programs were used to coordinate the production of this book, including Dropbox Paper, Google Sheets, Airtable, Google Meet, Zoom, Signal, and various email providers. Liza Olmsted and Anthony Francis have been your hosts for this experience; thank you and good night.

Printed in the USA
CPSIA information can be obtained
at www.ICGtesting.com
LVHW012343140824
788186LV00002B/6